Ingredients for the Making of a Woman

Ingredients for the Making of a Woman

Suzanna Saumarez

Copyright © 2003 by Suzanna Saumarez.

Library of Congress Number:		2003093875
ISBN:	Hardcover	1-4134-1469-9
	Softcover	1-4134-1468-0

All rights reserved. No part of this book may be reproduced or transmitted in any form or by any means, electronic or mechanical, including photocopying, recording, or by any information storage and retrieval system, without permission in writing from the copyright owner.

This is a work of fiction. Names, characters, places and incidents either are the product of the author's imagination or are used fictitiously, and any resemblance to any actual persons, living or dead, events, or locales is entirely coincidental.

This book was printed in the United States of America.

To order additional copies of this book, contact:
Xlibris Corporation
1-888-795-4274
www.Xlibris.com
Orders@Xlibris.com
19464

Acknowledgements

To the memory of
Warren, Clive, Danny, Bernard, Billy, Iony, Simon and Tina C, Simon W, Dick, Rachel, Richard, Rikki and Nick.

And with thanks to
Christopher, Maggie, Patrick, Camilla and the late Jim Byford for encouragement, editing, reading and spelling.

I

1

Oh the law does punish the man or woman
Who steals the goose from off the common
But lets the greater thief go loose
Who steals the common from the goose.

(Anonymous)

Friday, 28 Feb 1995. Southwark Crown Court.

"Beam him up Scotty, beam Minu up, now . . ." I gave God one last chance to prove his existence, but nothing happened.

If you thought Minu looked a wonder to behold in a suit, and his spiky orange hair all gelled down, you should've seen the Judge. Plum-black, he wore a long white wig, a dark satin cloak, and a hat he must have borrowed from a Star Wars movie. Judge Dread's outfit was obviously designed to intimidate the riff-raff. He was a scrawny, dusty old black bird, who shuffled needlessly and endlessly with a pile of papers that became increasingly disordered, as they fell like autumn leaves all around him. I watched my character report float away, which had taken hours of painstaking concentration to write, and that was soon followed by the drifting references of his employers and teachers.

Through the windows, a chilly February sun filtered through the grey sky, suddenly illuminating and brilliant; floodlit dust-spangled shafts raced across the empty air, only to vanish behind the clouds again. Dr Dee, a psychiatrist and an old friend, was speaking eruditely and warmly on Minu's behalf. I was glad he was there, articulate and sure. But the Judge suddenly interrupted. "I have no references, where are they?" The clerks scrabbled around under his table to retrieve them, and while he read them through as slowly as he possibly could, there was complete silence in court, the alive and wired kind of silence. After some time the Judge looked down his glasses and said to nobody in particular, but loud enough for everyone to hear, "Well, just because he's an educated white middle class boy, don't expect me to treat him any differently to a poor homeless black boy from Brixton." There was something wrong about that remark, and other people thought so too, because they stiffened and the silence suddenly prickled with hostility. "Of course there's a difference, you bloody idiot," I thought, not because of race but of circumstances. "And anyway, everybody has a right to justice individually, don't they?" Minu sat isolated and very still, his activity lay in his blue eyes which were focused intently on the Judge, while his open face, full of trust, looked confident that everything would turn out all right in the end. His friends were all there, in their war paint and feathers, and those who had donned their formal gear wore it in such a way as to convey a general sense of anarchy and express their solidarity. They were usually such good company, bright, funny and sincere, but they were sober then, and vulnerable in the confines of Southwark Crown Court.

We'd had to go to Southwark, because our local court at Knightsbridge was being refurbished at the time. I think we would have done better in Knightsbridge; they were more used to middle-class boys there, and also it's closer to Harvey Nicks. Southwark, however, is a purpose-built high-security place, easily defendable and set in an open space to make it hard to blow up, and easier for the marksmen on the roof to see what they are aiming at. It's where the heavy brigade go on trial: hijackers, hoodlums, gangsters, terrorists, war criminals, the I.R.A., some of my dad's best friends and now my son.

Eventually Minu's barrister and the prosecuting barrister were *both* defending him, but that Judge remained completely disengaged—almost absent from the proceedings—except for giving off an air of unreasonable and personal dislike for the accused. The barristers tried to focus his attention on the point that although Minu had broken the law, it was not too serious. I waited, thinking, "You're wasting your time, boys, his Honour has some other agenda going on here. Something we don't know about, that's nothing to do with us." I doubted if he could see Minu for what he was. And I wondered what was really going on. "Silence in court please." Here comes a candle to light you to bed, and here comes a chopper to chop off your head . . . And it did. "Ahem . . . This is a very serious matter. With such a privileged upbringing good education and fine references, it is obvious that you are intelligent enough to understand what is the law and what is not. I must therefore sentence you to two years in prison, with one year suspended."

Turning around, I caught a look of total shock on Minu's face. He reeled, his legs giving way beneath him, while his face gave new meaning to the words a whiter shade of pale. Then he reached out his hands to hold on to the two policewomen who had been guarding him in the dock, and they obligingly propped him up on both sides as they led him away. "Where . . . where are they taking him?" Finn put his warm hands over mine, his eyes full of love and gentleness, and my friends, Romany, Saskia, and Pearl caught my eye in disbelief. The huddle of hushed teenage friends sat bemused and still and Sorrel, Minu's girlfriend, broke down in tears, slowly bowing her head whispering over and over "Oh no, oh no, no, no, fucking bastard". I put my arms around her and held her as tight as possible, sensing that she would fall apart unless one took a firm grip on her. She felt of nothing but skin and bones, with no protection on her at all. Trying to reassure her and the others, I said, "It'll be ok, it will be all right." Leo, Minu's best friend embraced me saying. "I'll be in touch, take care now." Then he shook Finn's hand and guiding Sorrel out they all left, mute. I asked a policewomen if I could say goodbye to him, but she said, "I'm afraid not. He'll phone though, in the next twenty-four hours." "Oh . . . but where are they taking him, where is he going?" And how on earth did we get here?

2

I am a baby, and my brothers Caspar and Jake are carrying me upstairs. They think that I'm tired, and are kindly taking me to bed. Jake has my legs, Caspar my head, and we are making slow progress around a bend in the stairs. "Careful of her head, Caspar," says Jake. I'm worried.

All the houses in Star Road are the same. Our sitting room has green curtains, and there is a play-room with a fireplace that Caspar throws things into when no one is looking. The kitchen looks out on the back garden. Upstairs, I sleep in a cot, with a picture of an elephant on it, in Mum and Dad's room. Next door, my brothers share a room with a view of the street. This is the room I was born in.

Granny has green earrings, and looks down benignly at me in my hospital cot. I can remember learning to say "Hospital". There is thick yellow smog that hangs on the rooftops. It lurks in the alleys and creeps down the roads, it slides under doors and climbs up stairs. It is so dense it's hard to see the other end of the ward. And it is in my lungs.

I am a baby, in the pram, and I'm too hot in all my gear. I can't articulate this, so I howl and cry with frustration, and soon learn to talk.

Dad has made a "sculpture" in the garden. It consists of a forked stick and a bicycle wheel. He has painted it all white. I have to keep explaining to all my three-year old friends that it's something to do with art.

I'm back in hospital. They are binding bees-wax leaves onto my chest. The wax slowly melts into my skin, and it feels great. I feel warm and protected, like I have extra skin. I wish I could always have it.

We have lovely roses of all colours, opening out in our front garden. One morning they are all gone. It's a mystery.

Dad takes me surreptitiously to the circus. Wowee! A beautiful lady in a turquoise sequinned swimsuit lowers herself elegantly into a tank of swimming snakes. I'm riveted; so is Dad. Her long black hair floats out around her—she is a mermaid, a high-heeled mermaid. We go home on Dad's motorbike; he holds me in front of him. "Don't tell ze others, darlink," he says, and I don't.

My Dad has meningitis, Caspar has rheumatic fever, I have the German au-pair, Mum is "worn out with it all." And she is.

Jake breaks both his arms falling from a high chestnut tree. I was not there, but I saw him in my mind. The tree is wet and glistens darkly from rain, I can hear his heart beat, he is so high and he is unhappy, his foot slips and he loses his breath from fear, he falls like a stuffed toy. He knows he's falling seriously, and so do I.

We move to Woodbrook in Sussex. I never have to go to hospital again. It must be the country air, they all say. Maybe they're right—who cares?

We've come here so that my parents can lead a more holistic and spiritual life amongst a community of like-minded people who have settled this part of Sussex.

We have a brand new house. (Actually it's not really even finished). We meet his majesty the lord architect; I don't know what an architect is, but it sounds grand all right. He is called Byron Gibbons. I like to roll this name around my head. "Gibbons, Gibbons, Gibbons."

Mum is masterminding the garden. We wade around in the clay. I have to leap onto the spade to make any impression in the earth. "The lawn is just the right size for a tennis court," I hear Mum say. I see plenty of mud, but no lawn.

Recurring dream: it is a silent dark night. At a distance the forest, brooding and sombre, surrounds the house. It is very still. From behind the trees, slowly and menacingly, step out the hooded men. They are wearing long white robes with red crosses splashed across the front, and hoods with black eye-holes, and they carry burning torches that smoke darkly. They have come for me. There is no chance of mercy. I awaken in despair, crying. Mum begrudgingly lights my candle and makes me hot milk and honey, but my heart is afraid.

I am surrounded by other children from zero to six years old: Rayette, Max, Liza, Rohan, Emil, Luke the baby, Charley, Saskia and Pearl and Dean, who are twins; their mum is Swedish.

My life is centred on the stream. It runs through our land, under the road and into Rayette's garden, whence it joins the Medway. I can splash through the tunnel, catch minnows and lampreys, and find caddis-worms, which make a beautiful soft shell of tiny stones around themselves. There are water boatman, who walk on the water, and in the deeper pools trout that swim up from the Medway in the winter, when the stream turns into a raging torrent. I play on my own, or with the gang of friends. I dam it up, and make a world of harbours and piers with stick boats. I have waded up it all the way to its source in the heart of the forest.

My Dad is hugging me. Unwaveringly, I stare into the ice-blue of his eyes. He crushes the air out of my lungs, and my ribs bend easily between the power of his arms; it hurts. Loosening his grip, Dad pauses to slick back his blond hair, which has fallen across his face. Wriggling to catch my breath, I kick him good and hard. He smiles his wide generous smile with dimples, the one the ladies can't resist—a smile of danger—as my feet thrash about flailing the air. He laughs but it isn't funny.

I am listening with my whole body to Mum telling me the story of the Frog Princess. "Oh no, oh dear, this is terrible," I say to myself, "she's dropped her shining ball like the sun into the dark dark well." My eyes are smarting. "And now she won't let the frog into the Palace. She has to"—"You have to," I say out loud, "You promised!"—"Oh no, she's throwing the poor poor frog. Oh this is just the worst, how can she? And she promised . . ." I'm always exhausted by these stories.

I wake up, open my curtains to a bright sunny day, and see Max Rye digging a really large hole under my swing. He must have been at it since about six o'clock. Then I remember Jake telling him that there was a lot of treasure buried under there. "Hey, Max," I shout, "you're too late, I dug it up yesterday. Want some breakfast?"

We have a pony, a stubborn brown gelding with mean eyes and ears that always point backwards. He is called "Bucephalus". I bet Alexander the Great didn't have to put up with this kind of creature. We also have a Golden Retriever called Morgan, and two cats: O'Brian, who is spry and smart, and Eliot, who looks like a mangy blue owl, with yellow eyes and fishy breath.

Caspar and Jake find an old car chassis. We put wheels and a steering wheel on it, and spend days pushing it up the hill and jumping on for the electrifying wizz down. Sometimes there are piles of us hanging on and flying down the road. We call it the Blue Bird.

I am lying face down on the lawn, my arms and legs spreadeagled. I am listening to the Earth rumbling as it slowly turns round. It is enormous.

The little village of Woodbrook lies scattered haphazardly along a valley. At its centre is the Village Hall, Church and the Green Man pub, and the village green is surrounded by local shops. The Steiner community is fairly well integrated, except you can tell our shops a mile off on account of the hand-carved signs and modest, wholesome window-displays. So you get our craft shop, with a weaving-loom in the window, sandwiched between the flashing sign of the garage and the local butcher, who sells our grass-fed organic beef and free-range chickens alongside the New Zealand lamb and Wall's Sausages. We've also a health-food shop which sells produce from our farms. The blacksmith's, timber-yard and farm-suppliers' are all places where the older kids from school can get jobs. Soon we will have a bakery too.

I fly down our road for the first time on my bike. I reach a death-defying speed and am hoping to go into orbit. My bike squeaks and rattles like crazy, I pull up my one trusty working brake and I go into orbit all right, arcing over the handle bars until BAM, my head hits the road. I am crying, blood starts to drip into my eyes, and I am running home. I get three stitches and a sweety for bravery.

All through the spangled summer, various grown-ups smile down from a great height, and say things like, "You'll be starting Kindergarten soon." This vaguely registers on my horizon, menacing as a distant storm, but not as yet something that's really anything to do with me.

We are running in the woods, just my gang and me. Snaking our way through the hazel and fading bluebells, we notice a rubber thing, like a long brown balloon, tied to a low branch and filled with something we decide is snot! We give it a few good bashes with our sticks; it's most curious.

I have lost all four of my front teeth—"Very early," Mum says, like it's my fault, or there's something I can do about it. Rayette's Dad keeps calling me the toothless hag; I will gum him to death, if he keeps it up.

The pond is flooded over with rain water. Caspar and I are poling our way across it on the discarded lid of a grand piano.

Jake, Caspar and I are stealing wood from a building site. We make a fine raft, and eventually set sail on the Medway. "Yo heave ho, Yo heave ho, heave my brothers . . ." "Shut up, Sunny."

Mum plays the piano, and sings opera arias. I often go to sleep to the sounds of "Cosi Fan Tutti" or "Fidelio" drifting up the stairs. Dad tries to teach us Cossack dancing. We all line up beside him, clapping and pumping our legs in and out, falling over and larking about. He is semi-serious about it; we are not.

Dad blames every little misfortune on "the bloody Russians." Mum tells him off for saying bloody. "Misha, really," she says, but in my head I say, "bloody bloody bloody."

Our houses are side-by-side with those of the local inhabitants.

There are five biodynamic farms within a ten-mile radius. Some families live in way-out, isolated places, though most of us live within walking distance of the village and our school. With slight variations, we've all got the same routines. By Easter, for example, every Steiner household will have painted Easter-eggs and baked Easter-cakes, and an Easter-egg hunt in the garden will have been organised for the children. Some families will walk to the forest spring, in silence, to bring home the Water of Life. Others will have silent supper on Good Friday, and read the relevant passages from the Bible. Every family says the same grace at meal-times, and I can already say it in French, German and Norwegian:

> "It is not the bread that feeds us
> What feeds us in the bread
> Is God's eternal Word,
> His Spirit and His Life."

Then everyone joins hands around the table and says together, "May the meal be blessed."

Mum knows the ex-prime minister's family who live nearby, and we go to meet President Kennedy at "Our Lady of the Forest," the local Catholic church. I like President Kennedy, he seems all right. We are not Catholic, and they are a mystery to me. I like the name of their church, and it has a statue of Jesus Christ, rolling his eyes up to heaven like he's really had enough, plus a load of blood trickling down from metal thorns on his head, and a really ghastly gash in his side that also oozes a load of blood. "Oh poor Jesus, no wonder he looks so fed up, why doesn't he do something about it?" I wonder. I really want him to.

I can feel the underground rumblings of something that sounds very evocative to me: "THE COLD WAR". I imagine the weary soldiers with ice in their beards, wading through the endless blizzards in the midnight sun at the North Pole.

The Cuban crisis weighs heavy on my heart too. I can see the missiles hidden amongst the banana trees, the rough army chewing cigars and their glittering sun glasses, bayonets, tanks, sweat and dust. They look like the baddies in the *Tin Tin* books, as they point their deadly missiles towards Woodbrook.

Russia is a very exotic and mysterious place. I love the stories of Baba Yaga, the Fire Bird, and Princess Vassylisa; I have often journeyed with the youngest son across Russia, searching for a stolen Tzarina, or the Magic Ring. There are bears, wolves, ice, wind, the deep dark whispering forests, steppes and mile upon mile and wave upon wave of sighing collective wheat. But one thing's for sure: you cannot trust the Russians, so I don't.

I go to Kindergarten. I'm surprised to see it's in a wooden hut. I do not hold Mum's hand as I go in, but one little girl says to another, "We don't like her, do we?" I am way above this kind of remark from strangers, but I don't forget it either. I survive the morning with what I hope is dignity. Mum and my good old dog Morgan are waiting for me when I come out. Well, I think, that wasn't so bad. I have no idea that I have to go back again the next day. Bloody bloody bloody.

There is a lovely lady, with smiling eyes, who comes to my Kindergarten every day. She seems to have four legs under her copious skirts, but then I realise that there is a boy under there who they try to coax out in various ways. I'm fascinated, and want to tell him not to trust them; after all, nobody told me this was going to be a regular thing. After a while his face emerges. He looks dead cross, but I can tell he's nice. He's called Rory. Eventually he joins us in "In and out the Dusty Blue Bells". I don't say anything, though; he could be dangerous. He still looks cross, anyway.

> "O Michael the victorious
> I make my circuit under thy shield
> O Michael of the white steed
> and of the bright brilliant blade
> conqueror of the dragon
> be thou at my back, thou ranger of the heavens
> thou warrior of the king of all
> O Michael the victorious, my pride and my guide
> O Michael the victorious, the glory of mine eye."

We are celebrating Michaelmas day. The sky is both light and dark, and the wind blusters through the falling leaves as they cascade, yellow, brown and gold. It's a mighty day. I am inspired and enraptured by the fiery figure, liquid light, of the archangel Michael. I see him, armed to the teeth, with stars in his hair, God at his side, and all the forces of good around him, slaying the cringing, crawling, bloodthirsty dragon of evil and darkness. I too will fight like St Michael; and I do.

Every morning I wake up and decide to be good, really good, like St Michael. I'm usually in trouble by breakfast, though.

Mum has sold her diamonds, and bought all the wooded land opposite our house. It becomes a home for the ponies.

I am losing a fight with Jake. He is sitting on me and has my arms pinned to the ground. "Do you give up? Do you give up?" he shouts. "No! Never never never," I shout back. Jake plays by the rules but I do not, and I am pleased at his exasperation.

I am listening, taut as a bow string, to "Little Red Riding Hood". "No no don't, oh please, please don't stray off the path. Oh god, she's going to stop to pick those flowers . . ." I can hardly stand the drama of it. I wonder why they think this will help me fall asleep?

Alone in the forest, I walk like a Red Indian, silently. I know if I do this it will not startle the deer. In the distance I can hear the wood-cutters, coppicing the chestnut trees. They use the wood for fencing, and make a bit of charcoal on the side. They also make besoms for sweeping and fire-beating. There are besom stands all over the forest, here and there (which is just as well because my brother Caspar is a pyromaniac.) I climb up an enormous beech tree and tingling from the effort, curl leopard-like along a spreading branch and watch them working far below. They are a surly lot, and follow their own rhythm of work, with hatchets, knife and wire.

> "The men of the forest, they asked of me,
> Saying how many strawberries grow in the salt sea?
> I answered them back with a tear in my eye,
> How many ships sail in the forest?"

"Hey kids, come down to the station with us," my parents say. "We've got something to pick up there." A new pony arrives by train; she emerges from the dark box-car, white and perfect. We call her Shadowfax.

It is the Advent festival. A soft path of moss and pine lies at our feet, spiralling inwards, inviting and twinkling with the crystals that lie amongst the greenery like stars. The School hall is dark, save for the one candle that shines in the centre of the spiral. In my hand I hold an apple, with a dip candle that I have made in Kindergarten stuck into it. I await my turn with the other quiet children and then walk slowly into the spiral, I light my candle in the centre and walking slowly back I place it with reverence amongst the greenery. Eventually the whole green spiral shines with the light of everybody's candles. I am conscious of being part of a ceremony for the first time, and outside I feel the cold of winter-time.

"Guarded from harm
Cared for by Angels
Here are we
Loving and strong
Truthful and good."

We are bought up to know Truth, Beauty and Goodness.

Throughout the year, the seasons and festivals, meals and bedtimes are marked with Bible readings, services, graces and prayers. I don't mind Jesus and that lot, really, but I know that I'm not left free here; it is firmly imposed, with no respect for my own sense of what is holy. There is a lack of trust in my natural reverence for the divine.

Sometimes old Inga comes into my Kindergarten with a basket under her arm, which always has something special in it. Today, she brings out some moss, a gnarled little tree-root, and six woolly gnomes. We sit down around her, and she tells us all about the elemental beings who dwell alongside us, and who, like us, have their tasks to contribute to the Earth's well-being. Gnomes feature importantly in our lives. They work away within the earth. "Why, without gnomes," says old Inga, "the soil would become sterile, the rocks would turn to dust, and everything would fall apart."

There are also undines, who live in the water. They cascade down waterfalls; then, dividing themselves up like drops of spray, fly off over the countryside before becoming whole again. Without them constantly enlivening the water, it becomes stagnant and dead. Salamanders are fire beings, quick and lively; but they can also consume, like a drought. And lastly, the sylphs bring life to the air. They have the same colour as lightening, and guide the migrating birds to their distant destinations. We learn from old Inga that we have all these beings around us, and inside our bodies too.

The trouble is that although I know I shouldn't, I fall into every temptation that comes my way. It's more interesting—much more than trying not to.

I lie in my bed. Tonight, instead of opera, I get Mum and Dad shouting at each other downstairs.

President Kennedy gets assassinated. Everyone is deeply upset. I am bored by their sadness and long faces, even rather irritated. I don't really take it in, but I have a very vivid picture of Oswald lying chained to damp walls, the rats scuttling across his legs as, unshaven and repentant, he awaits the electric chair, and eternal damnation.

I am playing Snakes and Ladders with Caspar and Jake. Caspar is winning; I am suicidal with despair.

Mum is on the phone. She's saying some dead interesting things: "Yes, we had roses in our garden in London, and one night the gypsies came and cut the whole lot." Wow . . . I go off pondering a mystery solved.

The rabbit escapes and raids our neighbour's vegetable garden. Harry Singleton owns the pumping station and is not a man to be taken lightly. He is stalking around in his pyjamas, with a shotgun at his shoulder. (Cuba has got nothing on us). I waltz in exaggeratedly, pick up the rabbit by the ears and shake him. I stick my tongue out at Harry, who is still pointing his gun at the rabbit. I keep my tongue out and walk really slowly backwards down the garden path; the gun still points at us, and my tongue still points at him.

Shadowfax escapes all the time and keeps trotting off to the station, where she arrived from. Dad spends all his spare time fixing fences, but Shadowfax always pushes and pushes till a post topples over. She works hard at it, and stops if she sees any of us coming. P.C Stoat brings her home one night. Mum is apologetic and gracious: "Oh, how very kind of you, I'm so, so sorry, naughty little pony," she says. Mum is enormously aristocratic but P.C Stoat is not, and he doesn't know how to deal with her, so behind her I'm smirking at him.

Dean Lowen often comes down to our house, dressed up in his armour. He likes to sit on Shadowfax. He doesn't want to go anywhere, he's just passing through his mind's eye battles and the knights of the round table, damsels in distress and fearsome dragons. Shadowfax, the noble charger, stands patiently for him.

Mum is searching all over the house for her rubies, earrings, necklace and bracelet; they have all disappeared. I like to sit on her bed with Caspar, and put on all the rest of her jewellery. We help each other, draping emeralds, diamonds, pearls and gold over ourselves; we are princes, pirates, kings and queens. Caspar's eyes sparkle at the jewellery, all inherited from Granny, Great-Granny and Great-Great-Granny—forever, it seems.

Analise and Manix are Dutch, and have built the bakery themselves—brick by brick, stone by stone. We have watched it rise through the wreck of the semi-detached house it once was. They made the brick ovens and wooden storage-racks for the bread, which they start baking at four in the morning. Upstairs, their Spartan living quarters lie snug next to the moderate granary, with its surprising Sheila-na-gig carving above the grain-bins.

Their books are about baking, anatomy, mythology, farming, and astrology. They plot the course of the planets through the zodiac, and waxing and waning of the moon, daily. Every little thing they do is in harmony with the heavenly rhythms. 'It's hard to bake when Mercury is retrograde or the Moon is waning, and don't even try it when Saturn is square Venus.'

These two like to work themselves to the bone; they are skinny and sinuous, with hollow cheeks. Perpetually clad in faded dungarees, and with their short blonde hair on top and clogs below, they look like a pair of bones. And now that the whole village smells of their fresh bread, and the Ceres Bakery is up and running, they are already finding life too comfortable.

I am lying on the bank of the stream, with Caspar and his friend Kevin, a village kid. Kevin has his arm in the cold water, his hand is under the earthy bank, where he is rubbing the belly of a blissful trout so slowly that he closes his hand around it and brings it up flapping out of the water. We watch it gasping; it looks like it's talking, and then Kevin gently puts it back again.

All the children I know have a common enemy: the adder. In its fangs lies our death; we are frightened and fascinated. We kill them on sight by stamping on their heads; they writhe around for hours after death. We throw them at each other. We leave them on our doorstep, ring the door bell and run and hide. Mum opens the door, and seeing the writhing snakes, to all our delight, she screams. Her scream is both primal and furious, and very satisfying.

We are the Grim Reapers of the adder world.

I am blowing down the overflow pipe. You can play it like a trumpet. It resounds with a fart-like resonance, its sounds emerging in the downstairs loo. I usually wait for a visitor to go in there before doing this.

Walking up the hill towards the forest, the snow lies "deep and crisp and even", and it's still snowing. I have my own wooden sledge and Morgan runs by my side. I am already freezing. It is so quiet when it snows. When we get to the forest edge, I lie down on the sledge, take Morgan's collar in a firm grip and say to him, "Dinner Morgan, dinner!" He runs for home. I have learnt to stay on the whole way, as we hurtle along at breakneck speed. When we get home, we start right over again.

I have a high temperature. I get them often, and whenever I do, the same dream comes. Two old witches (my idea of toothless hags) are playing catch with a leather ball, very smoothly and slowly over my bed. I am hypnotised by the motion; sooner or later, this crushing ball will land on me, and I won't be able to breath again. The witches silently laugh and gesticulate at each other. I struggle to wake up, and cry for help.

Mum is cooking the Sunday lunch. It sounds like some maniac is having a drum rehearsal in the kitchen. Us kids are not allowed in there, nor are we allowed to know what's cooking. My job is to set the table, having made out that I'm too young to understand the subtleties of washing up. The boys wash up and they like to squeeze extra washing up liquid into the water and have soap-sud fights . . . really fascinating. Dad carves, expansively. But today he looks sheepish as he approaches the very shut kitchen door, and when he opens it, wonder of wonders, a plate comes flying through. He deftly closes it, muttering, "Bloody Russian cow."

I have a friend that nobody else can see. He tells me he's called Peter-David. I think he just made that up when I asked him, not being used to human names. Peter-David comes from the forest, but he's not an elf or a fairy; he's a wild green boy, and gets to do whatever he likes. He says that he's been to Australia and the moon, and he gives me a certain amount of grief because he sulks quite a lot, and has a temper that can be malevolent. I ask his opinions on weighty matters, and his answers are usually right. Mostly he's around, lounging about in the garden waiting to play, or lurking just out of sight, but if I look for him he's not there, disappeared into another world.

3

We came out of Southwark crown court that evening into a different world. An early mist had crept up from the river, making the street-lights glow like oily moons. Everything had taken on that slightly unreal atmosphere of an Edward Hopper painting. Finn and I drifted off through the cold and damp towards the tube station. "How are you feeling, Sunny?"

"A bit, I don't know, trying to sort it out . . . You know those lines about 'We are the hollow men'?"

"Yeah, I know what you mean. Me too," he replied, putting his arm around my shoulder and making a space for ourselves against the rush-hour hordes descending at the Embankment. But I felt isolated even with Finn there, and random details of the trial kept pouring in and out of my mind. "What are we going to tell Scarlet?"

"I don't know, Finn. And we've just finished reading her *The Wind in the Willows*. She probably thinks of jail as a dark, damp Victorian place for baddies, where the only hope of escape is to dress in drag." Scarlet was only five then, but we both knew that she wasn't going to understand or take kindly to the sudden disappearance of her big brother. She would be waiting at home for us, left in the capable hands of my childhood friend Charley, and her little boy Shane.

"Well, I expect we'll think of something. But Sunny, you're going to have to tell your Mum . . ."

"Yes Finn, I know."

Hi Mum, I walked out of school and I'm not going back. Hi Mum, it wasn't my fault. Hi Mum, I've been arrested. Hi Mum, I hate everybody. Hi Mum, I've been suspended again. Hi Mum, look it's not serious. Hi Mum, I'm getting married. Hi Mum, I'm pregnant. Hi Mum, I'm getting divorced. Oh Mum, hi, I'm getting married again . . . Maybe she's used to it by now, I hoped, as I drove towards her Chelsea residence.

"Hi Mum . . . Jake, what are you doing here? And Caspar, how nice." It was quite a surprise, seeing as Jake now lived in Rio, and Caspar in the far north (Wales). Over the years, my two brothers had increasingly begun to look like Mr Steppenwolf (Jake) and Dr Zhivago (Caspar).

"I got a few days off, and Caspar just got here. Where have you been all day?"

"Funny you should ask," I said, wedging myself down safely between them on the sofa, and facing my tall and dark mother. "In court, as a matter of a fact."

"Oh my god, now what have you done?" asked Caspar anxiously. So I explained carefully that Minu had been sentenced to a year in jail, plus one year suspended, making it absolutely clear that it was for possession only and that there had been no question of him dealing. Jake, who always needed a drink to handle any news (good or bad), poured himself a shot of Jamesons, and one for Caspar, who radiated outrage, support and concern. Mum, who reminded me of an elderly Angelica Houston these days, admitted graciously that she had smoked pot once. "It doesn't look good, Mum, if his grandmother's a drug addict . . ."

"I'm not," she snapped, blowing her nose decisively. She was close to Minu, and close to tears. She'll be alright with Jake and Caspar, I thought on my way home. It was lucky they were there.

Finn and I curled up around each other, snug and familiar. "Thanks for coming today." "Well of course, I wanted to." Finn had been a good step-father to Minu over the years, supportive in a relaxed, easy way. I tried to keep my inner confusion and turmoil under control, and maintain a calm and normal atmosphere around the home for Scarlet, who was sensitive, and had a tendency to amplify whatever the mood was around her. Also to take my mind of everything, there was of course, decisive action to be taken and important things to do . . . like writing a letter to the *Guardian*.

I wrote in a fury and waited and waited for his call, turning the phone up so high that when it did finally ring it made me jump out of my skin. "Mum?" Minu's voice was a whisper. "Hi, where are you?"

"In Feltham. It's a detention centre for young offenders near Heathrow. I can't believe this is really happening . . ." He was in tears.

"Hey, you're very close to us, only twenty minutes from home."

"Yes I know. Look, can you visit tomorrow from 2 till 4? This is my prison number, you'll need it: LA 1242. Mum, I'm so sorry to have let everybody down."

"No, no blame. You're the best, I've never not once ever been ashamed of you. I'm the one who's sorry, OK?" He was running out of units. "Give Scarlet a hug, and say thanks to Finn . . ." I didn't sleep that much; just lay awake wondering and trying to imagine where Minu was sleeping, hearing the clink clank of his cell door, locking him in for the night. What must he feel like? Was he awake too? Well, I'd find out tomorrow. "Once you go in there, you will never leave again, not ever in your whole life . . ."

4

Today I start school. I'm both proud and shy about this. I have a brand new blazer, my pen knife in my pocket just in case, and a grey skirt, worst luck; I never wear anything but trousers. Mum's pleased about the skirt though, which makes me cross. Peter-David is skulking by the school doors, and as I go in he says, "Once you go in there, you will never leave, not ever in your whole life," before retreating in a sulk. I'm not sure what he's up to, and I'm completely fazed by what he's just said.

At the class-room door stands my new teacher. I can see that he is kind and that there is no fakeness about him. I can also tell immediately that like me, he thinks nobody is more important then anybody else. We shake hands firmly, and look at one another directly; we will trust each other for the next eight years. "I'm Mr Shepherd," he says, "how are you?" "I'm Sunny, I'm just fine," I reply. I go into my pink class-room and see Peter-David out of the window, sprawling in the apple tree.

Mum is sitting by my bedside. My candle is burning. For tonight's entertainment, she is telling me the story of Sleeping Beauty. Once upon a time, there was a King and a

Queen . . . This is total immersion story-telling; I am riveted. Don't forget to invite the bad fairy, oh no they're going to forget! (I can hardly stand it.) Don't open that door, don't go up those stairs. She's going to prick her finger . . ." Mum, I'm going to the loo," I say firmly. "But I haven't finished yet," she says uncomprehendingly. "Never mind, tomorrow maybe."

I am never going to be able to write. I always have my crayon in the wrong hand, but it's comfy there. Over and over my teacher firmly places it in the right hand and I can't control it there, I want to push the crayon which makes the letters go backwards. When I do it with the wrong hand I can push it and the letters come out fine, but it's the wrong hand. Why?

We are in London Zoo. I enjoy all the animals and take my time to look at them carefully. I have been learning about the great flood, and how Noah saved all the animals, well, two by two. I feel terrible about the ones who were left behind to drown; I don't like it at all. It is cold at the Zoo, and a mother chimp is holding her baby to her for warmth. We go to the Bird House to warm up; blimey what a noise. There are finches from Africa, parrots from Australia, toucans from South America and a Mina Bird that says "Fuck off," to Caspar's and my delight. "Sixpence off your pocket money," I say in a parrot voice. There is also Josephine the Hornbill, who is exactly the same age as Jake.

Our community is vaguely Protestant but definitely Christian. There are people here from all over the world. We live our lives according to the teachings of Rudolf Steiner, who lived around the turn of the century. He was a wise man who taught about spiritual things and, well, there isn't much he didn't cover or have something to say about. We just call him "the Doctor".

We are not like other people. We eat health food and only wear natural materials, we have our own medicines and our own doctors, and our farms are biodynamic, which is better than merely organic. We believe the Earth lives and breathes, a bit like a person. And if you care for it properly, your yield will be better. So we've got all sorts of composts, herbs and natural potions which we make and dig or water into the land to treat it and enliven it—a kind of homeopathy for the earth.

Our school is different to the village school. We learn all the same subjects as everybody else, but in our own way. And we have eurythmy, where we learn how every tone of the scale and sound we speak, and the natural rhythms of the body and the earth, have a realm of their own which we can step into, move with, so that we can be at one with ourselves and the world.

Our parents dress in Laura Ashley-type stuff and the dads look like Swabian peasants. "Chic Frump." Nobody is allowed to watch television. We rub along more or less with the local people, but occasionally clash with the village kids. There are communities like ours all around the world, something of which I am very aware, especially when we celebrate the seasonal festivals, because I know that we all do them the same way, at the same time.

My Community is centred around our school, the Steiner teachers' training at William Morris college, and the priest seminar (where they train the priests for our celebrations' services). But others work with the handicapped, or in a hospice, or farming. The schools for handicapped children are known as Community Schools, the schools for normal kids like me are just called Steiner schools. Our lives are simple, even austere, and have the same atmosphere as the Amish or Shakers, with a heavy dose of the idealism so strong in the 1960s.

I'm waiting for my school report. Mr Shepherd's is good, but my French teacher's is not. It says, "Sunny does not take French seriously enough to make progress." I phone him up and complain; I say nobody takes "Savez-vous planter les choux" very seriously, actually.

When I practise on the violin, the dog Morgan howls. I try not to take it personally, but I do.

Both at home and at school, people are forever saying, "Doctor Steiner said this", or "Doctor Steiner said that". Whatever he said is gospel around here.

Caspar, Jake and I trudge up to the Forest. We are fetching fir to make our Advent wreath. It is tough and springy to cut, not to mention the needles and sap; it's hard to make the wreath too. We twine the fir around the moss-and-wire frame very carefully, and eventually it looks great, with its four proud candles, red ribbon and pine—cones. Each Advent Sunday we light a candle, and by Christmas all four are shining.

I am playing by the frozen stream. I have built a palace of snow, for the Snow Queen. I've been at it all afternoon. As soon as the sun sets it becomes freezing cold. The stream tinkles along. I jump out of my skin when I hear Dad's voice behind me. "Why don't you come when you're called?" he says. "I didn't hear you, Dad". He kicks me below my ribs so hard I fall backwards into the stream, banging my head on a stone. I cannot catch my breath and the water floods in; it is surprisingly warm and welcoming. Dad pulls me out and turns me upside down. I cough the water out, struggling to get out of his arms, but he holds on to me and runs for home. "Don't tell ze others, darlink," he says. And I don't, not ever. When we get home, Mum asks Dad, "What happened to her? She's soaking, get her warm, can't you stay out trouble for one second?" "She fell in the stream," he says looking at me. "That's right, I fell in, Mum." I am shivering; a temperature is on its way, but I don't care, I feel so far away and small inside.

"Sunny, you mustn't use your left hand for anything any more." I'm all wrong all the time and I can't tell which is the right hand or the left any more. Everybody's reading and writing is much better than mine. I struggle on; it bothers me but I pretend not to care. I have mixed feelings about it any way; I am very aware that for every word I learn to read and write there is a price to pay, and I'm not sure I want this yet. Peter-David becomes more and more aloof, peeved that he can't write at all, I think. I am losing him, and his long absences leave me empty and lonely.

My family know about Peter-David, but they think he's imaginary.

We are in the class room, everybody boasting about how great their dads are. Michael says his dad's a robber. "Bollocks," I say, and push him in the rubbish-bin so hard he folds up, with his bum at the bottom, and legs and head sticking out of the top. "That's what you get for talking crap," I explain. (But there's nothing to boast about when it comes to my Dad.)

My class stands in a perfect circle, quiet for once, and waiting for our eurythmy verse to start the lesson. Their eyes are closed. Slowly and surely I draw my water-pistol, and shoot every single one of them. Yee ha!

"Oh good, a puppet show in the Gypsy Caravan. I wonder what story it will be?" We sit in silent expectation, on the bright cushions in the dark caravan. The lyre and flute play a little tune, the curtain goes up . . ."Once upon a time, there were two little girls. One was called Rose Red, and the other Rose White . . ." The beautiful handmade puppets appear before my delighted eyes. Puppet shows are my favourite, and I never miss one.

Whenever I get ill, the doctor always prescribes my constitutional homeopathic remedy, which is Phosphorus. I look its meaning up in Mum's medical book. It says, among other things, that Phosphorus people can be show-offs, and—get this—sex maniacs. I'm an eight-year-old sex maniac? The doctor must be wrong.

My Dad is gently putting Combudoron on my hip that he's burned. He sticks on a plaster. "Soon be better," he says. "Don't tell ze others, now will you?" "Nope." I want him to trust me. "I won't tell."

I am knitting a flannel. It's a mess, I drop stitches, and the thick cotton is manky. On the one hand I wish it was perfect; on the other, I know these flannels are useless, because my brothers have had to knit them before me at school. The boys like to drop their scissors on the floor so they can look at Miss Speck's underwear, which they say she knits herself.

Outside the snow falls endlessly, icicles spiral down from the green art-deco roof tops. The house smells of sweet sugar-biscuits cooking. I am in Czechoslovakia, visiting my grandparents. My Grandfather is Russian, Grandmother is Hungarian-German. The whole family sleeps in the same bed, which I mind but they don't seem to. My Uncle Vlad slips vodka or rum into my tea when no one's looking, and my Granny cries with joy and sorrow most of the time. I feel prickly; everybody is too close. I know they are poor, and I'm embarrassed by the constant presents they give me; I think they would give me the world if they could, and I don't know how to handle it. Dad has twin sisters and a younger brother; they in turn are married with children. Dad's oldest brother was killed in a war. They are tremendously jolly, and warm, noisy, and defiant. They cry like babies and laugh like giants, they sing and drink and talk politics non-stop. My Auntie Petrushka is a glass designer. I have never seen such beautiful glass—there are worlds engraved, etched and coloured into everyday objects like glasses, bowls and vases. None of them have seen my Dad in a long, long time.

Dad was born in the mountains. After his christening they drove back, dead drunk, on their sledge. When they got home, Dad the baby was no longer with them, so they drove back and found him peacefully sleeping in the snow. They laugh now at the bears and wolves that could have eaten him, ho, ho, ho!—just like Father Christmas. I wish he had been eaten slowly, by hungry wolves.

Back home we are decorating the Christmas tree. First the shining copper signs of the zodiac, one for each of the Apostles and the months of the year. Then the thirty-three roses, for the life of Christ, plus don't forget the Alpha and Omega symbols, and the shiny red apples to hang on each branch. We have real candles, and guess what: a five pointed star on top to represent Man. It's OK, but I want tinsel, and lots of it. No chance, I know. "Right, that's it, I'm not helping." "What's got into you?" Mum asks. No point in explaining, because they will just say no.

Father Christmas is reading my letter that I sent in secret up our chimney. "I don't think her parents would like it much, no, I can't. Every year she wants the same sort of things: last year a scimitar, this year a six-inch sheath-knife, next year a chain saw . . . I think I will give her these beautiful coloured pencils instead, and perhaps this drawing-book, and a chocolate penny . . ." I have a feeling I'm not going to get it, but that's all right with me, I think, opening up my stocking at five o'clock on Christmas morning.

My drawings never turn out anywhere near how I want them to look; they don't seem to match up with what I had in my imagination.

Mr Shepherd has taken us bird-watching. He is fairly deaf and we are crashing through the undergrowth, no birds in sight for at least a hundred miles. I blow through my thumbs and imitate the wood pigeon, others start with gentle whistles, a macaw screeches, owls hoot, chimps chatter, low growls rumble, Tarzan gives his call . . . We are having an excellent time in darkest Africa.

We have started a high-pitched hum in the class room. Mr Shepherd fiddles with his hearing-aid. We tell him it's the radiators. The next day we all pile out for a walk while Mr Marsh bleeds them. The radiators hum from time to time from then on.

Mr Shepherd shepherds us along—every single class has walked this way before us, over the years—down to the farm. I am eager and expectant as we enter the cosy barn. The geese, ducks and chickens scatter, fussed at our appearance. "Children, over here please, and choose your quill," says Mr Shepherd. We pick carefully through the pile of feathers; and then, with a very sharp knife, cut and split the ends into nibs. Back in the classroom, the inkwells are filled. The quills feel lighter than the crayons we are used to, and a hush falls as we scrawl and blotch our way through the words: "In the beginning was the Word, and the Word was with God, and the Word was God . . ." I wonder just exactly what word it is.

The whole house is being turned upside down and inside out. My brothers' two christening cups (that look like holy, holy Grails) have disappeared. You can't use them; in fact, one of them leaks. But they are beautiful, and belonged to Grandpy.

Because we are carefully and gently awakened to all that is true and good, it is easy to recognise those qualities in our teachers, and in those who are around us. It is also easy to know who are the cartoons, who are only pretending. The fakes demand respect; the others are simply respected. The fakes are heavy on punishment. We rarely misbehave for the others. The fakes put on airs of spirituality. The others are striving people, and make every effort towards you; you can also share a joke with them. But they are few and far between. I am mostly in trouble with the fakes; they are big on discipline. I don't pay any attention to anything they say. In my heart I feel let down by them, and wish they were different. They don't like me, and I don't like them, for lying. They call me arrogant, but they're wrong. They just don't operate along the same lines as me and Mr Shepherd. Nobody is more important, but they think they are, and it irks them that I don't.

It's the first full moon after the autumn equinox. I walk as slowly as I possibly can over to Staplehurst Farm. The mist hangs low over the fields, making my knees damp, and shafts of the pale autumn sun break through the misty vapours overhead. I take my time, because I don't want to have to stir this particular preparation for the fields. It's called One Hundred, and has to be stirred for hours in a rhythm which ensures maximum life-forces. Its ingredients are secret, but it's thick and pongs to high heaven. Unfortunately, I arrive right on time for my go. Everybody takes turns, but some of the adults can't do the rhythm properly, or keep it steady, or even stir in the figure-of-eight form required. You've got to be relaxed and strong, or your arms will drop off. When it's all ready, we pack the stiff mixture into old cow horns, which are then buried all over the crop-bearing fields. It's a magic ritual, because these fields really do yield far more than anybody else's.

I look through the ice crystals on my window. In the full moon of November, out on the lawn, a twinkling star-shaped man, skates. He scatters powdery dust as he goes—it must be Jack Frost! I am so delighted, right through me to my bones.

My brother Jake's teacher runs off with my brother Caspar's violin teacher. And the science teacher with the eurythmy teacher.

I am walking home from school one winter afternoon. In a house on Monks Road, I see a man running down the stairs; he only has a towel wrapped round his middle, and he's chasing a lady. And that's my French teacher, I think.

Some of the kids put blotting paper in their shoes; they think it will make them faint. Nuts. "It's blotting paper, not blotto, you twits." But they all seem obsessed with fainting.

A crazed Japanese Samurai has invaded my dreams. He is murderously intent on his job of exterminating me. I spend my dreams rigging traps with fishing wire, bolting doors, endlessly securing my home, which is situated on a muddy mountainside in a forest. Whatever I do, he gets in, and his face with a knife in his teeth comes closer and closer until, sitting on my chest laughing, he gets ready to deal the final blow. I wake up, "Help, it's the Japanese!" I yell.

Mr Shepherd asks me a question I can't answer. I'm so exposed in front of everybody that I get up from my desk, leave the classroom, and walk home. He tells my Mum it's his fault, and he wants me back.

My French teacher asks me a question I can't answer. I fall off my chair backwards and lie dying and writhing on the classroom floor. Because I think I know what he was up to in that towel.

Saskia and Sinbad have come to live with us for a while. They have emerald green eyes, sparkling white teeth, clean nails, angular bodies, and shining black hair cut neatly, with a ruled straight fringe just above the eyebrows. They are resigned to their mother's obsession with hygiene, and her constant battle against germs, understanding that she'd rather give them a scrubbing then a hug. Saskia is a year younger than me, and Sinbad is way down at the bottom of the heap somewhere. None of us know why they are here, but their parents are always getting divorced or remarried; we think it's something to do with that, maybe. It's great to have them, anyway, and we get along just fine.

They have an older brother, Jeff. He lies in a cot in their kitchen; he can't walk or talk or do anything for himself, because he fell down a lift-shaft when he was a baby, but he knows what's going on all right. Whenever I'm over there (not often), I always stop to say hello to him; he can smile the best smile I've ever seen. I think their Mum loves him wholly, and doesn't have any room in her heart for the others, of which more keep appearing—soon after she remarries their father, usually.

I squeeze between Mum and Dad, who are arguing about money. Their voices, loud and tense, jolt coldly in my ears. I cover my ears with my hands, and start shouting, "Blah, blah, blah, blah, blah!"

I struggle on with my reading and writing, but on the whole I do not engage fully, even with things I am good at. Sometimes I do, though, so long as it doesn't intrude too much. I am not pushed, either, but I do take time off lessons with teachers whom I feel are likely to invade.

Dr Blau lives amongst his plants and seeds, which trail down from stone window-sills in a variety of containers: margarine tubs full of seedlings, test-tubes of white-green stalks and roots, bulbs suspended in wine-glasses. Even the light in his rooms seems green.

Dr Blau is always immaculately dressed, in elegant Viennese-style circa 1930s. In the summer, he wears white suits and a Panama hat; in winter, a loden coat with those trousers that buckle up just below the knee. I'm surprised he can still get hold of this stuff.

His black poodle, Mephisto, snuffles around the place, and Faust, the black-and-white cat, sleeps on Dr Blau's lap. He sits at his desk; in his typewriter, a half-finished page entitled "Hermes Trismegistus" sits in stasis. "Who's Hermes Trismegistus?" I ask.

"Vell, I'm not sure yet. But I'm beginning to think he was not a person as such, but rather more a being or spirit who worked through a few people."

"Oh, my Mum says the same of Christian Rosencreutz." Dr Blau twinkles at me.

On his wall in a frame hangs a yellow star, roughly sewn onto a piece of blue cloth. Neatly arranged on the bookshelves are endless botany books, interspersed with dried leaves and flowers, along with volumes on the masons, Jacob Boehme, John Ruskin, Zoroaster, Meister Eckhart, Agrippa of Nettesheim, Theophrastus Paracelsus, Valentin Weigel, Giordano Bruno, Angelus Silesius, and Rudolf Steiner.

"Dr Blau, what about John Ruskin? Was he a person?"

"Oh yes, my dear, a very great person indeed. Come now, we will go to the garden for some apples. Come along, Mephisto." I climb the old apple-trees for him, and he points out the good ones with his silver-topped cane.

I am keeping a sharp eye out for those heroes and characters from myths and stories who became immortal. Where are they? I know that they're around somewhere. I scrutinise the elderly, but nobody seems quite old enough, really.

One of the farms has two Clydesdale horses, which they use for ploughing. One is called Lucifer, the other Ahriman. And I am learning to plough, trying to keep my furrows straight, and knowing full well that any curve or wobble will be plainly visible to the whole nation all through winter.

Lucifer and Ahriman don't really appear to need me, except to steady the plough. But every time we get to the end of a furrow they turn sharply, the plough swings round, and I fly into the hedge.

Once a week we who eat in the canteen get roast chicken. There are six children per table. Mr Rose sits on a "throne" at his own table, from where he keeps order, and gets his own individual roast chicken. One day, I run in and steal it. Nobody sees, and I run off down the Water Meadow with some friends who, by coincidence, have stolen an Arctic Roll from the freezer. We have a picnic. These things really cheer a girl up, and we don't even get caught.

I've unscrewed the little ball and chain from the centre of Mr Rose's hand-bell. When he rings it for silence, nothing happens. Good grief, what a surprise!

The boarders at school live in the Manor. It's made of warm sandstone, a beautiful old harmonious building, full of secrets. There are nooks and crannies and a cellar to explore. I climb onto the roof and attach a fishing-line to the centre of the big bell, chucking the reel to waiting hands in a nearby window. The bell rings mysteriously from time to time afterwards, adding what we hope is some concrete proof to the boarders that the Manor is haunted.

Tomorrow is my birthday. Downstairs I hear Mum making my cake, the sweet smell drifts up to me. I cannot get to sleep because my mind is racing with pure pleasure—my birthday at last. In the morning, my place at the breakfast table is laid out with flowers, and leaves around it; a birthday candle shines brightly. I've got a variety of presents too—"Oh wow, look at this"—and then a party. Mum works hard on her cakes, icing them expertly with different colours and designs. The trouble is, I don't like cake; but I dutifully take my slice, and off-load it on Caspar or Jake when she's not looking.

We are at Winchester. I'm dead disappointed with the Round Table. It's too small and too new to have belonged to King Arthur, so it's a fake and won't get past me. I like the statue of King Alfred, though; he looks like the sort of king a nation could be founded on. But I love the Cathedral, and I'm not that interested in them usually. I wander round with my head in the air, looking at a man's face who looks out from behind the stone leaves; his face looks down from above and there he is again, on the wall at my eye level. Then I am face to face with three of them, and I put my fingers out and run them over his features. The pillars rise to the ceiling, still and lofty; it's like the Forest in here. "Mummy, who is that leafy man?" I ask, but she doesn't know.

Caspar tells me that the Zulus in the film are really being killed. "Oh yes," he says, warming to his theme. "They are prisoners who have been condemned to death." For months after, I hear the tramping feet getting closer and closer in my dreams.

I am helping with the sheep-dipping. They bleat piteously as they go down the ramp. We push them under the chemical purple-blue water with long-handled brooms. And to fend off their fear I chant every single swear word I know: "Fuck, damn, shit, bollocks, bugger . . ."

Caspar and I board at the Carters' farm now, while my parents live separately—Mum in one of our communities in Scotland, Dad in Yorkshire. Although I feel very indifferent to them at the moment, I want to know what's going on. I wonder about it all the time.

I am plucking chickens in the barn with Mr Carter. The feathers fly just like in "Mother Holle". The earth on the floor is warm, we work quietly, and I am very careful not to rip the skin.

"Hey, Sunny, you should read this book," Jasper Carter says brimming with enthusiasm. "OK, what's it called?" I ask. "It's called *The Little House on the Prairie*." "What's it about?" I want to know. "Well, it's about people who live like us."

We are hay-bailing in the top field. I lie on the bailer, as Mr Carter drives the Massey-Ferguson, and I watch the bails drop out behind us, oblong and neat. Later, I stack bails on the trailer. I can lift them and use my knees to jerk them up to those who are grown-up enough to build a load that won't keel over. The sun beats down, and my throat is dry and dusty.

After a year, we are all living at home again, but Jake goes to boarding-school. Jake does his fair share of naughty things, but he's neither a child nor a grownup; he lives between the two. Mum makes a big deal of how responsible he is. I don't think it's so great, myself.

I need a cold, cold drink and open the fridge door (our good old familiar fridge). Ha, the boys have been slacking; only two kinds of maggots writhing and wriggling in their containers. Mum hates them keeping fishing bait in there.

I'd forgotten how loud my Mum's sneeze is. It reminds me of the Big Bang theory, thousands of particles distributed over the universe. "Hachoooo!" she goes, and Caspar always pipes up, "Sound the Trumpets," and I say, "Blessyooooo." "Really, dears." It's the old familiar sneezing ritual.

At school we are submersed in Medieval History. Mr James begins by telling us the legend of Parzival . . .

A long time ago a young boy grew up amidst the sighing wind in the trees and the scent of pine-sap in the air. With mud between his toes and a spear in his hand, he hunted along the shadowy paths and fished in the shaded pools of dappled streams. Wild and simple, he lived with his mother deep in the heart of a great forest, and his name was Parzival.

Right to the depths of his very soul, Parzival yearned to become a shining knight, which was the one thing that his mother had always been afraid of. So when Parzival prepared to leave, his mother sewed him a fool's garment and gave him a ignoble pony to ride upon, and thus garbed he rode away to seek his destiny.

At first, because he was a simpleton, he caused a lot of harm, but soon he was taken under the wing of a wise mentor and with hard work and gentle guidance Parzival soon became a most powerful knight. In fact he had grown so skilful at warfare that he was able to rescue Queen Conwiramurs from her formidable foes. Soon afterwards they found they loved each other truly. Then they were married and Parzival remained faithful to her throughout his whole life.

Now one evening when the darkness began to draw in, Parzival rode into the Grail Castle where he was greeted with warmth; an air of expectancy seemed to fill the faces of those who saw him. He was treated with great honour and seated beside his uncle the Fisher King, who was afflicted with such a terrible wound to his groin that he could neither sit nor lie down in comfort. That evening Parzival saw the Holy Grail and the bloody spear that pierced Christ's side, but he did not think to ask what lay behind the mysteries he beheld. Nor did he ask the Fisher King, "What ails thee, uncle?"

If Parzival had asked these questions he would have become lord of the Grail Castle and his uncle would have been healed. But he did not, and the Castle became veiled and disappeared out of his reach. At this Parzival's heart was sore and full of sorrow, but he pledged his life to a higher and more spiritual ideal and set out to find the Holy Grail again, and to heal his uncle who still lay in great pain, awaiting the day of Parzival's return.

For the next month my class is immersed in the darkness of the ninth century. In handwork we learn how to cut and sew a fool's hat. Mine is green and gold and wonky. We go to the farm for sheep shearing; sometimes the men can take a whole fleece off in one, other times the sheep get gashed by accident. Then we learn to card the oily wool and how to spin a decent thread. In woodwork we make long bows and cross bows; Rohan's is so lethal it is immediately confiscated. In maths we study the map of the battle at Queen Conwiramurs castle. How many gates does the city have? How many soldiers are in the inner army? Given that there are four besieging armies, what is the ratio of knights that Parzival and his knights must fight? In the evenings, Dean rides around on his bike with a dustbin lid slung over his arm and a long pole sticking out over the handle-bars. "Joust to the death!" he challenges everybody he meets. We make painstaking illuminations in the no-perspective style of the time, with gold or blue backgrounds, using bright but earthy organic colours. Mum orders tickets for Wagner's opera. And our religion teacher takes the opportunity to point out, "You must always look for the meaning behind things, because what we see is only the final result of a far wider process... You see children, when Parzival was a young boy he only asked, 'What is it that I can get from this world?' instead of 'What is it that I have to give?' You must always seek for self-perfection, keeping your thoughts set on the highest ideals and then you will be calm and purposeful in your lives..."

Our neighbours are great. Rohan is the oldest. Everything about him is long: his face is long, and his eyes are brown and long like an Egyptian's, but they are for looking inside not out. Like those of his brothers and sister, his smile is very wide and his face framed by an unruly tangle of long loose curly hair, only his is dark brown. Rohan is in my class at school, and his thin elongated fingers can bring to life, like magic, the Plastacene, beeswax or clay we use for modelling. He can shape anything from it, while his legs stick out from under his desk as though they don't belong to him.

Then there's Liza, who radiates warmth. Her mouth is too big for her face and her smile is for the whole wide world, as is her friendship. Her eyes are golden brown and her hair tawny; just like a lion's it sweeps around her face and pours over her shoulders, curling in all directions. She laughs at everything, but like a queen she has her dignity. Her brothers have a go at it sometimes, and then she gets stubborn and bossy.

The third one is Emil. He is so beautiful that other children and grownups turn their heads for a second look, as though they didn't trust their eyes the first time round, or perhaps to make sure that he really is a boy and not a girl. His features are finely chiselled, his eyebrows curve delicately over his hazel eyes, he's skinny and his tousled dark blond hair shines like an untidy hallow around his head. His mother is always saying. "We must cut your hair, Emil." But she doesn't quite dare to yet. Emil himself is unaware of how he looks, and doesn't care either; he's a loner, preferring to remain on the edge of our games. He likes best to be with my oldest brother Jake, but we others will do when Jake's not around.

Last but not at all least comes little Luke, who's got Liza's tawny looks but not her lion's temperament. He's the only child in his family who has grey-blue eyes like his Mum. Luke is easygoing; I've never heard him cry or get cross and tired like other little children. Mainly I hear him talking to himself at the top of his squeaky little voice while he plays in his sandpit or in his tree-house, which partially overhangs our garden. As soon as anything is going on little Luke is there, ready and waiting in the marvellous wooden peddle-tractor that his Dad meticulously made for him. Luke follows us around everywhere, and is included in everything. Although he's much younger than me, we get on just fine; our friendship is unconditional, which is special for me. "What we doing today then Sunny? How about damming up the river for good?" he enquires, hopping from toe to toe, his tawny head bobbing up and down and his blue eyes dancing. "OK, Luke Peterson, whatever you want."

Mr and Mrs Peterson, their parents teach at William Morris College like my Mum, who is a psychoanalyst, and has a thriving practice up there.

William Morris College is run by a man called Edward Francis. His atmosphere is like Merlin's; he is a very powerful man. I can feel the fayness of untamed boggarts, pookas and faeries surrounding him. He is a spiritual person, and kind, but I am nervous of him, because his inner intensity makes it hard for me to concentrate on anything he says. I wonder if he knows about this?

We children build camps and dens endlessly. They have to be underground and as dark as possible; sometimes they are big, with several rooms inside. Once the general structure is built, Liza gets inside and points out where light comes in and we pile on bracken and leaves and turf until darkness is achieved. Occasionally a parent appears in order to spy, I mean to bring orange juice and biscuits for us. Harumph. We all smoke and drink cider as much as possible.

I make sure that I'm never alone with Dad. It's a strain, but he's got it in for me.

The Abels are down from London for the weekend. There are five children, mostly older then me. Their Mum is Chief Druid at the moment. We find out that the adults have planned a secret trip for themselves, to look at the eclipse of the Moon through our telescope in the forest while we lie sleeping. As soon as they leave, we all jump out of bed and go down to the pony field with a selection of saws, axes and knives. We select the tallest Scots Pine in the wood, and chop it down. We work hard and fast, yelling "Timber!" as it crashes to the ground, splintering in all directions. We troop back to bed, adrenaline surging through us as we lie "fast asleep" and the lady of the lamp peers down to check the sleeping babes. The adults don't notice for a couple of days. We remain silent as Stonehenge on the matter.

"This is really the limit, I can't find the bone-handled fish forks," my Mum says, verging on despair. Tum de da te da te da, there is an explanation for this: tire levers. "Come on Caspar, let's put them back. Mix them in with the other knives and forks."

The Twins Pearl and Dean are small and wiry. Everything about them is delicate, like a mouse: sharpish features, quick deft hands, skin as white as milk, lively grey eyes and fine, fine Swedish hair. They go to great lengths to explain that although they are twins they are not the same at all, pointing out their differences. "For a start I'm a girl and Dean is not. And look at my hair, it's much much darker than his . . ." There is an exception to this which I don't think they are aware of, and that is that when they dress up, they do it as if they were one person. For example, to be a King, Pearl wears the crown, Dean the Cloak, Pearl carries the Sceptre, and Dean has a sword tucked into his belt. "I'm the King," they announce simultaneously. It's the same when they are Cowboys, Indians, Knights, or the World War One Flying ace: she's got the goggles and he's got the leather flying cap . . .

    Dean has a nick-name for just about everybody; his mum is called the "Governor" and his twin sister "Brian". He likes to make out that Pearl has just recently crawled out of the evolutionary pond, but we all know who's got the brains. Why, she's one of the few genuine intellectuals in our class! But they're both original and perceptive about other people, and share a quick quirky sense of humour.

They live up the road a bit and have to do a lot of work at home. They are always digging, sweeping up leaves or gardening, while their Dad has a mini-tractor to garden with. They seem to be condemned to hard labour for life. They all build their own Swedish-style house, which expands as the years go by. They have also built their own swimming pool, and if you pee in the water it will go green. I don't believe it, but I'm not going to test it either.

There is a boy in my class who goes around saying "Aries are best". I would like to bop him on the nose for talking crap but I'm an Aries myself, which makes it a tricky old conundrum alright.

I am sitting through Wagner's "Parzival". My bum is numb, I have pins and needles in my feet and every hour or so Mum leans over and says, "Here comes an exciting bit!" Caspar sings quietly along beside me, with the wrong words and out of tune.

Mum is big on culture. We go to concerts, the opera and art galleries. We have visited every cathedral, spiritual centre, historical monument and castle in the whole of Europe. We go to Greece and scramble about amongst the ruins. I like the country, the heat and the warm people, but I expected a glorious culture: the Acropolis, Spartans and Gods. Naturally, I get the chicken pox in Delphi. They decide to go on a ten-day cruise, so that I can recover as we float from one island to another—definitely OK with me. One day, a fierce wind blows up across the sparkling Aegean and the boat begins to roll excitingly, so I slip on my swimming-trunks (I won't wear a top) and head for the onboard pool. The water slops over the edges, and the waves splash onboard from the sea. "Great, my kind of swimming." I dive in. Mum stands holding the rail, looking like an illustration from "The Boy stood on the Burning Deck". She wants me out but won't let go of the rail. "Sunny," she calls, "Darling!" I bash on regardless; I'm having a really, really great time.

My parents are arguing about money. They sell our V.W. van. No more diamonds in the mine for Mrs Fire and Mr Ice.

Dad can suddenly wallop me out of the blue. I detach my angry mind from my body, and never cry. I also never tell anybody. Because I promised him not to, I pretend that everything is just fine, and that I'm the greatest. I dream I'm walking up our leafy road. Four older boys appear at the top walking towards me. They are wearing leather jackets. As we pass each other one of them hands me a piece of paper. I walk on and open it up; when I read it, it says: "SATAN."

Everybody in the world has only got one Devil, but Rudolf Steiner said there are really two. We've got Lucifer, who pulls us away from the Earth through sensationalism and too much spiritual stuff. And we've got Ahriman, who turns us away from heaven and deeper and deeper into the physical with too much materialistic stuff. We've got to stand upright between these two, and get things just right. And by the way, they are fighting each other constantly for power over us.

Ahriman is the reason we are against machines, especially for children. We have to do it all by hand. In our woodwork class, for instance, we have to cut, saw, gauge and sandpaper without the aid of power-tools, and at home, there are no electrical kitchen-gadgets, because these things are purely of the material world. They encourage laziness, and you won't develop your will-power if you use them.

    Lucifer is why they are against anything frivolous, like make-up. Saskia and Rayette often have a stab at wearing it to school, but have to wash it off under disapproving glares. Any kind of a thrill is really wrong, including transcendental meditation, because it pulls you off the Earth, and then you can't develop your feelings.

In school they take great pains to develop our feeling, will and thinking. (Only they aren't too hot on thinking themselves.) "Sunny," Mr Shepherd says, "you are resisting the offer of help to work on your concentration and thinking." "No, no, I'm just very, very busy at the moment." I say, beetling off on my bike into the freezing winds and pouring rain.

5

In the needles of freezing rain driven by a February wind the families and friends queued up, sheltering like poor beasts of burden along the length of the twenty-foot-high fence. A chimney loomed up from the centre of the redbrick prison buildings. The architect of this place had not been exposed to Richard Rodgers or Gaudi, and Frank Lloyd Wright had passed him by. In fact he must have spent his formative years playing exclusively with Lego, because he had cleverly incorporated motifs from the Asda Supermarket kit and Viking Burial box . . . Or perhaps it had been designed by a child. You know, like a community project. "Now children, for the local borough geography competition this year, I'd like you all to design a prison tonight."

In their terminator outfits, the young guards stood around, aware of their power. Provocative, insolent and aggressive, with "Don't fuck with me, or I won't let you in" written all over them. They searched us, hands up and down the insides of our legs, impersonally: it was like being searched by the dead. After that they had let us in through a series of electric gates which opened before us and closed, bang, bang, behind. Our valuables were stored in lockers. And these were the rules. No goods to be given to inmates—all items must be handed in at the desk. Only cassette-recorders, cassettes, ten pounds a month, rolling papers, board games, books, writing paper and stamps, were allowed. I couldn't understand why they weren't rioting and burning up the furniture—until I noticed that it was all made of metal.

I'd been into the Eastwood police-cells on numerous occasions and for various reasons, sometimes visiting friends, collecting people, and for personal reasons, but this was something else. Sorrel, Leo and I found our way into the large freezing visitors hall and sat down at our table, which was divided by a transparent plastic window with a U cut into it. One by one the prisoners came through the double doors their eyes immediately sweeping round to pinpoint the whereabouts of their visitors—some were very young, maybe only 15 or so—and most bought with them an anger and despair that nearly knocked me off my seat. At last Minu appeared. He looked dazed, but seemed alright and we hugged through the U in the Berlin Wall. "Hi, how are you? Hey, great threads man!" Like everybody else there, he was dressed in an ill-fitting royal blue sweatshirt and trousers which were held up by a string belt. We settled down with an ample supply of tea, coke, crisps and chocolate from the slot-machines, and talked. "Minu, it's great to be able to see you so soon, I felt so bad because, we weren't allowed to say goodbye to you, I wondered where you went after the trial?"

"Basically, after a change of handcuffs, I went straight into a cell in a security van." "Oh. Can you see anything out of those windows?"

"Yes you can. I mean I made a point of watching our route. I was so numb after the trial and kept trying to make the situation real to myself, by taking on board where I was. We went over Blackfriars Bridge. It was misty but I could see the Thames at low tide, and the city lights reflected in the water. We stopped at the Old Bailey, but I couldn't see who came on board, then we drove up Holborn and through Russell Square, down the Euston road, and past Madam Tussuads, and at Paddington a boy came in shouting and screaming, he cried the whole bloody way here. Then we went over to Hammersmith. We were very close to home . . ." He collected himself. "I'm going to appeal." Oh no. My heart sank at this idea, because there were no grounds for it; but then maybe, it would keep him occupied until he came to terms with what had happened to him. Leo, Sorrel and Minu talked to each other, old friends, and each of them cautiously struggling to find a way to deal with this new and unknown situation. It seemed like no time at all before our two hours were up and we were saying, "Bye Minu, call me soon." "Bye Mum, Leo, Sorrel thanks for coming". Poor Sorrel's eyes started to fill up as we prepared to leave. "Take it easy for a sec Sorrel, will you?" Leo told her firmly. We watched until they finished searching him and then giving a final wave, he disappeared behind the security doors. "OK Sorrel, you can cry now," and she did. The tears just rolled down her cheeks like a personal monsoon.

Leo handed round cigarettes, saying to Sorrel warmly, "It's not as bad as all that, after all it's not Treblinka, is it?" "Might as well be," she'd replied. "Turn up the music Sunny, let's get out of here . . ." (I bet Ayrton Senna didn't have a co-pilot who snivelled.) That night, back home, I was very glad of the comfort of cooking, the quiet of reading a story to Scarlet, and singing her to sleep: our normal routine. Sometimes I was more domesticated than originally predicted. Later on, after telling Finn all about the visit, we ended up making love in a way that was entirely out of order, and also perfect.

6

"Sunny, that was entirely out of order and uncalled for." I often get detention on Saturday morning, usually for answering back or not doing my homework, or cutting lessons, or general attitude. I always go (except for the French teacher) because I get out of my Saturday morning jobs at home. Detention lasts an hour or so and then I get to wander around the village, go to the Inner Man cafe for a while, and return home for lunch.

Miyumi and Dan are an interesting pair. They do exactly what they want with their council-house, because Dan is in a wheelchair, which gives them license to bash down walls and dig a sunken bath in front of the fireplace. Their brightly-coloured floors and walls clash violently, and the overall effect is like a giant Smartie-box. On the walls are prints by Klee, Leger and Miro, which I don't like, being a Botticelli and Raphael fan. They've got a sort of leather-and-stainless-steel chair—you can tell it's a copy of a Corbusier because it's so uncomfortable to sit in—and a recording of T.S. Eliot reading "The Wasteland". He sounds like an American gangster. You can plot their campaign of self-development along the bookshelves: Ouspensky, Gurdjieff, Bennett, Sufism, Alice Bailey, Reichian therapy, and *The Road to Self-Development* by Rudolf Steiner. They both work in the local sorting-office, and take some courses at William Morris College. They get angry on my behalf—"Oh really? Well that's outrageous! And they made you apologise? Where are these people coming from?" Dan is American, Mayumi Japanese-American. Her clothes and my dressing-up box have a lot in common. She told me that she went to Japan in search of her roots, but had a terrible time. "They were really unfriendly, and so conservative. And everyone kept staring at me!" They do here too, I think to myself.

I am having a long objective look at my class-mates. Bobby has his head in his desk, and is stuffing his face with organic peanut-butter sandwiches. Rory is rolling his eyes in a demented angry way, probably about to succumb to spontaneous combustion. Boris (formerly Bob) is jigging on his chair, Aries is making "V" signs at Katya and nobody listens to the teacher. It occurs to me in a flash of inspiration that we are in fact in a school for handicapped children, and nobody is telling us.

I am also convinced I'm adopted. Or I may have been left on the doorstep by the wild creatures of the forest; that would explain everything. I put on an attitude of "Who are these people?" around my family. Not that they notice.

Rayette and her brother Max and I sometimes play in a derelict house. It is like the Marie Celeste, everything just as it was left during the war. We think it was a doctor's house, because of the bits of medical equipment that we discover around the place. We lark around with a dried severed hand—"It's coming to get you", "Eeck!" One day the police show up and we all get done for breaking and entering. Then the house gets demolished.

I am lying on our oil tank, saying to myself, "If I died now, they'd be so bloody fucking sorry."

Like Sweeney, condemned to live in the trees forever, I am climbing round all the neighbours' gardens, on hedges, trees, fences, stepping stones and walls. If I touch the ground I will die a terrible death in the tentacles of the mighty Kraken. The Kraken is a Norwegian sea-monster that even the psychotic Vikings are afraid of. It has unfortunately recently taken up residence in Woodbrook, Sussex.

Shadowfax is a great pony, even though I wonder who is in charge of whom sometimes. She tries to determine the length of our rides. When I want her to trot, she walks incredibly quickly. If I kick her up to a canter, she trots a little faster. If I wallop her she can go on strike. But sometimes she can fly over a five-bar gate or leap the river; it just depends on what she feels like. She will not walk over the drains in the road, though; even if there is a double-decker bus behind you, she calmly makes a wide detour into the road. People honk and I give them the "V" sign. Life goes on. Shadowfax is my escape route—I ride her away from home, away from school, away from homework.

We are riding Shadowfax eighteen miles to visit her Arab boyfriend. When we get there, I can tell she likes him by the way she ignores him, and looks about ready to bite him. Actually she kicks him in the end—a good decision, I feel. I learn a lot from Shadowfax.

I am playing "Wildlife" with my whole family. I have just one more animal to buy for my zoo: the Monitor Lizard. I have been saving for it, but oh no, Caspar lands on it and buys it, which doubles its price. Suddenly an earthquake shakes the table and the game-board slides to the ground. They all start bellowing at me.

I have decided that I'm going to be a trapeze-artist. I practise: back flips, front flips, rope-climbing, the high bar, and standing up on Shadowfax as she dashes towards a low branch. I ride my bike with no hands; I swing upside down to a great height, tucking my shirt in or it falls up; practise forward rolls, etc. Mum does not approve, but then she disapproves of just about everything I do. She should encourage me, I feel, because it's something I could be really good at. I get as good as I can without a decent catcher. I can somersault from high off the trapeze, but I must have a catcher who knows what's what. Dad offers, but I tell him no thanks.

I have noticed that older men do not really see me. They smile and pat me on my fair head like I'm fresh from heaven. They seem to have no idea that I'm a raging tiger who has been known to bite.

Mum reads to us every evening. We sit by the fire, as she conjures up Curdie and the Princess, the Black Bull of Norroway, King Arthur, Robin Hood, Swallows and Amazons, Oliver Twist, Mowgli, Captain Hook and all the others.

Sometimes Mum organises all the local children, and we do a play. But for now, she has organised us into an orchestra and we give concerts. Mostly I sulk, because I want to play first violin, but Lucy Carter is. She also gets to be first violin at school. I pretend not to care, but I do.

Little Luke and I are flying a kite. We tie on extra fishing line every time it gets high enough to need more. It's miles up in the air. When we run out of line, we let go and charge off on our bikes after it.

Aries and I jump over the electric fence into the pig pen and kick the pigs until they squeal with rage. They can really bite, but we work them into a dangerous fury and then jump out over the electric fence. The pigs shout after us, "Little buggers, little bastards!"

Aries and I are holding the electric fence, with one hand only.

We are seeing who can hold on the longest. "Thwack, thwack, thwack", it goes.

Mum is rummaging through the kitchen cupboards. "Where's the little silver sugar bowl, and jug and matching spoons?"

From time to time, my Dad says, "Don't do as I do, do as I say." He thinks this is hilarious. (Crackpot Nazi . . . He even looks like one.)

We have a huge tractor-tyre which we roll up the hill. It almost wobbles over, but we somehow manage to get it to the top anyway. I can easily squash myself inside it, facing outwards and holding the rim with my hands. When I'm all set they let go, and I shout at the top of my voice as I roll down, gathering speed, "Old Uncle Luke he thinks he's cute but Grandpa's even cuter, He's ninety-eight and stays out late with Grandma on her scooter . . ." It bumps along down the road, straight across the main road—"No cars, good"—and finally falls over in the field opposite the farm.

I creep into the factory hen-house of a neighbouring farm. I want to know about it. The chickens are in tiny wire cages; they are stacked in rows on top of each other, like council flats. There are conveyor belts that carry off the eggs as they are laid, and take them to the cleaning barrels which rotate slowly, half in water. The chickens are almost bald, and their beaks and wings are clipped. In front of them, another conveyor-belt goes around with grain on it. I am ashamed to be human in front of the hens. I creep out, go home and head for our chickens. I clean their house, feed them, and pick up Queeny, who's white and clean, and pet her on my lap.

My Dad is technically a Russian now, much to his fury and our delight. The Russians have swallowed up his Czech birth place by moving the border, and well, it's Russia now. "Hi, Tovarish (comrade)," I salute him as he goes by.

Shadowfax has a little black foal when nobody's looking. She has very long spindly legs, a lovely head and a small foxy tail.

Little Luke and I have a small tin, in which we pierce three holes and attach strings to them. We tie the strings to a huge plastic bag, and I put fire-lighters into the tin and light them. The bag fills with hot air and takes off, floating over the ground at about three-foot altitude. Later on we perfect our hot air balloon, and this time it disappears towards William Morris College.

My brother Caspar is afraid of black people. That's because at school they go on a lot about the light; all the forces of good come from the light, and everything that's loathsome and evil comes from the darkness. But if you're ill a lot, you get to know that in the dark of the night healing comes softly to lay his dark hands upon you, and then in the morning you are born again.

I always wanted to know what's inside a fire extinguisher. We let one off behind the main school building. Foam comes gushing out, the ground gets whiter and whiter, I think its never going to stop. I run away, and just in time too, as Mr Bean comes sloping round the corner.

We are poking sticks up through the holes in the eurythmy hut floor, which is full of pine knots. Sometimes a kid above us says "Ow" when they step on one.

Emil likes to run cross-country, so he dashes all the way to the Cole-Hole post-office, and with a selection of pens crosses our names off the list for us. We stroll down to the Inner Man Cafe, for an afternoon of pinball, tea and smoking.

My Mum has hennaed her hair. Why would she do that?

Caspar and I wind Dad up. We stir our tea, scraping the spoons in the bottom of the cup; squeak, squeak, they go. Sooner or later, Dad will either leave or explode, but this time I get a too hard slap on my head. I'm reeling, and it's me that explodes. He doesn't usually wallop me in front of the others.

There is a red-headed girl who is new to our village. She sits on the pavement in her beads and long dresses, kindly and sweetly wishing us peace and love.

Below the swimming lake, surrounded by rhododendrons, lies the scrying pool—still and silent, a man-made pond, now completely hidden. We lie beneath the branches, throw the question stone into the water, and try to see the answers in the swirling mud-clouds that rise. "Will I ever get a girlfriend?" "Who will it be?" "Will I be rich?" "Tell me I'm OK". "What are the chances of the French teacher dropping dead before the next French test?" I ask.

I can speak French pretty well now, but I sure can't write it. I still can't write English very well either.

Every time we have French dictation, my French teacher phones me up at home and says, "Sunny. One 'undred mistakes in ze French dictée. Only one sentence, and one 'undred mistakes." I hold the phone away from my ear and wave it about making faces at it.

My French teacher and I have massive arguments. He rants and raves, and I argue back. I wait until he's really in a wuss, and then turn my back and walk slowly away. He shouts, "Come back! Listen when I'm talking to you, you will do what I say." "Why, what's so special about you? I know what you're going to say anyway," I reply, and keep walking.

Most of the time, the real me seems quite invisible to the adult world. But I can see them allbloodyright.

I like my woodwork teacher—he's fine. He teaches me painting as well. He makes it interesting, and I get the confidence to work at these things by myself. Mr Robins teaches so you know how to go about things, and he doesn't put on any airs either. I'm never in trouble with him, although he's a bit barky sometimes; he tells me not to worry about the reading and writing too much. Because I could have a career in art.

I am sailing off New Haven. Bossy old patronising Lucy Carter violinist extrodinaire, is in the boat with me. The water slaps the sides of the boat and it's quite windy today, which I like. We are about 3/4 of a mile out beyond the pier when, with a twang, the main stay breaks, and the mast comes crashing down. I tidy the boat up, noting that we will drift in slowly with the tide; this sort of thing happens all the time. "What will we do, I mean should we wave for help? We might capsize or something," Lucy says, trying to conceal her anxiousness. "I dunno," I say, lighting up.

Mum is on the phone, and she's talking about me. "Well, you know, Sunny was completely allergic to my milk. No, I couldn't feed her at all . . . Yes, she spent her first two years in the Homeopathic Hospital, none of us thought she'd survive, really . . ." I always feel guilty about being allergic to Mum; it annoys her and she takes it personally, as if it was my fault.

Mum is always dealing with someone else's problems and we have to be quiet around the house, because Mum's private practice is at home, so she sits closeted for hours with her adoring patients.

Every morning, Chiron rows us across the Styx from the land of the living into the realm of the dead. Mum never dresses to drive us to school: she puts on a big coat over her nightie, and red wellies. One morning we get a puncture, and Mum refuses to get out of the car. She sits there, an immovable force, while we scuttle about fixing it.

Dad has a new job in Eastwood. He's running an import-export coffee business, and has employed some of the handicapped adults from the Community. I see him less than when he worked in London. I can feel this tension like electricity that sparks around my Mum and Dad, or Dum and Mad, as they have become in my mind.

Dad puts his cigarette out on my hand. I climb to the top my Beech tree in the forest, swaying in it gently, eyes smarting, but I don't cry. Below me the forest rolls like the sea. I sing over and over, in a quiet voice,

> "The sun is in my heart, he warms me with his power . . ."

I dream I am lying on the golf-course. I have little Luke tucked under my arm, and I am shielding him. The sky is dark dark dark, and from it the planets hurtle towards Earth. They are huge and whistle like the winds of a hurricane; around us huge cracks open and close like crusty jaws in the earth.

I've got a big burn mark on my hand, and Mum doesn't even notice.

"Good Morning, Sunny, how are you today?" Herr Wissenschaften Junior enquires. "I'm fine, just fine," I say. It's Religion Lesson, and we start by singing:

> "The Sun is in my heart, he warms me with his power
> and wakens life and light, in man and beast and flower
>
> The Earth whereon I tread let's not my feet go through
> but strongly doth uphold the weight of deeds I do
>
> Then must I thankful be, that Man on Earth I dwell to
> know and love the world and work all creatures well."

Some older boys are pushing Mr Robins's car up some planks into the Black and White Hall in the Manor. I think this is a mistake. And I'm right, because all hell breaks loose. Nonetheless, one day they winch Miss Bell's cranky old Triumph car onto the school roof, where it sits, defiant but pathetic, for some time.

It's always best to be told off by a spiritually-minded teacher. They address your higher self, and know you will never do it again. With the others, well, anything could happen.

Mr Shepherd always thinks the best of me. If I do get into trouble it's like an incredible surprise for him. "My dear," he says, "you're letting yourself down. It's not like you at all." I resolve to do better in the future.

We have a hole in the top of our paint-cupboard; you can climb up the shelves onto the inside of the ceiling, and have a quiet smoke. Bobby is in there now, and when the lesson begins, he doesn't come out. We can hear him chinking about and sighing, all through German.

We are having a painting lesson with Mr Shepherd. We load up the sponges with water, and drop them out of the window on passers-by. Some idiot drops one on the German teacher Herr Doppelganger's head. Wowee, now what? He stalks upstairs to complain to Mr Shepherd, who looks horrified, and then says calmly. "Oh no, it must be another class, my children would never do that." Herr Doppelganger looks mystified. We are embarrassed, and look to our painting. We never do it again.

There are families who have been here for many years and are not hostile or cynical about our lifestyle, because their ways of doing things which have been handed down through the generations are not dissimilar to our own: the Casts, who own the broomyard; the Tompsetts, who own the timberyard; the

Woolvines, who have their cottage right between the golf-course and the Forest.

Old Mr Woolvine was a forester and green-keeper, as is Mr Woolvine; and his son Tom, a year older than me, already has everything he needs to carry on. Tom has a younger brother, Titch, who at four years old also knows that he can work this land till the day he dies. Old Mr Woolvine says, "Well, before the War everything was organic. But we didn't have enough to eat. But there ain't no call for DDT or fertilisers round here, so we don't use them." (I wonder which war he's talking about?)

They have a well-ordered and abundant vegetable garden. Mrs Woolvine bakes her own bread, keeps chickens, and makes jams. She is secretly in love with Che Guevara.

P.C. Stoat is in my house. I'm skulking about, guiltily. But he's saying to my Mum, "So valuables have been disappearing over a period of some years now. Well, it must be someone in the house, I think. Have you got a daily help?"

"Yes, but she's new. What about the paper boy, he's a bit of funny little fellow?" My Mum suggests vaguely.

"I quite agree he is a funny little fellow an' all, but for all that he happens to be my son."

"Oh yes so he is."

"Do you employ a regular window cleaner perhaps?" That's me, I'm the window cleaner. I didn't bloody do it, though, so they'd better not blame me.

7

Another funny little fellow used to deliver the papers to the slumbering denizens of London W.14. He was diminutive and his bike so big that his hands couldn't reach the brakes, so he'd developed a method of breaking which involved the of use a hedge or wall or, in our case, the front door as his buffer. He wasn't too fussy either about which paper he gave you; just so long as one paper or another was delivered he felt the satisfaction of a job well done.

The papers arrived accompanied by the usual muffled thud, so I settled down with my coffee to see if I was in them by any chance. Sometimes when I spotted articles on or by friends I'd get wildly jealous, and Finn's letters were always printed because he called himself Dr. But I was in them that day, because the *Guardian* had printed my letter.

. . . Don't waste your time telling your teenager drugs are bad for them, just take them to the law courts to watch judges in action, then ask them if they want such narrow-minded and out-of-touch people deciding their futures . . .

That would show that judge.

It was early for the phone to ring the rest of the house was still asleep when Liza and little Luke phoned from Australia. "Sod off . . . Oh, it's you. He got a year in jail."

"What, for possession? They must be mad." Liza had developed a slight Australian accent, and I mumbled sleepily to Luke for a while, but when Liza got the phone back I asked her, "Why doesn't Luke have a girlfriend?"

"I guess he only likes really strong, bossy, good-looking women. It's our fault for bringing him up so badly . . . What's happened to Rayette, I haven't heard a thing about her in ages?"

"Oh, the New Age Queen of California. Well, the last I heard she was divorced with three kids. Her husband ran off with a eurythmist from Mill Valley, and she was bonking some crusty low-lifer."

"Hey Sunny, I'm a member of Amnesty. I'll write to Minu instead of the axe-murderer of Tehran who hasn't done it. Look, I'm really sorry, it just seems ridiculous to me. Give him our love and I'll be thinking of you both. Bye . . ." I was loathe to put the phone down.

The post bought my *BBC Wildlife* mag. And an unexpected amount of letters for me, as well as one addressed in Minu's neat hand.

> Dear Mum,
> Thank you so much for coming, I don't know how I'm going to manage in here, it's so full on all the time. And one of the many things I've got to do is work on my cockney accent.
> Although I'm six foot tall and can look reasonably tough when I need to, they sense that I'm not and I am afraid of one of my cell-mates, a Scottish bully, who is overtly racist, the screws do nothing about racism here in fact they are often actively racist themselves. I can't sleep it's freezing cold, and so noisy. I wish that I could be out of here so I that could look after everybody while

things are so difficult . . . I've got a job on the cleaning team. It's better to have a job, otherwise you're locked up (bang-up) either on your own or with one other person for twenty-three hours a day. There is absolutely no education programme here at all, and some of the boys are really young. Many of them can't read or write, without any education they have no resources, and therefore nothing to do. What will they do when they get out?

The cleaners share a cell. But I'd really like to wrangle a job in the kitchen, then I'd show them a thing or two about cooking. At least I can read, write or draw when I'm locked up. I'm so sorry that I let you all down, I love you very much, and I know that this must be difficult for you too. Thanks for standing by me.

All my love always
Minu xxxx

Dear Minu,
YOU HAVE NEVER LET US DOWN. I've always been proud of you, you are the best ok? Interesting you should be cleaning, it's good to get a wide variety of experiences in life I suppose . . . Liza and Luke just called; they send their love and are thinking of you.

I love you,
Mum xxxxx

Then I opened the other letters. To my surprise they were in response to mine in the *Guardian*. "Dear Mrs McCabe, my son Jason is in Manchester for possession, and we have to travel four hundred miles round-trip to visit . . ." "Dear Mrs. McCabe, I read your letter in *The Guardian*, my son Tim is in Sheppey for possession, first offence. Although there are no grounds for appeal it seems steep to us . . ." "Dear Mrs McCabe, our daughter . . . just fifteen . . . still a child . . ." The letters were quiet and confused, with an unwritten hope—perhaps there had been some mistake?—from families who just wanted to write to somebody. And although I was used to being able to do something about things, I felt powerless, useless and locked in. There was absolutely nothing I could do, except chain myself to the Houses of Parliament until they let him out.

My *BBC* magazine was full of beautiful images of wild animals from far away places, and an article called "Consuming Passion." "After mating," I read, "the female Tarantula will sometimes consume her mate. But recent observations show that she will sometimes eat him up BEFORE mating . . . Hey Finn, take a look at this!"

"Come on Scarlet, finish up your breakfast, we've got to get a move on." And while Scarlet went to work at her nursery school, I went to work in my recording studio. I was working on a tape of traditional children's songs at that time.

> "There was an old women tossed up in a blanket
> Seventeen times as high as the moon,
> and where she was going no mortal could tell,
> for under her arm she carried a broom.
> 'Old woman, old woman, old woman,' said I, 'Oh Wither, Oh Wither, oh wither so high?'
> 'To sweep the cobwebs from the sky.'
> 'Can I go with you, can I go with you?'
> 'Aye, by and by.'"

I knew that song was about death, and sat at the mixing desk with hot salty tears streaming down my face. I wiped them away but they just kept coming, overcome by my loss and wishing and wishing that I could be with Minu.

8

I wiped his face with my sleeve, but his tears just kept on coming. I sat with Csasper, waiting for Jake to fetch some help. And he was sweating and all hot. Although I had seen what was about to happen, there was absolutely nothing I could do to stop it. I was powerless and now Caspar has broken his arm for the fourth time. He's always kind of wobbly, really. This time he fell off his bike, and the spiky roller that they use for the golf course rolled right over his arm, just missing his head. His arm is full of holes and really smashed up.

His arm in a sling, Caspar tells me there are snakes under my bed, that the Mafia are after me, that Adolf Hitler has had plastic surgery and lives above the sweety shop, that certain spiders attack you at night and suck your blood away, and that you can be possessed by voodoo gods. Caspar also writes beautiful poetry, but Mum makes such a big deal of it that I get miffed.

Caspar looks a right twit, trying to work out with his chest expander. I just know its going to ping shut, and he'll get clobbered by it. Clunk, "Arrgh!" "Ha ha, told you so, Cassius bloody Clay." "Fuck off Sunny!"

Why does Dad always smirk when I say I've nearly finished knitting my Ball Bag at school?

Liza and I have decided that Rayette Rye is in her own movie. Her life is made up of a series of tragedies, dramas, conspiracies and mysteries. Her watery blue eyes are forever scanning the astrology column in *The Evening Argos*, while she holds back her dusky blond hair with a pale finger. "Oh my god . . ." She breathes as though the end of the world for Pisces is nigh before concluding, "It's a good day to spoil myself and go shopping. As if there were any shops worth it, stuck out here on the Isle of Avalon in the middle of a mucky forest . . ."

"Well we're not entirely backward. There are a few shops, I mean the bicycle shop's pretty good," responds her brother Max, entering their kitchen and turning a chair round to sit with his legs around the back of it and his chin and arms resting on the top. Everything about him smacks of adventure, and he's always in trouble for being cheeky and rude to the teachers. He bounces when he walks and his hands are always deep in the pockets of his oil stained Levis. He's been wearing the same faded red bandana for so long it's part of his physiognomy now; without it his straight blond hair would fly off his head. Like Rayette, he's slight and the same height as me, although he's older then any of us. When you see them walking together they remind you of a pair of jackdaws, hopping and scurrying along in fits and starts, with no particular destination in mind . . . Any way the wind blows is fine.

All summer long, Jake and Caspar have been patiently fishing for a fat trout that lives in a deep pool of our stream. They ground-bait the pool, they try worms and maggots and make some amazing flies, but old Mr Trout is far too wily for them. I get the thinnest fishing line and the smallest hook, with a tiny worm, and go down to the stream in the evening. I tie my line onto a tree root, and go home to bed. Next morning the trout is on my line. I bring it home, and Mum cooks it for my breakfast. I eat it slowly, with Caspar and Jake's burning black eyes glaring at me.

My teachers and parents don't think much of animals. We humans are above them, and we mustn't behave like them or stoop to animalistic behaviour, like fighting or gobbling our food. This is a puzzle for me. Lots of animals, I know, mate for life; and I feel sorry for the swan that's lost her mate, she will never get another one. They only kill and eat the weakest, unlike us—we eat the strongest; I've been at Staplehurst farm, and know how they select the beef for slaughtering. Animals only eat when hungry, people seem to eat whenever. I don't feel above them; maybe alongside.

I have to sit on the foal, because I'm the lightest. She bucks and kicks and prances around; she has perfected the vertical take off, and flies around like lightening before stopping dead. I fall off a lot, but Mum says, "Brave girl, up you get dear, hold steady, well done." I don't know if she's talking to me or the foal sometimes. It takes me a while to learn to control her with my will and not my body; then it's quite easy, but you have to concentrate all the time and stay inside yourself. I'm the only one who can ride her, unless they know the will-power trick; Mum does.

Sometimes Mum uses her will-power to control me too, unfortunately, and unfairly. She calls me a half-tamed wild thing. But I'm not going to be broken-in like the foal. They can try, I know that's what they want. But I'm never going to yield an inch. I need to know things for myself, not because they say so.

We are celebrating Doctor Steiner's birthday. He died in 1925, for God's sake. We light a candle, the teachers' chamber orchestra plays some muted Bach, and somebody reads something that the Doctor wrote, as well as something about his life. And then before anybody can stop us, the whole school—all 500 of us—sing him Happy Birthday, adding a verse: "We wish you were here, we wish you were here . . ." which falls to pieces at the end, because we can't get it to scan.

We are into weed-killer and sugar-bombs at the moment. You need to drill a hole at one end of a piece of copper piping and pack it with weed-killer and sugar; next you stuff the pipe into the ground until the drill-hole is at ground level; then you lay a fuse from the hole, light it and run like crazy. Once the copper pipe flew right past my ear. "A bit close, Sunny," I thought.

Caspar and Jake once blew up a whole tree. They packed their pipe in its roots. The farmer was a bit annoyed, because it fell on the road.

We find an old rusty incendiary bomb on the forest. We wonder if it's a live one, so I chuck it out of an upstairs window, hoping for a crater in the drive. Nothing happens. One day the police come and take the bomb away, and it does turn out to be live.

Liza and I steal Jake's motorbike. We drive with wild abandon all over the forest and golf course, shouting and singing, "How much is that doggy in the window?"

I am learning how to hot-wire a car from Oily Rags. "You connect the battery to the coil, like this, then put that white wire into the black one," he says, and lo and behold, the engine starts up.

At school we follow the stream into the tunnel, under the "Ha Ha". There are piles of us down there, larking about; you can get in all right, but may get caught getting out.

We are worming our way between the walls of Snailsbrook, a big old house that belongs to the priest seminar, where they train the priests. I can just about get around the whole place, and into the attic above the chapel, where they hold the Sunday service. Max falls through a ceiling and knocks a huge wardrobe over—man, what a mess. The man in the room looks gobsmacked, as we haul Max back through the hole and disappear again. Maybe he thinks we are a heavenly visitation. Max's dad gives us hell for this little escapade.

Mr Shepherd is walking down Monks Road, going home from school. I fall in behind him, and another kid creeps up behind me, until we have a long, long line, all following the leader. Suddenly Mr Shepherd puts up an arm, and we all put our arms up; he hops on one leg, we hop on one leg. We follow him right to the bus-stop, and line up behind him. The queue goes half way through the village.

There are four hundred and seventy eggs in a woman's body. Whatever next?

I know all about Ragnarok, but the First World War is a complete mystery. My school somehow manages to make all subjects lead to the same thing, which is that Jesus Christ is the centre of life, the universe and everything. It's awesome how mysteriously and elegantly they do this. Eg., Buddha was only around to teach about love, you see, so that when Christ came along people had been primed by Buddha's teaching, and were now ready for Christ. I think, "No, Buddha was a man in his own right, and Buddhism is just as rich and sophisticated as Christianity. I wonder what he would have thought?" Buddha just smiles and says, "Let those Steiner people think what they want, I don't mind."

> "Sit
> Rest
> Work.
> Alone with yourself,
> Never weary.
> On the edge of the forest

Live joyfully,
Without desire."

Oh no, it's Michaelmas again. We are modelling St Michael and the Dragon. The cold, fresh clay forms quickly and easily, like quick-silver in my hands, into an enormous gruesome dragon. I model St Michael's leg and stick it in the dragon's gapping jaws; good, just enough clay left for an arm and spear which lie at the dragons feet. It is no longer clear to me that the forces of light are on top of the situation at all; I'd say they're about equal right now.

Every year, the whole Community gets together for our own performance of the Mystery Plays. They do the Paradise Play, the Shepherds' Play and the Kings' Play. I know them off by heart, and look forward to them with eager anticipation. I enjoy the different accents; the Devil has a French accent, Mary is Dutch this year, and Joseph is Israeli. But the Angel is played by a shining man, with a beautiful voice. I'm entranced. And Christmas comes with the peace of Christ after all.

I hate picking teams for hockey. I want to win, but don't like leaving the weaker friends out. I'm embarrassed by how they stand, dishevelled, miserable and last in the Siberian winds of the hockey-pitch.

My school is non-competitive, but they don't realise how competitive the children are—even in handwork, for God's sake.

We are driving through the night with the Abels, to watch the sun rise on the summer solstice at Stonehenge. I'm placed in a good position to see, and when the sun rises, its majesty and magic fill me with silence. I am acutely aware of the many people who have done this before me, since the dawn of time. I'm drawn to them in my mind by the crackling sun.

We are staying at the Manor House with Grandpy. All his servants call me "Miss Sunny" and I get waited on at table; I'm dead embarrassed. If I leave my shoes outside the kitchen door, they are cleaned in the morning. I sleep in a beautiful four-poster bed, with rosy curtains around it which match the window curtains and carpets and rugs. There is a walled garden, and a river with a punt and a wooden suspension bridge leading to the island. I like to take the dogs there (they have about ten or so)—it's peaceful. Grandpy always hides half a crown for us somewhere in his vast sitting-room. "It's going to take days to find it!" Sigh . . . At breakfast, I can help myself to bacon, eggs, tomatoes, kedgeree, kippers, and toast, all kept piping hot in silver salvers. I also help myself to the cigarettes that lie around, conveniently, in various boxes throughout the place. Grandpy is the slowest driver in the entire universe. If I go shopping in the village there, I get introduced as "Sir Kester's granddaughter". I do my best to behave, but I'm not quite sure what's the right thing to do or say. I copy Mum, she knows what's what. She was presented to the Queen, no less.

"Queen, this is Mum." "Mum, this is the Queen."

My Mum actually looks like a queen, She is very tall, six foot. Her face is long and you can see her fine bones which cast shadows down each of her cheeks. Her eyes are huge and black, inside they smoulder like embers. Her black hair falls straight down over her shoulders to her waist, and her skin is white and delicate like the bark of a silver birch.

There is a rope fire-escape there, on a winch. I'm being winched slowly down in my pyjamas and dressing gown, my slippered foot in a loop and my hands holding the rope. I come face to face with Cook, who is glaring out of the kitchen window. I shake the rope twice, and am inched very slowly up again. I try to act nonchalantly and casual on my ascent to heaven. Ho hum.

There are a couple of boys around here who think I'm a boy. I'm exasperated by this, but maybe it's a compliment—I just don't know.

We have just had another French dictation. I am snipping our telephone wires with the rose secauteurs, eliminating all possibilities of any further French nuisance calls.

I play fiddle for the barn-dance at Stablehurst Farm. I'm always part of the band, and I really enjoy it. I know all the tunes but no steps, and I watch as they dance—"The lady round the lady, and the gent around the gent, the gent around the lady and the lady round the gent, and you circle round and you circle round, and you swing and you swing, and you promenade around. Two Buffalo-girls go round the outside, round the outside . . ."

We are chewing Morning Glory seeds, they taste like mustard and are very ghastly and bitter. You have to chew about fifty or more to get any effect, but then suddenly and gently the world turns an intense and beautiful blue. You feel delicate and fragile, and you know how it feels to be a Morning Glory flower. My mouth aches from smiling at Peter David, who has reappeared to warn me: "Never make a deal with a fairy." "And don't ever make a deal with a person," I say, and ask him how he is. "I'm fine, just fine," he replies across an increasing distance.

Caspar runs out of school choir, bent over, pretending he's about to be sick again.

All the local gardening shops have run out of Morning Glory seeds, but it doesn't matter at the moment because right now we are busy sniffing the glue in bookbinding class instead.

"Well this is the limit," my Mum wails. Her beautiful gold bracelet has gone.

Although I don't like my French teacher, I can see that he is an excellent artist and craftsman; his copper work and silver jewellery are second to none. I can learn these skills from him happily, and I do.

We have decided to stare, unblinking and merciless, at Mr Cato. He is teaching us history of drama. We stare, he teaches. After about ten minutes, he draws a big eye on the blackboard, and the spell is broken.

Mr Cato has a brother whom I stop and chat to when he's around. He's a film-maker from the outside, but he talks to me seriously, and makes me think about things in a new way. He's called Miles.

Good old Shadowfax has another little black foal. This one has a white star on her forehead.

I have a lamb, "Baarbara", who needs bottle-feeding, and a duck who steals chocolate biscuits when you're not looking. "Lobo", the duck, is lonely, so I give him a long mirror which he sits in front of, preening and talking and communing with himself. Shadowfax takes over the lamb and mothers it, resenting my interference. "But it's my lamb," I say, as she noses me out the field.

I am driving through the Alps with my family. We stop for a picnic in a high and silent pass. Far below, a miniature life goes on: tiny train, tiny trees, tiny farms, and I stand up above, concerned only with the mighty. I am trying with all my concentration to move a mountain with the power of faith. It's very disappointing when nothing happens.

Our closest neighbours the Peterson family are all gifted artists, and I can see they get it from their father. His work is so fine and intricate, and so far reaching—he weaves into his work designs from Africa, Australia and faraway places, and his woodwork may incorporate some Asian carving, or neat no seam Japanese joints. My eyes are opened; I didn't know you could do this with art and still have your own individual style shine through.

I am lying on my back, on the sweet-smelling, dewy grass, contemplating "the starry firmament" (as Mr Shepherd calls it), and picking out the constellations. It is Guy Fawkes night, but the bonfire has died down to a smouldering glow in the dark. I have been learning about Tycho Brahe at school, and something about him is important to me. I soak in his biography in fascination, and go eagerly to school for more about him every day.

I take great care over my St. Martin's lantern. Using a compass and Mum's best nail-scissors, I cut geometrical forms into the black cardboard. I stick coloured tissue-paper, oh so carefully, behind the various patterns, and Mum tells us the story. "A long time ago, a Roman soldier was wending his way home through a freezing blizzard. By and by, he came upon a poor beggar. He was so cold that the soldier cut his cloak in half, and gave half to the poor freezing beggar, and then continued on his way, and eventually reached a shelter. Well children, when he awoke, he realised that he had crossed a great lake in the darkness, and it was a miracle, so he became a Christian . . ." We join the other families, and walk with our lanterns through the dark, up the track . . ."But why lanterns, Mum?" "Will you be quiet, and sing with the rest of us," she replies. Why am I walking round with a bunch of lunatics, with this lantern? I wonder. "But why lanterns, Mum?" I insist. "Will you shut up now," she hisses at me. "No I bloody won't, and you can keep your stupid lantern." I stamp home.

"Hey Mum, one of the William Morris students taught me the grace in Chinese." Folding my hands, and keeping a straight face, I wing it. Only Caspar is suspicious.

I am sawing off the front forks of an old bike I've pulled out of the dump. I weld them seamlessly onto the front forks of my bike. I put the wheel back on and paint my whole bike red; it looks brilliant. Now I'm the only person in the kingdom of Woodbrook to have extended front forks. Cool, really cool.

At school, we learn about the Greek philosophers. I can understand why Pythagoras thought the world was made of music and maths and I like Plato, but have no time for Aristotle or Socrates who said, "The unexamined life is not worth living." I have no idea what he's on about.

9

We were allowed to visit Minu every three weeks, for two hours. But none of us were prepared for that second visit. His head had been shaved, his blue eyes peered out of dark sockets, his skin was white, and he kept his head down. A haunted man. I'd never seen him look like that before, there had to be a way to warm him up and keep him human . . . hold him in my heart somehow. He talked non-stop, and not all of it made sense. "I feel threatened all the time by this guy they call Scottie". My alarm bells rang: I used to feel like that around my dad. "I know now who's safe and who's a grass, which one of the screws will give me an extra blanket and who will take it away". I listened to everything he said, quiet and focused. "The other night when I was in my cell, a ruler came flying under the crack at the bottom of the door. It had been booted over from the cell opposite mine, and on a cigarette paper stuck to the ruler was a note, "Want some dope mate?" I wrote "yes" and booted it back. I've been offered the lot here, drugs, sex, anything".

"Minu, I love you, it will be all right," I said, trying to be strong and together for him, but my heart was breaking.

"I know . . . You know what? Everything I own gets stolen— my phone cards, rolling papers, tobacco, and the stamps we trade in. I spend my whole time cleaning or working out in the gym, and opt for bang-up as much as possible. Bang up is at least safe and I can get away from it, because I can draw and read in peace. Mind you I'm so fed up with all these endless paperbacks, it's all they have to read here."

"We can send you books, any books you want, is there anything that you might want to learn about?"

He was quiet for a while before he said, "I'll think about that, maybe I could study something, I've got all this time on my hands."

"That's a very good idea."

"Oh Mum, it's almost time for you to go again," he said the tears right behind his eyes. I just wanted to hold him close to me, and make those tears go away. "Minu we are both just going to have to be braver than we really are, have you made any friends here?" I didn't want to leave him, with no one to talk to.

"No not really, except on a superficial level. There's no one I can really relate to, you know they're all lads, and it's a detention centre so everyone is always on their way somewhere else . . . I'll be alright though, Mum."

"He looks like one of those soldiers returning from the trenches in a first World War newsreel. Like he's shell-shocked, Finn."

"I'd like to see him, and I want to know where he is, I'll go next time. Sunny, would it cheer you up to go down to the forest tomorrow.?"

Walking in the forest, we headed straight for the big beech tree. I swung up into its branches—a good and easy feeling—and Finn handed Scarlet up. We hung out up there in the dry crisp spring stillness. "Mum, I miss Minu, he should be here. It's not the same, it's all crooked without him."

"I know, sweetheart, I miss him too. Let me tell you a story." She nestled into Finn's lap, listening quietly, her invisible antennae waving. "Once upon a time, a king had twelve beautiful daughters. Every night they went to sleep peacefully and quietly, but in the morning when they came down for breakfast, they looked wrecked and weary and their shoes were all worn out. Nobody knew where they had been . . . They walked through a forest of gold, a forest silver, and a forest of twinkling diamond trees, and twelve princes in twelve boats were waiting for them, and they danced the night away . . . Scarlet in the night, when we sleep, we meet our friends and everybody who we miss and love. We can be with them in our sleep. Just like the twelve dancing princesses." "Yes,"she said, content with this idea, "that's true."

"Look at this up here, Finn." Clearly and neatly carved into a branch, quite high up, the boy Minu had carved his name. I marked the moment, and carved under Minu's name that of Scarlet, and under hers, mine. "And what about carving Finn up there too?" "Finn it just seems ridiculous to me that after sixteen years of marriage and constant propositioning, we still haven't done it up here. I only carve names up here for a good reason, see."

"Mummy, you carve Daddy in as well . . . done what up there anyway?"

"Oh, nothing."

"OK then, Sunny I will. But could we have a team of paramedics standing round at the bottom?" It was hard being a child-bride, sometimes.

When he was seventeen, taking a leap into independence and making a major statement about freedom, Minu moved out, sharing a house with other students, exactly fifty yards away from home. "Hi Mum, mind if I use the washing machine? How do you cook Duck à l'Orange? Have you got a recipe for tempura? Are you using this paint-brush? You haven't got a fiver, have you? Hey Scarlet, do you want to come over to my place for a while? Forget the soufflé, take a look at the sunset, Mum. How's the music going? Nice painting. Come on, Scarlet.

Bye!" Minu and I became semi-detached. He had eleven G.C.S.E's, and a B.Tech. in Art and Design from Chelsea School of Art. I was proud of him.

Sorrel, some other girls and I had to sort through Minu's belongings, and retrieve some of mine. We packed his stuff away carefully, Sorrel lovingly folding his T-shirt with the words "FUCK PARENTAL ADVICE" on it, and put it carefully into her bag. Bugger, I thought, I wanted that.

10

Every time Jake comes home from boarding-school his hair is longer. He's got a T-shirt with the words. "WE ARE THE PEOPLE OUR PARENTS WARNED US AGAINST" written on it and he wears a combat jacket all the time. But I know he works hard at school, and this sort of makes up for Caspar and me. Mum says to me. "Well one thing that's clear is you'll never get an O'level." It makes me feel really stupid all the time. (But I might in art and music.)

You can lift our classroom door off its hinges. I am doing this just before French, sliding the door back in place very carefully. As it's been done on a regular basis, the French teacher knocks before coming in. "Is the door on properly?" he enquires. "Yes, come in," we reply, all innocence, and BAM, he enters.

Saskia is covered in makeup. Glaring out from below her pencil-straight black fringe, she is moaning her head off: "Honestly, I've never been so embarrassed in my life. My Dad [who was big and South African] was wearing a kilt, claiming some Scottish ancestry I've never heard of, and Mum was singing Schubert Leider, and they walked ahead of us to church. I mean everybody saw them. For Christ's sake, these are my parents, this is my family!" I deeply sympathise, making a point of walking on the opposite side of the road to my own family, and trying not to be seen out with them. Ellie Winner asks me if I believe in life after death. I say, "Yes, this is it." This is not the answer she wants, but it's what I think. We came out of death into life.

I am watching the moon landing on telly. They have sent back the most beautiful pictures of the Earth; it is a vast planet of calm, inviting, a good place to live. I am fearful for the lives of the astronauts, as they make their way out of the rocket and down Jacob's Ladder, and I'm deeply disappointed that they have to wear space-suits and breathe our air. To me this means they haven't really been to the moon at all; they have just taken the Earth up there.

Off and on I feel sad for Leika, the Russian dog who was sent off into space and death, and even now forlornly orbits the Earth where I live.

We are lying in the pony's stable, sprawled in the hay, secret and silent. The sun pours through the knots and planking, lighting the dust. Jake turns the knobs of his home-made crystal set, and the valves alight like a city from outer space. There we have it—Radio Caroline, Bob Dylan, Mick Jagger, Sergent Pepper's Lonely Hearts' Club Band, Pink Floyd, Leonard Cohen, Free, Ten Years After, Them, The Moody Blues, and Jimi Hendrix—all of them flying across the air-waves to our eager ears, intermingled with many languages, the police, whistles and crackles, and the BBC World Service.

"I shall be released . . ." The Band plays just for me.

11

I am in Prague with my family. It is 1968, and I am twelve years old. The Russians are invading: tanks rumble through the narrow streets, there is intermittent machine-gun fire, and on every roof a soldier stands. Jake, Caspar and I sneak out all the time. In Wenceslas Square wreaths from many countries, with messages of solidarity, lie at the feet of the statue of the saint. But wreaths are not enough, they need action. I wonder why England isn't helping? And what about the Golem, the clay man created by the legendary Rabbi Lowe? It's supposed to come to life when the people of Prague are in most need. "Time to activate the Golem," I say out loud. "Don't be daft Sunny, the Golem is just for Jewish people." Jake is a such stickler for detail.

The atmosphere has become interestingly menacing when Jake says, "We'd better get back now. Come on, you two." We trot off, passed coffee shops with the blinds pulled down, chock-o-block full of people, and the puppet shop with its wooden puppets leering through the window, cheerily colourful and surreal.

When we get back the whole place reeks of smoke. The adults are so engrossed in their politics nobody bothers about us. We talk in halting German to our very old quiet and smiling grandparents and help them to prepare supper, making up dumplings, sauerkraut, salamis, ham and frankfurters, and opening jars of pickles.

Prague was always beautiful but grey and decaying. People used to be so grim; everybody was afraid of everybody, and nobody went out much. But in this crisis, it's alive and buzzing like an ants' nest that's been poked by a stick. People are excited and friendly, smiling at each other and smoking on street corners, jeering at the Russian soldiers when they try to tell them to move on. My Grandmother is taking Jake, Caspar and me to church; we walk past the crowds milling about in the old town-square and stop below the old horologe. It's a clock of hours, seasons, zodiac signs and planets, and when it strikes the hour, you really do know exactly where you stand: it's seven o-clock, spring-time, the Earth—with you on it—is circling along the zodiac in cycles between the planets, and the moon is in its first quarter.

Under Russian communist rule, nobody was allowed to worship. Every church was closed and locked up. My grandmother has always been deeply religious and in this capacity she is head of the secret service. (Holding her own secret service at her house, ministered by an underground, travelling priest.) She stands at the alter rail and weeps and prays, then she takes communion in public for the first time in many, many years. Jake and Caspar are up there with her. Because I have steadfastly refused to be confirmed, I'm left leaning up against the red marble tomb of Tycho Brahe, Royal Astronomer to the Emperor and Bohemian King, Rudolph. "Hello Tycho, I know you." I fit my fingers over his cold stone hand, which rests over a globe of marble. "Is your skeleton really in there?" By the time the service is over, the town-square is empty, and the deserted streets are silent, nervous soldiers stand looming in the rising fog which has curled up from the Vltava.

"Do you know any songs by the Beatles, Sunny?" Uncle Vlad asks. "Yes, I think so . . .

> "Yesterday, all the Russians seemed so far away
> Now it looks as though they're here to stay
> Oh, I believe in yesterday.
> Why they had to come I don't know,
> They wouldn't say
> We said something wrong,
> Now I long for yesterday . . ."

(Eat your heart out, Paul McCartney.)

Caspar and I are looking for a Statue of the Black Madonna and her Black Child that we spotted simultaneously a few days earlier, up on the corner of a house.

"It's a blasphemy of some sort, Sunny."
"I know, what would they say at school?"
"I dare you to ask Mum if Mary was really black."
"Hey Caspar, here we are again at the old Jewish cemetery." We sit behind the gravestones, sharing a ciggy and a quiet moment in time. The enemy is trying to make friends with us. "You English? Vat's it like there?" he enquires, giving us a cigarette each. "Me, I will not go home after this, because they are sending us to the Mongolian border, so that nobody at home will know what has happened in Prague. Please, you write to my family and tell them where I am going."

"OK," I say, responding to his heart even though he's a Russian. Reaching out and taking his address, I fold it up carefully, and put in my pocket realising how important and serious this is. He shakes my hand. "Sank you." I'll give the address to Mum when we get back to England. Caspar and I set off again on our quest for the Black Madonna, and poke our heads inside the door of the puppet theatre as we pass by. "Come in if you want, it's just a dress rehearsal, sit down." So snug in the cosy darkness, we put our feet up on the seats in front of us and settle in to watch. Puppet shows in Prague are different to English ones. The puppeteers are dressed in black, and their faces are blacked up too. With a combination of marionettes, glove and rod puppets, they are doing the story of Mother Holle, and it's about halfway through; good, we've missed the part about Golden Mary and how boringly good and dutiful she is.

Out zooms the ghastly stepmother, busty, red high heels, thin lime-green lips and squinting eyes, with her hair held up in a dishcloth neatly pinned together by a large red communist star. And here comes her equally attractive daughter, as they go huffing and puffing about taunting Golden Mary, their cackling falsetto voices gradually dwindling as they disappear into their house. The squint-eyed daughter—after some gold for herself—sits spinning by the well for about five seconds before she "accidently" throws her spinning wheel into it. Up it flies, out of her hands and several feet into the air, falling into the well as it twists and turns. Kersplosh! she jumps in after it. Caspar and I laugh out loud. The whole stage whizzes about, trees go up, her house and garden disappear and the well vanishes from sight. Then fish swim into view: crocodiles, goggles, flippers, mermaids, submarines, you name it, and it really looks like she's sinking down and down, until at last she comes to rest at the bottom with a loud thump.

The dirty lazy girl lies in a crumbled marionette heap, inanimate for a while before she slowly uncurls herself, tests her limbs, cracks her fingers and stands up, shaking herself off before adjusting her head and stepping out from the bottom of the dark well. The lights come up and birds start twittering from backstage, cows low softly, and little woolly lambs careen about in a most beautiful countryside. An apple tree calls to her, "Pick my apples, pick my apples or they will fall and bruise!" But she thrusts her warty nose high in the air and ignores them. The apple tree blows raspberries at her.

On she goes, stomping along as fast as she can towards a cottage where Mother Holle, a strange, kindly old troll-like lady, looks out from the doorway, and opening her arms invites the dirty girl inside. They do a little dance with brooms, dustpans and mops, the dirty girl slapping her thighs and showing her knickers. Mother Holle explains that she can stay if she will work for her, and that everyday the feather beds must be shaken out very well, for only that way will it snow on earth. At first the dirty girl works quite well, unaccustomed as she is to cleaning and cooking. Everyday she shakes out the feather beds, even falling out of the window in the process. (Feathers fly out all over the theatre, I think they've got a fan back there.) But soon she's dragging herself about the place with heavy sighs. Eventually she doesn't get up at all and remains in bed, refusing to get up for Mother Holle; she shakes her head vigorously from beneath the bed clothes.

Mother Holle sits down on the bed, and the dirty girl starts crying loud crocodile tears, pretending that she's missing her home, her mother and Golden Mary her step-sister. (You almost feel sad for her.) "I want to go home," she wails. Mother Holle, breathing a sigh of relief, leads her to the garden gate where they say goodbye. But when she steps through it, she does not get covered in gold like her sister—oh no, no, no. (The sounds of soldiers' voices talking loudly outside can be heard, and the clink of their buckles and boots as they trudge off somewhere towards the river.) The director and puppeteers come out from back stage, swearing at the interruption and lighting up. "How you like, so far?"

"It's brilliant" says Caspar. "It's really great!"

"What you think, when she is falling in the well?"

"It really looked like she was going down and down."

"Hey you two, you smoke, you want coffee? You want to stay for the end, or go in your home now?"

"Stay, and coffee please," said Caspar, overcome by the dusky blond.

"Here, do you want to try an English cigarette?" (I offer them round.) "My favourite part of this story is the frogs and toads, I don't want to miss the ending."

"Well look, come with me, I show you how we do the frogs and toads. Here, you be Mother Holle, put on your hand like so . . . You can speak her in English." I make Mother Holle breath an enormous sigh of relief and say, "Come my dear, let me take you to the gate that leads from my garden back into your world." The dirty girl is eagerly anticipating a rush of gold as she passes underneath the gate, and I wave her towards it. "Here, your brother, come and work the soot . . . all you do is pull this . . ." The dirty girl passes through, Caspar pulls the string and soot falls all over the puppet. The Rooster is thrust into my hand, and quickly holding him up, relishing my new role, I shout as loudly as I can, "Cock-a-doodle-do, your dirty girl's come back to you!" "Is that what you say? Fantastic, I must learn zat. So what do you say ven Golden Mary goes through?"

"Cock-a-doodle-do, your boring girl's come back to you!"

"Hm. Boring, huh?"

"Yes, but what about the frogs and toads?"

"OK, go back and watch now." After the dirty girl gets covered in soot, every time she tries to speak frogs and toads come out of her mouth instead of words. And boy do they come. It's a simple device involving the blowing end of a hoover, and frogs and toads shoot out all over the place, canon-like. "Hurrah!" we shout, clapping wildly.

He comes out laughing. "Vell, it still needs a bit of vork." On our way back Caspar stops and looks up. "Look Sunny, there it is again, up there on the corner of that house." The Black Madonna, and her solemn Black Child.

Here's what you've got to know about Czechoslovakia. Children are not separated off from the adults; they are precious and everybody loves them. They are welcomed and included in everything, you can be friends with anybody, and people take time with you like they want to instead of it being a bother.

There's none of this "respect" crap either, and you can stay up late and hear all the dirty jokes, sharing in the conversation until it's bedtime for everyone.

One day a stranger shows up. Nobody knows who he is, and immediately the household starts to bristle with suspicion and hostility. "Is Misha here today?" he inquires, in perfect English. My father takes him and *my* suitcase outside.

I wake up later; it's one o'clock in the morning and my mum is hissing like a spitting cobra at my dad. "Have you gone out of your mind, Misha, smuggling mercury into Czechoslovakia in her suitcase?"

"Vell my darlink, it vill pay for all ze school fees, and our stay here. Even a little extra for my parents. Zer is no mercury here at all at ze moment."

"But Misha . . ."

"Hey Mum, were Mary and Jesus black?"

"What ever are you talking about? Of course not darling, go back to sleep."

We keep our noses down and wait for the right time to go home. After three weeks all foreign people are asked to leave.

12

In Grosvenor Square—and I'm definitely not supposed to be here—it's chaos. There are hundreds of police on huge horses lurking in the side streets, like a medieval battle-ground. The crowds are shouting over and over, "LBJ, LBJ, how many kids have you killed today?" Through an opening in the crowds I catch a glimpse of my brother Jake. "Christ I hope he hasn't seen me. What's he doing here anyway?" I get through the seething violence, and run like crazy towards what I hope will be Regents St. When I get there I am amazed at the normality of it all.

Watching the Paris student riots, at a safe distance, on our neighbour's telly. I am with them all the way, and hope they win.

My family and I are climbing up Mount Vesuvius. Caspar keeps saying, "It could go off at any moment you know, Sunny." I know he's frightened that it will, and ignoring him until we get to the top, I make my way down a little into the crater, where there is a narrow lava ledge, and dance around completing an entire circuit, making a racket and hoping for volcanic reactions. My family are all peering over the edge, looking like a bunch of owls. Dad's laughing, but Caspar beetles back down the mountain at a hundred miles an hour in case I set it off.

Mum tries to hurry us by some truly fascinating mosaics in Pompei. "Come along now dears, look at this." We catch glimpses of women doing it with dogs and things anyway. Caspar and I double back later for further study.

Caspar is very ill with a brain tumour; I think he's dying. He lies in hospital, his head is shaved, and he has felt-pen marks all over it, to direct the beams for his "Ray Treatment". He also has hundreds of stitches up and down the back, around the sides and over the top. His skin is pulled so tight across his face he looks transparent. He tells me quietly that he is frightened that the ray treatment machine will fall on his head and crush him. He dreamed that he was walking over a barren land along a path with lots and lots of children. They were making their way towards a shining boat, with angels in the rigging. Caspar was last to go up the gang plank, but an angel stopped him, saying, "Alas, there is no room for you," so he had to turn back. He is sad about that, because he really did want to go. "But we want you Caspar, don't we Jake?"

"Yes. Anyway, it looks like you're going to live now." Jake's metaphysical reply is a surprise to me.

Mum takes Caspar to a clinic in Switzerland. He takes a remedy called Iscador, and gets slowly better.

I have gone to live at "The Cottage" with old Miss Wilder and Miss Watson. They built their cottage themselves. It leans up against the forest, and they have seven other boarders. I love it here. I help milk the cows, and dig in the vegetable garden; I bricklay, cement, lay floors, practise my violin, and do my homework, and if there is anything I don't understand,

Gabriel, a very kind boy who never makes me feel bad, explains and helps me patiently; he is my special friend. The whole place always smells of fresh baking bread. I miss Shadowfax and the foals, but don't go to visit them for fear of meeting Dad. Life is peaceful here—a refuge. I make new friends with children I've been at school with but didn't know too well, like Jay and Neville, who turn out to be quite unique characters; and in the night, Gabriel creeps to our room for whispered conversations, with an interesting unspoken new flavour. One day Gabriel gives me a crab claw in a match box, and when I leave he gives me a beautiful piece of agate which he's been polishing for months. It's wrapped in moss, and I treasure it.

We are blowing the Easter eggs for painting. I never have enough puff, and the eggs are fragile. I like to paint Celtic designs and crosses on them, or dip them in wax and scrape a pattern. Some people boil them in natural dyes with grasses and flowers that leave a delicate print on them. I enjoy it very much, it's tricky, intricate and challenging.

Oh no, not Good Friday, the worst day of the year—doom and gloom, wailing and gnashing of teeth, alas. None the less I always try to be outside at three o'clock on Good Friday, because I've heard that Richard Wagner saw the Earth shimmer at this time, and that's why he wrote the Good Friday music. It never shimmers for me, but it can be very still. The whole Steiner Community all over the world, like us, will be having their silent supper; you are supposed to look out for the needs of others, and be aware... We are. I am passing the potatoes for the third time to my neighbour, and he is passing me the spring greens, which he knows I don't like.

I have been at this school all my life. Why don't the teachers who do like me see how the French teacher haunts me? He is as violent with his words as my father is with his hands. I feel confused and betrayed by this.

I am shaving my legs. Man, it looks like a suicide attempt.

On the Forest, under the heavenly firmament, I am losing my virginity to some one who clearly needs it more then I do.

But now, three weeks after doing it, God points his finger at me: my first period. But contrary to the rumour, I do not feel in touch with "the all-creative feminine." I am a loner, Artemis–like. But I'll try not to destroy all my boyfriends, although I know how she feels.

Everybody seems to have taken up making love (our new discovery) in a big way. We go at it like it's never been done before, and no man, youth or boy is an island round here. We swop partners, we're not fussy—that is, me, Liza and Rayette. They are sorting the men from the boys; I, on the other hand, am in search of the cold indifference of sensationalism. We make love in the hay, on the forest, in cars, up the big tree, in the bracken . . . all except for Ellie, who is keeping herself pure until she's married. "Married?" I say, completely mystified. "I'm never getting bloody married."

The boys are too shy and under-age to buy their rubber johnnie's in the chemist, and they're too young to get them from the gents' in The Green Man pub either. So Rayette, Liza and I sit on a skip and watch them go through the back door. First they have to scale a six-foot brick wall, then jump into the courtyard, brave the jaws of the Alsatian, and finally run like mad to the outside door and the almost empty slot-machine.

We are at Ellie's house, our fingers aching as we stretch them for the bar-chords we need to play Leonard Cohen songs on our guitars. We sing "Suzanne" and "Nancy", solemnly imitating the sexuality of his voice, and trying to intensify the subversiveness of his lyrics.

After 13 years of constant campaigning, we have a telly. The modern materialistic world has finally arrived in our house. Once a week, Mum goes out to join the more spiritually minded-members of the Community for their meditation. I encourage her off benevolently, because amazingly, it coincides with "Monty Python's Flying Circus", which we are all glued to in astonishment. No wonder we've never been allowed a telly.

Pearl and Dean have got a T.V. now as well, but their Mum insists on them wearing woolly hats when watching it to protect them from the radiation.

I tell you, when I grow up I'm going to let my children do whatever they want to.

Sex is a big deal in the adult world, and you can tell they don't really enjoy it because of the agonised faces they make, and excruciating difficulty they have with words, when talking about it.

It is midnight, and I am sitting outside my parents' door to see if they do it. Mum is so holy, I have my doubts.

Riding my bike home from school, and whizzing down Monks Road, I hear an ominous gronking and a "fring" . . . The welding on my front forks has cracked. I careen over the road and half way up the bank on the other side, narrowly missing that girlie Hamish McTavish. Instead of helping, he runs off down the road squeaking, "Sunny's fallen off her bicycle!" Twit.

Yannis is divorced. He has his workshop way out in the middle of nowhere. He's Greek, and a Communist, and prefers men to women. He has dedicated his life to making magnetic wooden fish. He doesn't fit in anywhere.

I read *Oz* religiously, whenever I can get my hands on it, but this week's cover is so outrageous I have to rip it off before taking it home.

We all await the Michaelmas festival with impatience. It has now become the herald of the psychedelic mushroom season. We eat ourselves sick and get stoned out of our minds on the school Michaelmas walk.

"Lets just talk about this calmly," my French teacher says. He's holding my French book, onto which I've written in red, "IN CASE OF FIRE THROW THIS IN FIRST". "You know Sunny, you have a real problem with authority, which you must try and come to grips with." "I'VE got a problem with authority?" I bellow at him, "YOU'RE the one with the authority problem around here. You try and come to grips with it yourself." "You are burning your bridges in front and behind you," he says ominously. "Cheerio," I say, leaving.

Rory Twyford is always on the verge of losing his temper. I really like him. He can be completely outrageous and funny, and doesn't take any crap either. He makes a big deal of lusting after the girls, though, and it's hard to get through this. I went off to look for his company during lunch break, but changed my mind when I ran into him in the Water Meadow with spittle and grass clippings all over his chin, rolling his eyes and going up to girls saying, "Cor blimey, I luv's you darlin', give us a kiss".

I am the Queen of the Night, swathed in a black and purple satin cloak studded with stars. Walking to the Halloween Ball, I can hear music already, and I've got my fiddle under my arm. When I open the door Dracula and Frankenstein whirl by, followed by a vampire clutching a small Egyptian mummy, and there's Merlin and Baba Yagga complete with metal teeth. Some ghosts are apple-bobbing (there's a trick to this they haven't cottoned on to yet), and look, there's Death sipping mulled wine with the Devil. I join the band, taking my place next to Max for "The Gay Gordons", to welcome in the spirits of winter . . . and have nightmares for months afterwards.

Whatever the festival, Caspar always goes dressed up as Tarzan, or else a savage.

Max Rye and I are good friends. The trouble is, though, he always smells of engine oil. He doesn't get on with the French teacher either. In fact the French teacher has it in for quite a few of us. I think of us as the French Resistance.

I am playing Monopoly with Caspar. He mortgages everything in sight, and buys up Park Lane. I wish he'd fuck off and die.

Caspar's friend Kevin has died. He drowned while swimming in the reservoir; he dived in and got tangled in some fencing wire. Kevin was like an elegant seal when he swam; I used to think that's why the trout liked him. Caspar is bemused and numb; I am angry, burning with rage.

Sometimes on a Saturday morning, I get a guitar lesson with Ed Leichner. Ed is a Czech friend of Dad's. He has loads of kids, a big wife, and a big rambling house in Buckfastleigh. He runs a translating business simultaneously with teaching me. I get coffee, which I'm not allowed at home, and his lessons are really something; he teaches me three chords at a time and says, "Now see how many songs fit those chords." Ed goes off to chat in Czech on the phone, bits of which I understand, especially the swear words. He organises the family—"Everybody happy?"—chats to the typists, and comes back to me. "You vant more coffee?" he says, and then picking up his guitar, he improvises along with me. We can go from "She'll Be Coming Round ze Mountain" into "The Brahms Lullaby", and then on to "These Boots are Made for Walking", not a bother on us. These lessons take all morning, and I often stay for lunch; maybe with luck we play some more after. He says, "You're good, zat's very good, you are a regular Chet Atkins."

It is the evening, and Dad has really lost it this time—he's thrown Caspar down the stairs. I'm so worried for Caspar's head, it gets an awful fucking bang. Dad drives off. Mum and I stand there aghast before she swoops into action cradling his head and checking it out. "It's OK Caspar, it's OK," I say. What I want to know is, why does Mum let it happen? Why doesn't she do something? Maybe because it's mostly me that gets it, and that's what you get if you're only a half-tamed wild thing.

Dad knows all the Czechs in the south of England, and has loads of wheeler-dealer dodgy friends too. He meets them gambling; he bets on anything: dogs, horses, whether it will snow at Christmas. He's got a friend called Larry the Cheese, who smuggles Pakistanis into the country. Larry once landed an aeroplane on the motorway. Dad's friend Sid's wife was mysteriously murdered, but it turned out to be Sid in the end. These guys sometimes turn up at our house in their suits and Rollers, but this usually means they're going off to the casino in London. Sometimes Dad disappears for days. Mum doesn't like it, but I do.

I come home from School, and let myself in. I know something's wrong; the moment I open the door, I can feel it. I go to the kitchen, and then through to the sitting-room; by now my heart is racing. Mum is lying on the floor. She is unconscious, and there is blood every where; I can see her nose is broken. I call Dr Thomas, and an ambulance. I know it was Dad, and so does Dr Thomas. Suddenly I'm all bound up with Mum in a way I don't want. I'm left alone in the house, and when the doctor goes, he prescribes me some tranquillisers called Oblivon. I save them all up and take them at the weekend.

"Hey Mr Cato, congratulations! I hear you and Romany had twin girls last night. That must have been really something, what are you going to call them? You look knackered.

"We're thinking of calling them Misty and Phoebe, I hope that meets with your approval?" Mr Cato is tired, but he's also shining, like when he was the angel in the Christmas play. "And how are you today?" he asks.

"Oh fine, just fine," I reply, wondering if Mum will be back from the hospital when I get home.

Jasper Carter and I are giving a gig in the Green Man pub. We play jigs, reels and dance tunes on trumpet and violin, and guitar. We are a hit, and get a fiver each.

Aries and I are snogging on the forest. Things are getting pretty hot. When he gets his thing out I realise that he's circumcised and say, "Hey, I've never seen one of these before." He misinterprets me, I laugh, and the moment passes.

Rayette is worried about her biker boyfriend's fidelity. She asks Saskia to go over to his place to test it out. Noel can't believe his luck, and Saskia has no trouble at all in seducing him. Now Rayette isn't talking to Saskia.

"Darling, what do you think I was in my last incarnation?" Mum enquires. "I don't know, Mum. Boddecia, Lady Godiva, Cleopatra, the Medusa, Grendel's mum?" "Oh," she says, disappointed. "Not a Cathar?" "Oh yeah, sure, a Cathar. A Parfait even." We are getting ready for Carnival. This year's theme is "What you were in your last incarnation". I think I'll put on my raincoat and go as a flasher.

I can't get the image of Mum all covered in blood out of mind, it's there all the time. I wonder why I have to go to school if I'm never going to get an O'level? I don't go to loads of lessons. I just can't get my mind to work; even if I like the subject, it seems meaningless and hollow, like I'm in a tunnel and everything is happening at the far end of it.

Saskia's class have it in for Miss Bell, a mousy maths teacher. They are always writing off to computer-dating services on her behalf. When it comes to the question, "What are your hobbies?" they write down with glee, "Rally-driving". Nobody knows her home address, so the replies come in sackfuls to the school office.

I'm on a French exchange. I enjoy the ferry boat and train ride through the night. I change trains in Geneva for the mountains. I really like the family I'm staying with, and I'm good at skiing. I fly down the mountain as fast as possible, at top speed, and if I get up really early I can get the lift up to the glacier. It's very cold this early, and down below, I can see the footprints of little animals in the snow. It's so quiet in the mountains, the peace and majesty settle warmly inside me. Higher up and always at a distance the Chamois mountain-goats forage with their slender legs and long spiralling horns. One day I find a horn; it's so perfect, like the sea has made it.

No skiing to day, the snow-storm shrieks outside the chalet. I curl up by the fire and read *The Lord of the Rings*. I'm in heaven, and I don't want to go home.

Home again. I bought some Camembert cheese home for Mum, put my goat horn on my dressing table, go to the Forest and take a tab and a half of LSD. I go whooshing up out of myself, from the bottom of my stomach through the top of my head. Breathing with the Forest, I know that I do have a place in this world, a rightful place.

We buy a load of slimming pills off "Big Bertha". (Dr Thomas can't understand why she never loses weight.) You can get quite a wizz if you take two or three of them. We start stamping on puff-balls, the clouds of spoors exploding under our feet. Stamp, stamp, stamp, squelch—"Oh God, that was an egg, what stupid chicken laid its egg here? Man, look at my desert-boot, I hate chickens." Stamp, stamp, stamp.

I wear desert-boots, Levi's, T-shirt and a top hat at all times. I have a gorgeous uniform jacket from Carnaby Street, which Mum throws out; she's in horse-breaking mode, so there's nothing I can do about it.

Some kids pinch money from their parents. I don't, though; I just go on and on and on, and Dad usually gives up and gives me a fiver.

Mr Harman, our maths teacher, is clearly colour-blind. He wears pink shirts, yellow ties, purple hand-knit jumpers and tweed trousers; we put on sun-glasses for his lessons. He can teach maths though; I understand most of what's going down.

We are convinced that the maths teacher is having an affair with the school secretary. We write notes from her to him, putting them under his window wiper and on his desk. Unfortunately we don't know her first name. "Darling," we write:

> I love your mathematical rhythym, your precision,
> the way you measure my cones and triangles.
> 1+1=2, let's equalize later in the office, where legs meet in infinity.
> I love you to the power of ten—
> Yours ever, Mrs Rose.
>
> p.s. Divide me. I am a fraction of my former self.

One day the maths teacher says to us, holding up another letter, "Who is this marvellous Mrs Rose? She's just my type, I'd love to meet her." All notes stop forthwith.

That Australian geezer is teaching us about Darwin's theory of evolution. I'm interested, but he keeps picking holes in it and pointing out where it's wrong, as if we can't see for ourselves. After all, we've all been brought up to suspect Darwinian evolution, where one species comes out of another; he's teaching the experts. I let him fumble along for a while before asking him what he does believe in. It's clear he doesn't know exactly; he doesn't appear to have even thought about it. I tell him, "We don't want information you've read the night before, what about teaching us something you've passed through your heart?" This time it's the teacher who walks out, which is different. I feel guilty, but I want the real thing.

Mum and I beat the pants off Caspar and Jake playing Bridge. Yee ha!

In my dream, I am walking the length of Newhaven pier, along the top wall. My legs are so stiff I can hardly move them, and a strong off-shore wind blows against me. In the harbour I can see the ferry boat and junky old fishing trawlers. Eventually I arrive at the end of the pier, and stand on the edge. The sea begins to crawl and boil, and a massive tidal-wave creeps up slowly from the sea; it rises, seething and immensely powerful, way over my head, until it arches above me and the end of the pier ready to break. I struggle with this wave until it slowly recedes, inch by inch, back into the sea.

I have painted a landscape in oils. The yellow sun sets over the Alps, on a winter evening. I show it to Teddy, who runs the Inner Man cafe. He likes it immediately, and offers me a fiver for it. Secretly, I think the sun-set looks like a fried egg, and that's why Teddy (who fries eggs all day) likes it so much. I try not to smirk, and accept the fiver.

Teddy is an ex-con, and can forge any hand-writing; he forges our sick-notes for games (which we spend in his cafe) and even thank-you letters from his own children. He and Noreen let us pile into the kitchen if a parent or teacher comes in search of us there. Teddy is blind in one eye. He and Noreen send their kids to our school, but I can tell they won't last. We're too weird and spiritual for them.

Mum has a crashing migraine. She lies in her darkened bedroom, clutching her Codeine and Bidor tablets. I wish I'd known or I would have stayed longer in the cafe, knowing she couldn't come to hoik me out. As it is, I have to tip-toe around the place ministering to the half-dead, who are not very grateful.

Man, you should see what Rayette Rye is wearing. She has the smallest mini-skirt I've ever seen, her black polo-neck is so tight I'm surprised she can get her boobies in there, and then these platform boots which go up to her knees. She totters up to the village while all the older holy-rollers in the Community drive by, just about bumping into each other, trying to get a look before registering their disapproval.

Liza and I know that there is less to Rayette than meets the eye.

Myumi has some pretty amazing gear as well, but she is generous with it; and Dan, knowing how Mum has thrown away mine, gives me his uniform jacket. It's just like one off the front of the Sergeant Pepper Album. I spend time up at their house. It's very hip now; they know the Maharishi.

I pay for my cinema ticket to see "Easy Rider". I head straight for the ladies' loo to open the window, and an unending stream of kids climb through and settle down for the movie. It's always really noisy when we go, what with peanuts flying everywhere and Coke spraying in all directions. We hiss, we boo, we sing along, we snog—none of us is allowed to go to the cinema, so we may as well get my money's worth. It's a riot. We follow the same procedure for all the films we are not allowed to see, like "Woodstock", "Kes", "Miss Jean Brodie", "2001", etc.... and best of all, the Eastwood Cinema is haunted, so when we get bored we make ghosty noises.

I'm completely stoned in maths class. The numbers on the blackboard keep dripping into each other like Salvador Dali's clocks, leaving me to wonder what he was on.

Us girls are swimming at midnight in a local lake. We are not wearing anything, this being a spontaneous decision. Wouldn't you know it but the boys have come down with the same idea; they soon realise we've got nothing on, and put all our clothes up the surrounding trees. Ha very ha.

I like Rory Twyford's Dad but he never teaches us, which is too bad because I could learn from him, he's not a fake, and he's always been fair to me. But he's around all right, and that's good to know.

Toya collapsed of an overdose today in Art. I thought she was looking a bit pale, well, white actually. I hope she's going to be OK. But I guess they will expel her. I wonder who else comes to school in an altered state?

Another school report has arrived, and I'm crying. They say I'm lazy, because I don't hand in my work. But I'm not lazy; I try, but I can't do it. I write letters backwards, sometimes whole words. "You must try harder," it says. "Oh shut up and try harder yourbloodyselves". I'm very offended at being called lazy.

My trapeze hangs forlorn from the pine tree. I climb the rope ladder, trying to control my tears. I swing gently, trying to gain inner and outer equilibrium. I ease myself down to hang by my feet, I swing, I hang by one foot, I swing, I put my hands behind my head, and place my free foot on my knee. I am the Hanged Man from the Tarot pack. I swing, and I'm not lazy. Then, bang! I fall off.

In our mechanics lesson we are building a car; well, Oily Rags is, actually. The girls are standing round daubing psychedelic paint on it. It only has a driver's seat and was once a Vauxhall Viva. It doesn't look very Viva now, but miraculously works. We even get permission from B.R. to drive it on the old Eastwood to Oldbridge line, now that the tracks have been taken up, so we spend the whole summer happily driving up and down it. Even little Luke gets to learn to drive, smoke and drink cider; he inevitably throws up.

It is the Mid-Summer Festival. I look forward to the fire we light at night, and the Shakespeare play the older children perform in the outdoor theatre. Pearl Lowen, who is politically-minded and a feminist, suggests we burn our bras in the fire en masse. I don't know what to say; I don't wear a bra.

It is dark and warm, the stars shining high above in the cloak of the sky. We stand together, most of the Community, hushed, waiting around the unlit fire. From the distance, the oldest class carry their burning torches towards us. They move together in a line as one. They criss-cross, loop, make a figure-of-eight, and slowly they approach. All I can see are the patterns of the burning torches. But now, as they circle the fire, I can see Charley, Angy, Calvin, Jason and all those ready to leave School. Tonight they stand on a threshold, and plunge the torches into the dead wood; the sparks rise upwards to meet the stars.

We have just changed the lyrics of Paul McCartney's "Let it Be". It now goes:

> "When I find myself in times of trouble,
> Rudolf Steiner comes to me,
> Whispering words of wisdom,
> Anthroposophy..."

"Come on Mum, the elder-flower is all ready to be picked." I love elder-flower juice. I like to pick it, the yellow pollen staining my fingers and going up my nose. And the smell when you boil it up—man, it's delicious. Plus it's a fine sunny day. "Let's go now, come on Mum."

I am on my bed; the blows rain down upon me like the blacksmith's hammer, merciless and relentless. My Dad beats me all over my face, my head, my body. I am fighting back and my Mum is shouting at the door, "What has she done?" I don't know. He just carries on and on and on. I drift up to the ceiling, and looking down I can hear myself snarling and swearing, fuck you, fuck you, but I never give up or give in—never. He is beating me with the beautiful horn I found in the Alps, and now it is covered in blood. My nose bleeds, I have two gashes in my head, and my backbone is raw.

Mum tries to make me stay home but I can't stay there, so I go to school. I'm black and blue. I say I fell off my bike, "But I'm fine, just fine." Every bone in my body aches, but this is nothing compared to my heart. Where will I go after school, now that nobody wants me?

Serafina Windfall picks me up in her Merc. Her son Ralph is in the back. (Ralph and I have a long-standing relationship; we have been friends since I was six.) They have got my gear from Mum; I'm being rescued, but I'm worried about

Mum. I snuggle up to Ralph, this is his job in my life: total unconditional love at all times, while Serafina administers Arnica pills in extravagant handfuls. We drive slowly over the Forest to their pink Manor House. I'm so cold I can't believe the sun is shining. Ralph and I curl up in bed, the fire lighted and furry hot-water-bottles everywhere. He knows not to ask for details of what's happened, because he won't get them. I'm too sore and out of it for any of the usual, relaxed, hilarious love-making we can get up to. I go there quite a lot, because I can't sleep alone when I have bad dreams. When we first did it Ralph was rather miffed to find that he was not the very first one. He'd been waiting all those years, you see.

My parents are getting divorced. I'm ashamed of this, and worried. My Dad lives in Eastwood now, and our house is so quiet and strange—just Mum and me, and we're strangers to each other, really. But I can smell traces of my father all over the house, and I don't like it.

When Dad finally goes the silver tea-service with the family crest also mysteriously disappears.

I steal Mum's car, pick up Aries, Liza, Rory and some others and drive up to the Ridge Road. After the pub, couples go to snog in their cars up there. We turn off the lights and inch the car slowly in, right behind a car with a writhing couple in it. We watch for a time and then flick on the full beams and toot the hooter; to our amazement, the couple shoot out of the car with nothing on and run off at full speed across the heather.

I take a tab of LSD but this time the gates of hell open, and the Devil rides out. I live in hell for the next eight hours, but with the help of the American teacher I'm OK. When I finally come down I sleep, and when I awake it is to the words, "The sun is in my heart". I know this to be true.

I have to go to court to speak at my parents divorce, but it will be Christly awful to see Dad.

I am so ill—I have pyelitis, a kidney disease. My temperature soars, it feels like I'm dying and my back is so painful, throbbing, throbbing, throbbing. Dr Thomas comes; he's very kind, Mum is worried, I drift in and out of sleep and pain for days and nights. The homeopathy doesn't seem to help much. "Give me normal medicine, I want drugs!" Finally I get real medicine; man, you have to be really sick in this house to get antibiotics.

Everyday Ellie Winner comes to visit me. When I get a little better, I ask her why. She explains that she thought I was dying, and was writing a speech about how brave I was. "I'm sorry to disappoint you," I say, and she is very disappointed. I'm almost well again now, grace of a cocktail of homeopathy, antibiotics, acupuncture and a load of other stuff. And I learned a secret from being ill: which is that life itself is the holy thing.

When I go for a check up the doctor asks me, among other things, "How's your sex life?" I reply, "Fine thanks, how's yours?" I'm rather embarrassed by his question, actually.

It's the end of the summer holidays, and I stagger off to The Green Man. Rayette is there and all the gang; while I get myself a Coke, Rayette is asking her biker boyfriend if he loves her. "Course I luvs ya. I fucks ya, don't I?" he announces reassuringly to the whole pub.

Loads of people have been to see the Maharishi. I'd like to go too; maybe, just maybe, he might have a mantra that would be good for me. You're supposed to keep your mantra secret, but everybody knows everybody else's.

I have had a painting accepted in the village art show. I phone up the village hall and enquire in foreign accents who the talented young artist is, and if the painting is sold yet, adding comments about its composition in an Italian voice. "Sunny, for Christ's sake, you sound like the Mafia." Oh bollocks, how do they know it's me?

I've just passed my Grade Five violin. Mum promised me a new, expensive, posh violin if I passed, and where is it? Nowhere to be seen. But now she says she won't get me one, because I'm only really interested in "that folk music."

We often get together for a jam, and now The Green Man has given us a spot on Friday evenings: Liza on side-flute, Max on autoharp, Jasper on trumpet, Caspar and Charley fighting over the accordion, Jake on guitar, me fiddle, and Rayette sings. We all play grouped around the old fire-place, the flickering firelight hot on our faces. "Scarborough Fair", "Sounds of Silence", "Suzanne", "I Once Loved a Lass", and "There is a school in Woodbrook, they call St Georges School"—our own particular version of "The House of the Rising Sun". When we run out of songs we move onto country and western, which Rayette booms out in husky American accents.

It's breakfast time, and who should come nonchalantly out of Jake's bedroom but Rayette. "Hi," I say. Mum raises her eyebrows but seizing the opportunity, says, "I don't mind you staying here Rayette dear, but could you cut Jake's hair before he goes back to school?"

"Now that you're fifteen, there's a few things you ought to know." I'm sitting on the sofa with Mum. "Christ, she's explaining the facts of life to me," I think. She says it's very spiritual, and rambles on about love and the union between a Man and a Women. And that," she concludes, "is how a baby is born." I'm trying to arrange my face into an expression of mature surprise; I keep trying to catch my reflection in the window to see how I'm doing.

We believe in reincarnation, and that we have a certain destiny, with tasks to perform, on this earth. We have gifts to give and old karmic debts to pay, personal development to work on, and we must help each other along life's pathways. We choose our parents carefully, arriving in the family where we can best learn to develop what we need for life, our families are people with whom we have been on earth before. And that is why we are absolutely against abortion; we do not believe that any human being has a right to take the life of another, it is murder.

I work hard on my music and art because these are the gifts I arrived with, and they must not be squandered. Whereever we are, we can always work with what we've got.

13

We can always work with what we've got, so we could make something positive out of this too, positive for all of us; I knew we could. Minu's friends were brilliant, especially Leo and Sorrel, and mine as well. We started on a campaign of total support: "the war effort". Christ, we sent him stuff every day, postcards, tapes, books, drawings, games, and poems.

"Please could you send me something on Buddhism?" he wrote. He must have received enough information on Buddhism to become an incarnate master. "What's Christian Gnosticism?" Copies of *The Gospel According to St Thomas* and *The Gnostic Gospels* flew off to jail. "What about Ouspensky?" "The Knights Templars?" "The Rosicrucians?" "Who were the Cathars? Who was Mani, and the Albigenses?"

"Dear Minu, Mani believed that you could transform evil into good from the inside . . . and he was right."

"Has anybody got a copy of *The Doors of Perception*, by Aldous Huxley?" Finn rushed him one.

"Dear Mum, What do you know about early Celtic Christianity?"

Dear Minu,

    Only the first four hundred years after Christ are interesting . . . Even St Pat says, "They found it of themselves." You see, it's the only place in the world where Christianity wasn't imposed on the people. Celtic Christianity arose from a deeply spiritual relationship to nature, and around the time when Christ was born they experienced a shift from their old gods of the past to something new that looked ahead to the future. But after about four hundred years, the power-mad Roman Catholic Church came along and wrecked a really good thing. It is not possible to have power without tyranny . . .

Love Mum.

P.S. Here's a Celtic poem, to illustrate my point of view.

> I am the wind that blows upon the sea
> I am an Ocean wave;
> I am the murmur of the surges;
> I am seven battalions;
> I am a strong bull;
> I am an Eagle on a rock:
> I am a ray of the sun;
> I am the most beautiful of herbs;
> I am a courageous wild boar
> I am a salmon in the water;
> I am a lake upon a plain;
> I am a cunning artist;
> I am a gigantic, sword-wielding champion;
> I can shift my shape like a god.

"Anybody got a copy of *The Celestine Prophesy*?" Certainly not! Although I'd never actually read it, I hated that book.

Dear Mum, have you got any thing by Terry Pratchett or Steven King? . . . I've been on bang-up now for thirty-six hours. It's peaceful, and away from the agro. The white boys pick on anybody who isn't white, especially the Indians, and the Somali's wind up the Jamaicans—the blacks have a pecking order too, and the screws turn a blind eye. There are no wacky theories of evolution or convincing arguments for angels around here, the main topic of discussion being football and women, which is all right sometimes, but I do miss everyone a lot. It's not that I have to be constantly surrounded by artists of some kind, but it cheers things up. I miss the gay boys too (darling), and Nicky from the recording studio. They sent me a card, it said 'Minu, we miss you, it must be really horrible in there . . .' Mum, I'm going to be 21 in a few weeks, and moved to an adult jail. I am afraid of what I'll find there . . .

I made up my mind there and then to handcuff myself to the Home Secretary until he released Minu. And swallow the key. That would show that fine upstanding pillock of society.

> Dear Minu,
> You are going to be twenty–one soon and I know where you are is perhaps not what you anticipated for your twenty–first birthday! Never mind, it is none the less a landmark, on a long and open road which lies ahead of you. There are places to see, triumphant successes and spectacular failures to achieve, people to meet along the way, friends to make, and much, much more. Perhaps this seems empty and meaningless to you. Sometimes I've been very afraid too, but most of my fears have come welling up from the past and from things that have already happened; I am not afraid at all of what the future may bring. Just maybe, in the immediate future, you may find an adult jail is less threatening then a youth detention centre. And in the long run, being twenty-one is a fine step forward on an

open road. I think that one day you will be able to look back along that road, and see your prison clearly defined, along with all the other experiences good and bad that you will have, but I know that they will be set amongst a truly unique and beautiful landscape.

I love you, Mum.

14

My Dad is telling me his life story. He lives with an Indian women in a flat above the Eastwood library. It's decorated Czech-Indian style, a novelty of Ganesh and cuckoo-clocks, incense sticks and pictures of Prague. I hope none of my friends ever sees this place, and I don't want to know about his life at all, but he just goes right ahead. He tells me how he was champion boxer of Czechoslovakia (and Woodbrook, I think); and how, because he could speak fluent Russian and German, he was recruited aged seventeen by the Russians to spy in the Foreign Legion, they being in training for the Indo-China war. Dad went to the Sahara and Algeria, where he had a cannon and a mule, caught malaria, and relayed information back to his Russian bosses. After his training he was in the queue for the boat to take the Foreign Legion off to war when a diplomatic car pulled up, and a Russian official pointed to Dad and some others, saying, "These boys are under-age, they must come with me." They were then taken to Marseilles, where they were closely questioned, and then all sent to Brandenburg in case they had been double-agenting (which, knowing Dad, is a likely possibility).

They stayed in Brandenburg for nine months before they were released with no passports and only Russian papers, but he had some agreement that his next job would be in England. He went back to Czechoslovakia to see his family and give them money, but was arrested again—this time by the Czech police, because of his Russian papers—and put back in jail. Eventually he got to England, where he was immediately approached by the Czech resistance. So he started working for them.

Dad was sent back to Czechoslovakia one more time to rescue an eminent scientist, but when he got there it was too late, the Russians had already got him. He saw his family one more time, then with the help of friends stole a plane and flew to Stuttgart, and on to England. He got a job in a brick factory, and wheeled and dealed on the black market, where he made so much money that when Mum met him he had a flat in Mayfair, and was living like a king.

I'm pleased he turns out to be somebody, but what I say is: "It's no excuse Dad, you know. It's no excuse at all".

My class has been up and down the country visiting various other communities with our play, "Le Petit Prince". For transport, the powers-that-be have decided on a removal lorry. Every single person in the class has a role to play, or something incredibly vital to do. Tonight is the last night, and we are back at school. I am standing on top of a ladder behind the "Mountains". To make mountains the floor of the stage is covered in a huge sheet, and various kids hold it up with broomhandles or fingers. Mr Shepherd sits in the front row, clearly moved, and dewy-eyed at his old class's performance. I play my Little Prince role as deeply and seriously as possible. Unfortunately, one of the stupid mountains having farted, the whole range has got the giggles and is heaving about hysterically. A great actor like me has to work under all sorts of trying conditions.

I am watching and listening spell-bound to Herr Wissenschaften's history of art. He starts at the very beginning: ancient Chaldea, Mesopotamia, Ancient Egypt, the Greeks, the Romans, and the Italian Renaissance. We spend three weeks immersed in the science lab in the dark, watching the slides that Herr Wissenscaften has lovingly put together over many years. He teaches like he's about to die and wants to tell you everything, which is great because I want to know it all. I soak it into my heart; every single word is like sweet honey in the rock.

Just back from the Isle of Wight pop festival, where I have been having sex more or less continually for three days. My throat is sore and I'm muddy. I'm shouting outside the bathroom at Mum, who is not in a hurry. "Let me in the bathroom, I want a bath now, you've been in there for years. I've got things to do, let me in, let me in. Rudolf Steiner said!" "All right darling, I'm just finishing, calm down." I can hear her wallowing like a manetee, the slowest sea-creature in the world.

I'm having my breakfast when who should come out of Jake's bedroom but Liza. I'm annoyed he's pinched my friend. "Hi Sunny, how was the Isle of Wight?" she asks.
"It was great. I met Hannah there, and she's got a little baby. When I asked her who the father was she said, 'Oh, this is everybody's baby'."

I'm having a rant at my French teacher again. "I just think differently to everybody else around here. I am full of doubts, but you are not. I don't know about St Michael's dragon, except perhaps it's in all of us and we have to work with it every day. And I'm not sure about Jesus Christ either, or anything much. I used to think I knew everything, but now it's like I know nothing for sure . . . You adults who surround me are like moonwalkers, clomping around in your own little world and belief-systems, sure and secure in your space-suits, not really letting things show themselves to you. You don't see things that are right under your nose. We live in our little community, grow our own pure food, and have our own doctors and remedies, we wear our natural clothing, and this school has two fine orchestras, and produces some extraordinary theatre productions, and who is it all for, may I ask? Us, and we offer nothing to the outside world. Our local community is never even invited in, in fact they are completely ignored."

"Well anytime you want to share anything and do something in the local community, be my guest. Feel free, there it is down the road and off you go, Sunny."

"That's such a cop out, and you know it."

"If you really want to know about the world, you have to look inside yourself, not outside."

(Oh bog off.)

My class has to do a week's work experience. The school clearly thinks we want careers as Amish people. Here are our choices of what to do:

1. Work at Raphael Medicine, with the herbs and flowers. Learn about complementary planting, keeping ducks to eat the slugs, etc. In other words, pretty much what we do at home.
2. Work on one of the farms.
3. Work in the local timber yard. That could be good, maybe.
4. Go and clean the Long Man Of Wilmington, an elegant man carved out of chalk on the South Downs. Sounds great, but a real preparation for life, in a working environment? I wonder who's in charge. Good, it's that pseudo-intellectual American hippie. So I opt for this, and spend a happy week weeding and whitewashing, camping and swimming. I come home refreshed.

I feel indifferent to school; and at home, alien to Mum. I'm always being told off. I resent my teachers and family for not knowing me, but it's my fault because I never tell them anything. On the other hand they do not ask either.

We sit in the school canteen, "Oh cor blimey, it's food again, can't they think of anything else to give us? Look at this green potato, man. Do you think it's radioactive?" "Dunno," my neighbour says, "chuck it out the window, maybe it'll explode." So I bung it out, and it wizzes past Cromwell (another American teacher, but definitely not the hippie) who happens to be passing by. He calls me out. "Did you throw this?" he drawls.
"Maybe," I say.
"I'm taking you home," he says.
"Your place or mine?" I enquire in an American accent. "Woo woo, Cromwell is taking Sunny home!" The kids in the canteen start wolf-whistling.
"Come along now, Miss."
"Hands up, I'm arresting you for a spud felony," I drawl.
"You always have to have the last word, don't you, Sunny?" I count to ten before saying, "No".
I get suspended for three weeks.

Rohan, Liza, Luke, Jake and I go to Brighton for the day. After larking about in the ghost train and playing the slot machines on the pier, we try the new Dolphinarium to watch Baby, Missy and Marlon do their tricks. And when the dolphin trainer says "Does anybody in the audience have a birthday today?" I shout out "Yes!" "No you don't," says Luke. ("Shut up, idiot.") The dolphins line up in front of us and standing on their tails, sing "Happy Birthday" to me.

I'm writing to every single one of our communities for handicapped children. I lie about my age; I will be sixteen in March, but this is only December. So I tell them that I'm seventeen, I'm good at art, music and woodwork, etc., and I'd like very much to help with sick children. And I would, too.

The rest of the time I spend over at Ralph's. Inside myself I feel a failure, and hurt over being suspended.

Mum gets a letter from Monsieur le French Dictator, saying the School has nothing more to offer me. Well that's a weight off my mind, I didn't think they did anyway. But Mum is fuming and fully garbed in battle dress. Man, she sallies forth like the ride of the Valkyries. She makes such a fuss that I'm summoned to a meeting.

I approach the Coach House. It's shrouded in fog, I feel like I'm going to have my soul weighed. I give a knock like thunder on the door. "Come in," says Death in a gloomy German accent. I go in, and "Oh bollocks, look at this lot"—a line up of all the teachers I don't get on with. I've been set up and betrayed. No allies, no Mr Shepherd, no Miss Hendle, no music teacher, no Mr Twyford or Miss Myron, no Herr Wissenscaffen or Mr Harman. And I know they don't know what's going on here. The massed forces of darkness are sitting on high wooden thrones in a semi-circle, and facing them in the centre is a tiny little chair they must have borrowed from the kindergarten; that's for me. It doesn't take much imagination to know what they are going to say here. "If you crawl on your belly and lick the dust, live in humbleness, and never talk again . . ."

But I do not even let them get started; I am burning like a volcano. "I know you, but you don't know me. I have been with you all my life but you have not been with me. This education is based on developing each individual character, and now that you've got one, you don't know what to do with her." I wave out the foggy window, "All these new buildings you build—just signs of your inner weakness. You try to make up for it with material strengths, your college of teachers is a festival of fools, the college means you can all support each other and nobody needs to take individual responsibility for what they do. Like a proper head master, who is answerable for everything." I go on and on and nobody gets a chance to interrupt, because right now, for this moment, I have God on my side; my thoughts are clear, my words fall coherently, and before I leave I fix them with my horse-breaking will-power and say, "I hope you are ashamed."

As I leave I hear a melancholy sigh, and a voice says, "I thought something like this was going to happen." I peddle off on my red bike, ting-a-ling, ting-a-ling. It's a bell of freedom.

It is the summer. We are all camping at Deepmere, the whole gang. The Ryes, the Petersons, ourselves and others hitch down for a day or two. No parents, of course. We have one sailing boat and one rowing boat, fishing tackle, all our musical instruments, enough hash for an army, and white bread and white rice—another new discovery. Liza and I jump in the river and let the strong current pull us miles out to sea. One night Jake says, "Race you all to Sweethaven pub." They all hare off in various cars and ramshackle heaps like Max's black hearse, while I put little Luke on the back of a motorbike and drive hell-for-leather along the cliff path; we fly over the Seven Sisters, with the sea way below and the sun setting huge and red over the sea. We get there "hours" before the rest of them pull up in the dusty car park.

Little Luke and I sail up the coast gently. We have the sails full out and are running before the wind. By sitting right at the back of the boat, we can raise the front out of the water. Passing Beachy Head, we sail on to Eastbourne, where we leave the boat on the beach and make our way to the Grand Hotel. I have discovered that for a few shillings, you can get a civilised tea there, including various cakes which Luke likes, and smoked salmon or cucumber and cheese sandwiches. I like camping, but this is nice too.

I am sitting on the beach. Everything smells of mackerel and smoke. I am looking out to sea; way out there something is not right, it's someone caught in the tide. I plough my way out there, but when I get close this person looks dead. I know exactly what to do: lift her unconscious head above the water and swim on my back to the beach. When I get there, I pull her legs up above her and all the sea water comes shooting out of her mouth, then I pinch her nose shut and give her mouth-to-mouth. I keep on and on, using my will power . . . and look, a miracle: she comes alive again! It's Sally, Paul's girlfriend.

Mum suddenly appears at the beach, waving a letter. "You've got a job," she says, "in Switzerland." "Don't read my letters, Mum," I growl at her.

> "Dear Sunny,
> One of our co-workers has fallen ill. We would be very glad if you could come to help out, and see if you like working with our children."

I drive back with Mum, and read the bumpf on the school.

> We are a Community school, who live our lives according to the teachings and philosophy of Rudolf Steiner. We have a hundred and fifty children in need of special care, and about fifty handicapped adults. Our Community is set in three hundred acres of land by Lake Geneva. It is divided into twelve family houses, a biodynamic farm, market garden, workshops, school house and therapy buildings.
> The children live together with their helpers and house parents, and each child goes to school every day, and also works with one of the many therapies we have to offer, such as Physiotherapy, Art therapy, Music therapy, Massage, and Curative Eurythmy. We also have our own pool for Colour Therapy.

> The therapists work under the auspices of our own resident homeopathic doctor.
>
> Our handicapped adults work at the farm or market garden, or in the pottery, weavery, and woodwork shops. We are not self-sufficient, and maintain firm links with the local Community.
>
> A three year training course in special education is available to all those who work here and would like to participate. It is run in conjunction with our local education authority and leads to a Diploma in Special Needs Education. Courses, lectures and classes take place three evenings a week and two mornings.
>
> Year 1: the study of general child care, students have the responsibility for a dormitory of three or four children, working in and around their family home.
> Year 2: education; students work in the school helping the teachers and assisting the children.
> Year 3: therapy; students work alongside each of the therapists, helping them with their work and gaining some therapeutic experience.
>
> Our aim is to nurture the individuality of each child, and to awaken the thinking, feeling and willing—an education towards freedom, in a quiet atmosphere of healing and dignity, and respect towards the soul of the handicapped child.

Well, I'm up to it. Perhaps they'd let me do the training course too?

My Mum is giving me three pieces of advice:

1. Never let anybody take photos of you with nothing on, because they could use them for blackmail.

2. Don't have sexual intercourse unless you have a relationship with the person.

3. Never get a tattoo, or you won't be able to wear a ball dress. I swivel round and gape at this last one; I mean, when am I going to wear an effing ball dress? But I think about the tattoo for a while, and eventually go out and get one on my left arm.

15

Minu lay within my conscience like a piece of grit within an oyster, and I thought about him all the time. The poor chap had never been punished in his life; surely everybody in the universe knows that that doesn't work. Why hadn't he been given community service? At least it would have been constructive. And perhaps being constructive was what I needed as well?

Like a lot of others from my school, Paul was a builder. At a leisurely pace—fussing over the minor details, making trips to and from the timber yard, and drinking a lot of tea—we were building an "art-studio" on the side of the house . . . when we'd nothing better to do, or in Paul's case, when he needed an excuse to get out of doing something else. After a while, certain unnamed parties in the home quite unreasonably complained about living in a building site, so we got going in earnest. I buried myself in the hard physical labour; it kept my mind off things, and we enjoyed working together. "Sunny do you remember how you saved my wife from drowning? Well I wish you hadn't."

"No kidding! She phones up and blames me every time anything goes wrong in her life . . . Paul, do you think perhaps some aliens could be persuaded to abduct the Home Secretary?"

"I don't see why not. You never know, they may even take Sally along too."

I ached from mixing cement, my hands were full of lime sores, cuts and blisters from cracking bricks into shape for bricklaying . . . not stopping for one second. Because an abyss had opened up inside me. A hushed velvet blackness waiting in the wings, waiting to swallow me whole.

I didn't want to tell anybody about this growing inner darkness; perhaps it would go away soon, or just sort itself out (fat bloody chance). Finn and my friends probed gently about my feelings but I made them back off. "Outta my face, I am fine, just fine, drop it, let me get on with my building."

I lost a lot of weight, thinking it was because of all the hard work on the house. A pain developed under my arms which spread down the side of my ribs, making it hard to breath sometimes. It never occurred to me to ask for help, though, because it was almost a point of honour to be able to carry everything for myself and be totally independent. Also I wanted to help Minu inwardly, to hold him in my heart somehow. One day I found a meditation by Rudolf Steiner for those in danger; it was perfect.

In my dream, the long dug out canoe carried the two children serenely down a wide fast-flowing river. The tangled jungle crammed along the red mud banks, the first birds began to call in their vibrant and exotic voices, and the dark of the sky slowly fled before the pink and crimson spilling across the horizon. The Amazon sun rose, highlighting every drop of dew, each leaf and cobweb. An early mist burned off from the river's surface, which glinted with the sunlight. One of the children, the oldest a boy of about ten, was Minu, wearing animal skins and a Davey Crockett hat. The other, a little girl sitting behind, was Scarlet. Both children were at home and relaxed, as they looked forward towards the rising sun and opening sky in silence. Standing at the back, steering, was the enormous winged figure of an Indian whom I didn't recognise—he was a bit like Hern the Hunter or a Green Man, but definitely good and in control . . .

16

I'm sixteen. The plane thrusts forward through the air, and I'm glued to the window as the land I know slips away beneath. Part of me is leaving but another part is pulling the other way, back to the beach and the Forest.

"Hello, velcome, I am Elfrida. Zis is Johannes, my husband. Ve are your houseparents here, I vill to your room help you. Oh, you have a violin, how lovely."

"Danke, Ich kan Deutch sprechen," I say, as Johannes shakes my hand vigorously.

"Actually ve are supposed to speak French here." He smiles warmly, and a helpful committee of children drag my rucksack upstairs. My room looks out over Lake Geneva to the Alps on the other side. I can live here; everything's going to be fine. Nobody knows me—maybe I'll reinvent myself. Dead pleased to be treated as an adult, I slip into my responsibilities with ease, making an effort to get along with Elfrida and Johannes, trying to be grown-up and self-contained.

The children show me around the place, taking me to the farm and introducing me to everybody who works there. It provides us with milk, eggs, etc. Today they are bringing in the last of the hay. Enjoying the familiar smells and noises, we join in for a while. I grab a bail to toss up to the top of the stack; it's good to feel the rough string in my hands again.

The children take me over to the school-house, and look, they are taught in the same way as I was, following the same curriculum that the Doctor laid down. There are also lots of workshops. I take my time, familiarising myself with all of them: the industrious woodwork shop, with its sawdust and chippings, the peaceful weavery and the centred concentration in the pottery.

Then on to the well-ordered market gardens. "Hi Swiss Chard." (It's good to talk to the vegetables, the people in Findhorn get great results.)

The garden grows, overflowing and bursting with life, thanks to the green fingered handicapped adults who work here. It's a noisy gregarious garden, because they talk to each other at the tops of their voices, across the rows of vegetable, chatting away, or complaining—"Tony, Didier's eating the onions again"—as they weed between the rows of sweetcorn. "Hello, are you Sunny?" They introduce themselves: Felix, Didier, Margaretta, Collette, and Tony the head gardener. We pick up the vegetables and herbs our house needs for today, and leave with the basket overflowing . . . . It feels something like a scene from "The Sound of Music."

They have the same daily rhythm as I did at home, celebrating the same festivals, with the same kind of prayers at night and at meal times. Only where we say, "Earth who gives to us this food, Sun who makes it ripe and good . . ." they say, "Ce n'est pas le pain qui nous nourrit, C'est la parole éternale de Dieu . . ."

"Sunny, now that you have been here nearly a month, would you like to stay? And you could start the training course too, if you would like to," Johannes says. "I think you would enjoy it."

"Yes, I most certainly would," I reply.

I receive my first wages with pleasure and satisfaction, and I'm even enjoying my courses and classes. The trouble is, you have to write a thesis in French alongside your studies. I have great difficulty with my writing, but everybody helps and I'm determined to manage. About every five minutes I get discouraged, and think, "I'm never going to be able to do this." But Johannes helps me to persevere.

There are three boys in my care who are my special responsibility. They have a variety of special needs. Johnny doesn't talk and he can inflict damage on himself, like biting his hands and through his lower lip, or hitting himself. Hugo is paraplegic and generally quiet, but he can get very angry. If I ask him to do something he isn't into he will reply, "I can't do that. I'm handicapped, I am." Which he knows is a real wind-up. Then there's Dominic, who's Downs Syndrome and a lovely kid, fun and gregarious. Pretty soon, as their personalities shine through, you forget their different problems.

Ten-year-old Johnny goes riding every day. At first he winds his arms down behind his back and stalks around Blanche the pony, like a strange bird. Taking his unwilling hand in mine, we feel gently down the soft velvety nose. "Breath into her nose gently. They like that, and get to know you." Johnny puffs up his lungs, and then lets the air out in a tiny jet stream. "And ponies really like peppermints." We hold out our upturned palms together, his on top of mine, Blanche picks up her peppermint gently . . . and we have contact. Like Johnny, you have to relate to ponies on their own terms.

They will tell you that an autistic kid does not relate to people except sometimes as objects. Johnny doesn't speak, avoids your eye, is self-destructive, rocks his bed at night, and on the face of it has no contact at all with you, but we most definitely do have some kind of friendship and a lot of understanding. He also has a sense of humour, because he laughs when Blanch starts to nibble at his pockets for more peppermints. His contact with the animals is that of a normal boy. Eventually he sits on her like a prince, and smiles and comes alive; happy and confident with his own achievement, he trots round with outstretched arms.

"What's in your package Sunny?" says Hugo, opening it carefully. "Oh look, you've got a book. Who's it from?" It's very beautifully made; the cover is woven in shot silks of ocean colours. It's from my class at school; they have made it for me. I open it carefully, and on each page there is something from each one of them: a poem, some pressed leaves from the forest, a photo, a feather, thin birch bark, some dried seaweed, a drawing, a Celtic knot of gold and green thread. They have sketched and collected bits from my local landscape, sheep's wool, horse hair, moss—things I can smell, and feel.

I read their letter about twenty times.

>Dear Everybody...

OK, then, I force myself to write. I'm embarrassed about my spelling, but tell myself they won't mind.

>Dear Everybody,
>You'l have to hack your way through my spelling. Thanks very much for the beautifull book. And thanks for sending me the bits of forest, field, and earth I love so well, and miss so very much. I miss you all too. I'm allright here, I like my work and the country side is different from there but beautifull to.
>On my days off I travel all over the place, visiting and seeing as much as possible. There are three good jazz clubs in Lausanne, I did'nt know I liked jazz but its great when its live.

There are Advocado Pears growing in the greenhouses here, and red, green and orange Peppers two, which you can just pick and eat. The Swiss eat their bread and butter with a knife and fork, I'm not kidding. Although lots of the kids here are very handicapt, they are also bilingual, French and German, and a few have Italian as well. The other young people who work here are mostly nice they come from allover the world, I'v got a good friend Lilith who knows the Dali Lamma, and another friend called Pan who's really lovely and also a Steiner school survivor like us . . . There are of course the older Holy Rollers, who go by the book and what the good docter says, and drive us all crazy. Some of them are nice too though.

Yes I have a boyfriend and love has raised it's ugly head. He's not a boy though he's 29, and comes from Algeria. He's been in the military for the last nine years. He's called Fart Face, I mean François.

I just read a book called "The Wizard of Earthsea," and I also read one called "Memories, Dreams, Reflections". Both are really good. I had to work hard on the second one though, but it's so interesting it pulled me along.

We celebrated Michaelmas the same day as you! I thought of you all getting stoned. These festivals we celebrate so beautifully, seem to bind us together weather we want it or not.

I am missing Marmite, McVities Chocolate Biscuits, and fish from the sea. They only have perch here, next time send a mackeral.

Thanks again for the beautiful book. Have a good time, and take it easy.

I love you,
Sunny xxxxx

PS. I had a great time on the Areoplane comming out

here. I really enjoyed taking off, and the wings shaking like they are about to drop off in the turbulence over the Alps, and the Landing. Also I got a small bottle of wine with my lunch.

François is one of the best-looking men I've ever set eyes on. He's supposed to be white but actually his skin is the colour of cinnamon, his hair is black but has red in it too, and he is lean and tall, with green eyes. He's white Algerian, in slang they are known as "les pieds noir", on account of the shiny black shoes the colonials wore. His military haircut is growing out now, and his neat clothes are taking on a certain cowboy aura. After nine years in the army, he's hungry for a more spiritual and socially aware life. He's so laid back I'm surprised he can get out of bed. But if he wants something he absolutely has to have it; he buys whatever takes his fancy, and the things he can't afford linger in his mind. This is different to me—I've been bought up and encouraged to suppress all material needs, and I do; they are only things. I am flattered by François's love for me. I don't want to question it either; so I let it happen. When he says he wants a wife, I find myself replying, "OK, yes." We get on just fine, despite the language barrier; I understand about half of what he says, and vice-versa.

Our sex life lacks chemistry; he takes forever, and my mind wanders, contemplating life, the universe and everything until he finally arrives, but I don't think it matters much.

All my life I've lived with other people. At home there were always lodgers from William Morris College busy with their teacher training courses, and others like Saskia and Sinbad who just stayed for a time. I like it that way, it's more fun for the kids, better for the adults, and makes sense ecologically. But I do need some space of my own, to paint and do music in. My room here, however, is like a mainline station. People seem to have a different sense of space; they just wander in and out, and so do the kids, sitting on my floor drawing or playing Jacks (the in game at the moment), while people dump their toddlers for a while.

Pan wanders by with a deadly hot curry. I hate hot food of any kind. "Hi. Want some?" he enquires, as Lilith drifts in and settles down to read *The Way of the White Clouds*. Pan is blond and very beautiful. "Well, shall I read your Tarot?" he drawls in his Swiss/American accent. "NO, thank you very much!" I hate the strong images of the Tarot pack; I can't get them out of my mind. The Tower of Destruction, The Hanged Man, Death: who needs it? And another thing I don't like (will you turn off this music?) is the Incredible String Band. In the evening, we usually settle down to discuss philosophy, reincarnation, freedom or religion, smoke a joint or two and sort out the world's problems.

The only source of information I have about what's happening in England is through my subscription to *Private Eye*. With its send-up style of journalism and Lord Gnome's letters, it's rather hard to tell exactly what's going on back home.

One day, this arrives: "TELEGRAM. Nov.1.1972. Sunny, Jake in motorbike accident. Been in coma for three days. Your Mum."

I'm on the plane. The stupid flight was delayed, and the plane is only going 450 mph, practically motionless to my mind. I've got to calm down, better check through the papers my Dum and Mad have to sign if I'm going to marry Fart Face. At 16 I'm a minor; how will I get them to sign? They'll never do it.

Jake lies in intensive care. He is not with us; his total absence takes me aback. Boy, is he gone. He's got seven tubes sticking out of him, "One for each colour," I think vaguely. Mum and Dad sit on opposite sides of the bed, glaring at each other across his body. "No wonder he's in a coma with you two for a welcoming committee," I say. I'm in double shock here. Dad gets up, saying, "Sunny, darlink, how lovely." "Not for me it isn't," I reply, before remembering that I need something from him and adding nicely, "See you later". Mum is explaining Jake's damage to me. She's so cold and clinical. My mind always has to struggle to understand the contents of this kind of information. "Broken ribs" (blah blah blah) "punctured lungs, and stomach" (mumble mumble) "exploded spleen . . . cracked pelvis . . . no damage to his head." "Thanks, Mum. You look tired, get some sleep now, I'll see you later too."

"Jake, you've got to wake up." I feel like Orpheus, slipping into the underworld to retrieve lost property. "You've got stitches from your navel right up to your chest, it looks like a zip. How's your boat, where are you keeping it this summer, do you have any time for sailing, with all your exams coming up? You should see the sailing boats on the Lake Geneva, they're so naff, they wouldn't last a second in a Force 2 out in the Channel, at the moment we can't swim in the Lake. Because of a mercury spill, 'Beautiful Lake Geneva' is full of dead fish, and smells."

I tell him about my life in Switzerland, and try to fathom him. Jake is a hard person to get to know or understand, it's difficult to know what makes him tick, or what goes on inside him. When my parents divorced, I remember him methodically and neatly packing up our father's belongings; it was pathetic, and Mum should've done it herself. He even had to take the spark plugs out from the car so Dad couldn't steal it. He was usually away at school, always taking O or A levels, and now he was studying for a couple more because his sights were set on a degree in Economics and Politics at the LSE. And I respect him for that, because he's done it all through hard work. "Hey Jake, you've got to wake up . . ."

"Hi, Dad. Will you sign this please," I say casually.
 "Vat is it?" he asks suspiciously.

"I need my parents' permission to do the football pools in Switzerland."

"Vell of course, darlink. "

"Thanks, bye."

I go to Mum's house. She's just woken up. We sit and drink our tea, a good English cup of tea. "Sunny, you'll have to sleep in the sitting room," she says nervously. "Why?" "Well, I rented out your room, to a nice student from College." I'm very surprised, and immediately feel hurt and insecure. The 'nice student' comes in; he's dead handsome, maybe about forty-five, and I can tell right away that Mum and him are bonking furiously away—I mean, having a deeply spiritual, karmic and meaningful relationship . . . I hate this fucking house. It's not my home, I don't even have a room here any more. "I think I'll stay at Liza's."

Liza, little Luke and I stay up all night exchanging news and having a great time, laughing at old jokes. "Do you smoke after sexual intercourse?"

"Don't know, I never looked," I reply. Luke starts to get hysterical. "How many psychiatrists does it take to change a light bulb?"

"Um, one, but the light bulb really has to want to change . . . A white horse walks into a bar, and orders a whiskey. 'That's a coincidence,' says the bar man, 'There's a type of whisky named after you.' 'What—Eric?'"

I wander off to the Inner Man Cafe. "Hi Teddy." He looks up through his one eye, and grins. (My "Sunset over the Alps" still hangs above the till.) "Where have you been all these months, not in trouble are you love? Sorry to hear about your brother, he going to be all right then or what? Bloody bikes, terrible fings they are you know." He pours me a very stiff cup of tea. "Give 'im me best all right?"

"Sure, I will. Hey Teddy, this is my Mum's signature."

"Yeah, I know it well, all them games excuses," he chortles, like Captain Hook.

"Well I need it here next to my Dad's, here's her pen." I love watching him do this, as Mum's perfect signature appears delicately from his huge hand. I give him a fiver. "Thanks a lot, oh and Liza needs an M.O.T. for her car."

"I'll have it ready in the morning."

Caspar sits at Jake's bedside and ponders out loud. "I have the feeling that Jake can hear me in some way or another; I'm sure he can. It's very difficult talking to a missing person, but I have something I want to say."

"Sure he can hear you Caspar, go on. He's never been a great listener anyway."

Caspar smiles. "Well we've got him at our mercy now. Jake you have got to make an effort, mate." He says urgently, trying to force Jake to regain consciousness. "You have to make up your mind, I wouldn't blame you if perhaps you don't want to, you mustn't let go . . ." He pauses. "You say something to him."

"And another thing: you won't be able to take those A levels, and you'll be so fucking pissed off, and Caspar and I will be even more pissed off, 'cause we're never going to be able to do them. It's your duty."

Caspar nudges me. "You shouldn't swear at him, Sunny, it's not very pedagogical, and besides the nurses might hear."

"Jake, I'm going back to Switzerland in a few days, dead or alive, OK?"

Caspar puts his elbows on the bed, and lowering his voice he whispers, "Jake, in some ways you're quite lucky. Some of these nurses are gorgeous, why they're like little blue and white goddesses, I'd like to unveil their hidden charms and feel their cold little hands running over me . . ."

"Oh cor blimey, come on Caspar."

Ralph and I have abandoned ourselves to a wild sexual extravaganza. So far we've used up one bottle of Mateus Rosé, two tabs each of Dexadrine, five condoms, half a jar of chocolate spread (don't ask) and more or less totalled his room. We lie puffed out, naked and glistening, smoking dope, with Venus in our troubled hearts, drifting off to sleep to the words, "I'll see you on the dark side of the Moon..."

Serafina (Ralph's mum) and I sit drinking our Perrier and Ribena, something we have been doing together ever since I was a child. She is enthusing about the various natural disasters that will take place at the end of the century. "The whole of southern England will be flooded, and there will be huge earthquakes. You see, the Earth is a living being in its own right and it will fight back against the way it's being abused. Also Rudolf Steiner said that the climate will change, the indications are all there, even the psychics are agreed and they've all had similar visions of California dropping into the sea when the San Andreas fault goes. There will be an enormous planetary line-up, a very powerful one. Of course I won't be around for it but you will, and Lucifer and Ahriman will have their final fight for our souls. I think it wise to start preparing for it, anyway." So Serafina was losing no time in stocking up her cellar with tins of food, and getting her Portuguese staff to pickle and preserve anything they could get their hands on from the garden.

We wander off together to see the new rose garden. It is the work of a true artist; the rose beds had been dug out in the shape of a huge and beautiful Celtic knot, which weaved around and was interlaced with an ouroborous of lavender. My spine tingles momentarily. "Oh Serafina... One day, I would like a garden like this."

A few days later Jake regains consciousness. The first thing he says is he wants Liza, and can he still take his A levels? Poor guy, he must have had a nasty crack on the head after all.

We have a party at his bedside. He looks ready for the mortuary, and the nurses finally bung us out. Caspar, blushing, arranges a rendezvous with a rather friendly little blue and white goddess. We leave singing "Bye Bye, Miss American Pie" at the top of our voices.

I fly back to Switzerland, thank God. I am not at ease at all with my Mum. She is so critical; everything I do seems to be a reflection of her, and her remarks hurt. But she is the same with all of us; if you want her love, you have to change into what she wants you to be. She does not simply love you for who you are. She tries to organise our lives, and gets heavy and negative if we don't do what she says. She's very positive in front of others but puts us down when we are alone. I do fight back, but it's hardly worth it, because I can never win against her, and if I do she sulks for weeks after. To keep the peace, we end up leading a double life: one for her and one for ourselves, which she knows nothing about.

I read in *The Prophet*: "Your children are not your children, they are the sons and daughters of life's longing for itself..."

17

17 Jan. 1973. François and I are getting married in the local registry office. It doesn't feel like a proper ceremony to me; in fact, I'm having a hard time trying to make myself believe it's actually happening at all. But I do believe in this all-consuming love. I've never felt like this before.

When the first new shoots appear through the melting snow, with a ring of flowers woven into my hair, we celebrate the traditional wedding festival of the Steiner Community. All the children I love and the adults I have come to know and respect are assembled. It's the custom to tie together two small apple branches with a red ribbon so that they form an X. Everyone is quiet now while an Elder performs this ceremony. He searches my face. "Keep out, don't look inside me now, stay out of my head and heart," I think. I really don't want him to do this. Once he ties those branches . . . Oh well, what the hell. François is pleased as punch. I abandon myself to the feasting and dancing.

Ralph is on the phone. He's very upset, and I'm unable to deal with his pain. "But I wanted to marry you. You're too young, why the fuck do you always have to go at such a rate? Are you expecting a baby? I can look after you . . ." I cut in, "No, I'm not pregnant, OK? I have to try and make a new life for myself."

"And that doesn't include me," he sobs. Ow, I didn't want to hurt him, I don't know what to say. "Ralph, I love you very much but you've got to make your own life too, you're not doing anything, get another girlfriend for God's sake!" I can feel his fragility. "Ralph, I have to make a life away from home."

"But you could have one with me," he replies. This is hopeless. What have I done to him? "Thanks Ralph, I know that. But I have something to see through here, a different path to walk on." I'm the one who's crying now.

"But you still have something to see through with me." And he hangs up.

Practise Right Mindfulness.

In my dream, I'm on the beach at Seaford. The freezing wind is whipping my hair in my face, my back is to the sea. I pick up a handful of pebbles; they are burning hot, and as I let them go my hands continue to burn. Then a roiling wave catches me from behind and pulls me into the sea; I am churning over and over in the undertow, which is phosphorescent and full of sharp stones. I struggle to breath and to come awake. When I do wake fully there is a wild wind sweeping across the lake and over my house, a hollowness in my heart, and a sleeping husband. I remembered my Mum telling me once when I was scared in the night, that fear was a form of sensationalism. (We are against sensationalism.)

I enjoy my classes. We are studying the senses today. Everybody in the world has got five senses except us. The Doctor says we've got twelve: 1. Hearing, 2. Warmth, 3. Sight, 4. Taste, 5. Smell, 6. Balance, 7. Movement, 8. Life, 9. Touch, 10. Ego, 11. Thought, 12. Word. (Tough on you lot, but there it is.)

Everybody's got one body too, but the Doctor says we've

got loads. Too bad for the lumpen proletariat again. There's an astral body, and an etheric body, and any number of spiritual bodies. We've got bodies on our bodies. Which is interesting, but the down-side is the labelling: "God, you're so astral/ Luciferic/ sanguine", or whatever. It pisses me off, this constant fixing of types.

The young co-workers here have the use of a 2CV and a moped. One day about six of us set off on another exploration of the surrounding countryside. We jack up the music: Jerry Lee Lewis, an excellent choice for those Alpine hair-pin bends. Crammed into the 2CV, we stop at a garage for petrol. François, phlegmatic as always, is at the wheel. The garage owner comes flying out shouting and dancing. "You're supposed to switch the engine off!" he bellows, giving the car a hefty kick. I jump out, and start kicking the car as well. "Stupid fucking car!" I yell, ignoring the garage-man's consternation, and the others follow suit. We're having a great time. I don't know why, but he refuses to give us any petrol.

Every time we get to a steep hill in this car, we have to jump out and walk. We have been to Paris, arriving at three in the morning, and Milan. There are a lot of Alps on the way there, and both places involve a lot of walking. Nonetheless, we plan on Vienna next.

After years of committing themselves to live with the handicapped children, there are people here who know how to say yes to an individual's destiny and stand by their problems, helping a child to try and try to overcome a hurdle. They do not impose, and take the children from where they are, working with what they've got. And they do the same thing with the young people working here. Some of whom have "special needs" too. I'm encouraged to make use of my abilities: painting, music, woodwork, weaving, cooking, riding, gardening, farming, building, all of which I can use with the kids. The atmosphere here is one of quiet healing, and it works on all of us.

When I'm asked about my parents I say, "My parents did their best for me."

We also study Freud and Jung. (Isn't it interesting how nobody had a subconscious until Freud came along?) I don't go much on how he relates things to really obscure mythology, but Jung's ability to pick the important moments in someone's life, I think, is not only great diagnostics, but borders on divination . . . from which you could all learn a whole lot.

Hans the farmer is taciturn but nice; we work well together and I'm confident around him. "Sunny," he asks, "have you ever helped in a Barn Raising?"
"Yes, yes of course, two or three times," I reply.
"Did you have a special job?"
"Not really but I understand how it goes. Last time I banged the pegs through the crossbeams, because of being good on a trapeze."
"I see," he says. "Are you confident up high then?"
"Yes, I love it."
"Good. We have plans that still need work but I think we shall start building soon, then."
"All right, but will you explain to François that it's not dangerous?" Hans looks at me, and says, "You try first." He's right.

I open the fridge door. My God, it's the head of Orpheus . . . No, only the baleful eyes of a Conger Eel. "I 'ave found you a sea fish, Sunny."
"Yeah thanks François, I saw it. Love you."

It costs ten francs each to go to Lausanne on the train (which really does run on time). So we tend to go by moped, two sitting on it and one on a bike hanging on. It's a beautiful trip. We stick to the farm tracks, progressing quietly, like a very small funeral cortege, through the vines, ambling along in the private grounds of a small medieval chateaux, coasting downhill to the lake, through the municipal park and here we are at Ouchy. Park the moped, and take the funicular into town and the jazz club.

We often get caught by the local bobby, who carries a gun. He is a kind, tolerant, rotund man who writes down our names solemnly: Karl Marx, Dolly Parton and Mahatma Ghandi. He always fines us ten francs apologetically and benevolently, but the fine is in fact a saving of twenty francs by train.

It's bedtime. The dormitory is candle-lit. Hugo slumps on his bed leaning on the paralysed side of his body, quiet and melancholy cradling his paralysed arm, his eyes cast down. Johnny lies sprawled, with his hands twisted behind his back, so they won't hit him. And Dominic, rounded and ever jolly, his mouth wide open, sits cross-legged like Buddha. They are all listening, intense and involved, to the story of the Sleeping Beauty. I tell it slowly and gently, unfolding it like an opening flower. Wanting them to enjoy it, and not to worry about it ending happily. We sing a bit and say the prayer.

> "In the still and quiet of night
> When the stars are shining bright
> Gentle friends with love draw near
> With wings of warmth to guard from fear
> And when to sleep in peace I go
> My love shines out to all I know."

They are all asleep. I tiptoe out, the sandman.

I am a great believer in angels and try to give my own guardian angel some feedback from time to time. I can't say I've ever seen one, or indeed had any spiritual experiences at all, but just because you've never been to China doesn't mean it isn't there. And after all, everybody knows that Dr Dee's assistant Edward Kelly actually did it with angels, although I understand that Pookas only need a feather. Personally, I'd prefer an octopus; imagine all those arms.

> Dear Sunny,
> You should write more often. Jake is much, much better now. And Caspar is seeing a rather sweet little nurse. Your Father (she continues) has bought himself a cafe, right in the middle of the Village. It is most embarrassing. Every time I go shopping, he dashes out, hailing me in hearty Czech tones, "Darlink, come and have a coffee mit me" . . .

Our room is big enough, with its own fire place and wooden beams, sheep-skin rugs, and killims. Lilith and François are having an animated discussion about where exactly Marx went wrong. "No respect for individuality, maybe?" And Lilith has no respect for privacy.

She also treats men like dogs, as if she didn't like them. I don't like this about her, although she is my friend. "They're only men, Sunny, it's no big deal."

"François, pretty soon there's going to be a Barn Raising. It's not dangerous, I've done it before, so don't try and stop me," I explain.

It's the summer holidays. François "has" to go to Krishnamurti's summer school in Saanen. I'm trying to be mature about this, and Krishnamurti is definitely on the side of the forces of light, but François "has" to go alone. And I'm hurt about that, but you've got to respect other people's freedom, right?

Everybody else is leaving too: the Steiner people to various spiritual and cultural centres like Iona, Chartres, Delphi or Montsegur, while the young helpers headed for the Italian beaches. So I go to Sussex, to catch up with my friends. I am aware that I can be very destructive when my pride is hurt, and that I have to watch it. But I am saying "Fuck you François" inside myself.

Liza, Rohan, Luke, Jake and I are at the Battersea Fun Fair. Liza and I have taken a fair bit of speed for the occasion. We ride on the Ghost Train, screaming our heads off all the way round, and then go into the Hall of Mirrors; it's a lot of fun. Jake looks much better now, though he's still very thin after his accident. "And look, stand right in front of this one, over here . . ." We laugh at Jake, who is now almost circular. Moving right along we pay for three rides on the roller coaster, my favourite. I'm enjoying it, but the third time round I throw up. Which is odd; I never throw up. I feel woozy for quite a while after; maybe it's the speed. But nonetheless I'm definitely up for a whirl or two on the Meteor. Yeeeehaaaaa!

Liza is catching me up on the gossip. Saskia is now having a half-hearted affair with Ralph. "Hey, do you remember the time you sat up outside your parents' door all night just to find out if they did it?"
"Mhm."
"Well, did they?"
"Yep, but it wasn't what you and I would call sex."
"Ah, no chocolate spread . . . Have you ever tried those luminous condoms? The phosphorescence rubs off inside you, you know."
"Yeah, I know. When I opened my legs it was like opening the fridge door."

One night Rohan and I go to see "A Clockwork Orange". We find our seats and sitting down, Rohan stretches his long legs comfortably under the seat in front of him. At seventeen he has an upright noble bearing; his long eyes fit his face now, and have become more outward looking

It's a strange film; with an edge to the imagination behind it that was magnetic and disquieting. I didn't like the violence at all—in fact, I blocked my ears and closed my eyes a lot of the time. "Do you want to go, or what?" he grumbles. But we stay, and afterwards he takes me to see his sculpture. He is becoming a marvellous artist; his work is sensuous and exquisitely made. "These are lovely, Rohan . . . You always were pretty good with the Plastacene in Kindergarten."

I am walking up to the Forest. It's a fine summer's day. There's Rayette, wandering along like a dandelion seed ahead of me. "Watcha Rayette," I yell. She waits for me to catch up, and we walk in mutual consent to the big beech tree. Both of us are rather the worse for wear. We swing up into the folding green arms of this enormous familiar tree and settle in. "Sunny, have you ever kissed a guy with a quiff?"

"Nope."

"It's complicated. I have to avoid getting poked in the eye, and he has to sleep on his back dead straight." Rayette giggles and sighs. "On the other hand, it's the only thing I like about him." We stay up there all afternoon, tête-a-tête, comfy and cradled in the Tree of Life.

"Are you going back to Fart Face?"

"Yes, Luke, tomorrow the holidays are over, and I like it out there. But we have kept up with each other, so it's not a problem, is it?"

"Yes, it is."

François waiting at the airport, looking good and expectant, gets cold-shouldered by his wife, who doesn't want kind gestures from someone she's miffed at. He doesn't know what's going on. Tough luck, twit. "I was hoping to take you out to the movies to night," he says.

"What's on?"

"I don't know, let's just go and see."

Later, they are sponging me down with cool water and lemon. "No, no Belladona, it makes me delirious, like I'm inside a Hieronymous Bosch painting . . ." I have a high fever. I'm not ill, it's because of going to see "The Exorcist". I've never seen anything like it.

I am scaling the ladder, my bag of pegs and wooden mallet clipped on. The late August sun rises, "Great Hawk of the Morning . . ." To my right, the grape vines stretch away to the shimmering lake shore. On my left, the ripening ordered fields flow, undulating towards the rolling hills of the Jura. This is the longest fucking barn I've ever seen. I clip myself onto the safety line, and set to work. The Swiss pegs fit perfectly; I bang them through the rafters to the main beam. I've got about three hours work up here, and today I'm cautious. I don't muck around, pretending to slip, because I woke up with the certain knowledge that I'm going to have a baby. I'm thinking about it, taking it into my soul, up here where I can be alone. I gain confidence as I go along, and my mind wanders on into feminism; I get into a rage with Germaine Greer, and bang in another peg. I'd like to see her up here (bang), female eunuch my foot. By now my arms are aching, and it's so hot I have to push my T-shirt sleeves above my shoulders. But I'm in top form physically, and when I get to the end I absail down, Spider Woman on a silken thread, landing lightly on the good Swiss earth next to Ave. "Sunny is zat a tattoo, I vas just seeing?" "Nope."

18

"I didn't know you had a tattoo, did it hurt?"
"Not as much as all that, about the equivalent of getting your legs waxed."
"It's gorgeous."
"Do you think so? Thanks, I designed it myself. Had it for years. Say, have you got any more of that bright red lipstick, Sorrel?"
"O my god, can you see anything with all that mascara on?"
"Nope." We were going to give those prisoners a thrill. Having put on our shortest mini-skirts, skimpiest tops, high-heeled boots piles of make-up, the works, off we went.

That drive to Suffolk was so loaded. Apart from the blokes honking at us as we hurtled by, every time we got stuck in as traffic jam on the M25 I began to sweat, and Sorrel would rummage through the map looking for alternative routes, because we knew that if we were late he would think we weren't coming. Driving recklessly, it took roughly two-and-a-half hours to get there. And he was waiting like a child in boarding school.

It was a much better place; we didn't even get searched on the way in. "Hi Mum, You've lost a lot of weight, that's a nice outfit you're almost wearing . . . Hmmm, I see the local whorehouse has come to visit today." We embraced each other closely, and I felt tears pricking at the back of my eyes. "Hey Mum, Thanks for what you wrote to me, and look you were right—it's OK here." Seemed to me like everybody was enjoying a physical closeness round here. We had not been allowed any physical contact at all in Feltham. But people were having a good snog with their wives or girlfriends and Sorrel sat down on Minu's lap. He looked much better; in fact, our visit took on such an air of hilarity that I began to wonder if he was taking it all seriously enough. "Do you know what? Some of the men will be here for as long as ten years. They're completely different to the boys in the detention centre, which was a bit like the Shepherds Bush Youth Club, everybody going off like fire crackers for no reason at all, same sort of types really. There are some pretty heavy characters here, but they're much less volatile. And there's more heroin and cocaine about, to suit the nature of the clientele." We looked around more closely and it was true, there were some pretty tough looking guys of all ages; nonetheless, it felt a lot less threatening then Feltham. "I've never taken hard drugs and the guys won't give it to me anyway. Apparently it's bad for me! But smoking dope helps to pass the time away, while I serve out my sentence for dope . . ."

Instead of slot machines the visiting hall had a little shop. We trooped over to it and bought fresh-made sandwiches, decent tea, crisps and loads of chocolate bars. The guards kept an eye on things but they weren't intrusive. We could all sit round a table like normal human beings, and it was such a relief to have no barrier between us.

"Sorrel, how was the journey? I'm worried it's too far for you all to come. I don't know why they sent me up here so far away from my family."

"No no, it wasn't that far a couple of hours that's all, no problem."

"Well I was handcuffed the whole time, and it seemed to take ages. I'm not even exactly sure where in Suffolk this is."

"You're about ten miles north of Ipswich and in the middle

of miles and miles of M.O.D territory."

"Oh. And close to the sea, because I can see it from my cell. It's lovely and warm at night here. And there's an education programme of sorts. Come and have a look." We got up and followed, as he led us over to the window and pointed out a collection of buildings, a farm and what looked like an enormous market garden. "That's the open prison and because my offence is pretty mild, even a joke round here amongst the screws and the inmates, I stand a good chance of being moved there, if I keep my nose clean."

Minu already looked brighter, and a bit less anxious. For the first time I was able to drive away feeling that he was at least safe. We were allowed three visits a month, which was good for all of us. Finn and I swapped turns, taking two of the friends and their horrible music. Once I flicked on the radio and there was John Martyn singing, "I don't want to know about evil, only want to know about love." So did I John, but it wasn't turning out that way. Perhaps John Martyn was a Buddhist.

> "Shun all evil
> Do good
> Purify the mind."

19

All around our house the grapes are being harvested. The pickers are all hearty Swiss convicts (who do not try to escape) and Italian immigrants; they send every penny they earn back to Italy, for the children they've left behind with the grandparents, and for the houses they hope one day to build. The Swiss exploit them and use them to do all the jobs they would never do themselves. They live in poor flats that have become ghettos on the edge of the village; a fire is always burning in an oil drum in the empty car-park outside their homes. We know most of them by name, enjoying their warm hospitality and I learn a few folk songs off them. These people are completely at home with the handicapped children, totally accepting them as if everything was quiet normal. (The Swiss like to hide their handicapped children away, and get this: they are not allowed to walk by the lake on Sundays, in case it upsets someone.)

The pickers pour the grapes into huge copper vats with fires underneath them. The grapes give off an incredibly intoxicating vapour, and you have to watch the kids like a hawk during this time because they slip off down the vines. They have learned you could get drunk by breathing in the vapours. We spend our afternoons pulling intoxicated kids out of them—the brain-damaged, the hyperactive, the psychotic, the epileptic, the spastic, the deaf and the dumb all pulling together for once, unified in their desire to get totally rat-arsed at breaktime. (I have a jolly good snort myself when nobody's looking, or go down later at night and steam my face in it.)

The class I'm helping with is studying Norse mythology—something I like too. I help them with their reading and writing. And look, I too begin to shape my letters better, and I've stopped putting some of them backwards. Dominic looks approvingly at my writing. "You and I are doing pretty well with our writing, eh?"

"Yes, we really are."

"Sunny," he says, "relax your hand a bit more . . ." I finally gain writing skills, with the help of a Downs Syndrome child.

We are making jam from the enormous harvest of berries we've had this year. "OK Dominic—Dominic, stay with us—one kilo of sugar, Johnny for God's sake you'll just have to get your hands dirty. One kilo of raspberries, good, a squeeze of lemon. Now Hugo, stir. That's it, good. Dominic set the alarm for twelve minutes, now." "Say please," he grins. "PLEASE." The whole house smells of jam. The other kids join in, washing jars and testing for a set, and when a jar explodes in the oven, Hugo says in his best English, "Is fuck, eh Sunny? Is fuck." "Yes, Hugo, is fuck."

I find the hugest laundry basket in Switzerland. And screw wooden battens firmly along the bottom, cut two moon-shaped pieces of soft lime-wood, and fit and screw them onto the battens. Then cut a V-shaped frame, and cover that with wicker work. Fitting it to the end of the basket, and covering the whole thing in peach-blossom-coloured thick cotton, there it is: a rocking cradle for the baby. Perfect.

High up the in the silence of the mountains, I find a shell. Part of the mystery of the Earth, a geophany. I place it on my ear and hear the sea draw breath, the voice of a mermaid, a storm off the Cape, the Seven Sisters, full fathom five, the bells of lost Atlantis . . .

Did you know that when the angels seek human company, when they are lonely for the Earth, they too walk in the mountains?

"Sunny, will you be Mary in the Christmas play this year?"
  "No, can't I be God, or the Devil?"
  "Don't be silly, you're pregnant."
  "OK, Grumpy Innkeeper or nothing." I end up being a fat Angel.

I throw up every day and lose loads of weight. What goes down must come up. Meanwhile, François reads up loads of information on babies. Like, how to have one.

Here comes a gang of strapping toddlers. These rosy-cheeked bruisers are carefully carrying back the eggs they have collected from the hen house. Dressed in their home-spun clothes, they run and totter down the path, followed by the clucking hens and hissing geese because one of them forgot to shut the hen house door . . . Pandemonium. The staff children lead a good life in our communities, with many waiting hands to pick them up if they fall. Later on, though, they can get surprisingly wild, I notice.

The 2CV shakes, rattles, and rolls its way down from a mountain pass. "Ladies and gentlemen, please fasten your seat belts, here comes another of those views the Swiss are so fond of."

The whole household sits by the fire, making our St Martin's lanterns. Elfrida tells the story of St Martin and the beggar. "But why lanterns?" little Cecile asks Elfrida. "We light our lanterns and walk together in the dark, lighting our way towards Advent." Oh, so that's it! I'm glad we try to answer the children's questions here. Now I understand know why I'm wandering around in the dark, waving a lantern and singing with a bunch of lunatics.

Man have I got a craving for sea fish. Apart from Conger Eel, this country doesn't have any. I'll just have to fumble by on smoked salmon and prawns.

> Dear Sunny,
> Yesterday the whole class and all the teachers sat round in a big circle. Herr Wissenschaften asked us what we had decided to do once we left school, or as he put it, "Vat is your destinies bringing to you?" Saskia set the ball rolling. "I think what I'd like best is to live in a mobile home in Scunthorpe. I could be the mistress of a lorry driver, maybe have eight kids or so. I'll probably wear loads of makeup, and lots of nylon things." "Sank you very much, Saskia . . ." Then Aries said that he'd like to be a dustbin man. Most of the class are going to be artists, actors or builders, though; and a few are going to university, more power to them. Liza and Jake are still together, but Saskia has broken up with Ralph and is now with Rohan . . . what goes around comes around.
> Lots of love, Rayette xxxxx

Speaking of Ralph, François' and my sex life is still nothing to write home about. He doesn't seem to notice though; I don't understand.

There are about twenty of us "adults" lying on the floor. I have my grandfather's binoculars trained on the screen of the smallest cinema in the world. We are watching "Lawrence of Arabia", in black and white, dubbed into French, on a six-inch screen, attached to a radio, that we have confiscated off one of the kids. "No TV allowed here."

I dream I'm by a fast-flowing river in Yugoslavia, sitting on the shale. In front of me, a small boy with red hair is trying to skip stones. I go down to help him, and show him how to flick his wrist. The hills around us are green and sparkling in the sun. This boy is my son.

There's this German woman called Ave. She's a maniac masseuse and energetic eurythmy teacher who lives in our house. She decides to spring clean the whole house before Christmas. "Christmas von't come properly if ve don't clean ze top of ze doors," she explains. "Yes it will, don't be so bloody stupid," I say. A few minutes later I hear her explaining to a startled trainee she's pounced on exactly how to clean a toilet out. I stick my head around the corner and say, "Christmas von't come unless you clean ze bog out properly." Ave turns round and glares at me, saying, "And how are you helping mit zis cleaning poosh?" "I make vishy vashy on ze vindows, vorky vorky vorky, eins, zwei, drie."

The English in this place is brilliant. Everything is a rough translation from many other languages; I love how it sounds. Ave's is the best. She sits at the table and says, "Can I ze cabbage become?" "Of course you can Ave, anytime," and I pass it to her. In our seminar eurythmy lessons she exhorts us to valk on our balls, and I once heard her calling, "I'm coming every moment." Good for you Ave, that's amazing.

One time she remarks, "Ze English have never understood Shakespeare."

"Oh bollocks to that."

"You shouldn't be so hyperzensitive all the time," Ave admonishes me.

"Moi, hypersensitive!" Annoying old bat.

There are a few people hanging around in our room. Pan is explaining exactly why one painting is beautiful and another not, while Lilith, who has been smoking dope, is wandering around inviting everybody to take a bite from "the universal peach of love," which she carries about carefully in her cupped hands. Not only is this peach universal, it's also invisible.

Lilith saunters into eurythmy with a massive love bite on her neck. "Vell, vat happened to you?" Ave inquires. "Er, um, I got caught in the lid of the grand piano," Lilith explains. I snigger, and Ave gives me a right dressing-down for laughing at other's misfortunes.

Olivier is missing. There is a routine for this. Everybody knows his place: some to watch the other children, one to phone the police, some to search the houses and barns, etc., and some to search further afield (that's me). The more spiritually capable get together to meditate for the child's well-being. It works well. Olivier shows up by the lake with a fishing net and jar; he even has some tiddlers. Now, you're supposed to try to convey to him that what he's done is not OK. He's aphasic, brain-damaged, and in the first stages of muscular dystrophy. François and I don't say anything, because actually he's done really well to get here and catch the tiddlers. "Come on, lets put them back and go home, Olivier." I hold his hand; he's just a little chap, really. "Next time you want to go fishing take someone with you, all right?"

I am eighteen today, only everybody thinks I'm nineteen.

François is working in the garden; he looks like Wurzel Gummage. Oh look, I have visitors! Jake and Liza, Rohan and Saskia. They are on their way to Italy and the leaning tower of Pisa. (Jake often goes to the leaning Tower of Pisa, he's also fond of a drink or two, and I reckon that's why it appeals to him.) François is unfriendly; he can be possessive, but surely my friends are not a threat. I'm embarrassed because he will hardly talk to them. They stay for three nights and I take them to Lausanne for pizza and the jazz club. We go walking in the peaceful mountains, coming across one of those Swiss cafes at the top, which is chock-a-block full of families in their Sunday best, eating cakes and enjoying the clear crisp views. "How on earth do all the grannies get up here?" "Erm, they parachute them in, I think."

I'm very happy to see my visitors, and when they leave, I cry and cry in the bath so as not to upset François. I want to go with them. Later, a box arrives from Rayette: one packet of McVities Chocolate Biscuits, a pack of black condoms (with one missing), and a tape with the Moody Blues on one side and Pentangle on the other. "Far out!" But Rayette's presents and perhaps the taste of chocolate biscuits, or maybe just my birthday, make me aware that although I'm living here quite happily, this is not really my home.

Once again my classmates are studying *Parzival*, but from a different perspective—they are studying the form and shape of the text, in particular the parts concerning Gawain.

This is interesting to me too, and *Parzival* turns out to be a very precisely structured romance, divided into sixteen sections which are subdivided into parts of thirty-two lines each. Each section is complete within itself, and this meticulous outer framework houses the inner structure which is equally important. For example, Parzival's destiny lies within the Grail Castle, a secret holy place full of mysteries. And after he pledges his life to quest for it, the story turns to the adventures of Gawain, whose main adventure lies in the Castle of Wonders: an absolute mirror of the Grail Castle because it is an open place full of ladies, with a marvellous bed which Gawain, with much physical courage, must overcome.

Gawain is a man of great feeling and intuition, a healer with knowledge of herbs and medicine who is greatly loved by his friends. All of his adventures involve rescuing ladies, or winning them round, sometimes with great patience. Unlike Parzival, faithfulness is not part of Gawain's make up, but in his own distracted way he too is looking for the Grail with all the warmth of his heart.

My Mum and her bug-eyed Danish boyfriend are visiting on their way back from Assisi. "If your baby is a boy, why don't you call him Francis, I think we're all very connected to St Francis, and you like animals. Perhaps in another incarnation, who knows, darling."

"Actually I'm going to call him Egbert, Mum. Or maybe Spike."

20 April 1974 Anno Domini.

It's midnight but I'm still milling around. Ouch, what was that? ... and another one, ten minutes later. Oh yeah, contractions. Well, I'm tired, and at ten minute intervals, there's nothing to worry about. I go to bed and actually sleep. I always wake up at 7:10 am. It's no different this morning, except ouch, I time them at, oh, every four minutes. "Hey François, wake up man, we've got to go, ouch, oh shit." But, I'm cool ... sort of.

The very first thing the midwife says to me is: "Just because you're young, don't expect special treatment." "Nazi," I reply. But even though I've come back with a swift reply, I am still completely blown away by this welcome.

They've got this routine list of dehumanizing things to do to you in Swiss hospitals, sort of like entering Belsen:

1. Shave off pubes, as roughly as possible.
2. Surprise patient with an enema.

3. Measure for dilation, during contractions only.
4. Never explain, never apologise.
5. Make them feel as insecure as possible by making remarks about their age, and how complicated childbirth can be.
6. Put an I.D. bracelet on them, in case they die.

"You need a drip," says Rosa Klebb. "Why?" I ask. She just shoves it in my arm. "Well, fuck you too," I say. Then she puts something around my other wrist. "It's for your pulse," she explains. "There's gas and air if you need it." "OK Rosa, If I want to gas myself you mean." François puts it on his face and I laugh, but ouch, "I want a go with it." He gives it to me, and says, "Breathe." I hate it. Rosa puts two straps around my waist, one to measure the contractions and one for the baby's heart beat. At this point (I swear to God) they bring in twelve beaming medical students. "Oh great, a party, anyone bring any beer?" The last part of this sentence gets muffled as François firmly puts the gas-and-air mask over my face.

I feel like a lump of meat in a butcher's shop window, and it's very cold in here. I have to lie down, in fact I'm strapped down with all these drips and things; then the kind midwife flicks on the operating lights. Man this is something else, I'd like to go home.

Yes folks, Rosa Klebb, the psychotic baddy in "From Russia with Love", now works under an assumed name, applying her warped and twisted mind to innocent victims in a Swiss hospital. Not many people know that.

At about midday, a very smooth and confident doctor oils his way in. He measures for dilation, and smiles radiantly and rakishly, "You're nearly fully dilated, which is good, but your waters haven't broken yet, not so good. Maybe we will have to do that for you, OK?"

"Yep."

"Did you call my midwife a Nazi?" he enquires nicely.

"Oh no no, I said nasty."

"Aha, I see." I trust this smooth doctor, and he tries manfully to break the waters, but does not succeed. "You don't want to have a dry birth, I'm going to give you an epidural."

"I'm all right, I don't need one, no way no thank you, bugger off."

"Now are you going to be part of the solution or part of the problem?" he asks.

"Part of the problem, of course. Oh all right then." But I am upset, and as the fluid trickles into my spine I say, "And you can give François one from the waist up."

It's six o'clock, the waters break, I push, a child is born. Quite simply and easily, leaping into the world like a flying fish.

He cries a bit, and yells when they wash him off. I yell too, "Don't wash him off, give him to me!" I hold onto him, and get twenty-two stitches. He's beautiful, although he's got two black eyes, blue bruises, a head shaped like a honeydew melon, a few orangy-red spikes for hair, and yellow skin. "Is he all right?" I ask. "Oh yes, a fine boy." "Are you sure?"

François and my mother are asleep like a couple of drunks, on the bench outside. Leave them be, I can't handle them right now.

A few days later I bring him home, holding him close, as I have been doing more or less continuously since he was born. We are both relaxed and fine.

"Nice baby, Sunny," Lilith and Pan say, both desperately trying not to snigger at his spikey orange hair and black eyes. He gets nicknamed Minu, after the ginger cat with pandabear eyes that lives here.

I slip on my blue jeans—good, I can easily zip them up—and a green shirt. Downstairs I hear Ave's strident voice telling somebody off. "You can't expect a child to keep clean if ze bathroom's dirty." That's Ave, and she's right.

François puts Minu down in his cradle, and I fall asleep exhausted, like I'd been ill. It takes it out of you, giving birth, and I sleep right through supper, only waking when it's time to feed Minu. After feeding he goes back to sleep in the cradle. François who's been reading, lies down beside me and then on top of me. "Hey, I've got twenty-two stitches," I remind him, but he's not listening. Now we're fighting, but François is a big man. "It'll be OK," he says. "It won't, it isn't!" (This can't be happening.) I am quiet and afraid, silently fighting, but he's enjoying it; the more I fight the more he gets off on it. (Keep calm, it's only pain.) It's like being under water, struggling to breath, no sun, muffled sounds a distant reality, and when it's all over I feed the crying baby, and cannot look my husband in the eyes. My stitches are torn and bleeding, and I am ashamed. Carefully cleaning myself up (yikes, I'm so sore, calm down, ouch, take it easy). I try to return inside myself, holding my baby to me like it's him who's bleeding. I don't know what to do . . .

Just have to rescue myself. Starting with putting things to rights, changing the sheets first; got to get those blood stains out, put them in the Swiss washing-machine. (This particular machine takes hours and hours, and is really into it.) I clean and clean, Minu lies awake in his cradle, we go out to pick flowers and to get some vegetables to eat. By the time I've finished it feels like my home again, all outward traces of what happened have gone.

When Adam and Eve were thrown out of their beautiful garden, they were told, "It's your own fault, you created this for yourselves. You're on your own now. Go away." And then God added, "Till the soil, work it through, bring forth children, bear great pain, make sure you leave no stone unturned, turn each sod over one by one. If you want to get back to the garden you'll have to do everything properly. And a lot better then you've done so far. Good-bye."

"What happened here?" the Community's nurse asks as she sews me up.
"Don't know, perhaps they weren't put in properly," I replied unconcernedly.
"Odd, after four days . . . You've got an infection setting in too."
Luckily Minu starts to cry, and I can hide behind him. She gives me Arnica drops to take. "Good, has it got loads of alcohol in it?"
"Yes," the nurse replied. "Come back in two days, OK?"

François reappears a few days later. Maybe he's been staying with his parents, but I don't ask. He behaves like nothing has happened at all.

My body heals, my baby is fine and I love my husband, but I sleep on the floor.

We immerse ourselves in learning about the different therapies. Hugo heaves himself onto the massage table, this morning's therapy victim. We need to work on the circulation in his left side . . . gently massaging the distorted limbs in a figure of eight form, once you have found a rhythm of movement, don't interrupt it by taking your hands off the body at any time. Keep it light and etheric, always be aware of Hugo's whole system, and retain an image of both his limbs as healthy and strong. At twelve years old Hugo is a bit of a lad, and although he enjoys everyone's attention, he goes off grumbling in haze of Lavender Oil. "I may be paraplegic, but I'm not a woofta."
Johnny sidles in for his music therapy. He respects his therapist, and she can interact with him, more or less continuously through out their session. To start with she plays a few notes on

a sonorous marimba, and he answers back on the glockenspiel, then she plays a few notes up a scale and he continues them, then leaves a break for her to complete it. Johnny can talk at least to his therapist in music, and the last surprise is that he can hum clearly and in tune, holding his own part all the way through a difficult round, and he's enjoying it.

Dominic works hard on his concentration through walking and clapping different rhythms in his curative eurythmy sessions. He's all over the place, mainly because he can't be bothered to focus, and love and peace are his main gifts to the world. Ave gets him going, though. "Now Dominic clap your hands. Short, short, long . . . short, short, long . . . Good, now step with your feet, long, short, short . . . long, short, short . . . switch . . . again . . . Now both together." Dominic comes to a halt and smiles helplessly at Ave. "Pull your self together, Dominic, off you go again." Curative eurythmy is meant to consist of "gentle exercises that work on the whole being." Ave's sessions are rather vigorous, though.

The therapies seem to be working on me too and helping me to feel at home in my physical body once more. Some evenings I go to the therapy pool, turn on all the blue, green and purple lights, and dive in through the shafts of flowing luminous colour. It's colour therapy: twenty thousand leagues below sea, in fields of kelp, whilst on the surface through a distant purple haze, shines an ultra violet sun . . . All right.

Whatever the problem is with a child, if you can find a normal bit, that's what you can work with, a key to the way into them. Johnny's autism can be worked with too, like his fixation for pouring water endlessly down the sink, which can be channelled into emptying the rubbish for example. But the place where we really meet as whole human beings is in riding, humming and humour.

My thesis is about normality in the mentally handicapped child. While I'm struggling late at night with the final touches, Minu wakes with a piercing yell. "Sunny, we've got to get him to the hospital, I've never heard a baby scream like this." Francois and I take him off pell-mell.

"No you can't stay with him, I've never heard of such a thing, we are a hospital not a hotel. He will be perfectly fine with us, we don't need you, and it would be better for him if you didn't make a fuss." They are already carrying him off—where are they taking him, where is he going?

We wait while they operate. Then Minu comes round, opening his eyes like a doll; and then François leaves. I sit in the entrance porch of the hospital and smoke. I'm only allowed regular visiting hours. It's torture. I feel like a mother tiger, I want to be with my baby and feel torn in half every time I leave. "He is not better off without me! He screams the place down when I have to go. And look, he's got eczema all over him." "It's because you are putting all this stress on him . . ." They blame me! It turns out to be an allergy to penicillin. "But why did you give him penicillin anyway?" "He has an infection." Caught there, in their efficient Swiss Hospital.

I hang out in the hospital cafe, or the waiting room, or on the front porch. Then my Mum arrives (must have driven from England) and takes me back to my house, saying, "You've got to calm down dear, you must try and meditate for him, carry him inside your heart." I have a go but I'm not capable of it, trying for his sake but wishing I was back at the hospital. And François never comes to visit him or help me out—why? Where is he, anyway? Mum stays around until Minu is nearly better, and I am grateful for her company.

I have been stopped by our local friendly police officer for speeding slightly. He inspects my English provisional driving licence, "Where are you going?" he asks.

"The hospital."

"Are you ill?"

"No I'm fetching, my son home."

"Well everything seems to be in order, and I'll overlook the speeding this time."

"Thank you very much sir." The 2CV, just makes it up the hill to the hospital. Little Minu straddles my hip holding on around my waist. "It's OK, you're staying with me now." I collect his things, with a mounting rage inside me. Nobody tries to stop me from taking him home a day early, but they stand around uneasily and watch me through reptilian eyes, their tongues almost flickering in and out of their mouths as I say "Bye-bye, and thanks for nothing." Then we drive home slowly.

Minu is asleep as I carry him upstairs to our room but when I open the door, François and Lilith are making love—perfectly normally—in our bed. I shut the door and take Minu downstairs. With fury and despair in my soul, I go back to my room and ask them, "Do you realise that there is a child involved with this?"

Lilith replies, "Yes, we thought about that aspect of it, and we're very worried in case we get bad karma."

I am astounded at this selfishness."Oh for Christ's sake, wake up!" I yell, slapping her face as hard as I can. Lilith starts groping for her clothes.

"You know what Lilith? I thought we were good friends."

"Well I'm sure we can all still be good friends," offers Francois.

Lilith rounds on him, "Oh shut up, you cretin."

"Don't you talk to my husband like that . . ."

As it turned out, when I appeared they were so startled that Francois forgot to withdraw. So that is almost certainly when Jean, Minu's half-brother was conceived, with a kiss and a slap. However inadvertently, I am responsible for him being on the earth.

The thesis out of the way and in the hands of the local education authority, Pan and I have time on our hands to spare.

He is a good friend, and with our Steiner education in common we understand each other and enjoy preparing a treat together for the children. We had gone to town on our puppet show. Our puppets are second to none: the dwarves are earthy, with sheep's-wool beards, the stepmother surreal and terrifying, the king upright and full of inner authority, the huntsman a perfect Green Man, Snow White radiant and virginal, and the Prince warm with enthusiasm and light. Our sets were worthy of the Royal Opera House, and we had rehearsed every little detail. We put on black clothes, and blackened our hands and faces (just how I remembered it from Prague). "It's show time, folks—ssshh." And we slowly tell the drama of Snow White, with mime, marionettes, glove puppets and magic, while the children sit open-mouthed and silent. After several showings, we even get invited to other schools.

Resolving to put everything I'd got into making Francois feel great when we made love again, I finally pluck up courage to do it, but it turns out he only feels good when he hurts me. When he'd finished he calmly got dressed, saying, "I'm going up to Saanen again to hear Krishnamurti. I need some time on my own, and I like it there." I don't even need to ask; Lilith would be there waiting for him.

> "Must you weep
> and turn your face from the moonlight?
> You should know love is
> crooked
> frail as the little
> spines on a cucumber."

Like a mother kangaroo, I keep Minu with me all the time carrying him round, holding him, singing him to sleep. "Watch the stars, see how they run . . ." Gradually, we recover from our hospital ordeal; his scar heals slowly, and he's fine, healthy and easy again.

Sometimes he gets a really bad bout of hiccups, which go on for so long that he gets worn out. I look up hiccups in my Steiner baby health-care book; it says to place a camomile teabag on the baby's tummy. (Sometimes I wonder about these doctors.) I suppose it works because the baby is so surprised, and can't believe what's happening to it.

In my dream I was walking down the centre of a farm track that ran between the vines. It was autumn. The twisted roots and vine prunings lay glowing in bonfires that were smouldering in heaps at various intervals down the track. It felt like I was walking along the processional way at Avebury, in a ritual that I didn't know the meaning of, or what my role in it should be. In the distance a man approached; from far away he looked like a storm crow, and as we got nearer one another I became afraid, because he had an enormous head. He was holding out something for me to take: in his palm lay three gold coins, and I knew that they were evil. I took them anyway, because I was afraid that he would give them to some child who would not understand how bad they were, and then an evil infection would spread throughout the world. The man smiled; he had one brown eye and one green. I continued walking towards the lake, realising slowly that if I wanted to keep these coins safe I was going have to carry them with me forever . . .

I live in the shadow of that dream. It wraps itself onto me like a shroud for weeks and weeks, and I'm really scared of going to sleep in case it comes back.

Every single person in whole wide world has got a Time Line, maybe a bit like gossamer. It's born with you and stretches back to your beginning, and leads ahead of you to where you're going and your eventual death. It also reaches out from your heart towards the stars. Your life is not a random thing; it's taking you somewhere, and there's no point in fighting against it, it will take you there anyway, willy nilly. The trick is to put yourself behind it and make it yours, take what your being offered, and use your skills. And if you don't know what's going on sometimes, put your faith in where it might lead. Also, because of the way it reaches out from your heart you know that you are connected with something that is greater and wiser then you. So if our Time Line brings things for us to fight through, that is why we are here and what we have to do.

Making love, for me, does have something to do with love. People always look different, more open and beautiful when they are doing it. If I could show them how they looked, I'm sure they would feel better about themselves. Even after you disentwine, you can retain that togetherness for quite sometime.

This, however, was something else. It wasn't the pain so much as the total coldness of the way it was done. It made me feel like I didn't belong to myself. Then there came a night when it felt like I was being shoved off the face of the world, eliminated in some way. I heard myself react: "Why don't you just kill me and have a real thrill?" Which prompted a hurricane of violence. It was midnight, and over till the next time . . .

But there isn't going to be a next time. Calm, clear-headed and organised, I'm taking back control of my life whilst packing my bags and making up two bottles of milk for Minu. For a second I catch a glimpse of someone in the mirror and it's a moment before I recognise myself. Washing my face, tying the sleeping baby onto my front, and stepping out into the full August moon.

Hitching a ride to the station, we're in luck: this lorry and its relaxed American driver are headed right across France to the ferry. "Do you always hitch across Europe in the dead of night?" he enquires kindly after a while.

"Yup."

"Do you smoke?"

"Yes, I do." Now we're at Geneva, crossing over into France. "Right," he says, prizing off the top of the hooter and producing a large lump of hash. Roll us a big fat joint then."

Nestling in the green valley, the pink mansion-house glistened in the summer Sussex rain. Ralph was hanging out on the front porch. "Christ almighty, is that you?"

"No it's me. Why, were you expecting Him?"

"Come in," he said, taking the baby gently, and going into the cavernous kitchen. We get out all the frying pans and make a huge breakfast of eggs and bacon, sizzling mushrooms, tomatoes from the garden, fresh white bread and real coffee—and an Arnica chaser. The Portuguese servants take over Minu completely, saying, "Now you're coming to live here, yes?" "Don't know, not sure, just for while." I phone Ave to let her know where we are and what is going on. "Hello Sunny, congratulations you got your diploma, vat's up?"

"Ave, Francois and I . . . got a lift almost door to door . . . I don't know, but see you soon."

Serafina puts her arms around me saying, "Here, have some more Arnica. What happened, if you don't mind my asking? You look like you've been in a road accident."

"It was a sort of road accident . . . More of a head-on collision with Minu's father. But I'll be driving from now on."

II

1

Every Sunday night my father-in-law used to call from Montreal. I would look forward to it, because I loved him a lot. True to form, and despite his operation, he phoned at eight o'clock. "Hi Alex, how are you today?"

"It's a little hard to tell. They've got me all drugged up here. Pain-killers and all sorts of things." His voice sounded tired and slow, but we'd talked quietly for a while before I'd handed him over to Finn. They'd been waiting till he gained strength, before telling him about the liver cancer. And while Finn's gentle voice talked quietly on the phone my mind wandered off, to when I met his father for the first time . . .

Alexander McCabe was a tall, broad man with a mane of thick white hair, and he opened the car door with the style and natural grace of a gentlemen. "Well, hello. Come on in," he said with a welcoming smile. He was of Irish-Icelandic descent, which gave him good looks, charm and authority: a patriarch in the best sense. Struggling out of the huge Lincoln and leaving the luggage behind us, we walked up towards his country home, nestled above a wide deep blue lake amongst silent sweet-scented pines. Alex's house had been built out of the wood and rock, from the hill on which it stood, modern yet harmonious, part of the landscape. Minu and Tristan, my stepson, walked either side of Alex, keeping close, happy in his secure affability and taking on board the understated luxury of a self-made millionaire's retreat. The boys sat down by the pool, and privately I wondered why you would want a pool when your house is situated on a thirty-two-mile lake.

While my father-in-law-to-be showed me around, I became aware of how similar Finn was to him in many ways. Finn was darker and more effeminate, but he had the same dark blue eyes and thick hair as his father. They strode around, step in step, with a purposeful gait and their heads bent towards each other, mirroring a reflective listening pose. Tristan and Minu scampered off. "Watch out for porcupines, guys. Why don't you take a dip before you go exploring?" Then he had turned to me smiling and raising his eyebrows with the question, he'd said, "But you, I guess, would rather swim in the Lake?" I breathed out, relieved by the unspoken understanding, and aware that we'd taken a shine to one another.

We got into a routine. "Hey, do you feel like a dip today?" "Yup." "Don't say yup, say yes!" Then we'd whiz off in the boat, heading for the other side of the lake. (He was a laid-back sort of person, until he got behind the wheel of that boat. Some people refused to go out in it with him.) We would dock in the small harbour, surrounded by white timber-framed houses, geraniums, and antique shops. Once this place had been an old logging outpost, and the most imposing building was only three stories high; it was surrounded by old wrought iron balconies, a front porch, and had been the saloon, as well as home to the resident ladies of the night. Now it was a wholesome airconditioned restaurant called "L'Aubergine."

The little church had hidden gallons of bootleggers' whiskey and the Benedictine monks, pitching themselves against the local hoodlums, racketeers and gangsters, had run a lucrative, highrisk smuggling business. During the winter months the whole area was even more isolated, with freezing storms leaving snow-drifts ten feet high. Nothing daunted, Brother Hilarious and his pious gang would sledge their booty down the frozen lake and over the American border. But now the whole place was duck-boards, potted trees, and surreal piped music ("I just called to say I love you . . .") Equally determined, Alex made his way towards the store to buy himself a huge ice-cream with extra marshmallow, sprinkles, and lots of cream. Which his wife had banned for health reasons: forbidden fruit.

Later, in a forested bay out of sight, I would dive over the side of the boat into the cool clear Canadian water. Maybe this was what dying was like: plunging into another world, acclimatising in this new-found land, at home in a twilight world. Swimming along amongst the weeds and through the opaque azure water, occasionally catching glimpses of an enormous lake trout, veiled in shadows and glinting shafts of light muted, deep and peaceful as can be . . . And on finally surfacing, it was our world that always seemed the foreign place to me.

Minu caught one of those lake trout. He stood triumphant on the shore of the lake, his cries of "I got one, I got one!" echoing over the still grey waters. It weighed eight pounds and was big enough to feed us all: Finn's older brothers, wives, children, plus Alex's new wife and their two children. The Thai helpers cleaned and cooked it expertly, chattering, smiling and fussing over him. "Oh Meenu, some big fish you have caught for sure, my goodness!"

I started waking up to a new and altogether unexpected view of things. And Finn, even with his complicated, mixed feelings about Canada, was nonetheless proud to open the curtains on it for me.

I liked driving the Lincoln, although the hood was so long you couldn't see over the bonnet when going up a hill; one just had to hope that nothing was coming (and nothing ever did). It was like driving an enormous marshmallow. We got stopped for speeding once, in the middle of nowhere. The big policeman lumbered over, inspected Finn's British driving licence with interest, and after a while he drawled in his Quebec accent, "Well, I'm going to do my bit for international relations, so I won't fine you this time. Besides, there's an English guy who lives out here, and he tells us that you don't have any speed limits in England."

"Oh no . . . I mean that's right, we don't. It's a little hard to get used to it here. Thank you so much sir."

There were evenings at L'Aubergine, Thai cooking at home, and Trivial Pursuit. Once we got out the video of a film called "Witness". Every time it got to a part with the Amish people, I nudged Finn. "That's what it was like, Finn, that's how I grew up! We did all that barn-raising stuff, exactly like that, except they're not sweating and filthy . . ."

We flew through the heavens: the particularly heavenly California heavens. It was the last leg of our Grand Tour, and Finn's Mum and I were sky-diving. (Despite Minu's indignation. "How come she's allowed to sky–dive at seventy-two years old, and at *sixteen* am not?") I threw myself out of the rattling plane head first, diving into a higgledy-piggledy somersault before stabilising and spreading out my arms beside me to slow down, then tucking them in close for speed to became a comet, hurtling towards the welcoming Earth. Free-falling the ultimate joyride, and an unparalleled experience of freedom. Even at 120mph I could breathe long slow deep breaths. I wasn't even afraid.

I had convinced the pilot to take me up to 15,000 feet so I could have a good long free fall, giving me plenty of time to see how very beautiful the Earth looks. "A vast planet of calm, a good place to live." I felt reborn; the only thing was that I suddenly had to make a split-second decision, and surprised to discover that I did want to be here after all, I pulled the rip cord a little late. But the parachute opened triumphantly, and from then on it was rather like sailing peacefully, almost becalmed. "Am I moving at all? Ho hum, oh look that's my shadow way down there . . ."

Finn's Mum lost her sneaker somewhere on her way down (now how did she do that?). We scoured the alfalfa field where we landed for it; no luck, though. "A jogger in Golden Gate Park today was struck on the head by a sneaker which came from nowhere. His condition was described as stable but pissed-off..." We made up news-flashes all the way home from Davis, eventually winding up into the Novato hills, where she lived in peaceful isolation. The silver Merc purred along very nicely, thank you.

No, I wasn't becoming decadent with all this—just eager for the experiences, and dead pleased. But the boys were soaking it all up, one couldn't help but notice...

Finn came off the phone to his father. And I came out of my reverie. We both thought that they should've told him what was going on. Perhaps they knew what they were doing, perhaps they didn't... But I think my father-in-law already knew that he was going to die.

2

Now although I recognised that it was serious and important—or because of that—I had initially cold-shouldered Finn, as was the custom in those days. On the rebound from previous marriages, both of us were totally spooked at the thought of getting involved in any more long-term relationships ever again. So I responded very maturely by trying to ignore the situation while sleeping with as many other people as possible. But he showed persistence and imagination.

We had met because my Mum, after twenty-five years of living in Woodbrook, had suddenly upped and moved to Chelsea. The mother-figure was still into Steiner in a big way, but as she got older she was also returning to her aristocratic roots at an alarming. "What goes around comes around." The aristocracy has always moved in mysterious circles, heigh ho. Anyway, Finn bought her old house in Woodbrook for his ex-wife and little boy Tristan, destined for the Steiner School (poor little beggar). Though Finn himself lived in London, beavering away at the L.S.E, political, edgy, and brighter than some of his professors. And although I was living at Romany's, we kept bumping into each other at my Mum's new residence; he would appear from time to time with things she'd left behind, and then one day he came by to say that there was nothing left. Standing on the doorstep, and showing no signs of leaving. Which demonstrated, as I said, persistence and imagination. "You want a cup of tea then, or what?" I heard myself say graciously, inviting him in.

Finn was a social/intellectual historian. His study was viridian green, his windows shaded by wooden venetian blinds, and treasures from all over the world glimmered on dusty surfaces: duck decoys from Manitoba, a nattily-dressed fox from Japan, a weird aboriginal creature and all manner of stones, feathers, fir-cones, conkers, and acorns whose origins and significance had long since been forgotten. On the walls hung his collection of Japanese prints (lovely ladies, mostly), a large Modigiliani nude, Monet's water lilies, and the Venus de Milo. A couple of guitars rested on the dark green velvet upholstered chairs and a collection of pens in a Ministry of Silly Walks mug.

The Home Office was a hive of activity: phones ringing, faxes rolling, fans blowing, music playing and the PC on overdrive. "Goddamn it! That's good, if I say so myself . . ." His current problem was how to create an ecological society without actually imposing it by force. Reviews and articles rolled off the printer at a furious pace, as steam billowed out from the half open door. When Finn wrote his books he lived in them, so the entire house rocked and rolled along with him, and over the sixteen years of our marriage we had been through several different incarnations, his groaning bookshelves a testimony to them all: Aristotle, Plotinus, Chuang-tsu, Nietzsche, Gramsci, Wittgenstein and Foucault—and that's just the philosophers. Oh yes, and Dave Hume, an out-and-out scare monger who said jolly things like, "Just because the sun rose yesterday doesn't mean it's going to rise tomorrow." An ex-hippie, Finn had mystical leanings, but lately he had taken up with

Machiavelli, who said, "To make an omelette you've got to break a few eggs."

"Hello Finn. Conference go ok, you want something to eat?"

"Phew, home at last . . . It was pretty hard going. Some interesting people though. But all the way home I just kept thinking about my poor old Dad. Where has all the time gone, Sunny? Suddenly I'm forty-five and I really haven't achieved much, only a few books and none that great. And I found a grey hair the other day. I want to write something really good and make a difference, before I die too."

"Don't worry, you will, and you've achieved a lot already. Some of those books got excellent reviews. And Finn, you're not dead yet."

"Thanks . . . Oh, an omelette! Great, I'm starving." He settled down to eat hungrily.

"When you say you want to write a book that will make a difference, what do you mean?"

"I mean to the real world. I've been thinking a lot about green ethics. It's terrible the way we treat the poor old Earth, and ignore the common good."

"Most of the time I'm in overload about the state of the Earth. I just feel totally useless."

"Lots of people do. We get so much bad news from the media, it's too much."

"But what can we do to fight these terrible forces of destruction?"

"Well we can fight politically, of course. But Sunny, every single creative thing you do works against that destructiveness."

"Well now there's a thought, Finn. I can work with that idea."

Finn responded to emotional problems with logic and reason instead of feelings, which always made me throw a fit but that's just the way he was. If I was put on the spot, on the other hand, my faculty for logic just vanished into the Cosmic Midnight, fring! and I'd say any old thing that came into my head. Which always made Finn throw a fit. Actually I hardly ever met anybody who could deal with it.

Showing no signs of slowing up after all those years, Finn McCabe and I shared a love of the unusual kind. We were good friends, and our occasional rows never seemed to matter much because we'd always have such a good time making up afterwards.

There only ever had been one thing Finn missed from Canada, and that was the "proper snow" of a Canadian winter. And once on a February evening, to Finn's delight, the sky had gradually turned black as icy winds began to blow from the north, bringing lots and lots of snow to London. We had gone out in it for a while, Finn high as kite and looking like the abominable snow man, animated by the bitter wild winds. "This is more like it!" he laughed. "Yes Finn, but I'm about to go snow blind, as it happens..."

Eventually, frozen through, we'd come in to warm up. Then, while the blizzard worsened outside, sipping hot chocolate, Finn put the music on full blast, and that's why you can put the blame fairly and squarely on Van Morrison's shoulders. He'd been raving on with his usual wild abandon about "No Guru No Method No Teacher": an unlikely tune for attempting a tango, but we had stalked across the sitting room floor pretty impressively—until, that is, Finn dropped me. The next thing I knew, I was pregnant. (It's important to thoroughly discuss the more serious decisions in life, make them together, consider every angle... Harrumph, if we'd done that Scarlet would never have happened.)

"Minu, we need to talk." There had never been any use in beating around the bush with him. "Let's have some coffee then," he said, putting on the kettle, reaching for the mugs and starting to mash instant coffee and sugar together. "What's on your mind Mum?"

"You're going to have a baby sister or brother."

Then he handed me my horrible coffee soup, and slowly focusing his eyes on me, asked, "Haven't you ever heard of contraception?"

"Very funny."

"Well, if it's a boy we'll call it Minu, of course. If it's a girl, lets call her Scarlet."

"Where did you get that from? I like Scarlet, but lets see what Finn thinks." There had always been a slight confusion as to who exactly was man about the house.

Taking on the proportions of an African fertility goddess, as I ate up the entire EEC sweet-and-sour prawn mountain, we weighed up the pro's and con's about her entrée into this world: should it be at home or in hospital? "Or Finn, what about doing it at the ICA, as a piece of performance art?" But the hospital had a couple of birthing pools. I'd imagined myself lying around with my sunglasses and *Hello* magazine, but in the end there was no time for that, because the whole thing only took two hours. I felt elated afterwards, and could have picked her up and walked home. Things are very different these days. The midwives were laid back and gave me a cup of tea afterwards. No drugs, no stitches, no hassle, one baby, voila. Finn was relaxed and helpful. "It's a little girl!" he exclaimed, delighted. But to me it feels like she's always been around.

Scarlet's friends came in prams and pushchairs, in baby buckets, slings and carry-cots. They brought with them a variety of trendy bags full of food jars and bottles, creams, unctions, remedies and nappy sacks, they mainly came to feed and sleep. The house was full of breast-feeding Earth-mothers. Later, they came on tricycles, in peddle-cars, or standing like captains on the back of pushchairs behind their new and younger siblings; some with mothers and some even with nannies. The house was full of four-year olds, who came to fight and wind each other up. Much later, they came on roller blades, bicycles and scooters, and one or two suave experts on skateboards—mainly, by then, to play, while we sat over our cups of tea and gossiped. Then Minu was joined overnight by his girlfriend Sorrel, and some of their friends arrived in cars of their very own. Once again, they mainly came to feed and sleep, the house full of wiped-out teenagers.

We were the only people at home but Scarlet was in earnest conversation with someone, and I wondered who it could be. "It's Tail Woozy and Miluka."

"Oh? What are they doing?" I asked her.

"They're staying with their Aunties in Australia. They're called Susie-Anna and Daffodil Fanny."

"Daffodil who?" Scarlet had two imaginary friends and all their relations for company when no body else was around. "Do you know something? I used to have a friend called Peter David, and he told me once that he'd been to the moon."

She looked at me in astonishment. "So has Tail Woozy!"

We lived in horror of Finn's cooking. ("Mum, was there a fire here today, or has Finn been cooking again?") So he was dispatched instead to buy a load of beautiful flowers for Scarlet's birthday. And when he returned we set to, putting her birthday candle by her place, with some flowers and leaves scattered around it and a few Smarties for good measure, and arranging the birthday cards from all her friends. Scarlet was going to be five the next day, and liked everything just so. Even though she was not always just so herself.

The kitchen steamed up as Saskia, Charley, Marlene, Pearl, Romany and I made sandwiches, and discussed with enthusiasm the operations we were going to have when we got elderly. "Face lift"—"You needed one yesterday"—(fry sausages)— "Bum tuck. Look, does your bum really drop when you're forty?"—"Yours will"—(open up the bags of crisps)—"Fanny tightened"—"I'm going to get mine sewn up"—"Oh you don't still do it, do you?"—"Well it's a chance to put my feet up"—(egg mayo)—"Boobs like Dolly Parton's"—"In your bloke's dreams"—(peanut butter)—"Hands, you've got to stop the sagging between the fingers"—(chocolate fingers)—"Liposuction all over your body, or just suction maybe"—"You're so kinky, we don't want to hear about your sado-masochistic fantasies"—(jelly, of the non-mad-cow variety)—"You're a mad cow yourself sometimes, Sunny"—"I'm surprised you noticed Marlene"—"Party bags?"—"No. I don't do party bags, middleclass bollocks. They can all win something."—"I'm glad you're making a stand. Besides, it's not their birthdays."—"Ladies, please!" Minu came in from school and got stuck into making the cake. It was shaped like a train, he put a lot of energy and enthusiasm into making the carriages just so, and when he was finally satisfied they stretched the length of the table, and there was no room for anything else. Finn washed up and kept everybody supplied with drinks, and my friends (party addicts all) helped out.

The children arrived in their party clothes, shining, expectant and excited. Scarlet greeted them as though she was the Queen, and carefully put their presents aside. We had a magician friend who was so good at it that the kids sat hushed and awed, as doves, cards and rabbits appeared and disappeared from nowhere. Pass the Parcel, Blind Man's Bluff, and best of all, Wink Murder; then food ("I'm allergic to dairy"—"Don't like jelly"—"I'm allergic to chocolate"—"Well I'm not," Harry had said, stuffing his mouth), hose and calm them down, bye-bye.

Later, we two sat talking quietly. "I can't believe she's five years' old already, where has all the time gone?"

"Finn, for Christ's sake, Scarlet at five is at the very beginning of her life, your father at eighty-four has had a long life, and in between we are supposed to have the time of our life, get it?"

"Sunny, you are completely satisfied with the idea of reincarnation, but I am not, I just don't know. So for you when somebody dies they are still around somewhere, but for me they are gone. I see Scarlet on one end of the scale moving up, my Dad at the other end moving out, and me on this downward slide, driven by time."

"Ok Finn, ok."

Man, did I get a high fever that night or what? I'd always had to watch Finn, or he'd get hysterical and have me off to casualty. "It's only 104° Finn, that's fine."

"No it isn't!"

"Ok, how about you give me a paracetamol then, and some cool water with lemon in it?" Finn gently wiped away the sweat, carefully avoiding my eyes with the cool lemon-water, patiently and gently he worked around my neck, my back and legs, until the fever turned around, pouring all his love and concern into making me better, calming down and concentrating, until we fell asleep.

Maybe my children and I were over-bonded. Although Scarlet had been well-prepared, she howled her way to school for the first two weeks. One couldn't blame her. Anybody would rather have stayed at home making chocolate-chip cookies and having tea-parties. That summer we'd been particularly industrious, picking mountains of blackberries, raspberries, loganberries and later on apples and sloe, the whole house embalmed in the warm smell of fresh fruit. Just a couple of weeks before, Finn had announced, "Has anybody noticed the elderflower is coming out now? I reckon it's ready. Scarlet you want to go down to Sussex, don't you?" We had picked bags of it, and ended up at friends' in Blackboys. The kids played on the trampoline and the (ahem) grownups hung out in the hot-tub; later that evening, we made a sign which read "BLACKBOYS—TWINNED WITH SOWETO". So we'd been having a good time together. I was glad not to have to work;

I'd just wanted to be with her. Guess I am a post-liberated woman.

At the end of the summer Tristan went back to his Mum, and Finn went off to the library in search of lost times. Minu was studying for his GCSE's. Scarlet settled down at school eventually. And I got on with the tape of traditional children's songs I was working on in my studio.

Scarlet became firm friends with Katie and Harry, and a whole new school life opened out for her. I enjoyed picking them up from school and listening to the chit-chat in the back of the car. One time they were discussing theology, and Katie, suddenly seeing the light, said, "Oh, I know what Christians are, they're those people who go to church and sin a lot."

I also had job of sorts working for an ageing punk rocker. Nicky lived in a house-boat, and weighed anchor spontaneously and sporadically, and you could never be sure where he was when you were talking to him. I used to phone him up about my own engineering difficulties. "Nicky, help! I can't get the computer to play it back onto the eight-track."
"Have you changed over the input/output leads?"
"Yes . . ."
"How do I know you're lying?"
We worked extremely well together. He loved fighting with the various record companies and haggling over deals; I liked being able to do the music, and took a certain pride in mastering studio engineering. At first, all those winking lights and buttons were daunting, it looked like the Star Ship Enterprise—warp factor on track four, at five point three degrees, out of sinc and melting slowly, massive buildup of feedback from unknown source . . . My mind was not prepared in any way for sound engineering, but it was something new and challenging to learn and would eventually be useful for my own

music; I was proud to find myself perfectly capable of working this equipment. Nicky and I became firm friends, and if you are going to be locked up with someone, sometimes for thirty-six hours a session, it's a good idea for them to be gay.
"Nicky, I've been working here for three months now, and there are these lights, see—here, here and here—yeah, those flashing ones, and I can't work out what they're for or which computer they're attached to."

"Oh, that's easy, those are for P.I.V.," he replied.

I racked my brains; must be something I wasn't familiar with. "What's that?"

"Punter Impression Value. They don't do a thing, kid, just make the place look good."

The Thames looked beautiful in the rays of the sunset, as we strolled across the Hammersmith bridge. When we were almost across, Nicky suddenly stopped dead in his tracks and mumbled in alarm, "My God, that duck, it's taller then me!" He was not a healthy guy, so it was surprising how fast he could run, when he took off back across the bridge, every so often staring back over his shoulder. The little Mallard looked up at me quizzically. "It's nothing personal," I explained. "Probably a mixture of Ecstasy and Tequila." And we watched Nicky recede, zigzagging through the pedestrians, into the darkening distance.

We spent a lot of time making demos for teenage bands. They arrived at the studio with their precious pennies all saved up, hoping that they had a hit; and once in a while they did. We could tell almost immediately if a song had a chance, but whatever the material we did our best. Nicky was an excellent guitarist as well as sound engineer; I learned a lot and enjoyed the sessions, as well as the company of other creative people. There was an understanding and humour between us that I felt secure with, like being with my friends from school. But what I liked best was the fact that I had a bass track playing on a Japanese demo, and acoustic guitar on a minor hit in France, and some music in a Spanish film. Bits and pieces of myself spread out all over the place.

One day a young man walked into the studio, and Nicky asked, "What are we doing today, a song? A commercial?"

"A song," he replied.

"OK, what would you like to start with?"

"Effects," came the emphatic reply.

Nicky had a cult following of gay teenagers, who showed up and hung out at the studio. He used to deal with them calmly, accepting their love with equanimity, because he hàd always been loved. Some were in long-term relationships, others on the loose; some were HIV, some had AIDS, others a bad drug habit, but they supported each other gently, with humour and great care. Which was interesting to me, because society always seemed given to understand that most gay people were only interested in cruising and the next sexual encounter. Even if they were, I had known plenty of straight men and women like that. What mattered was whether you were a decent human being or not.

"Sunny, we've got a gig in a club in town on Saturday, OK?"

"Oh good. Can I oil my body, put on my bondage gear, and play topless fiddle?"

"No you can't, you can play bass fully-clothed on the floor. It's a gay club, they don't want to see your uggsome female body. Course, they might want to see mine."

"Now you have seriously fucked with my ego . . ." He got out his guitar, and tinkled about on it. "Nicky, someone once told me a good guitarist is exciting, not excited."

"Sunny, someone once said, if you don't know what to play, don't play anything. Come on, let's finish up that rock video."

"Nicky do you think you could pay me sometime?"

"Shut up, ssshhhhhh, 4, 3, 2, 1, we're rolling . . ."

Nicky didn't do anything without consulting the *I Ching* or the Tarot. He pored over his hand-drawn Tarot pack, and then emerged, his narrow hawk-like face beaming. "It's going to be a great gig. Look at this, we've got Death, the Tower of Destruction, the Dancing Man, and the Fool." I could see what he meant: it was the perfect reading for a punk-rock concert. "What about the Nuclear Explosion, did we get that?" I'm really a "Nuclear Power No Thanks" person, but flexible when it came to rock concerts.

"Gentlemen and gentlemen, will you please welcome, the fabulous and amazing, the really incredible, Nicky Sly and The End of the Universe!" That was me: the end of the universe.

Once in a while I used to go to the Fifth Floor Cafe at Harvey Nicks with my women friends: "Five jumbo cappuccino's coming up."
 "Hey Sunny, what's the strangest place you've ever done it in?"
 "Well, I once did it with the captain of a Sealink ferry, on my way to France. My Mum and Jake were on board. What about you?"
 "Up the big beech tree in the Forest."
 "Well, how about the waiting-room at Eastwood station?"
 "I once did it in Buckleberry Church."
 "But any old bat could have walked in there anytime."
 "I know."
 "I bet it was with the Virginian, that country and western singer."
 "'You'll go to your church, and I'll go to mine, but lets walk along together . . . ' Did he sing that to you?"
 "Sure he did, all the time".
 "Finn is dead scared of flying."
 "Just like Erica Jong."
 "Very droll. I love winding him up though. 'Finn, I can't

find your life-vest, it's a bad omen. Let's do it now, it may be the last chance we ever have to join the mile high club. Hurry up, while all the kids are sleeping!'"

"Another five cappuccino's, please."

"Poor old Finn."

3

Once, in the holidays, we took off for Skiathos, where Finn's Mum had a fabulous house. The girls were dead impressed by my welcoming party at the airport: three Greek male friends. Even if the oldest looked like Isaac Bashevis Singer and the youngest looked (and sang) like Pavarotti. With "Greek Clint" (as he once called himself) in the middle. "Welcome, welcome, who is everyone?"

"This is Marlene and her daughter Phoenix, and this is Charley and her son Shane."

"How do you do? . . . Sunny, why you so thin? How is Finn? Oh Scarlet, you are a beautiful girl now! Hello Minu, I see you cut your own hair now, where is Tristan this year?"

"Oh, he's working."

"Working? Tristan? I not believe it. But why you only come such a short time, a week not enough." They loaded the suitcases and kids into the car. "Bye-bye, ladies, enjoy yourself. Oh Minu I have lovely motor bike for you to use, I bring it up later."

"Bye bye, boys, thanks," and we finally drove off. Skiathos only has one road, on which you drove as fast as you could. It's part of Greek culture, to die driving; a noble thing.

The whole island shimmered with a silver light. Up in the hills the cicadas sang, and the black figs ripened. My green-fingered mother–in–law had planted a wonderful garden, roses, wisteria, herbs, and all manner of fruits and flowers and blossoming trees, pomegranates and avocados; the sweet smell of orange and lemon trees filled the air. Surrounded by the old olive groves she and Pavarotti lovingly maintained, overlooking the sea, the house was a peace-haven. Finn's mother lived six months of the year there at that time, and the rest in California. Much to her chagrin Finn had never liked it there, but I was welcome to go whenever. Minu searched about for his flippers and snorkel, and Scarlet for her buckets and spades, Shane in tow, as they reacquainted themselves with familiar shady paths at the back of the house. Then they all went down to the pool for that first evening swim after a long journey, when the sun sets behind the hill. I thought of Finn at home enjoying having the place to himself, not shaving, drinking a beer at ten in the morning if he felt like it and playing his Grateful Dead records (or worse, the Incredible String Band) at full blast.

Marlene, Charley and I bought a postcard depicting three curvaceous models on jet-skis with their bums in the air. "Dear Finn, here we are in Skiathos. I'm the one in the G-string . . ."

The kids played in the sand, and Scarlet showed off her recently acquired swimming skills. Minu spent his days floating around on an inflatable Pocahontas "canoe" recovering from the night before, and the tumbles he took from the enormous motor bike. Occasionally, with Phoenix in my arms, I'd carefully carry her around up to her waist in the water. She was dead scared of swimming—"Help I'm drowning!"—and clasped me around the neck in a death grip, but we made good progress. Otherwise we opted out on our deck-chairs, chatting and having a laugh. "Have you read *Miss Smilla's Feelings about Snow?*" Charley enquired.

"Yes I have. There ought to be a help-line for that book."
"Yeah! What on earth is Cryolite?"
"I haven't a clue."
"But I thought you read it?"
"I did, but that don't mean I know what Cryolite is."

I was trying to read a dead stupid book called *The Horse Whisperer*. "Shut up for a second, will you? She's doing it with a horse."

"Is she really? I don't remember that . . . Thought you'd gone rather quiet."

"That reminds me, did you ever find your cap?"

"Well, I looked for days, it was putting quite a dent in our conjugal relations. But I finally found it in the only place I hadn't looked . . ."

Marlene and I had worked with special-needs children in different Community schools and Charley taught the "normal" ones, so we had a load of friends and experiences in common. "Hey Sunny, let's phone up all the schools on Good Friday during the silent supper, then chat inanely for hours and hours. They can't answer back!"

"One of the good things about teaching is that you get to confiscate the children's chocolate and cigarettes," I mused, broiling myself in the sun like you're not supposed to. Marlene and I shared the same bad habits. It was a relief not to have the husbands around, vibing us to eat better. Charley wandered off topless to the beach taverna to show them how to make a proper cappuccino; no doubt about it, *la belle dame sans habilles* had them all enthralled. You wouldn't necessarily have predicted Charley's smouldering sexuality and voluptuous curves from the spiky, porcupine-like kid she had once been; in fact, if you saw then-and-now pictures, you wouldn't have connected them at all.

"After my family," mused Marlene, "kids with special needs were easy. My father once nailed the Christmas tree into the floor of our apartment in New York, when it wouldn't stand up. He stood back to admire it, saying, 'There, that should do it,' while we had to deal with our downstairs neighbours whose plaster had descended on their Hannukah supper... When he was dying in hospital, my Mum and I went to see him. He was bald from the chemotherapy, which was probably killing him too, and my Mum sobbed, 'Oh Tony, Tony my darling, I wish it were me instead.' He replied, 'So do I.'"

On the beach, we were the sort of nightmare women you dread ending up next to. There were sixteen sandy beaches in Skiathos, and by about midmorning we'd usually made such a racket, and our patch such a hive of hyperactivity, that most people had cleared off somewhere else. All except Helmut, that is, who was very large and about sixty, and lay on his deck chair enjoying our water fights, paddle-boat races, and the show in general. "Help, the mighty Kraken has his testicles wrapped around me, oooh he's pulling me under..." (Brunhilde, his wife, just had to put up with it.)

I was trying to make an effort not to swear at the time, because when you do you use a bit of brain that's very crude and underdeveloped, left over from Neanderthal man. Who is still around, Charley pointed out: "Just cast your eye along this beach, will you."

One day we buried Shane up to his neck in sand, and then shaped two huge breasts with shell nipples over his body, a mermaid's tail, extra fine and curly red seaweed for pubes and long seaweed tresses. He was so cross, a scowling, swearing mermaid. "You stinky fish face, Sunny!" he bawled. But with his arms firmly buried he couldn't do a thing about it. "Look who's talking... Oh-oh, I think the tide's coming in." Honestly kids are so uptight these days, maybe they should be encouraged to smoke more and mellow out a bit.

Sidling up to a stiff, middle-aged British businessman, with Charley and Marlene a few paces behind, and all of us as close to naked as you can get without actually being it, I asked, "'Scuse me, would you take us for a ride in your power boat please?" I writhed politely. "Er, yes, if you like. It gets a bit cold out there, you know . . ." "OK kids, come on!" "Oh. Are they coming too?"

Back at home, Minu went off to his room with a pile of official envelopes, Finn and I could hear him opening them up at a furious rate. Then, after a rather breathless pause, he sauntered downstairs, saying, "Mum, Finn, I failed every single one of them." Then he'd smiled widely at us. "Just kidding. I passed, look seven A's and four B's, and" (by now he could hardly contain himself) "I've been accepted by Chelsea School of Art to do a B.Tech. in Art and Design. YES!"

"Congratulations! You worked so hard, and you got into Chelsea too! You can be proud of yourself, and I am too," Finn said, keeping his wits together. Because all I could say was. "My son is a genius, an absolute genius . . ."

4

Marlene was a petite redhead. Everything about her was firm but fairylike: a sort of fiery New York fairy. She and I were on our way to the Royal Academy to pick up a copy of *John Constable's Suffolk Landscapes*, which Minu had ordered from jail. "I got the all-clear from my endoscopy this morning, which was relief I can tell you."

"I'm so glad, thank God for that, Marlene. What did they do exactly?"

"OK, first they anaesthetise you. Then they stick a cheese-grater up you and turn it round four times."

"Well, that's different, anyway."

"Yeah. And then my Iranian doctor said, 'No sex for two months. The vagina is a warm moist place full of germs, and we don't want a penis up there . . . '"

"You know, I never did hear how Minu got arrested in the first place."

"Oh God, he was on his way to a rave at Chelsea School of Art to celebrate finishing his B.Tech. He and Leo had been rigging up a sound system, you could probably hear it on the moon."

"I can imagine—the end of civilisation as we know it. And we thought our music was loud!"

"Anyhow, he was walking down the Wandsworth Bridge Road, and the police were looking for someone with ginger hair, so they jumped out of a van and searched him on the street. They kept calling him Jason! It didn't take them long to find the Ecstacy and dope that he was taking to the party. Then they bunged him into the back of their van, telling him not to lie about his name and took him down to the police station. Minu says they were pretty rough."

"The fucks, I can't bear to think of him in their hands."

"I know. He kept telling them that there was no need to be like that, but they kept on at him. And what's more, they told him that he could have a solicitor but it might take two or three days, so he would get out a lot quicker if he didn't wait for one. He was scared stiff, of course, so he made a statement there and then."

"But I thought you weren't allowed to be interviewed without a lawyer present these days."

"I don't know about that, but he played right into their hands, he said he was shaking with fear."

"Poor Minu, oh don't cry Sunny, it's not your fault. It's just something to do with his life, something he has to go through with and learn from, don't you think?"

"Yeah, I know. OK, I forgot to teach him to always have a solicitor there. That's very bad parenting but you just can't think of everything. I thought he knew that, anyway. But the worst part was that he had to go through it all alone. In court they called it "a fortuitous arrest"."

"Where did he get his dope from in the first place?"

"Some dealer the students used, I don't know why he couldn't have bought his dope off the milkman like everybody else in our neighbour hood."

"No kidding?"

"No, you just leave a note in your milk bottle saying you

want "Two pints of milk and an ounce of Black Moroccan please."

"And to think I blamed Mrs Thatcher for blindly encouraging private enterprise. Wish I lived in your street! Bloody Northampton. You know Sunny, I've written to him a few times, how's he doing really?"

"Not too bad, I guess. But I'm planning on cementing myself into the middle of Oxford Circus during rush hour until they release him. Fancy joining me?"

5

"So, do you fancy joining me?"

"No, I most definitely do not Mum."

"Good, well that's settled then. We can all go in your car."

And that is how I had been trapped into a Sunday lunch with my mum's sister, Lady Macbeth. Goddammit. Staring down from the hall walls, the ancestors had me surrounded. My auntie's ancient seat had been recently renovated, and firmly leading Scarlet by the hand and stepping over a pile of slumbering dogs, she led the way upstairs with Mum following her, then Minu and Tristan trudging unwillingly behind, then me and Finn. "On the first floor, we now have the master bedroom, and new bathroom suite . . ." she boomed in stentorian tones. I mooned Finn behind me.

At lunch we were served pheasant from her estate, and Scarlet lost her first tooth on account of the lead shot she came across. "Are you going to put it under your pillow for the tooth fairy, Scarlet darling? What on earth does she do with all those teeth I wonder?"

"Why Auntie, don't you know? She sews them onto her dress of course."

All the way home, Scarlet sang, "Welcome to the Addams family..."

I've always had a strange attraction to Punch and Judy, in all its non-PC glory, so Minu, Scarlet and I set off gleefully for the Punch and Judy Festival in Covent Garden. "Ah, putcha putcha putcha," said Punch, as the policeman entered stage left. "'ello 'ello 'ello, I'm your friendly community policeman I am, and I'm going to do a bit of friendly community policing on your 'ead..." Looking around, I saw Saskia—well, her lipstick actually—and Pearl, with some bloke they had in tow. "This makes a great change," she declared, "from all those woolly puppets we grew up with," and introduced me. "Hi how are you," he said, "glad to meet you at last. Did you go to one to one of those funny schools, too? I hear you do a lot of knitting there. Still, I suppose it's better than maths and French." "Yeah, we had to knit French," I replied. "And maths, and hockey," the others joined in, "and singing and woodwork, and"..."Man, we even had to knit lunch"..."And then in Class Twelve, you cast off!"

Saskia didn't talk to either of her parents any more, and was always moaning in exasperation at our "fucking spelling and writing. Thank God for spell-check!" She earned her living as a researcher, but her main interest was in producing the most brilliant operas. She was trying to persuade Tina Turner to do Brunhilde in the Ring cycle, and I think she'd got the Gay Bikers on Acid for the chorus. Alongside this she was writing a book called *A Year in Peckham*.
"Sunny, do you lot fancy coming over? I think I've just knocked down a supporting wall..."

The car was rather overloaded when we puttered off towards Hyde Park Corner. "Go on, go down the Burlington Arcade, it's more direct." "No mum, don't do it!" squawked Minu, as the half-timbered car swerved across the pavement down the oldest little pedestrian shopping street in London. "Charge 'em and they scatter!" And we almost made it, before being stopped by a security guard who was rolling his eyes in a crazed kind of way. Saskia leaned out the window waving an *A to Z*. "Hullo, excuse me," she breathed huskily in a broad Bronx accent, flashing her big emerald eyes. "Could you pul-lease tell me where Piccadilly is?" Then he gaped as we angled the car expertly down the two steps. You can't do that now, though, because within days of our little escapade they put up concrete posts across the entrance.

The journey continued uneventfully across the river, to where she lived in a block of Victorian flats. She had been rebuilding her place for about eight years by then, and it was lovely: exposed brick—work, sanded floor-boards, neatly cemented corridor, raised bath with bleached wooden panelling. Her opera scores lay on the carefully chosen rug, and the whole place was neat as a pin; a real home. Except, of course, for the wall that she'd just removed. "It is a supporting wall, Saskia," I said easing my way around the ultra-sized anti-Steiner T.V. she had bought. "Come on, lets find some four-by-fours and shore it up . . ." Rebuilding bits of houses was an enjoyable sideline for lots of us, involving lots of power–tools that we were never allowed at school.

In London, it's hard to maintain a sense of the seasons. The rhythm of the inhaling Earth, withdrawing into itself gradually through autumn towards the winter solstice, or exhaling and opening out through the spring towards the Midsummer solstice: it all gets lost here. Even the daily rhythm of sunrise and sunset gets mishmashed with all the street-lights and continuous bustle that goes on all day and all night.

Neither Finn nor I had regular jobs, either. We worked at odd times, which made it even more important to maintain a daily rhythm. I liked to celebrate whatever festival I could, so my children had some sense of what season it was; and apart from being fun, it may have made them feel more secure. It was something I was going to do anyway; more a question of me sitting down to paint an autumn picture and them joining in. I wasn't going to impose Christianity upon them, because it neglects the Earth, and excludes every other religion which might pollute their minds. Above all, don't trample on a child's own ideas and sense of the sacred.

Our daily rhythms and routines were helping us to move along and not get too down about Alex dying, so I hung on to them determinedly. One morning I walked into our bathroom, and sitting on the floor on either side of the loo was a pair of little red shoes. Christ, I thought, Scarlet has either been blasted into outer space or stolen like Faust by Mephistopheles. I glanced at the ceiling for a hole—no, no hole, so she must have been swallowed up by the bog. "Mummy, have you seen my red shoes anywhere?" she asked, toddling up behind me. "Oh there they are, good. Now can we go to Holland Park and look for things to make an Easter nest with?"

The sun came out as Scarlet, Finn and I walked in the late spring air, collecting moss, leaves and feathers for Scarlet's nest. In the distance there was a young man under a tree, totally involved in his Tai Chi. He had the same concentration as someone meditating, his movements fluid and beautiful to watch. We waited until he'd finished his form before approaching; he looked up glowing, embarrassed but pleased that we'd seen him. It was Tristan, Finn's son. He gave us all a hug. "Yeah, yeah, I love you too Tristan, save a tree."

Back at home Tristan and Scarlet blew the quail, duck and chicken eggs for us to paint. Something had been puzzling me for a while. I bet Tristan knew the answer, because he often went to places like Twyford Down and spent time with people who lived up trees. In fact he was involved in lots of environmental guerrilla activities, which often seemed to demand throwing himself in front of a computer. "Tristan, when people cement themselves into the middle of the M4 extension, what happens when they need the loo?" "I don't know. Perhaps if you're planning some sort of action, you'd better plan on cementing yourself into the bog."

We put some tissue paper in a frosted glass bowl, then Scarlet sowed wheat grain into it and carefully watered it. The grains would germinate, and by Easter there would be a fine, light green forest. And then she made her nest, for us to put our eggs in when they were finished. Tristan painted some tiny little magic mushrooms on his. Finn's was complicated, like a Hokusai-style Japanese landscape, Scarlet's in the image of Kandinksy, and mine spiralled in colour and lots and lots of gold.

Finn had been closeted with his publisher more–or–less the whole day (whom I noticed was extremely handsome and interesting, the strong but sensitive type). When they'd finished he asked me, out of politeness, what I did. I told him I'd just finished a children's tape, and was looking for a deal on it. "We might be interested in that," he said. "Could I have a copy?" I liked these deals that took place in the comfort of my own sitting-room. And he had a nice voice too.

I left a message on Nicky's answer-phone: "NICKY GET IN TOUCH I HAVE A DEAL." I wanted to tell my Mum about it too. She didn't like my music much, disapproving of the amount of technology it required; but the children's tape was different, because it was hand-made and unplugged with no effects, all played on acoustic instruments. But no-one answered the door-bell, so I let myself in and went upstairs to her sitting room where she was sitting on her white leather swivel-chair, in front of the TV. Rigoletto was weeping at the top of his voice over the dead body of his buxom daughter. Mum had strategically placed her two radio speakers on either side of her, because she had discovered that Radio Three sometimes broadcast the same opera simultaneously with the TV. Everything was turned up full volume—it was like a hurricane in there. "You ought to strap yourself in that chair and wear goggles and a leather flying-hat if you're going to do that, Mum." "What's that dear?" she shouted. Sometimes, apparently, one made exceptions for technology.

"Mummy, help! It's the big bad wolf!" "Where?" "In my bed, and he's all snarling and toothy." Scarlet flew up the stairs, hurtled into bed between us, and then proceeded to wriggle around for the rest of night. "Mummy, I've got an ear-ache now . . ." This wasn't the first time, and I reminded myself that these were the normal bad dreams that children have. "Daddy, are you awake?" "No." Maybe she needed a good homeopathic doctor. The problem was that all the ones I knew in London worked with my Mum. There was nothing wrong with them as such, but it was a challenge to be honest and open with them when they'd known you most of your life.

Two weeks later, she was perched on the edge of a chair in Dr Martin's office, her feet hanging in mid-air, her little fingers twisting nervously around one another. "If I settle down, she will," I thought. She checked him out one more time, but I already knew he could be trusted and would be fine for her; full of empathy, he listened with total attention as she answered his questions. "Are you scared of thunder?"

"Oh yes."

"Do you like the hot weather or when it's cold better?"

"When it's cold," she replied.

"Why?" he asked.

"Because it's fresher." She settled into it and started to enjoy herself, and from then on every time she got a splinter or grazed a knee she'd say, "Perhaps we ought to take this to Doctor Martin." (Oh, and his remedies worked.)

After her visit to the doctor, I decided to take a chance, based on my own experience that when confronted by reality I could usually handle it, but if left to my imagination things sometimes got distorted way out of proportion. So we went to the zoo, to see the wolf. As luck would have it, he was running along the fence playing with a dog on the other side; they leapt and ran together, rolling over, and dancing madly. "Isn't he beautiful, Mummy?" The magnificent, dignified wolf and the crazy Jack Russell made us laugh. Then, when the show was over, we found our way to the bird-house, and Josephine the hornbill was still there. "Scarlet, this is Josephine. She's exactly the same age as Uncle Jake, forty-three. She's been here, all this time . . . ever since I was little. Come on, I wonder if the Mina bird is still here too . . ." Well it was, but it didn't say "fuck off" this time, because it had been busy working on its vocabulary, and when Scarlet said "Hello," it proclaimed in a broad Dublin accent, "Feck, Arse, Girls!" What a success the Zoo was . . . And Scarlet never had another bad dream about wolves.

Very late one rainy night, there was a shy knock at the door. When I opened it the hall light fell across the dishevelled figure of Phoebe. She was one of Romany's daughters, together with her twin sister Misty and Ariel, the eldest. The rain poured down, mingling with her tears, her bag in her hand and her fiddle slung across her back. "What's the matter? Come in." She plonked herself down at the kitchen table and wiped her face with her hands, smearing her makeup. I'd known Phoebe her whole life. Phoebe was vivacious, beautiful and vulnerable to disastrous and dramatic affairs. She'd been in my band since she was fourteen, and the band had been very accommodating to a variety of doomed musical boyfriends. She was studying for a music degree. "Alcohol or coffee, darling?"

"Alcohol, please. Got any whiskey?"

"Yes of course. Irish OK? Erm, you might want to wash your face. What's going on?"

She looked in the mirror and laughed, only to immediately start crying again. "I'm pregnant, and I'm going to have to have a termination . . . Sunny, what do you think about abortion?"

Despite her firm decision, she was asking for my opinion. I knew that this particular person would listen most politely, really thrash things out with you, and then pay absolutely no attention at all to what you had decided together was the best way to proceed. So I was wary about handing out advice. "Phoebe, I think the decision to have an abortion is as important as the decision to have a baby. I had Minu when I was seventeen, I've never regretted it, and Phoebe, you would be just as good a mother as anybody else."

"Oh, do you think so?"

"Yes of course I do, why not?"

"But what about my music degree?"

"You can do both."

"And it was only a one-night stand, with a Cuban guy... Look, I'm booked in for the morning, will you drive me to the clinic tomorrow?"

"OK, I will." But I didn't want to. I really didn't want to have anything to do with it.

"Where've you been Mum?"

"Out with Phoebe, why?"

"Phoebe was here? I wish she'd waited for me to get back before going. Did you tell her about my results?"

"Yes Minu, the whole world knows by now."

"Mum, remember when we used to live in the house up on the Forest?"

"Yes, 'Mellow Cottage.' What about it?"

"Oh nothing, it's just that I've known Phoebe, Misty and Ariel such a long time. Remember when we all used to sit in Titch Woolvine's tractor as he worked on the golf course? Titch was in love with you wasn't he?"

"I don't know, was he?"

"Yes, him and Luke. There were loads of people always coming and going for painting or music lessons, I must have started painting then alongside them, and we always seemed to be cooking massive meals for every one. Every day we all went to the Forest for a walk. I can remember climbing up the big beech tree with you and the girls, and once Ariel wanted some water lilies and Luke went right into the pond to pick some for her. It was always sunny, and Mum, I had two daddies!"

"Yes, that was when we came back from Switzerland...."

6

The weather was gorgeous. The British sun rose majestic in endless blue skies, day after day; it was the beginning of the drought of 1976. Minu was three years old then, and we had settled in at my Mum's for the summer. My oldest brother Jake had also moved in, making it a full house. Relationships with my mother had not improved over the years, and not altogether pleased with the invasion, she was bossy, forever trying to dictate the course she felt our lives should take; and as usual, we resisted. Luke, Liza and Rohan were still living next door, but their brother Emil had moved to Rhodesia. Rayette was just down the road with a brand new bloke in a brand new place of their own, and we were all expecting her brand new first baby. We went to the sea as often as possible. Rayette floating around like the Ark Royal, while the rest of us stretched out on the beach drowsy and half asleep, only very occasionally stirring ourselves for a swim. Minu plashed around in the rock pools, sometimes lying inside them, quietly observing the miniature water-worlds for hours. His long hair glistened bright gold, bleached from the sun and salt water. We walked in the cool of the forest, hauling him up into the arms of the great wilting beech tree; he looked like a dusky wild boy. Some evenings we'd go down to the Green Man to play pool and hang out, and on Saturday nights we hijacked the music session. Earlier we'd been staying with Seraphina; it would have been easy to get together with Ralph again, but it didn't feel right. Anyway, I was off the whole idea of relationships and had been without a lover for over a year, celibate for the first time since I was twelve. The days grew longer and hotter as the summer drew towards the solstice, the Midsummer Festival, and the Midsummer Fire.

Luke, Liza, and I walked over the forest through the twilight. During the last four years I had been surrounded by majestic mountains and living by the shores of a wide sparkling lake, but this close green forest was my lovely landscape, small, cosy, and part of me. We made our way through the school grounds, and waited in darkness. The whole Community was gathered, hushed; far in the distance the burning torches flared and flamed, tiny flickering pin-pricks approaching in their criss-cross patterns. For a Christian community it was a rather pagan ritual, the torches interweaving and spreading out in the complicated and intricate forms of the ancient and silent line dance. I counted twenty-four of them—a lot for Class 12. As they solemnly and silently drew near, I warmed to the familiar smell of smoke and paraffin. Upright like the flames they carried, the young women and men circled slowly around the waiting unlit fire, and when the circle was completed they ceremoniously plunged their torches into the old dry wood together. They did not know that when they went out into the world they would find themselves alone.

I watched until the fire died down a bit, and then felt a friendly hand on my shoulder. "Sunny?" I turned around to find an old friend whom I'd completely forgotten looking at me. "Oh, hi Miles." I got a warm, full-on hug, definitely more than just friendly. "I thought you were living in Switzerland. Are you on holiday?" "No no, between jobs, my divorce came through and I have a little chap to support". When I was a child Miles had always been easy and interesting to talk to, and he had the knack of making me see things from a different and wider angle. He was still in the film business and living with his brother Crispen, who used to teach me. "Do you want a lift home?" I looked around for Liza and Luke hoping I think for an excuse not to make a decision, but they had disappeared. "Yes, that would be nice." Only we didn't drive home but up to the Ridge Road and turned off, and made love under the stars in the heat of the summer night. I was nervous about it at first for a very good reason, but overcome by the chemistry I got into it; all the time in the back of my mind, though, I was acutely aware that at any moment a car load of teenagers could sneak up silently, toot the hooter and flick on the full beams.

"I thought you were never going to have another relationship," Luke said, glowering indignantly at me. "Well I've got to do something to amuse myself till you've grown up, got rich and are worth marrying, haven't I? Anyway, it's only up the road, you can come anytime you want to." And he did.

We moved in with Miles and Crispen. "Mellow Cottage" was a lovely place, practically in the forest. I was pleased to have a home of my own, a new experience; all my life, I'd lived in a communal situation. I got into cooking in a big way—the way to a man's heart is through his stomach and all that—and it was stable and almost normal, a proper grownup situation, for a while at least: gardening, watching telly in the evenings and sometimes going out to dinner. "Hello, can I make a reservation please? For three." "What name please, madam?" "Plantaganet. Thank you, goodbye". I learned to deal with waiters in restaurants. "Can I have that lobster, please? No, that one. Actually what the hell, I'll have them both, thanks."

I found my way around London, and sometimes met Miles after his work. I learned to talk to "normal" people from the outside world, like the BBC people who Miles worked with, and his friends. At twice my age, Miles had savoir-faire; gently, and with humour, he showed me the ways of the world. I took on board what I wanted to. He was on his own particular personal search, and seemed able to have a spiritual life—one that expanded outwards rather than constantly narrowing down and closing off; because he was also firmly rooted in the real world. At that time he was making a series on the different religions of the world. I liked the way he worked with people: he included each member of the crew, asking for their advice and opinions, keeping everybody involved with the whole process of film making all the way through. Along the way he introduced me to Taoism, which I felt a strong affinity with.

Ever since Crispen appeared as an angel in the Christmas play, I had maintained that image of him, but he had become a rather crumpled sort of angel: miserable, extremely complicated, and still smarting from his recent divorce from Romany. His oldest daughter Ariel and the twins Phoebe and Misty used to come up to stay on weekends. Romany and I had become best friends—friends for life, as it turned out. I taught painting and music, and had loads of work, even a waiting list. In the mornings I worked in the crèche at William Morris College, so Minu could be with me, but the highlight of his day was driving around on the Golf Course in Titch Woolvine's Tractor. Old Mr Woolvine was semi–retired by then, and seemed philosophical about his wife's desertion for Cuba, so she could be closer to Che. "Better off without her, she was always here but not here, know what I mean?" I taught Crispen guitar, and he was gifted at it; we played a lot together. Deeply into Jungian analysis, he was head over heels in love with his analyst, a steely-grey woman with a bun on the back of her head, which I thought was hilarious. Crispen swore up and down that it was Platonic—"No such thing, you bloody twit." Miles supported me reasonably, but I was glad to be able to pay my way, and increasingly uncomfortable with the idea of being dependent on others for anything. As the summer drew on Minu and I made elderflower juice, blackberry jam and stinging-nettle soup. The local harvest that year went from abundant to out-of-control. There were parties, and holidays rambling about in Cornwall. I was twenty-one, and I had two lovers.

Once I dreamed that Liza and I were running around London, in search of red cabbage. And why red cabbage, you may ask? Well in my dream, everybody was transparent, and the fashion was to eat as many colourful foods as possible, thereby creating interesting intestines. We eventually found our red cabbage in that vegetable shop at the corner of Ladbroke Road and Pembridge Road; then we both had rainbows inside us. Far out, man.

I drove up the lane to William Morris College, passing an endless stream of women, all of us on our way to the same meeting. Every year the women of the Community met. Our women's movement was called Ariadne. That year Romany and I counted 247 women in total—more then ever before, I can remember us smiling at each other across the entrance of College's main door. This was going to be good . . .
When we had all settled down the women who led the various groups, which took place once a week in their own homes, stood up and one by one introduced themselves. "Hi, I'm Bernadette, and my group will be looking at the role of women in making the personal political." "Hello, my name is Daisy, and my group will be studying Esther Harding's *The Way of all Women.*" "Ya, I am Uta. My group vill be looking at single parenting, making festivals, ze four seasons, and story telling. Ve are a practical creative group, especially interesting for young mothers." "Hi, I'm Jude, I come from Texas and I'm ovulating. My group is an open book, we discuss anything from power struggles in the home and divorce laws to how best to nurture the feminine in men without emasculating them." "Good evening. My name is Maddy, and I lead the all female Woodbrook Morris dancing team . . . Sunny, could I have a word with you after about some music?" I immediately became prickly, annoyed by Maddy's presumption in front of everyone

on the platform. They were all mad that lot any way, and extremely embarrassing in their Doc Martin boots, sleeveless T shirts, hairy armpits and revealing flowered miniskirts—I wasn't going to play for them. Being a flibberty-gibbet, I didn't fix myself in any group but enjoyed spending time with each of them: the man-haters, the perfect mothers, the intellectuals, the artistic ones and the radical feminists. (Watch your mouth, anything you say will be taken down as evidence against you.)

Serafina dropped by from time to time, bringing me news of the latest predictions of disasters for the end of the millennium, and memories of Ralph. She always thought that we would end up together, but despite the debt I owed him from the personal rescue service he operated on my behalf, it was not to be. After Ralph went to live in Cape Town, apart from the occasional letter and a couple of nights together—including one really memorable one in Claridges, which I was thrown out of— we didn't see much of each other. And then it was too late, because he died.

Serafina and I sat drinking our Perrier and Ribena. She seemed distracted. "Listen Sunny, this is serious. Did you ever talk to anybody about what happened with you and Minu's father?"

"No Serafina, I don't need to. It's finished, all over with now" (back off).

"Well, I think you ought to. I'm a lot older than you, and things have a habit of coming back to haunt you, only worse. It's just better to talk about things, and sort them out."

"Oh my god, look at the time, I've got to go, see you around!" I fled.

Some of the older kids at school once sent me off to nick a large adjustable spanner for something they were up to with the fire alarm system. On my way out from the maintenance room with the spanner, I walked slap-bang into Ralph, a "big boy". He knew I was up to something right away—psychic about my doings. He quietly removed the spanner and put it back where it belonged, to protect me from more trouble. That's what he was like with me: responsible and protective; faultless. Which sometimes got on my nerves.

Seeing Serafina reminded me that there was something I needed to do for Ralph. I bought a shiny adjustable spanner, three red roses, and a small tube of chocolate sauce, then tied them together with a red velvet ribbon, making a sort of bouquet that looked like an entry for the Turner prize. Then Liza, little Luke, Minu and I made our way across the water meadows, passing the charred remains of the midsummer fire, and on through the woods. Luke and Minu ran on ahead towards the lake where as a child I had looked for the Lady of the Lake, and where we all used to swim as teenagers in the steamy sultry summers. I threw my offering way out into the middle. It was received with a splash, the ripples circling out and out, over and over the still water and the surrounding quiet. In memory of Ralph, whom I didn't treat quite properly. I loved him all right, but didn't want a life with him: chocolate sauce on my body, but a spanner in the works of my heart.

Minu and I walked down the road to visit Rayette and the brand new baby. We went through the back gate and into the garden where Rayette was digging a large hole in the ground. "Hiya. What you doing?"

"What do you mean what am I doing, are you crazy or something? I'm burying these nappies, and if I never see another fucking nappy again it'll be too soon. We are moving into the twenty-first century soon and I am too, with disposable nappies. I've had enough of this Plymouth Brethren lifestyle." She was dead cross, but laughing as well.

"Take it easy, I don't blame you," I replied. "Can I have a coffee and a go with the baby? What are you going to call her, by the way? (Minu, get out of that hole, will you?)"

"Something normal, like Wendy or Tracy. Names are important, look at me named after my grandfather Ray. Will you be godmother? I've asked Liza as well. Hey, guess what? You know that new American homeopath that's around? Well his kids are called Arnica and Ignatia. I tell you, the Steiner people get weirder every day." She handed me the baby, who felt soft and smelt sweetly of milk. I took a long look at her, and decided—"OK, I'll be godmother if you call her Iscadora." Rayette grinned. "She could have a posh, triple-barrelled name, like 'Lavender Bath Milk'."

"How's your brother Max doing in Canada?" I wondered.

"Oh fine, and Max is called after my grandmother Maxim. Anyway he's fixing Canadian cars now instead of Sussex ones. Erm, Sunny, are you . . . well, are you . . . you know, with Miles and Crispen?"

Rayette was not the only one wondering about that. And I didn't say a thing about it, enigma is far more sensational then reality, and besides I liked to tease the nosey parkers.

"Look, do you get the Health Centre bugging you about getting Minu vaccinated?"

"Yeah I do, they sound like the voice of doom—'woe and death to all those who don't vaccinate! I tell them I haven't had any and I'm still alive. I mean it's a free decision in this country, and they harass you. They're persistent about it because they get money for every vaccination, you know, and I've worked with kids who are vaccine-damaged. You have to be firm with them, Rayette. Some people say that their baby has developed loads of allergies, so it wouldn't be a good idea at this point."

"I think I'll do that, then. I don't want her pumped up with all that stuff, and it fucks up the immune system, doesn't it?"

"Yes, and although they deny it, it can definitely cause brain damage. The consequences of some of these vaccines are scarier then the illnesses they are supposed to protect you against . . ."

Romany and I sat painting together in the kitchen. She looked like a robin, with fine bone-china features. Her cheeks were red, almost scarlet, and her eyes, dark and alive with intelligence, were almost oriental in shape; which gave the wrong impression, because she was a true aristocrat and a direct descendent of Anne Bolyn. The only real hints of her aristocratic roots, though, were the incredible amount of stuff lying around all over her house (subconsciously waiting for a long-dead nanny to tidy up) and her total disdain of the middle classes and anything conventional. All traits familiar to me from my own dear Mama.

As we painted, we talked about the end of the century, reincarnation, flagellation, education, emancipation, intuition, superstition, dissolution, revolution, and what a bunch of fuckers men were. If you had a sensitive one who was in touch with his feelings, the chances were he didn't go out to work. If you had one of the old models, the chances were he'd be chauvinistic, insensitive and try to dictate your life to you BUT he usually had a high income. What a dilemma! I was glad not to be a man, poor things. They didn't know it, but they were about to find themselves on a steep learning curve. We cheered ourselves up with the thought that in our next incarnations we would be men and they would be women—according to Rudolf Steiner, anyway—so we could get them all back. It was a long time to wait but we could do it, so watch out.

While we had been sorting out the world, Misty and Phoebe the five-year-old twins had undressed the three-year-old Minu, and covered him from head to toe with mud; he looked like a tiny cheerful Golem. In retrospect, I think being covered in mud by twin girls affected the whole of his sexual development. Romany and I had to abandon our spiritual research. "Right, get in the bath all of you." We made shampoo horns on the side of their heads, and then they all started crying when we had to rinse the shampoo out. "Hello it's the social services. What's going on here?" Luke called up the stairs. "Luke, save us!" they wailed. "Tell you what, I'll go light the fire, and put the kettle on if you all shut up." The little beggars brightened up (which was not necessarily a good thing).

In general, apart from un-blocking the drain in the bath afterwards, I didn't have to much house-work to do because Miles and Crispen, who were in a silent power-struggle a lot of the time, dusted and hoovered, mowed lawns and cleaned cars, and kept the whole place spick and span. They could fight over a dustpan and brush. Once Crispen (his brotherly rivalry getting the better of him) asked me who was the better lover, him or Miles. "You are of course my darling . . . No, just kidding, really you're both useless . . . Well, I don't know maybe Miles is, just a bit." He was genuinely offended, for Christ's sakes.

Deep in the heart of the Forest lies a quiet, still pond. At one end stands a dark yew; oak, chestnut and beech trees enclose it all round. The whole place lies in a hollow, and its peacefulness works on us. Luke in his waders stands in the middle surrounded by a cloud of water-lilies and attendant dragonflies. He stands perfectly still, like a blue heron, before gently bending down to pick the five lilies he has come for, a present for his friend. This is a lasting image . . .

7

I had replaced my Sussex forest with the urban jungle, and Scarlet and I would go out hunting and gathering. We'd buy ourselves a steaming salt-cod fritter each, and then carry on past the fresh vegetables, the sweet potatoes and sugar cane, the reggae bass booming out and a local tribesman calling, "Spare change mon, spare change?" Past Arran jumpers, velvet leggings, saris, the head shop and the excellent hat-stall ("Red Hat No Knickers"), I threaded my way down Portobello Road, followed by a small savage, in search of the best deal in fir to make our Advent wreath. Having bought what we needed, we'd proceeded to the cafe which sold my paintings. I had some money to pick up there: good.

In the cafe, we ordered a hot Ribena and a cappuccino. And then we'd sat looking through the window, as a tall African lady passed by. She was dressed in a British Rail uniform and carried a long bamboo pole like a spear under her arm. Scarlet turned pale at the sight of her and whispered, "Mummy, is that Mrs Thatcher?" "Yes, it is," I whispered back.

We knew by then that Alex had at the most only another year to live, and although the reality of his worsening condition could be heard clearly on the phone, I was unable to get my head around it and secretly hoped for a miracle.

"Hiya, love of my lives, how are you doing?"

"Well, I get tired easily, and sometimes short of breath, but basically all right."

I was taken aback by the frailty in his voice, and waited for him to catch his breath. "You know, my father hasn't been a lot of use to me, and I'm glad I've got you."

"I'm glad you do too. How's Minu enjoying art school?"

"Oh he's loving it. Doing very well."

"And what are you doing with yourself at the moment?"

"Well, painting like crazy as well, because ages and ages ago I got invited to do a show in a gallery, and now that the children's tape is just about finished I thought I'd better get on with it."

"Oh I'd like to see them. Will there be a catalogue?"

"I expect so, I'll send you one. Here, Finn's waiting to speak to you."

"Hi Dad. I'm in a minority here, Scarlet's a furious painter as well . . ."

8

Dear Mum,

I've been moved into the OPEN prison. And I have a most wonderful art teacher here. I have a room with a view, and it's really nice to have a lock on the inside of my door for a change. I can walk out of here any time I want. Some of the people here are in for non-payment of TV licences, or poll-tax dodgers. Lots are dodgy solicitors. I'm learning a lot. In the mornings I work in the market garden here, there is also a prize-winning herd of cows on the farm, but I'm going to work with the horses! We have thirty-two Clydesdales. You can't ride them, of course, but we took them out along the beach for exercise, it was magic. I can also sketch and draw outside again, and continue my lucrative business of drawing portraits of the inmates' wives and girlfriends from photos, which is a cinch. Will you tell your girlfriends to send me some lighter reading, please? I'd like *The Mists of Avalon*. So far I've read Primo Levi, Caspar Hauser, Brian Keenan and Victor Frankl's *Man's Search for Meaning*, and I get the picture —one can make something positive out of the darkest experiences, and

I am, in my own way. Sometimes I have been alone for long periods of time, locked in my cell on bang up and left to myself. I've often ended up thinking about bits and pieces of when I was growing up, sorting it through and finding a place for every memory and experience. Almost as if I will not be ready for release until I understand how I got here. All those authors could only write about their experiences, once they'd got some distance from them. I don't want to write a book, but perhaps something positive will come out of this for me as well. Look now I'm in open prison Scarlet can visit! I miss her so much, Mum. Thanks for everything. I get depressed sometimes, so many stupid little rules you have to remember, but basically I'll be OK now. I love you,

                Minu

The very next visiting day Finn and I took Scarlet to see Minu at his "job" in the country. She sat swathed around her brother in the bare room, no telling where one of them ended and the other started, two souls one heart, exchanging the latest jokes. "What do monsters play at parties?" "Swallow my leader! But why did the chewing gum cross the road?" "I don't know Minu, why?" "Because it was stuck to the chickens foot." "Minu, what do you call an exploding monkey?" "Don't know, what?" "A baboom!" "What do you call a fly with no legs?" "A walk! Ha, I know that one too . . ."

Finn and I sat back and watched for a while, but feeling like an intruder at a private party I went off for a smoke outside. Finn joined me and we left them to it. After we returned, I found ways to slip Minu extra funds. "Nothing to be given directly to the inmates" provided an interesting challenge. When our time was up and we had to go, Minu had manfully hid his tears and I too hid the sadness inside me. Enough was enough, and I decided I was going to chain and cement myself . . . but what was the use? And it was only drugs, for Christ's sake.

9

When Alex became ill, Finn had kept his mind off it all by filling up every little empty space in his day. He used to spend a lot more time relaxing with friends, a very social historian; in fact sometimes he didn't get any work done at all. But he became driven. I'd say, "Finn, lets go out for dinner tonight." Then he'd opened his Filofax, and I could see that his week, let alone day, was completely out of control. I wondered how to get him to slow down a bit. "Perhaps you could have your people call my people?"

"Look, I can't tonight, I'm going to the Zen centre for the evening meditation." (It was my karma to be lumbered with people who meditate).

"Finn, you ought to go and spend some time with Alex. It would be a help to both of you, and you could see your brothers at the same time. I reckon Alex's probably wondering why it's taking you so long to get out there..."

My exhibition opened in due course, and it ended up almost a sellout—eighteen out of the twenty-two paintings went on the first night! My friends and all of Minu's showed up, which was really nice of them. My Mum threw a fit because I had a short biography up on the wall with my date of birth (1956) on it.

She thought that everybody would immediately deduce her age from the information. "Oh look Mum, they've all got calculators and are working it out."

"Sunny, don't be so mean. What if my patients find out?" She did buy a painting, after Finn calmed her down in his firm but slightly short-tempered way. Next time I need an autobiography I shall write:

> Sunny McCabe was born in a small town just outside of Germany in 1930. HER MOTHER IS A HUNDRED AND EIGHTY-FIVE YEARS OLD. She was educated at Cheltenham Ladies College, where she was very happy, and at Oxford where she got a first in the philosophy of physics. She sold her first painting at age thirteen, entitled, 'Sunset over the Alps.' It looks like a fried egg and can still be viewed at the Inner Man Café, Woodbrook.

By the time the exhibition was over every single painting had been sold. And my autobiography had mysteriously disappeared! But there was also a sadness to it, because Alex had sometimes bought a piece, when he liked it. I missed sharing the opening night with him, and going through my work quietly with him beforehand, as we had so often in the past.

Once in a blue moon I used to accompany my mother to a lecture at the Novalis Centre, Steiner's London headquarters. This one was all about how important it was to control your lower nature. I bet I could have seduced the lecturer in about thirty seconds flat. On the way back Mum explained to me that there was no temptation in the spiritual world. "Hell's bells, Mum, one would like the choice."

I had nothing against Doctor Steiner himself, or any other spiritual path for that matter. If people are getting some kind of soul food, it doesn't matter too much which particular master they follow. Of course, the trouble is that everybody thinks that their chosen path is the best. But different strokes for different folks; luckily, there is as wide a variety of spiritual teachings as there are different people, and who you end up with is of course your own personal business and destiny, or karma. But there is one small (but large) additional point to make: this lot were so intent on developing and becoming, and so focused on the hereafter, that they forgot the here and now. They forgot to look at what was all around them, where all the action was.

Every single Steiner School pupil in the whole wide world reads *Parzival*. Sometimes as a child you can hear an extra set of foot-steps running with you through the forest. And just as Parzival stumbles his way towards right thinking, you learn with him beside you to ask the right questions. "What ails thee, uncle?"

But then, wide awake and armed with new powers of perception, you feel let down when the same person who tells you to "Always look for the meaning of what lies behind things" has yet to take his own fool's cap off, or when they blame you for your behaviour and do not think themselves to ask or question "Why? What ails thee?"

When you are sixteen everyone becomes so naturally attracted to each other. You lie with your clumsy lover upon a wonder bed and hear an extra heartbeat parallel to yours and Gawain goes through his adventures of joy and pain beside you, in search of a soul mate, an ideal love straight and true. But some in time are greatly disappointed, because they never do. You are being asked to look for the Grail with your head and with your thinking, but also with love and with your feelings to warm the whole thing through.

10

I opened the front door and a Sherman Tank rolled in with its gun pointing at me; then it mowed me down and reversed backwards, before slowly advancing on my art. "Why would you paint a trout?"

"It doesn't matter what you paint, so long as you catch its spirit," I defended myself feebly. "And anyway I'm thinking about becoming a chain saw artist."

"That isn't Art, dear." The gun lowered its sights: "I understand that it's better to steam vegetables."

"I am steaming them, look in the pot. YOU never steamed them when we were kids."

The tank then fired its big gun at me: "I've been reading John Scotis Erigena and Thomas Aquinas. I believe that Parzival and Erigena are deeply connected."

"Whatever . . ." She refuelled on black coffee (no sugar), and released another barrage of criticism. "You've been travelling too much, it isn't good for little children to be in aeroplanes. They lose contact with the earth's etheric, which weakens them."

"Good, my children are far too strong, a little weakening would help me enormously."

She lit a cigarette, and went off on a spiritual reconnaissance mission. "It's obvious that Charlemagne was the wounded king. He wanted to crown himself and not let the Pope do it, but the Pope did crown him in the end, thereby wounding him spiritually forever . . ." I had learned to listen to this kind of thing but not comment unless specifically asked, my opinions being deeply flawed on account of not committing myself to the teachings of Christ or Steiner. Then the tank rolled out, leaving me completely flattened. The smoke lingered.

Once I'd asked my Mum if could borrow fifty quid for the weekend? Without a moments pause, she'd replied.
"Don't be stupid darling, I just lent your brother twenty-seven thousand pounds yesterday."

Scarlet, however, was not fazed by my Mum in the least. One day, they sat having tea together. "Would you like another biscuit, dear?"
"No."
"No what?"
"No way!"

And another time: "My Mummy made my bed."
"You should make your own bed, dear."
"No, I mean she MADE my bed, out of six-ply. It has sides that curve like a moon, and the head and bottom are rounded. She cut stars and moons and planets into it and when I lie down, the light shines through, and I'm in heaven. And I varnished it myself."
"Is it safe for you to have varnish?"

11

Finn finally plucked up the courage to go to Montreal and see Alex. I wanted to go as well, but Finn needed to be alone with his old man this time; too bad, never mind. The day he left the rain just drizzled down, it crept into your clothes, into your house and into your psyche. I made a hot water bottle, one large mug of tea, wrapped myself up in a huge blanket and got totally immersed in *The Bhagavad Gita*, concentrating as best as I could.

"There is a wisdom which knows when to go and when to return, what is to be done and what is not to be done, what is fear and what is courage, what is bondage and what is liberation—that is pure wisdom . . .Krishna, the visible forms of my nature are eight: earth, water, fire, air, ether, the mind, reason, and the sense of 'I'." It was this sense of 'I' that interested me; the other forms were easy enough to understand, but the sense of 'I', I was sure, meant to be able to see the 'I' in others, not only your own. That was just ego. My education was based on the idea of individual development, but they didn't actually see me. That's where they let us down so badly—we were compromised on all levels for the ideal.

Finn returned home from Canada. "How was Alex?"
"Not so bad, you know. He's doing ok . . ."
I kept on waiting for more, but it never came.

"Every morning, Chiron rows us across the Styx from the land of the living into the realm of the dead . . ." But we had Classic FM and Henry Kelly, with his crash-bang-wallop classics to get us through the school run. Mothers shot by in their Volvo's and yuppie tanks with children pinned back in their seats, their faces distorted by the G forces, to the Thunder and Lightening Polka.

One morning, with our seat-belts firmly secured, Scarlet, Katie and I drove off to pick up Harry from the bosom of his warm, friendly family. He jumped into the car, saying, "Budge up, you fat lesbian." "Excuse me," replied Katie with great dignity, "I am not a lesbian, I'm a Leo."

Astrologers call it "time twins", when you share birthdays like Finn and I. But I was worried about making it to our next one, because I had had an endless night, restlessly lying between sleep and wakefulness, worrying about Alex and worrying about Finn. But then Scarlet had arrived with a grapefruit cut around the wrong way, and a morning cup of tea worthy of the best transport café. "Thank you so much my darling, it's just what I need."

"Hey kid, don't I get one?"

"No daddy you don't, because you have been very, very naughty."

"Goddamnit, I've been asleep!"

For the occasion of our birthdays, we hired a beautiful room above a pub. It was right by the bridge and overlooked the twinkling Thames. The whole of Hammersmith was grid-locked because they'd suddenly closed the bloody bridge, but everyone got there anyway, eventually: Saskia, Pearl and Dean, Marlene, Romany and Crispen (now friends again after years of strife), and the girls, Ariel (who had become an actress), Phoebe the musician, and Misty (actively avoiding taking charge of her life). "The last party we all went to was at your house, Romany."

"Yes, and between us we'd slept with every single man there."

"Well, it was good to see all our old lovers getting on so nicely."

"Really Mum," said Minu, drifting by with Sorrel like a pair of lovers from a Chagall painting. Then the rest of Minu's tribe had arrived (painted, pierced and polite). Old friends and new friends, neighbours, and people from far and wide, Caspar and his lot, and all the children—alright! Some people made an enormous effort to get there; Gabriel even flew down from Scotland . . . *Gabriel creeps to our room for whispered conversations, with an interesting unspoken new flavour . . .* " Can I have quick word in your ear, Sunny?"

"No way." Some things don't change. And the Fabulous Flying doctor of Ireland came over with all his family. "Go on with you, we wouldn't miss it for all the world!" (I loved his voice.)

Some of those guests used to fight each other in kindergarten but now, they were propped up against the bar, flirting, laughing and drinking together. The ceilidh band began to play, and the caller's voice rang out: "The lady round the lady, and the gent around the gent . . . two Buffalo Girls go round the outside, round the outside . . . ." Finn went round the outside with Charley, who must have been cooking for a week—she had prepared us a feast that Babette would have died for. Then a musician friend arrived. "Sorry I'm late, the fuzz have closed the Bridge and London's noble bomb disposal unit are this very minute disarming a massive bomb underneath it. Did you bring your fiddle?"

"Yup, did you bring the stilts?" We put them on in secret outside, then waltzed in to play a few swamp-cajun tunes. There were jugglers, and an attempt at fire eating ("Didn't burn your mouth did you?"). By now ninety people were there! "Thank you all for coming. I'd rather be here with you than with the finest people in the world . . . Oh no, no presents thanks. Cash only." Leo, stripped down to his trousers to show off his perfect black body, flew by with Saskia, who raised her eyes heavenwards, pretending to faint into his arms. (They danced again later on, too, one couldn't help but notice.)

Afterwards we had a full house, babies sleeping in odd places, children whispering to each other in their sleeping bags on Scarlet's floor, men laughing over another last whiskey, and women chitchatting, conspiratorial, and relaxed. The house lights finally dimmed, all quiet on the western front . . .

In the early hours of the morning Minu arrived home, rolling drunk and knocking at the door. "It'sh a foin fing," he said, glaring at his keys, "It'sh a foin, foin fing, when your own movver changes za locksh while her shon is out drinking . . ."

12

Charley and Shane, lived with her elderly parents in an imitation Black-Forest woodcutters' cottage. The pupils had built it on our school grounds for old Herr Wissenshaften under his guidance, when he was in a fit of elderly nostalgia for the fatherland. We would visit them often. Schloss Wissenshaften had porthole windows with red and white chequered curtains, and many little crooked leaded windows, framed by red geraniums in wooden window boxes with heart motifs lavishly carved into them. Scarlet and Shane would clatter about the place, the wooden floors, *gemutlich* pine-panelled walls and creaking stairs with pretzel-style bannisters, reacting like a drum to their footsteps. "There was an old women who lived in a shoe," Scarlet mumbled in her sleep beside me, as I lay listening to the chorus of snoring and whistling from the old folks, which resounded up through the floor-boards. The house was noisily sleeping and dark, the smell of the damp Sussex night outside silent and familiar.

It was four in the morning, and I got up to make myself a cup of tea. When I opened the fridge door, the green glow of kryptonite illuminated the kitchen eerily. It was a pistachio mousse. And I helped myself to a large slice. "I could hear you opening the frigging fridge door, right up in the attic," Charley said a minute later, lighting up emphatically.

"Honestly, I'm eating this in memory of Herr Wissenshaften, who left this world a better place."

"Well this place isn't it."

The next morning, I went to pick vegetables for Charley in the school gardens, and met up with one of the men who'd ruined my life, my old French teacher (quelle horreur). "You haven't changed a bit," he said. (Va te faire foutre.)

"I'm worse, actually."

"Perhaps, but let's not discuss your behaviour, look at this beautiful garden." (Comme, c'est Bonnard.) "You know, for a while every child had a little patch here, but of course they were all away on holiday during harvest time, and their plots ended up looking like graveyards."

I laughed. "Anyway, for some reason or another, most children hate gardening."

"You're right, you know . . . Have you got a proper cigarette? I've switched to these extra mild ones, which means I smoke twice as many."

We lit up, and continued our discussion on the glories of gardening. (Époustouflant!)

13

Dear Mum

Great news! I get one week's home leave. You have to pick me up at eight in the morning, at the doors . . . I can't believe I'm going to be allowed home and keep thinking something's going to spoil it or stop it from happening.

At the moment there is much to do in the market garden and I have to work there in the mornings, I'm not that keen on gardening but there's plenty of vegetables to eat. I can only work with the horses in the afternoons. One of them got stuck in the river. Clydesdales are so heavy we had to pull her out with the tractor or she would have drowned. It's awful when such a huge and majestic animal is so pathetic and helpless. I passed my tractor driving-test, just what I always wanted, and an absolute must for West London life.

There is a move here for the prisoners to have some kind of meaningful contact with the outside world sometimes. So those who take art classes, are doing a mural for the local hospital—a lucky break, and we are all enjoying it a lot, it gives me some experience on designing a very large piece of work. It's based on a sea theme. I do go swimming in the sea sometimes, when we take the horses along the beech to exercise them, but some of the artists can not swim and have never been in the ocean, or looked through a mask and snorkel. At the hospital there's an enormous and steamy laundry room. The nurses are very very nice to us. I've discovered a way of ordering take-away pizza and I get counselling here too. My first session was interesting, real Freudian stuff. She opened it by saying "Well, have you been beaten up by anybody lately?"

I'm so looking forward to my week's home leave I can hardly wait.

Your ever loving son,
Minu xxxxx ooooo

Good, he had a week's leave coming up, he was eating pizza, he was getting analysis, and maybe he was shagging nurses in the laundry-room.

"MINU'S COMING HOME FOR A VISIT, I shouted at the top of my voice. I put Kathryn Tickell on full blast and did a "Minu's Coming Home for a Visit" jig. Yes, we all knew he would be spending most of his time with his friends, but that was normality.

14

Once upon a time, a king had many daughters, and one day the youngest princess was playing with her golden ball in the castle garden. How beautifully it shone, as she threw it higher and higher into the sunlight. She drew near to the woods and when she threw her ball again, she could not catch it, for it rolled away and fell into a deep well. Down, down, down it went and her heart sank with it, as she watched it disappear into the murky darkness. The princess sat down at the edge of the well and she cried and cried, until she heard a funny little voice saying, "What will you give me if I fetch your ball for you?"

"What about my necklace?"

"I am a frog, and have little use for necklaces and trinkets. But if you promise to let me sit beside you at dinner, and eat from your golden plate, and drink from your little cup, and then let me sleep in your little bed, I will fetch your ball for you." So the Princess eagerly promised . . . but she soon forgot about it. And the next day when the whole Palace were gathered for the evening meal, there came a knocking at the door. The princess was struck with horror, but the king made his youngest daughter let the frog in. "If you make a promise, you must keep it."

"Princess, lift me up so that I can eat from your golden plate." The frog ate heartily, but the Princess could hardly eat a thing. "Now Princess, carry me up to your little bed, in your little room." And she picked him up, and held him by one leg, in her two unwilling fingers. "Lift me up so that I may sleep in your little bed." At this the little Princess, who was petrified of the frog, picked him up and threw him against the wall. And when she looked again, he had turned into a king, for she had broken the spell.

Then they fell in love and went to sleep. The next day the young king asked the princess to marry him and come away with him to his castle. Soon a beautiful carriage came driving up to take them away, and behind stood faithful Henry, the young king's servant . . . Now Faithful Henry had been so unhappy when the witch had turned his master into a frog, that he had caused three iron bands to be put around his heart. As they drove away the King heard a cracking behind him, and he thought the carriage was breaking . . . No Master, it is not the carriage. It is a band from my heart, which was put there in my great pain when you were bewitched." Again and once again, the king heard something cracking; but it was only the bands springing from faithful Henry's heart, because his master was free and happy.

Scarlet put her arms around my neck and gently whispered in an Italian accent, "My mama, my lovely mama. Not Minu's mama, no no no, *my* mama."

Finn never did say too much about his visit to Canada, but ever since he'd come back there was a solitary, thoughtful quality about him, and the weeks went by until one day he sat at his PC, shaking his head and said, "Sunny, I'm finding it so hard to work here, I need to look for an office out of the home." He had taken on more and more work, which kept him up late into the night, and sometimes till the small hours of the morning.

"Oh Finn, you're finding it hard to work because of your father being so ill. It will be alright, wait a bit before you decide to move office."

"You think so? Perhaps you're right, I don't know." And then he'd got ready to go; it was one of his days pretending to be a man about town.

"Are you having lunch with Emmanuel Béart today, or Michelle Pfeiffer?"

"Neither. I'm going to Sotheby's to see some drawings that Blake drew of people from visions. John Varley did their horoscopes . . ."

"No wonder you don't get anything done, Finn."

"It's for the book!" Finn took advantage of everything London life had to offer, because he had been born and raised in Quagmire, a small town in Manitoba, Canada, founded basically because the Pilgrim Mothers had said, "Stuff this for a lark, we're not walking another inch. We're settling right here."

When I went to sleep that night, Minu had Sorrel and their friend Fishy staying over; they had spent the day in search of a flat to rent. I ignored the smell of dope, and Finn crept into bed sometime around three A.M.

The thorn trees looked like something Mervyn Peake had drawn, only these were real. They grew twisted, dense and dark grey-green. Ash covered the ground, embers flickered dully, and wisps of smoke curled up through blackened branches towards a twilight sky. My hands had been glued and then clamped together with green G-clamps. I was being pursued by a 'man' in armour, only it was more sci-fi than medieval; the visor was down, which made it hard to guess what sort of a face was underneath, but I suspected it was that of Death, or else empty. Not too far up ahead, there was a hunting lodge with a single tower. It was on fire, and from the top most window—bowed and romantic, surrounded by blooming wisteria—a child was crying for help. I ran towards her, and looking up I saw that people had been impaled high up in the trees on the huge thorns, some still alive even though the thorns went right through them: the work of my pursuer. It wasn't hard to run through the flames, and up the winding stair-case to where the little girl waited. Because my hands were clamped it was tricky to pick her up and I had to open my arms in an O putting them over her before I could lift her. With her holding on to me, I felt her trust in my ability to save her, and I ran back down the stairs through the open door and slap-bang into the armoured 'man'. The only place to go was back through the flaming door. I must save this child . . .

"You have the most incredible night-life, Sunny," moaned Finn. "Calm down" he added, sounding more masterful, "It's only a dream." After a while I turned over and almost went back to sleep, until I felt this thing like a heat-seeking missile beginning to creep up my back . . . the whole nine bloody yards of it. "Finn, you chancer."

Straight across the street from us, a one-bedroom flat came onto the market at a price we could afford. We went off to see if Finn could make an office out if it.

On my way to pick up the kids from school. And up the High St. Ken, I got stuck behind some dangerous dude who should have had his car confiscated; he drove like he was on his own in the middle of the desert, taking up both lanes so I couldn't get past. "Get the fuck out of my way, bog rat," I swore under my breath. Pulling up next to them at the traffic lights, I rolled down the window to suggest a full frontal lobotomy before rapidly changing my mind. "Hi Mum," I smiled politely. "Oh, it's you," she said. "Let me give you a piece of my mind about your driving, it's very dangerous to tailgate like that." Then revving up her engine, she roared off like she was at the wheel of an ambulance. Ain't no flies on the Lamb of God.

I read somewhere (possibly a Celestial Seasonings tea-box) that "A man is at his most wily in his forties." So far, Finn, wily is not the first thing that comes to mind . . .

"Sunny, you need a break. Come on, I'm taking you out to Montiverdi's for dinner." When our food arrived, instead of the nice fish I thought I'd ordered myself it appeared to be a Kraken. Finn was in comfort and charm mode. "Sunny, you've been doing so well, keeping the house together and looking after Scarlet." (What?)

"I don't know Finn, I'm going to be upset about Alex when he dies."

"Don't worry, you'll be OK. But maybe you should go and talk to Dr Martin, there's bound to be a remedy of some sort."

"I can't eat these genetically modified bagpipes, look they're trying to escape off my plate now!" (But I'd rather talk to you, Finn.)

"Well let's order something else then. Look, what do you think about buying that flat for an office?" (Aha, very wily, that's why he suddenly took me out to dinner. Actually all my instincts were against it, and my whole life's insecurities flashed before my eyes.) "Sunny, I really do need an office outside of the house, I don't have enough room at home, and also I have to be able to shut the door on my work when I've finished."

"I don't know, I suppose it's alright. Couldn't this wait until after Christmas?"

"Yeah sure it can . . . Damn, it's so warm this year, where's the snow?"

"What are you doing, Scarlet?"
 "I'm writing to Father Christmas."
 "What are you asking him for?"
 "A dagger." (Didn't come from my side of the family.)
 "What do you want a dagger for?"
 "I want to be a hunter like Pocahontas." (Good; she doesn't need therapy.)

Secretly, I carved her a wooden dagger, with a simple Celtic design on it and a few jewels embedded here and there, and Minu set about making wood-cut of a shamanistic reindeer. It was really good. Minu's work had become more studied, I noticed a quiet introspection taking place, work done for the sake of itself rather than to create an impression on its viewer. Last year the reindeer would have been leaping madly through the sky, but this year it was full of peace.

Every time we went to a play or concert I got stuck behind some tiresome person who sat bolt upright and obviously took the Alexander Technique very seriously. We were at the Novalis Centre to see the Christmas plays. They were performed simply and beautifully, without any fuss. Scarlet knew them well now, and loved them like me. There was a surprise this time, for God was played by an enormous black man with an American accent; he was amazing, and the rest of the cast was the usual multinational eccentric collection of thespians. Afterwards I'd caught a glimpse of Holy Mary Mother of God, smoking outside the dressing rooms. On the way out, the house manager greeted me warmly, and said, "I haven't seen you for ages, how's your painting? Would you like to give an exhibition here?" "Thanks, yes I would, but I'm all sold out of work at the moment. Happy Christmas and good to see you . . ."

"Sunny, you've got too much tinsel on your Christmas tree, I can hardly see the Zodiac signs under all that." We all sat down for Christmas lunch. Tristan and Finn, Minu and Scarlet, Caspar and co., and the *materfamilias*. The general atmosphere kept on reminding me of something which I couldn't quite put my finger on. What was it now? . . . I had it. We looked like a scene from that James Joyce movie, "The Dead".

A post card from Australia, lay on the door-mat. On the back it said, "Ayres Rock". And they had added, "Clitoris of the world!!!!!!"

Dear Sunny, and all
   Happy New Year!
   Too broke to visit England at the moment, but we are saving up and the plan is to come sometime soon. Liza gets terribly homesick, we miss the forest and the beautiful colours from season to season, it's not like that here at all.
      Lots of love, and Happy New Year
               Liza and Luke xxxooxxxooo.

That New Year's eve, at midnight, we performed the annual divination ceremony. Here is what you do:

Get a load of old lead, old piping, roofing lead, or lead bars from your local hardware store, or church roof. Place old lead in old pot. Open all the windows. Heat up lead till it's shiny and liquid, on your cooker. Try not to die of lead poisoning.

Get a ladle full of aforementioned liquid lead, and pour it into a bucket of cold water. The lead will form a most marvellous shape. Now divine your fortune for the coming year.

Minu swooshed his ladle full of lead into the water, steam hissed out like Old Yeller erupting, and then the dust settled. "Oh, it's a monster from the deep, it looks like something I once saw in Antigua. Grandad Alex really loved it there . . . He's is going to die soon, isn't he? I think about him all the time, he treated me like his own grandson and I always wanted to do well for him, He's so kind, making sure that you were OK without it being a big deal. If I thought about what sort of adult I'd like to become, it would be like him. Can you remember going to Antigua for his seventieth birthday? And Grandad plastered and smiling happily with you, Finn, and your brothers. I can see you now, all standing swaying on the beach under the loaded coconut-trees, drinking rum punch at eleven o-clock in the morning. I'll never forget swimming through the coral reefs, snorkelling past hundreds of fish, and water-snakes, unable to name a single one. 'That was a swivel-eyed gogglefish!' And now look, I've pulled one out for this next year. What does it mean Mum? (This Mum had taken one look at it, and felt extremely uneasy about this unknown monster of the deep.)

"Keep swimming along and beware of deep waters, perhaps?"

Then Finn deftly cast his lead. "Oh Dad, how cosmic, look it's a perfect snow-crystal!"

"Scarlet can you remember the snow crystals on our windows in Canada?"

"Yes of course I do, they were just like that thing you've got there . . ."

Tristan, was hesitant. "I'm not sure I want to fix the future like this," he said, slowly poring his lead into the water.

"My, Tristan, that's amazing. Are you thinking of going into the 'Pet Rock' business?"

"S'cuse me, this is either a meteor or a snow-ball. Either way it's a definite message of some kind. Maybe my career will snow-ball, or I'll shoot to stardom in a matter of weeks."

"Any particular career in mind, Tristan?" Finn grumbled, as he busied himself with helping Scarlet, who held her boiling lead at arm's length and bravely plonked it into the water.

"Is it a bird? Is it a plane? No, it's Eddy the Eagle! Scarlet, you're going to fly through this year no problem, but you may have a few crashes and bumps on the way. Let's see what the year brings you, OK?"

Alex had spent one entire Christmas holiday following Eddy the Eagle's skiing career. "You Brits can sure ski. Think Eddy would cope with these conditions?" he queried straight-faced, as we skied gently down Owl's Head Mountain together, the Quebec winter mild at only twenty below. Minu wizzed by with his Walkman on as Finn skied up elegantly to take over minding the old man, while I flew off to race Minu, yahooo! Snowballs, hot dogs, grilled cheese sandwiches, maple syrup, roaring fire and frozen lake, and the warmth of human kindness. And occasionally my father-in-law would slip me a few notes, saying, "Here, this is for being married to Finn . . ."

Then it was my turn. I got a flaming Viking ship, which obviously meant Bash On Regardless, be brave in the face of death and have courage, like the Vikings. This ship will sail through. Happy New Year!

Finn and I sat by the smouldering embers of the fire, and talked late into the night. We were trying to come up with a solution for his son's future. "Hopefully he'll bump into Lady Arabella Swampy sometime soon, and all our problems will be over. Hey Sunny I'd like to go ahead and buy that place over road, if that's ok with you?" I decided to take the path of least resistance if that's what he wanted to do. "Yeah, sure that's fine with me. Finn, Nicky usually stops by at some point over Christmas or New Year. He's probably away or something, but I've left loads of Happy Christmas messages and I wanted to tell him about my tape coming out soon . . . I was really expecting to hear from him."

Did you know that making love attracts spiritual beings? It says so, right here in my Steiner baby health-care book. Is nothing sacred anymore?

After a long steaming hot bath full of lavender bubbles and absolutely essential oils, my hair still wet, I lay in bed thinking things over. The soft candle-light shone, making the wooden walls and ceiling glow like honey. Finn's arms gently circled round me, and I rolled over to face him. He slipped my T-shirt over my head and we kneeled upright heart to heart against each other. Outside the night was silent. Our hands met behind each other's backs, and my body became taut as I felt his hardness push up against my stomach. The room warmed with our shadows. My mouth and hands moved together, tasting, feeling, unhurriedly, lazily down his smooth chest and I heard his intake of breath. Somewhere outside a car started up, its lights briefly flickering through the curtains. Exploring across his ribs, and the vulnerable hollow just below them, I paused, breathing him in, feeling delicately aroused, warm and wet. Uncurling my legs behind me I lay on my front, my tongue tasting and circling the ridge around the top of his swollen penis, then I took him into my mouth and moved, oh so slowly, down onto him. The rain began to pitter-patter on the roof, echoing Finn's scattered heart beat. His fingers ran through my damp hair, and around the back of my head and ears, as I bought him to the brink of explosion and taking my mouth up and off, we folded around each other, breathing erratically, and fumbled to light more candles. The wind whispered over the roof while Finn, flecked in the candle light, warmed a pool of fragrant massage oil in his hands and worked it, deliberately and expertly, over my shoulder blades down my spine, over my buttocks, between my thighs. Then from behind he nudged my legs apart with his head; I quivered to feel his tongue inside me. The rain lashed down in the darkness outside, but we were infinitely quiet, silently creative, weaving ourselves together with love. He turned me over, and his mouth moved up over my stomach, I rose towards him, his fingers between my legs, his mouth over my breasts and nipples, the exquisite shock waves pulsing through me over and over. "I love you, Sunny..." "I love you too, Finn." We kissed again and he drew himself up the whole length of my body, until I had him in my mouth again, cupping his tight testicles in my hands, and feeling along the ridged vein, with my thumbs, I felt him ready to spill into my throat. But he withdrew. We had become anointed with sweat, sweet oil, and our own salty fluids for this silent ritual. I wanted him so badly now inside me that I could hardly stand it. Finn slid my legs over the edge of the bed, and parting the folds he guided himself in slowly, easily, while I tightened and felt him move all the way up inside me. The palm of his open hand upon my clitoris, he hardly moved at all, not even daring to breath, prolonging the completeness, until, with five or six deep thrusts we came together . . '. Content and harmonious, we fell asleep, he still inside me, to stave off the feeling of abandonment and separation when you come apart afterwards.

And that's how we were when the phone rang. "Hell," said Alex, "I ought to be dead by now. Can't understand why I'm still here. I'd like you to catch the first plane out, I want to see you again just one more time."

15

We were warmly welcomed by Alex's young wife and their two children, a girl and a boy. Alex was so thin he looked like a majestic ancient ship-wreck, with the wind and waves blowing through the proud ribs. His thick white hair, neatly combed by somebody else, framed his ravaged face and his blue eyes sparkled, enormous now in the drawn face. Always the gentleman, he had got dressed in a suit with a tie and all, just for us. We sat alone by the fire, and caught surreal glimpses of our youngest children, bouncing wildly around on a trampoline outside in the whirling, falling snow, as they appeared and disappeared in the window.

Alex was not an emotional man—or maybe he was, but in any case, he hated it—so our conversations were often about other members of the family, or art, or Power (which was the modest name of his business), or what I'd been doing. We had always been easy with each other, and it was no different then. He had the best sense of humour; I made him laugh, even when I didn't mean to. He used to try and wind me up about feminism: "Now that you women have got your fingers into all the men's jobs, the whole world's going to hell in a handbasket."

"Yeah, but you know, if you guys hadn't been so candy-assed in the first place it would never have happened . . ."

Alex made sure that he spent time alone with everyone, before we flew home. Finn stayed on with Alex right to the end until he died. The house had a calm about it, with his children helping and taking good care of him, and you know what? Although we were aware that this was the last time we'd see each other, we enjoyed each other's company so much it was really good to be there. I'd been worrying about how to say goodbye to him, knowing how Alex hated an emotional scene, but I got the chance to tell him I loved him, and he told me he loved me too; and he did. He was the one person in the whole wide world whose love I was absolutely secure about. We held each other for a long long time, until I said, "Well, it's been lovely for you to see me." "It sure has," he laughed. And that's how I will always remember him: old, and laughing, and mine.

But Finn's sense of loss had seemed immeasurable. He'd phoned after the funeral. "The whole service was completely meaningless, and there's something about those Christian words which doesn't meet the occasion. They're just superficial, and empty. Anyway I don't think Dad ever had a religious thought in his life, so why they had to do it in the Montreal Cathedral is beyond me . . . . I've been doing my Zen meditation, which helps a bit and I found some amazing passages in *The Tibetan Book of the Dead* . . . You want to hear them? Hang on, ok, listen to this . . ."

> "O nobly-born, when thy body and mind were separating, thou must have experienced a glimpse of the Pure Truth, subtle, sparkling, bright, dazzling, glorious, and radiantly awesome, in appearance like a mirage moving across a landscape in spring-time in one continuous stream of vibrations.

> Be not daunted thereby, nor terrified, nor awed.
> That is the radiance of thine own true nature.
> Recognise it."
>
> (from *The Tibetan Book of The Dead*)

Finn sounded distant, almost as though he was giving an academic paper, strangely detached, and then he added, "It's like I've lost something of myself along with him."

"What Finn, what part of you has been taken away?" But the line had gone dead.

III

1

The rain-washed street, a lonely blackbird (the piper at the gates of dawn) singing on top of a pale street lamp. Nobody stirred. Eventually a lone girl, skinny as a reed, appeared. We hugged, and settled into the car; plenty of Coke, plenty of cigarettes, plenty of music. The roads were empty, even the North Circular, and we made the M25 in record time. "Out of our way, we're on a mission from God."

A light breeze momentarily rattled the reeds as we waited in the still Suffolk morning. Then a young man swung through the clanking gates, his red hair catching the sun. "Oh Mum, Sorrel, let's get out of here, this place does my fucking head in." That's my boy: eloquent, like me.

During your one week's home leave you are supposed to rehabilitate a bit and sort out a place to live, perhaps if you have family let them get used to the idea of you being around again. But we abandoned ourselves to a week's worth general social whirl, good cooking and a house humming with young people again, although all the time in the back of our minds we were constantly aware that he was only home on loan. Minu was relaxed and considerately divided up his time between us all, even surprising my Mum with a visit. He played with Scarlet, reading her stories, and going for walks with us in Holland Park. Cheerful Charlie was with us again. No longer a boy now, almost a man.

"Mum, the house looks so beautiful, your art studio's brilliant, you've redecorated the whole place, I like the new curtains, and the kitchen looks really pukka . . ." I heard him on the phone to Uncle Jake, chatting at ease across the thousands of miles which separated them, in his friendly open manner: "I'm working with horses . . . yeah, we breed them. It's a stud. You know, those huge big cart-horses, yes it's good to talk to you too Jake, I'll write, OK? Bye . . ."

"Is Tristan around, at the moment?"

"I'm not sure, but if we make macaroni cheese for supper, where ever he is he'll appear. You may think I'm joking, but it's a psychic link we seem to have developed."

"I'll grate the cheese, then."

"But that's my job now, Minu," Scarlet said, a challenging edge to her voice.

"We've got two graters, praise the Lawd!"

We hadn't seen him for ages, but I swear to God the moment we put on the pasta Tristan arrived. "Spooky," remarked Minu. "Just in time!" said Tristan, who exuded warmth and embraced Minu. "What have you been up to, and where have you been all this time?" Finn inquired.

"Here and there, Dad. First in Avebury for the autumn equinox with the Druids, who've incorporated didgeridoos into all their rituals: 'Peace in the East (parrp), peace in the West (parrp), peace in the North (parrp), peace in the South (parrp, parrp).' After that I went up to Wales to help some friends who are starting a recycling centre in a lovely little wood they bought. I was living in a bender I made myself." He smiled at me looking for support.

When Tristan was sixteen years old he had dropped out of his Steiner school to become a dedicated New-Ager. He spent much of his time at festivals, Womad, Glastonbury, and the Fairport Convention annual gathering in Banbury. Then he'd decamp to Stonehenge for the summer solstice. Part of the new religion, he had a smattering of bits and pieces of information from many spiritual sources, and plenty of love for one and all. ("Pity you can't get paid for this, he puts enough energy into it," Finn once muttered, clasping his head in his hands.)

Both he and Minu had been reading all of Carlos Castaneda as if it had just come out. "Sunny, have you ever read any?" Tristan asked hopefully.

"Yes, the first three books. About twenty years ago."

"But . . . how can you live like this, then?"

"It's easy. You get old, you get decadent."

"But the world is in such a terrible state! Your generation really messed things up."

"I know we did. So it's up to you lot now to clear it up and do better than us . . . Look, I've got you a present." I had bought him a copy of Paulo Coelho's *The Alchemist*. He was very pleased; everybody was reading it.

Occasionally I'd catch a glimpse of Minu off-guard, and in these moments he had a sort of worried hangdog expression; but his face would lighten up immediately when he saw me watching him. "What you looking at then?" Maybe he was just making the best of it, but I was bothered by the things he said sometimes, too. "It's much easier in prison than out, because you have fewer worries. No rent, no laundry, a job to go to everyday, and they organise our entertainment. Everything is done for you—bedtimes, meal times, waking up, etc. There are strict rules to follow but it keeps you together to have them. It's just easier in lots of ways. I've learned a lot more in art, there then I ever did in Chelsea, my teacher is way better than anyone there . . .

When I first went inside the hardest thing was getting used to all that bloke stuff. I don't know, it's probably good to learn to get along with other men, I've been suspicious of them really."

"I'm glad us women taught you something useful, then."

He laughed. "You may be right, Mum. I thought it was because of my father perhaps. You never say anything about him at all good or bad. Sometimes I've wondered about going to see him but I'm not sure, he would've kept in touch if he wanted to know, wouldn't he?"

"Minu, this is probably one of those things in your life that you're going to have to find a place for. Why don't you go and see him sometime, and find out for yourself what he's like? It's better to know the truth about these things."

"You say that, but it's very hard, as you know. You never go and see yours."

"No, I know I don't, but at least I once knew my father . . ."

"Mum, what's up with Finn? He's a bit of ghost around here at the moment."

"Finn has been all locked up inside himself since Alex died. He probably just needs a bit of space and time."

"OK, I didn't think of that . . . You know, it's lucky I've got the horses. I love working with them, and around the stables. It's the best place to be, and the screws are frightened of horses. Murderers are fine, but horses . . ."

That week was up so soon. Finn sat in the car, the engine idling. Minu had his arms wrapped tightly around Sorrel. "Goodbye, I love you, see you soon." He hugged me. "I love you too." And although he looked straight at me he wasn't giving anything away. "Thanks for everything, after this boost I'll be able to see my way through, in four months it'll all be over." He said cheerily, but I couldn't bear the thought of him going back to that horrible place, and watched them go like a mother animal being forcibly separated from her young. Then a coldness filled my heart. It spread slowly through me, as though my veins were full of ice, not blood.

"Through and through the lady's heart/ the cold steel it did go . . ."

2

I couldn't go back into our empty house, and Sorrel's tears made it worse; they fell slowly down her lovely face. "Come on Sorrel, come with me. We can go to Harrods, and look for a present for Scarlet or something." So as Finn and Minu drove and talked their way up through the late January countryside, Sorrel tried on leopard-skin and gold bikini's, while I sat in the fitting room following Finn and Minu's journey in my mind, clear on all the details of the well-worn route outside London, where the world was still wrapped in winter. We went up to the toy department. "Sunny, do you think they're on the M25 by now, coming up to the junction for Chelmsford?" "Yes Sorrel, I've been trying to figure it out too."

It had seemed like a good idea at the time, but it was no simple task shopping for Scarlet; she had no use for toys at all, and never asked or wanted anything, except bits of string, glue, colours, and any old junk out of the skip which she could make something out of. "Look I've made a flying machine!" But we did find a really neat tool kit, with proper tools that had been scaled down for little hands to use. I wondered if the roads were busy or clear; Finn and Minu could be at Colchester by now . . .

I left Sorrel trying out the perfumes, and went to pick up the kids from school. "Has Minu gone back to his stupid job in the country side?" "Yes, he has. How's the play coming along?"

"Boring!" they sang in unison. With Scarlet and Harry in tow it was easier going back into the house. I imagined they would be in Ipswich by now, passing The Toys-R-Us factory. After that, the fields were full of frosted hollows and patches of mist that wafted through the treetops. We settled down to tea, and then immersed ourselves in the making of our silk scarves, an ongoing activity. We painted fish designs in gold on them and used silk dyes (the colours were great), putting salt on them to create patterns within the colours and then steaming them for a while: alchemy. The house looked like a Chinese laundry; mist inside and out.

The phone rang. "Hi Sunny, did Minu go back ok?"

"Yes I think he was alright. Oh Caspar, we had such a good time together."

"Look" he said gently, "I know this is a bad time for you, but you ought to know that Dad is having an operation tomorrow. He's got stomach cancer and they are going to remove his stomach."

"Cripes, I didn't know they could do that . . . Are you going down to see him? I haven't seen or heard a word from him in years."

"Well, I was wondering if you'd like to come with me? He's never even met Scarlet."

"Don't know, mate. I'll think about it."

"It's an opportunity to get in touch . . ."

"Thank you, Caspar," I said crisply and firmly replaced the receiver on the voice of my conscience.

I didn't want to get in touch. In fact I wished my Dad were somebody else, even if, as Mum always used to say, you choose your parents before you're born. Which was always bloody irritating, because it made you responsible in some way for what they do to you.

He sat in his bed, looking elderly, cheerful, and handsome. His long blonde hair was streaked now with white and grey; it curled down over his broad shoulders and marvellous HAWAIIAN pyjamas: clearly not a modern man. He was surrounded by most of the Czech community of southern Britain, plus a collection of semi-respectable elderly gangsters, accompanied by their hardened and dubious blondes. An uncertain nurse hovered in the background, arranging the red roses, cards, chocolates and champagne bottles. I smiled broadly on recognising Larry the Cheese (who had earned his name on buying a crate of Danish Blue, thinking it was Scandinavian Porn). "Hi Larry how are you doing? It's been years."

"Too long sweetheart, good to see you gal, you done the right thing in coming here," he growled in my ears, enveloping me in an enormous hug.

"Don't s'pose you're still in the extortion business are you?"

"No, why?"

"Oh nothing really, just wondered if you had any dirt on the Home Secretary."

"Sorry love, squeaky clean that bloke . . . Bad day for the old man, init darlin'."

The old man fixed me briefly with his cold blue eyes. "Darlink, how good of you! And who is dis little angel?" "Scarlet, this is Misha, my Dad" (I leaned over, suddenly disturbed by the scent I'd caught of him) "and your grandfather." Scarlet was charmed, and reached out a tiny finger to trace around the gold pineapple on his cuff. He took her hand. "Vell, you're very lucky I'm still here. I go home tomorrow, ze nurses are fantastic, such a service, come and sit up here wid you grandfader. I vas just wondering if you like horses?" A hush fell, as everybody suddenly became transfixed by the TV. Dad produced a score pad, saying, "Ladies and Gentlemen, place your bets for ze 2.30 Cheltenham Gold Cup."

"Come on Sunny, come on Scarlet, let's go, we're late." Sorrel was taking us to see the Circus School she'd recently discovered. We drove down to Hammersmith, parked under the flyover next to the graveyard ("Rest in peace, folks"), and walked around to the front of the church—curiously named "St Paul's the Divine Comedian". Inside, the joint was jumping: children on stilts, some as high as five feet, others on walking globes, and about a half dozen zooming around the Victorian church pillars on unicycles. There were adults happily juggling, and kids just hanging out and playing together. Sorrel introduced us to Oscar and Lucinda, who ran the place. They gave me an instant coffee, and as we chatted, it became clear to me that there were things I could learn here. "Can anybody join, or are these kids specially trained?" I asked.

"Anybody who wants to can join, we've got kids from all over the borough, and all sorts of social backgrounds. Nobody is turned away, even if they can't afford it."

"Really, open to anybody in the whole community?" Well that was a bit more bloody like it. I didn't often bump into people like that any more!

The children were all working and playing together. There was a quiet girl working and working in a corner on her juggling. A gang of naughty boys, playing football on their stilts. Two little girls throwing hoops to each other on rolling globes, and a roley-poley boy trying again and again to ride a unicycle. "Go on you can do it. Takes a bit of work and patience though. Here, I'll give you a hand, now give it some welly." CRASH.

Scarlet got some stilts on and was soon off with the other kids, as the sound of "Jive Bunny" floated up to the distant vaulted ceiling . . . I felt right at home. Oscar and Lucinda helped me have a bash at everything. Since Alex's death it had felt disrespectful in some way to enjoy myself, and I had to give myself permission to laugh and have some fun. I needed the challenge of learning something new and physical, something that I was going to have to work at, outside my daily life. It would help keep the growing shadows in my heart at bay. I placed my foot upon the tight rope and walked uncertainly across.

"Hello Sunny?"(It was Nicky's mother.) "Oh I'm so glad I've got you at last. I've been trying to ring you all week, Nicky was asking for you, Sunny he's dead, he died in my arms, he wanted to say goodbye to you. He got pneumonia in Belgium. I've been phoning and phoning you. It seems so strange, he died so quickly, and he was only forty-seven. He wanted to see you, Sunny, he wanted to say goodbye." She talked rapidly and then broke down.

"I'm so sorry, I would have come right away if I'd known . . . When did he die?"

"It was on Wednesday, between four and six in the afternoon . . ." Nicky's mum was in such pain, I could hardly find the right words. She was eighty-seven, and without Nicky would be completely alone. He must have died of AIDS, he'd been H.I.V for years. His Mum probably didn't even know. He had been ill—that's why I couldn't get in touch for so long . . . Oh no . . . Now the funeral will be held next Monday . . . Sunny will you read a Ginsberg poem? He liked Allen Ginsberg, didn't he?" "Yes he did, of course, I'd like that very much."

Hand in hand with Nicky's bravely smiling mother, Nicky's boyfriend was campness itself. "Sunny, Finn, Scarlet, how delightful of you all to come. So sorry Her Majesty is detaining young Minu at her pleasure, I hope she enjoys him thoroughly," he said engulfing us in a red Feather Boa hug, and releasing us eventually to come up for air, smelling of Chanel No 19 (pshaw).

"Mummy, I thought we were going to a funeral." It looked like the entire clientele of Subterranea had assembled at the Crematorium. Nobody had stayed at home or been left out, and in between the leather and spikes sat some very formal aged ancestors, with pursed wrinkled lips and skinny diamonded fingers suspiciously scanning the order of events.

Behind them, a couple of punks were shooting up in the back row. "Do you have to do that, dears?" Nicky's mother said. "We're about to begin." "Sorry..." The coffin of biodegradable cardboard was something else. It was decorated with his posters, album covers, stick on twinkling mirrors, and reflective stars. "Nicky Sly To The Ends of the Universe" flashed around its sides in leaded lights. The loudspeakers crackled, and John Lennon's gentle piano playing hushed the assembly. We stood up as the po-faced pallbearers, shouldering their light load, started off as voices rose on high. "Imagine there's no heaven, it's easy if you try, no hell below us, above us only sky..."

"Ladies, Gentlemen, and everyone who is neither one thing or the other, we are gathered today to celebrate a life and not to morn a death..." Finn turned his head and smiled at me, suddenly alight; I hadn't seen him look like that for so long. Nicky's boyfriend continued, "I'm going to start this ceremony by reading a poem by John Cooper Clark, after which those of you who have bought something to share are welcome to do so." He cleared his throat and began: "I Married a Monster from Outer Space..."

With heart and style, people took it in turn to pay their respects. Dave, the leader of The Monster Raving Loony Party, walked up slowly; then lightly touching the coffin, he bowed slowly and doffed his top-hat. Others were more elaborate: a delicate and beautiful contortionist routine, a kind of silent synchronised body ballet, a biography.

Elegy for Neal Cassady, by Allen Ginsberg

"OK Neal
    aethereal Spirit
        bright as moving air
        blue as city dawn
happy as light   released by the day
      over the city's new buildings..."

A boy read a letter he had written to Nicky, and someone placed a drawing of the Dancing Man from the Tarot pack on the coffin. Then all was still, silent and completed. The first few notes of a recording of one of Nicky's songs filled the air, his honeyed guitar-playing resounding triumphantly through the cold hall, around the dark pillars and the suburban stained class. It brightened the darkest corners, vibrantly alive and breathing light into the house of death.

When the coffin finally glided towards the flames, there were very few dry eyes. Tears glistened on Finn's face as Scarlet's comforting little hands sought ours, my heart blue as a city dawn.

3

A few days afterwards Scarlet sat in the back of the car telling Katie and Harry all about the funeral. "It was a very gay funeral . . ." A hushed and earnest conversation ensued. "Well, I think gay means men who are against women," said Katie. "And I think lesbian is women who don't like men," said Harry, and the girls agreed. "But . . ." and there followed some prolonged and frantic whispering. "No, you ask her . . ."

"Mum, what's a heterosexual?"

"I don't know, never heard of it. Sounds pretty kinky to me."

That night Scarlet arrived in our bed sick as a dog. And I had to call the doctor in his own home on a Sunday morning. I finally got through, after his wife tried to vibe me dead down the phone. "It's Scarlet. She has a high fever and bad earache, and there's a white fluid coming out of it."

"Otitis media," he replied.

I settled down, hearing the quiet reassurance of his voice. "What's that?"

"A burst eardrum. She needs a remedy," he went on.

"Is it serious?" I asked. But lost my concentration in the middle of his reply, and missed a bit of something or other about listening to a mother's instincts. Don't listen to this one. She's lost her touch or she wouldn't be on the phone to you... I didn't even have a sense of when it was time for her to go back to school, and kept her at home for so long that finally Finn had to say, "Look, she's completely better now. She's going back tomorrow."

I used to love cooking. It was art to me: arranging a meal like a sensual Modigliani painting, using the colours to create subtle or vivid combinations. I enjoyed the exquisite cold sharpness of the sushi knife on firm flesh, and the soft texture of the braised scallop as it entered your mouth, its salty taste lingering on your tongue and melting down your throat; and the feeling of well-being when you've finished. But I couldn't even think of what to make, my mind blank and utterly uninspired. Not hungry for anything, I could hardly eat let alone cook. What was wrong?

I looked up depression in a medical book. It said that it can happen when you lose someone you love, or because of overload, or as a result of the breakdown of a relationship, or because of poor self image, or a lack of seratonin, or it can just happen. And also that forty-year-old middle-class women are more susceptible to it (which is depressing in itself). More muddle-class in this case, but definitely a women—and as a matter of fact, rather proud to be forty and still alive.

Steiner says that life goes in roughly seven-year cycles. Loose teeth around seven, hit puberty at fourteen, etc.; and all these stages are part of your incarnating experience until you get to forty-two. Then you are as fully here as you can be, and after that you start to loosen up again because you are on your journey back to wherever we came from. Sometimes because we are so completely within ourselves we can experience a terrible spiritual loneliness. And that's when you might meet your Shadow. (The Shadow is a ghastly creature that we create ourselves out of all our unconscious deeds, all our negative thoughts, all the frogs and toads that come out of our mouths and every dirty low-down thing we ever did.) Of course if you're a materialist, and unable to accept the natural and inevitable course of life, you might go off and buy a sports car, cut your hair, or worse: like grow a pony tail over your balding head, wear a gold medallion and have an embarrassing affair. Basically, either you get on the boat at this point or you get left behind.

There were certainly some awesome shadows slipping and sliding around inside of me. It was indeed the pits. But even if I didn't know what boat this was or where it was going, I did want to be on it . . . I s'posed.

"Sunny, what's the matter with you? You look so run down, your glands are all swollen, you don't sleep and you've stopped eating. You need to stop pretending that you're just 'dazzlingly marvellous, darling'." I felt rejected and defensive. Then Finn added, "You know, it would help to know you were getting some proper help."

"Finn, I miss Alex too, and everybody else. Maybe all I need is a bit of warmth from you."

"But I've got to go to Zen now . . . What about homeopathy? Maybe you should go see Dr Martin. I'll give him a ring for you."

"Alright then, OK. What are you looking for there, Finn? Are you in search of the Truth?"

"Who, me?"

"Well, have a nice time." (A nice quiet hour of uninterrupted thinking about women, I bet.)

"Mrs McCabe?" said the voice. Being on first name terms with everybody, including her bank manager, Mrs McCabe was temporarily fazed at this. "Er, yes?"

"Dr Martin here, I understand you've got swollen glands," he said helpfully. I tried to settle down.

"Yeah, at the back of my neck and under my arms and in my groin. They're so swollen they make me limp, but it's not surprising really. My son is in jail, and I'm zonked out from the five-hour round trip to visit him, I get so anxious about getting held up and being late. Plus my father-in-law who I loved has died of liver cancer. Now my own father, who I don't get on with, has got stomach cancer, and it's so complicated with him. And someone I really love just died of AIDS, and I just can't get used to it, and I'm trying to care for Finn too who isn't right either." There were tears trickling down my face, and I was so embarrassed at offloading all this on him.

"Are you tearful?"

"Yes." I could feel his total alertness on the other end of the line, and was grateful for it.

"Would you like to come and see me?"

"Yes please." So we made an appointment, and he prescribed me a remedy in the meantime.

Some days latter an anonymous brown envelope, with four little packets of white powder, arrived in the post for me, along with a small bill payable to the homeopathic pharmacy, purveyor to Her Majesty the Queen. (The plot thickens.) "Well, this is a turn up for the books Finn, do you think I should snort it? Look, it's even organised into lines."

"Sunny, have you forgotten that we're going to hear the Brandenburg concertos tonight?"

"Yes I had, actually."

"It's on the calendar, why don't you look?"

"I don't even know what the fucking date is. Anyway I don't want to go, I can't deal with anything extra. And you, Finn, are just avoiding your grief by going to concerts and meditating and so on, instead of talking about how you really feel. You're the one who needs help around here, not me!" I had tears of frustration in my eyes.

"Well you may be right about that, but Sunny you like them. And I want to go anyway, so you may as well come along too."

In the Wigmore Hall. I sat down resigned to being behind the usual Alexander Technique expert. But it didn't matter one bit, because the orchestra played the Brandenburgs so well I heard things in them that I'd never noticed before. Maybe it was because I felt like I had no skin and was vulnerable to everything; at any rate, it was almost like hearing them for the very first time. I waited for my favourite bit: the maniacal harpsichord solo, like a bumble-bee on speed. He played it perfectly, *dementientaro*, bravo!

The Body and Soul Clinic was situated right in the shadow of the church I had been christened in. Every member on my mother's side of the family had been given the family name 'Saumarez' when they were christened. My Mum, Jake and Caspar all have it, but she did not give it to me; relegated to the stranger gallery right from the beginning. I was hurt by that, even insulted, and underneath it never felt like I belonged. So I arrived at my appointment already fazed by this memory. But I needed help, so I made a supreme effort to concentrate (get a grip, Sunny). Didn't really manage it, though.

I always felt at a loss when it came to explaining myself, partly because I was afraid of sympathy but also because people can hurt you if you are open with them. I kept telling myself, "It's all right Sunny, he will help you, talk to him," and I reminded myself over and over that I was not being judged. And I wasn't. Dr Martin was extremely patient with me, which may not have been his natural state of being, ahem. He was also very concentrated and quiet, which helped. I had forgotten about the intensity of a homeopathic consultation; he needed his whole picture if he was going to be able to help.

"Hello, come in."

"Hi." I hovered in the doorway. (I'm not going to be able to do this.)

"Sit down. I'm sorry about your father-in-law, and your friend. When did they die?"

"Alex? About a month ago. Sometimes it doesn't feel like he's dead, more like he's away on holiday or something. And Nicky maybe ten days ago . . . I get woken up by my own tears."

I cried then, and he waited before asking,

"Not sleeping too well? What time do you wake up?"

"On and off all night long."

"Do you like pickles?"

"Yes." (I have just about been living off them recently.)

"Are you afraid of thunder?"

"Yes." (Even in movies, and on records.)

"Where did you grow up?"

"In a Rudolf Steiner Community, and I went to a Steiner school."

"That must have been nice."

(No it bloody wasn't.) "It was like every other school, good and bad."

"How do you get on with your parents?"

"My parents did their best for me." (Why would I say that? Idiot Sunny, you missed an opportunity there.) "My heart is very sore, I feel so sad it just comes over me. Have you got a remedy for that?"

"Yes, but how do you feel about your parents?" I shot him such a glance that he had to put his hands up, but he smiled. "My father was a bit rough sometimes." And then like an idiot I said. 'But I don't want to talk about him . . . Look, I miss my son, and everybody's dying. I'm just sad. And I've got this pain under my arms like iron bands around my chest it makes it hard to breath."

"You're grieving . . . Have you lost any weight?"

"A bit." (Two and a half stone.)

"Are you eating?"

"Yes. Scarlet's a poor eater, and I don't feel good about sitting there not eating in front of her. It's not a food problem, I'm just not hungry." (I ate a bit of supper, nothing else, just when the family sat down together.)

"What about friends, are you seeing any at the moment?"

"Well, sometimes." (Tell him you're avoiding people because you can't concentrate, and you're fed up with pretending you're coping.)

"Do you tell them what's going on, or do they get a performance from you?" (How does he know?)

"I go into performance mode."

"How long have you and Finn been married for? Can you talk to him?"

"Finn's father just died, and he hasn't been the same since his funeral. I don't want to overload him with my problems, but we have a good relationship." (Couldn't he just give me a remedy and let me go? I liked the doctor, though. Wonder what his constitutional remedy is? For God's sake concentrate . . .)

"Is there something you're ashamed of ?" he asked tentatively. "Did something sexual happen between you and your father?"

"No." (Danger, Keep Out.)

"Look, I'm not a professional psychotherapist. Would you prefer to see one" (fucking hell, he doesn't want to see me) "or would you rather have some counselling with me?"

"What? Oh, I'd rather stick with you." (Don't let your fear of rejection take over here.) "If that's all right."

"It would be absolutely fine with me. Tell me, what about Minu's father?"

"I got married when I was sixteen and it didn't work out, he ran off with someone else."

"Have you ever talked about this with anybody?"

"No, I've not really told what happened. I'd like to talk about it, but I'm not brave enough."

"It would be helpful for me to have the whole picture." (And I thought homeopathy prided itself on being non-invasive.) "Do you think you could tell me?"

"I'll try..." (If I wanted to sort things out, I was going to have to talk.) "I'm worried about upsetting you."

"I'll be all right."

"Well you're right, something sexual did happen, not with my father but with Minu's father..."

Man, I never talked so much in my whole life. About growing up, and leaving home a.s.a.p., and going to live in Switzerland, and Minu's father. I've still got the scars... I can live with it, but I don't think I'll ever come to terms with it, why would one? You know Scarlet? Well, when she was eighteen months Leika, my jealous old Border—collie, bit her on the face. But when she needed to have stitches and a general anaesthetic, instead of being told that my baby would be better off with out me, I held her as they treated her. And she fell asleep in my arms, and woke up in them too. We were encouraged to stay the night right next to her, and Tristan and Minu came for a visit; we could even make ourselves tea and coffee. The doctors went out of their way to explain things clearly, and the nurses were warm and friendly. No one made us feel that we shouldn't have been there, or that this wasn't the right place for a mother to be. They should never have separated Minu and me like that, it wasn't right.

"Dr Martin, it took me sixteen years to pluck up the courage to have another child. I was afraid to because of being manhandled at Minu's birth, and the pain of what happened between me and his father when I bought him home..."

It was a relief to talk to Dr Martin. And he got his picture; or at least some of it, because it was not the whole picture by any means, and he knew it. (Next time you go there Sunny, you bloody well better tell him what you did.)

And I drove home empty as a pocket.

4

Surreptitiously, I looked up my remedy, Nat. Mur. It was for people who were grieving or depressed, but who didn't want sympathy, and bottled up their feelings. It also said that these people could be difficult to live with. What? Well bollocks to that, I was the easiest person in the world to live with; millions of people up and down the country were dying to live with me.

The bolts shot back on the prison door and a guard walked over to my bed. Placing his knees on my arms and sitting on my stomach he undid my shirt buttons one by one. Withdrawing the cigarette from between his teeth he laid it on my chest, where it burned slowly, I braced myself against the pain, determined not to react. I could smell myself burning. Taking a long drag to make the tip glow red again, he held it lightly above my skin until the skin peeled away. Sometimes he'd push it in further, sometimes it was just a singe . . . That's what I used to dream around that time. Serving my sentence too.

A young lad about nineteen years old stood shyly on the front door step and asked in French if I was Sunny. "Yes, I am." "Je suis . . ." I interrupted him, "You are Jean, Minu's younger half-brother. Come in." I'd never met this boy before but immediately recognised the mannerisms of his father, and although darker he looked very similar to Minu. I made Jean very welcome, admiring his courage. 'Where angels fear to tread . . .'

Jean was looking for Minu. "Unfortunately Minu is on holiday in Canada." But we looked at photos of him, and I found out all about Jean's life. I really liked him, and felt connected to him in a way he knew nothing about; after all, I was inadvertently responsible for him being here at all. Like Minu, Jean too was not in touch with their father, but he left his own address.

I wrote to Minu to tell him about it. "You have a really interesting and cool half brother living in Geneva, why don't you go and visit him sometime?" He hasn't yet, though.

Then I wrote out a bill for Minu's father. "For bringing up Minu . . ." And sent it off. I'm still awaiting a reply.

I had decided to take my old man gambling. It was important to spend time with him, so it seemed a good idea to do something he liked. Finn looked forward to seeing his father-in-law with relish and enthusiasm (I don't think). We walked into Victoria Station, where a useful notice said, "Some of the clocks in this station are wrong," and settled down in the train. Finn liked train journeys for reading, though, and had decided to start on Primo Levi. While Scarlet and I pulled slowly out of Victoria and over the river, Finn was already rattling slowly through Italy. When the train stopped at Gatwick, Finn crossed the Brenner Pass, Salzburg, Czechoslovakia, and arrived in Poland, I mean Brighton, where my father greeted us in his Black Russian hat and matching Black Sheepskin coat. ("Morning, Comrade Kalashnikov.")

As we ambled off toward the sea, Finn found himself in the sort of conversation unique to Misha: "Vell Finn, I vant you to know zat I vas instrumental in helping Mrs T'atcher and

Reagan. You see, I varned her zat old style communist military intelligence vas vorking against Gorbachev. I mean, Finn—ve all know zey killed Robert Maxwell. Vell, you know vat Mrs T'atcher said to me? 'Sank you very much Misha, I alvays listen to ze ordinary man.' Vell, I said to her, 'Mrs T'atcher, I ham not an ordinary man . . .'" Scarlet tucked her hand into my Dad's, and they walked along Brighton Beach, hand in hand. "Grandad, did you really grow up with the wolves and bears in the mountains?" "Yes darlink, ve had to dig our vay trough ze snow to school every morning, and ve ver chased by bears and wolves all ze vay home."

Finn, suppressing a grin, said, "Sunny, your old man is really something else. He doesn't hear what he doesn't wasn't to, but he's got a lot of charm. I don't know whether to believe him or not." You see the problem?

Misha took a circuitous route to the Brighton dog track, but we got there in the end. He seemed to have recovered well from his operation and the gambling was a big success; I lost loads of money but we were out and about with my old man, who turned out to be a well-known and respected figure, in certain circles. Man, you should've seen him being greeted by the bookies. "Misha, hello! How are you today?" "Vell, not so bad, zis is my daughter, and zis young man is Finn my son–in–law, he's a very famous journalist . . . Scarlet darlink come hand see ze dogs . . . So, vat are ze odds on Peeping Tom and Speedy Sam, today?" I didn't take anybody's tips but put my money on Martian Mystery. Yeah that's right, the Greyhound who lay down and barked as the others wizzed by. Well, he was only a dog wasn't he?

This was the only time I had ever seen my Dad totally confident and at ease, knowing what he was doing—a masterful person whom I had never met before. For seventeen years I'd buried him full fathom five and it would have been a whole lot easier to have just left him there. Because it's far more complicated than people think, coming to terms with the past, and even if it may be better to know the reality of your biography, if the price is too high you may not be able to afford it.

That day, the day of the gambling, I finally realised that our relationship would always remain on this level. He wasn't interested in anything more, and I would never even know if the past bothered him. It was so disappointing. I had wanted more, even though I had learned from working with the children to accept people as they are. Even if it was worth something to know that, I was disappointed. Fuck it. I wasn't looking for Superman, or expecting something we never had in the first place: just a father.

I wish he had put a tenner on me, though; it would have made all the difference.

In the supermarket, trying to remember what we needed for the weekend, my mind went blank, and just got all jumbled up; I ended up in tears again, unable to force myself to keep it together. I had to get out and leave. I just wanted my son back, and my father-in-law.

Finn was opting out of everything. "Finn, I need help with the shopping and the house for a bit."

"OK, let's get a cleaner then," came the voice from behind the newspaper. For the first time in my life I wanted some emotional and practical support, but my needs conflicted with Finn's increasing need to be alone, so he was unavailable.

Finn ended up moving his books, P.C, the Venus de Milo, the lovely Japanese ladies and all his bits and pieces over the road and into the new office, leaving an empty dusty room at home. The house was silent and I missed the rattle and hum of his writing ("Goddam Jesus Christ, the P.C. swallowed the whole bloody review!"). He still came in every day at supper-time though. "Hello darling, had a good day at the office?"

I didn't really feel like making love much—his warmth had disappeared, and I felt unloved. Finn didn't seem to sense that I wasn't into it. Being with him now was like travelling in a country that I thought I knew very well, but the sign posts were written in an unknown language, and all the roads led to different places. I tried to find my way through to him but just got more and more lost. I wanted to help him, but he resisted, and just kept letting go of more things.

The sadder I got the more people said, "Wow, you look so well!" Which was really irritating of them. And like one of those explorers lost in the snow, I lost my energy to move on. Not even to storm the House of Commons, and in full view of the cameras start taking off my clothes really slowly, one by one, until they agreed to let Minu out.

Scarlet cheered me up, though. She would come pootling up with her many questions: "Why is Postman Pat on the front of the newspaper, Mummy?" "Well actually, that's John Major, who was Prime Minister. You could be on to something, though." Or, "What's an egoist, Mummy?" "An egoist is someone who never thinks of me."

At Circus School, Dr Didge's music was on at full volume. The doctor, a great believer in the magic of the maximum dose, played his didgeridoo like an instrument of the vengeance of the Lord. Scarlet had become quite expert at the rolling globes, standing upright and confident, unselfconscious and delighted. I was improving too. Perched on high, you had to stay perfectly centred and poised; the first wrong footfall, and you trip lightly off the edge, tumbling into the night. How long, I wondered, can you keep this juggling, balancing act going, Sunny?

"Sunny, come down from there for a sec, will you?" I jumped off. "Do you want a job? Come and help out with the half-term course, and some of the classes, see how you go," Lucinda suggested. "Yes, I most certainly would."

"Good Morning Madam, I am Ezekiel, from the agency. I come

to clean your house." (Well I'll be, it's the African Queen.) "I like to work alone, perhaps you have some shopping to get on with while I'm here, cleaning for you?" "Yes, perhaps I do." Ezekiel entered, dressed in full traditional ceremonial cleaning robes, bringing his own cleaning kit, tall, thin as a bone and a quiver at his back which was full of an exciting array of psychedelic feather dusters. "Mummy, he's got ring on every single finger..."

"Beautiful place you have here Madam, lots of fine art."

"Thank you, Ezekiel, we have to go to Tescos now. Um, whereabouts do you come from?"

"Tooting, Madam, Tooting."

"Right-oh. Well, see you later." So he vibed us out of the place once a fortnight, and we let him get on with it. I was embarrassed about having a cleaner, though (not very left-wing or right-on).

"Hi Sunny, how are you doing?" "Oh alright thanks Caspar. I really don't like Finn working over the road though."

"Hey cheer up, we're all enjoying your kids' tape. Are you going to do another one?"

"I don't think so. It's just gone into a second edition and anyway I get plenty of music at the Circus, which has a sort of band. (My sort: they don't do rehearsals.) We're supposed to be rock and roll, but you should've heard our rendering of "Red River Girl": tribal, Cajun and keening subtly interwoven with the one chord we had all agreed was in there somewhere. Oh, it was sublime... Folk Thrash at its best!"

"Sounds right up your alley. Listen Sunny, I thought I should warn you I've had a huge row with the Mater Dominus, while she was up here inspecting the children."

"What about?"

"Well she lays down the law all the time about the kids, psychoanalysing their problems in a really negative and unhelpful way, and then I've been finding that Dad wasn't as bad as all that."

"Caspar how can you say that? He was so violent, once I found Mum unconscious on the floor. I thought she was dead . . ."

"Yes Sunny, I know but Mum was just as bad in her own way. Look how she was absent from the home doing her analysis training when we were little. Later on she was always tied up with her patients, and we were often alone. She plays on our weaknesses, like saying I don't remember things properly because of my brain tumour, and manipulates all of us emotionally all the time. She wasn't above smacking us either."

"Now hold on a sec Caspar, it was more or less normal to smack your kids for disciplinary reasons in those days. Still, I know what you mean by emotional manipulation. Christ, I was always afraid of her screaming and shouting if I didn't do just what she wanted."

"Exactly. And poor old Jake, can you remember him packing up all of Dad's belongings? It was pathetic, I would never ask a child of mine to do such a thing. And I would never smack any of my children for any reason."

"No, me neither, except I once threw a bucket of water over Minu, when he was being overly critical . . ."

Caspar laughed. "I'm going to try that on my oldest next time he has a go at me. But Sunny, Mum was always criticising us and Dad all the time, and she wasn't there for us, just for herself. I don't remember her ever doing something just because it would be a kind thing to do for one of us." Caspar was very upset, I could tell.

"I know that Caspar. That's one reason I miss Alex's kindness so much . . ."

"We only had ponies because she liked them, and 'everybody must be able to ride'. She took us to the opera and exhibitions and even Greece because it was educational and important to know that stuff, not because it would be a treat or a nice thing to do."

"That's true I suppose, but even if the motives were wrong I enjoyed the ponies, and even being steeped in the classics.

Mainly I just felt that most of the time, she didn't want me around . . . Heck and bollocks, I'll call you back, she's at the door now. Oi Caspar, did you know that moaning releases endomorphins? Bye!"

I let Mum in, blowing her nose, and clearly in a state like everybody else. So I gave her a coffee and asked her what was going on. "It's Caspar. He's been shouting at me about your father, saying it's all my fault, and banging his fist on the table, asking if Dad borrowed money off the neighbours and relatives, which of course he did. He doesn't remember things at all, because of his brain tumour.

"No Mum," I said firmly, "there's nothing wrong with Caspar's memory at all, and I hope you have never said anything like that to him, because it will just make him feel insecure."

"I don't know what to do, he's so anti–me. It's your fathers fault . . ."

"Mum, we see a lot of Dad at the moment because of his stomach cancer, naturally he's on our minds, but blame is not where it's at. The more we do that the more emotionally tangled it all gets. By the way, apart from asking after your well-being Dad doesn't mention you at all. "

"But Sunny, he was so violent with me. Did you know when I was seven months pregnant with Caspar, and Jake was just a baby, your father kicked me off the sofa onto the floor just because I didn't get up to greet him home from work?" (Why did you stay with him so long then?)

"Oh what? Well he was violent with me, too." (I thought it was my fault because of being naughty, and that's why you didn't do anything about it.)

"Misha was so impossible, it wasn't easy looking after you three, and Sunny you were very difficult, and I had my work to do." (Meanwhile your kids were compromised. And aren't you also responsible for what could have been prevented?) "Caspar just goes on about how bad it all looks."

"I don't think how it looks is what's bothering him, Mum. Nobody gives a flying fuck about how it looks, it was twenty-five years ago now anyway."

"Don't swear, dear."

"He once . . . Oh, never mind. (But why didn't you protect me??) Mum, you haven't seen Dad since Jake's accident. He's an old pathetic creature who's dying, someone who needs our best thoughts, not our hate."

"Harumph," said she.

"Any way I tell you what, Mum. Between you and Dad (who you won't talk to) I get fairly worn out, so I'm getting you both a nice double room in a maximum-security twilight home, OK?"

(And I'm not going to say anything at all about if she was a psychoanalyst, why didn't she know any better.)

If you look back you get caught in a loop going over and over the same old ground, struggling to deal with old wounds that never really healed. I was the girl in the fairy story, trying to climb a glass mountain with iron shoes on. It all came up involuntarily, and I was frightened. (You've got to tell him about what you did.) But I also didn't want to go back to Doc Martin because he had casually mentioned the word PSYCHOTHERAPY, and even though he had manfully worked through a load with me, if you wanted to wave a red flag at a bull, psychotherapy was the one to wave at me.

I knew millions of psychotherapists. Most of them were middle-class women whose husbands had disappeared (they'd probably eaten them), and after going through empty-nest-syndrome, they looked around for something to do with themselves. Their own children, moaning about the way they themselves were bought up, were nonplussed by Mummy's choice of a new career. Busy training at places like the Westminster Pastoral, those who did have families left their kids to be bought up by the nannies, neglected by their mums who were busy becoming experts on family therapy.

In fact, when they were not shopping and de-toxing at Planet Organic, most of London's chic "alternativa" were either in therapy or learning about it. They chose rebirthing, counselling, psychosynthesis, or something else worthy, and their lives were so fucking wholesome and different from mine they wouldn't have had a clue.

But here's the really important thing. If the time is right, and the chemistry between two people is good, and they have built up a working relationship of trust—which takes time and commitment—they can create a third thing between them, something which is over and above themselves, and *that's* healing. I'm talking about people like Nelson Mandela and de Klerk, who healed a nation, or John McCarthy and Brian Keenan, who healed each other: unlikely people alright, but look at what they achieved together. Anybody with the will to can do this. But it's not something that money can buy, and an hour a week with the therapist in their office is just not going to do it. So I'd be hornswoggled if I was going into therapy . . .

Well, I might have made an exception for one of those old, cultured, elegant, middle-European Jewish gentlemen, a couple of whom I knew. However, we always seemed to end up discussing art and music and how marvellous Vienna was in the 1930's, eating zachertort and drinking coffee in Fortnum's or Richoux, and gently charming the pants off each other . . ."Sunny, you have such an interesting vay of sinking about sings."

"Thank you darling, it's because I have Mercury in Pisces, it makes for muddled but very creative thinking."

"I don't sink ze stars are entirely to blame for zat . . . More coffee, my dear?"

Like rare gems, you do not find these people very often, and when you do, you do not want to let them down, and because they have faith in your abilities even when you don't, you remember them forever.

. . . Dr Blau lives amongst his plants and seeds . . . he is always immaculately dressed, in Viennese-style circa 1930s. In the summer, he

wears white suits and a Panama hat; in winter, a loden coat with those trousers that buckle up just below the knee. I'm surprised he can still get hold of this stuff . . . Someone, somewhere was still supplying this stuff though, here in middle England.

I loved those warm and elderly people. Five minutes with them and I felt like a real woman, the most important woman in the whole world. It was their old-fashioned charm, their respect, and their deep interest in humanity. And that, not psychotherapy, is what heals.

5

"I see it's a visit from the old people's home. How nice, what can I get you? A cup of weak tea, my dears?" Minu surveyed the array of wiped-out visitors. Sorrel and Leo, who had slept for the entire journey with their Walkman's on, had been up all night at World Dance, clubbing.

"Minu, I've got some good news for you. Grandad Alex left all nine grandchildren—blood relations or not—some money. Five thousand dollars each, which works out at about two-and-a-half thousand quids. So that should cheer you up, and you can put some thought and fantasy into what your going to do with it." That woke everybody up, I can tell you; the effect was electrifying.

"Are you serious?" He paused, running his fingers through his hair, and then pronounced: "When I get that dough, I shall buy myself ten Rolls Royce's and become a Guru. Om mani padmi Minu om . . ."

"No no, first you become a Guru, then you get the Rollers," Leo corrected him.

"OK, since you know so much about it you can be my driver . . . What's new at World Dance then?"

"Well they've got animated lasers now, with holographic people wandering along the beams of light. You hardly need E's anymore, you can get it all through the lights and sounds . . ." and they went off to the cafe, to return with coffee, crisps and chocolate.

"Mum, I keep wondering whether that judge was a bit racially prejudiced or not." That question had been hanging over me too. The judge had warned him not to expect special treatment "just because you are white middle-class boy . . ." But had the judge been prejudiced the other way? Was it really a fair trial? And then Leo, echoing our thoughts, said, "I've been wondering about that too. You know, some older black people are just over-zealous about trying to be fair, trying to make up for things. On the other hand, he was such a bastard it wouldn't surprise me in the least if he was . . . I mean, it did seem like he definitely had it in for you. I was afraid you might not want to be friends with me afterwards, you know, because of being black. Plus I was ashamed of that judge. I just haven't known how to bring it up."

"Now wait a minute Leo, you don't have to apologise for him. I'm sure you don't blame me personally for all the white judges that have stuffed up black people."

"No mate, I never ever personalised any of it, or thought like that at all." At ease and solid amid the woes of the world, Leo was Minu's best mate. He had a sensitivity towards my feelings and those of Sorrel as well, offering his arm just when you needed it.

Even if I was a great believer in reincarnation, the very next person who walked in here and told me that my dead friends were not really gone was going to get a surprisingly swift kick in the pants. I was fed up with it, and it was not at all helpful; I missed them physically, like chatting with my father-in-law. And I actually needed to talk to Nicky—my studio was giving me all sorts of grief at the time. The music computer had gone into a time-warp, and just would not play various notes like G and A that it had taken a dislike to. Nicky could have had it sorted out in a tick. So if he was not really gone, I wanted a phone number please, and although Ralph had been dead for many years now, I still missed him and thought about him too.

With Ralph in my mind I headed upstairs to my recording studio, tears springing into my eyes. Turned on the computer and the eight track, switched on the Roland and Yamaha synthesisers, hooked up the drum machine, turned on the effects box and plugged in the guitar: all systems go. I had 275 different voices up there (Joan of Arc would have been right at home).

I started to work on a song. It came slowly, alongside the music. And as I worked I wondered about Finn, shut away all day in his office over the road. He had hardly been communicating at all, at least not from the heart, since his father died, which I didn't seem to be able to break through. It felt like he no longer loved me.

> Oh sweet Venus, where have you been so long
> Wrought up from the silence, snow water,
> Spun out of space and light years, the rising dark
> Spindrift of my heart
>
> The city dreams under the moon and neon lights,
> The stranger, the night shift, the urban fox and silver fish
> Are sleeping, uneasy dreaming,
> Like salt upon the stone
>
> We lay entwined, just freshly formed from cold wet clay
> Adrift with no pilot, no anchor . . .

When Ralph had died, Serafina had gathered everyone up on the South Downs one summers evening. There had been a rich red sun-set joining the sea and sky together in a quiet carmine dance, a midsummer fire. A lone trumpeter had played the last post, as Ralph's ashes had been scattered into the sea. I couldn't get my mind around the idea that once I'd lain with those ashes.

Personally, I haven't decided yet whether to have mine scattered around the big beech tree or in Harvey Nicks. But now that I am a funeral expert, I would just like to say that I prefer the ones where the person had some kind of belief in the afterlife. They are more of a celebration of life, and not so stark as your regular that's-it, the-end-of-the-road, full-stop funeral. My Mum just says, "Well, they're going to get an afterlife whether they believe in it or not." She can be very forthright sometimes.

If you read anything about what happens after you die, you'll find all sorts of different explanations and descriptions, but one thing that everybody seems to be agreed on is this: if you haven't made any effort to have a spiritual life of some sort, you're in a whole lot of trouble.

The Tibetan Book of the Dead warns:

> "Then the Lord of Death will say, 'I will consult the mirror of Karma.' So saying, he will look in the Mirror, wherein every good and evil act is vividly reflected. LYING WILL BE OF NO AVAIL. Then one of his Executive Furies will place round thy neck a rope and drag thee along: he will cut off thy head, extract thy heart pull out thy intestines, lick up thy brain, drink thy blood, eat thy flesh, and gnaw thy bones; but thou will be incapable of dying..."

Here's the Revelation of St John the Divine:

> "And I saw the dead, small and great, stand before God; And the books were opened: and another book was opened,

> Which is the book of life: and the dead were judged out of
> Those things which were written in the books according to their works.
>
> And the sea gave up the dead which were
> In it; and death and hell delivered up the dead
> Which were in them;
> And they judged every man according to their works . . ."

And this is the *Bhagavad Gita*:

> "And if a man strives and fails and reaches not the end of Yoga, for his mind is not in Yoga; and yet this man has faith, what is his end, O Krishna?
>
> Far from earth and far from heaven, wandering in the pathless winds, does he vanish like a cloud into air, not having found the path of God?
>
> Be a light in my darkness, Krishna: be thou unto me a light. Who can solve this doubt but thee?"

"The world is the sum total of reality." That's Wittgenstein, and he is so wrong . . . Never mind, he'll be finding that out now, won't he?

6

I was fascinated by an article in the *BBC Wildlife Magazine* about seals, who apparently practise polyandry: females mate with several males, and the males mostly care for the young. "Hey Finn, you should count yourself lucky." "Why's that then?" "A female seal is only receptive for a couple of days each year." No reply, perhaps he was thinking it over . . .

But he wasn't. With a lurch, I suddenly intuited—I knew—that his problem was not only grief. Finn was thinking about someone else. "Finn, be honest. Have you met somebody?"

"OK, yes I did. A Czech girl," he said without looking at me. "Nothing happened, she's still too young, but she's the sort of person I would like to be with . . ." (And all this time, I thought I was the sort of person you would like to be with. I felt like a discarded doll, on the rubbish tip.) "I'm not managing here, can't seem to cope with the family." (Don't want any responsibility, you mean.) And then drawing in a deep breath he continued. "So I think it would be better if I moved out into my flat while I sort myself out."

"If you wanted to we could sort it out together." (Keep cool, and make him be responsible for his decisions.) "I think it would be a mistake to do that, but it's up to you. You need help, Finn, you're avoiding everything and driven all the time, there's no emotional feedback from you. Something needs to be done, but moving out is not the answer." (Or are you just setting me up so you can have an affair?)

And if anybody who's reading this thinks, "Well, you had a great sixteen years Sunny, you're lucky really," they can go take a flying fuck at a rolling doughnut.

. . . But the thirteenth fairy angry that she had not been invited, said. "On her fifteenth Birthday, the sleeping beauty will find herself alone in the castle, and come across a little winding stair case, and despite all warnings she will put her foot on it and climb those stairs. Then she will prick her finger with a needle and die . . . (Don't go up those stairs Finn, don't go up those stairs.)

As far as true love is concerned, fairy tales and reality are at one. If the lovers only play their cards right, love always wins through in the end. Because it is the most powerful thing, and it generates a force all of its own. But you have to work at it and always keep your mind and heart on the task, because if you 'Stray off the Path'—'Turn the Key'—'Eat the poisoned Apple'—'Let down your Golden Hair'—' Move, even a tiny bit'—all hell breaks loose, and the consequences are almost impossible to work through. But even when we know this, we just go right ahead and fall into the traps, because that's what we have to do . . .

"Finn, if you move over the road, you are not going to come over here and give me a poke whenever you feel like it. Things have to be clear, some lines drawn, some boundaries put into place . . ." So we ended up making love passionately.

I got in the car and headed off for a day in the Forest, it made me feel better being outside in nature, and helped me to breath a bit more. Except when I opened the car door, the whole place smelt of egg and bacon; bloody Boy Scouts. "Ignore it, rise above it," I thought, clambering up into the beech tree, my own personal *axis mundi*. "The leaves of the tree were for the healing of the nations . . ."

What had I been doing so often alone in the forest when I was little? When I first came across this tree, it was the largest and most inviting thing I'd ever seen. I'd had to leap again and again to catch the lowest branch. Clambering up and up through its outspreading arms was a tough and dangerous ascent, leaving my five-year old muscles shaking and my heart thumping by the time I reached the very top. I'd rested, coiled around a branch, and surveyed my kingdom. The forest below spread away, an ocean of green; there were waves and islands, tracks, a woodpecker, and silence. Sometimes I'd come here forcing back tears of rage, running away from my father ("I will not cry"), other times in peace, playing the long afternoons away. Sometimes we'd been up here on long summer evenings, draped along the enfolding green branches in the throes of childish love-making, or trying to steal the secrets of the gods with drugs. ("Hello Peter David, you up here too?") Other times, quietly sitting here with girlfriends sharing secrets. ("Never do it with Dean, Sunny, he just puts it in and leaves it there for hours and hours.")

Finn and I had always been so comfortable together, maybe it was because we shared birthdays that I felt like a twin being surgically severed apart, forced by clinical scalpels into a separation. "But Finn, whatever you feel about that Czech girl what we have is worth much, much more. You are breaking my heart, and you don't care . . ." The old branches creaked as a wind stirred, blowing hither and thither amongst the leaves, hither and thither about my soul. Sweeney astray.

I had lost my spiritual life completely, and I was desperately lonely without it. There were no gods anymore; they had gone away, creeping off one by one: "Sorry Sunny, you're on your own now . . ." They had always been there; then suddenly, nothing. (Where are you?) I wanted to cut this painful heart out of me. (If Alex hadn't died this would never have happened.) If

I can't trust the gods, who then? No Finn, no parents . . . You're supposed to be able to find everything you need inside yourself. Well I don't know how to. (Oh please just take this pain away . . .) The black hole's slipstream pulled me along. What's the point of doing a meditation for Minu now? (Up against a wall by any chance? commented my mind. Yes, and you can just shut up too.)

I was in the darkness, and the darkness was in me.

. . . I am holding a spoon of heroin over the lighted gas, and breathing in the warm acrid fumes . . . Oh, this is nice, no more pain.' Sharing a nice fat line of coke with my cousin, I throw up and then take a whole lot more . . . 'Oh man this is nice, no pain at all' . . .

Cocaine and heroin came up in my mind like an advert: "Feeling down? Take heroin now, to relieve all those little everyday stresses and tensions." It was so strange, I hadn't touched the stuff for at least twenty years. It became a constant struggle not to give in.

. . . At school, we learn about the lives of the Greek philosophers. I like Plato, but have no time for Aristotle. Socrates said, "The unexamined life is not worth living." *I have no idea what he's on about . . .* "But the examined life could make you want to die." (That's Saul Bellow, and he's right.)

7

I sat squirming, wishing I were somewhere else. Doc Martin explained that he had left his notes behind, because his car wouldn't start. I was about to remark that he was obviously not treating the whole car, but remembered that I'd decided not to go into performance-and-entertainment mode around him. When I was at the school doctor's, he used to make me go through this little ritual which went, "Do you agree to let the doctor help you?"

"S'pose so."

"Do you agree to help the doctor to help you?"

"'P'raps." And then I used to say to myself, "I now pronounce us man and wife."

So much for your goddamn self-effing-development—there simply hasn't been any.

He asked me a lot of questions but my mind was elsewhere. "I keep getting side-swiped, Doctor Martin. Everybody's dead or gone. Finn's moved out, and I know he's not coming back. I'm full of grief and trying to come to terms with it all. I have to fight this sadness . . . I'm afraid I'll be in the twilight zone for

297

ever, but I'm losing everybody I love, and people who loved me. I don't dare pick up the phone anymore."

"Sunny, there is no other way of asking you this: do you want to be with them? Do you feel like dying yourself?"

"Yes, sometimes I'm surprised that I'm still alive. But that's not an option."

"Why's that then?"

"Life itself is a holy thing. It's the one thing I've been given and therefore not mine to take. But I understand, now, my friends who have taken their own lives. You have this pain inside you and you just want it out. It's so strong that everything pales before it and turns to shadow. It saps your will-power, making you have to fight and push to do the smallest thing, as though you're wading through mud. Sometimes I just want to die because it would be a way of returning to my true self."

"Well, we don't know that for sure, do we." (I thought it was a dead cert, but he was right.)

"Dr Martin, I've got lots of good things going for me. My children's tape is doing very well, and I have a new job working part-time with the Circus. I have two brilliant children, a beautiful home, almost enough money, a car (and a great doctor)— I know. But the depression just happens anyway. And the pain is out of proportion with the injury. Will I ever be my real self again?"

"Yes, you will . . . Tell me, is there perhaps something else going on as well?"

"Yes, I think so. It's to do with my mother. I know everybody moans about their mothers, and then when you get to meet them they turn out to be the sweetest little old ladies one can imagine, but this is very different . . ."

There was once a man and a women who had two little boys. Now the women was surprised to find herself expecting again, and as she was very ill with gallstones, all the doctors advised her to terminate the pregnancy. Even the grandmother was against this child being born, and asked the woman, "What will happen to your little boys if you die?" Others said it would be unfair on the father and the pressure mounted all around her. But it was this mother's genuine wish to bring a new life into the world, rather then worry about her own. Termination was against her beliefs any way, and with the teachings of Rudolf Steiner, who made no bones about abortion being murder, to back her up there was no question about it, and she went ahead sure that she was doing the right thing.

In due course a baby girl arrived safely, but the mother did not find her easy to love after all. She just didn't have the same maternal feelings that had come so naturally when her boys were born. The child was sickly and allergic to her mother's milk, and hospitalised on several occasions and there was no bond between them. And when the time came for the child to be christened she was not given the family name.

The child kept telling herself "it's just a name." But it wasn't really; it was a mark, and she felt excluded, and all wrong. Plus she was left-handed and didn't look like anyone else in the family, which didn't help matters. Her mother was always cross with her, and told her how difficult she was; but she wasn't that difficult. It was the mother who had the difficulty with her. From time to time her father was very rough with her, but her mother did nothing to protect her, making the child feel it was her fault for behaving so badly. The child was further confused because her mother was always very positive in front of others about her and it raised her hopes that perhaps she was OK after all. This child did everything she could to try and please her mother, she learned to become a chameleon, but nothing was ever good enough.

So the girl decided that she would just have to do everything for herself, because she didn't trust either of her parents. She stayed out of the family home as much as possible and gathered another family around her, a circle of friends, children and adults that really did support her and some of them even believed in her as well. They were easy and friendly to be with, but even these she was often suspicious about.

Her mother told the girl that she would never get any 'O' levels, making her feel ashamed and stupid, but at the same time wouldn't help her with the things she was good at and wanted to do, suppressing any such ideas as ludicrous. The child asked herself what was the point of going to school at all, if she was never going to get any exams? And she felt let down by her teachers, who had known her all her life yet didn't see how tricky things were for her at home. She became indifferent. School was a struggle anyway, and she got so wild and bloody-minded that they finally chucked her out.

As soon as possible the child moved out and abroad, as far away as she could. Later, when her brothers as adults were in need of financial aid, the mother offered it freely, but to her daughter none was ever given.

All her life the child had made excuses for her mother, trying to pretend it wasn't true, hoping for a resolution, or that it didn't matter in some way, and asked herself can you blame the mother if she did not love her child? Perhaps not. But the mother did not work with it, and she should not have blamed the child . . .

"Dr Martin, I think this is where this depression comes from, what brings it on. I do not need unconditional love or even a family name to make my way in life, but everything is being taken away from me again. Bit by bit I'm being stripped down to the bare bones, until I will have nothing left at all and am nobody. Do you think you might have a remedy for courage?"

"Yes . . . Yes, of course there is."

I found myself standing in the silence that comes after the firing of heavy guns.

The snow fell all around, and the cold blue trail stretched ahead into the failing light. The silence was complete, and the snow-shrouded trees bent like ghostly old men towards the ground. Up ahead I thought I could make out the figure of a small child, and as we drew nearer I could see that it was a girl in a white paper dress. Her feet were bare, and frozen raw in the snow-drifts which had piled up along the edge of the path. She was a wild, strange, unearthly child, with raven black hair, icy topaz eyes and transparent white skin beneath which bluish veins flowed. A flock of seagulls flew all around her. She was screaming and screaming for help, but in silence, because whenever she opened her mouth a seagull would catch the scream in its beak and wheel off, disappearing into the snowy sky with it. I yanked on the guide reins to stop and help her, but even pulling with all my strength I was unable to bring the sleigh to a halt. My husky dogs would not obey my commands, and increasing their speed against my weight they ran on past her, set on some other course, which they insisted in pursuing, despite my best efforts. "Alex . . . Alex where are you?" I woke up tears pouring down my face. For days and days I felt empty and lost after that, just drained. I woke up in tears, and in despair.

Eventually, I gave up and lay down in the snow. Wrapped up tight in a blanket on my bed. Hoping for sleep, I had never been so zonked out in my life; it was only midday. The grief once again seeped through me. "Please take this pain away," I asked, "or let me die." And that's when it happened. Gently, between sleep and wakefulness, I felt myself being surrounded by strong arms, full of warmth and total security, and filled with a love that was different to anything I had ever known. I was held within it for a long, long time, until I had to know who was behind me, and turned over to see. There was nobody there, but the peace remained. Later, I awoke, after a really proper sleep.

Ask and you will receive. Only don't ask to win the lottery, or for a new car, or even for your son's release. Only ask for the courage to deal with whatever your fate brings you.

8

. . . Mum is sitting by my bedside. My candle is burning. For tonight's entertainment, she is telling me the story of Sleeping Beauty. Once upon a time, there was a King and a Queen . . . This is total immersion story telling, and I am riveted. "Don't forget to invite the bad fairy! Oh no, they're going to forget." I can hardly stand it. "Don't open that door, don't go up those stairs. She's going to prick her finger!"

"But she did prick her finger, and it bled, Scarlet, and she fell into a deep sleep and the whole castle fell asleep with her. The cook who was about to beat the scullery maid fell asleep, the little doves on the roof top tucked their heads under their wings and fell asleep, the castle dogs who were worrying the cat fell asleep. And while the princess lay sleeping, a huge and thorny rose hedge grew up around the whole Castle until even the highest tower with its blue and gold flags were hidden, and they slept for a hundred years . . . .

"Many a Prince tried to find their way through to the sleeping beauty who lay within, but they just got tangled and died caught up within the thorns and lost forever, until the right time came. The years passed and one day a shining handsome

Prince heard tell of the sleeping beauty and fell in love with her. He found a way through easily, the rosy thorns opening up in front of him to make a path to the palace. And with his love he found a way to her sleeping heart and woke her up, and all that was around them woke up too . . ."

"Mummy, Daddy is a bit in those thorns now, isn't he?"

"Yes, sweetheart you're right, I think he is too."

Scarlet and I sat in my bed together drinking tea, not ready yet to get up, still shrouded in sleep, on a Saturday morning. "Come on, let's do something. It's eight o clock already, we can't just sit here all day." She pulled a large colourful book off the shelf for us to peruse.

It was *The Book of Kells,* which she opened on the genealogy of Christ in Saint Matthew's Gospel. Fading golds, regal magenta, lustrous carmine, a hint of ultramarine, and shadow-black ebony. Like the Creation itself, out of the abstract patterning animals and people appeared, and there were letters in the spiralling forms of life. "This book," I told her, "was made from all sorts of things of the Earth. The tough leather-binding came from calves. Some of the colours were bought from as far away as India, maybe travelling at first on elephants, horses and camels along the traders' routes from China, then on ancient merchant-boats. And these reds are made from crushed berries and cold stones. Those ancient old monks were great artists. They used hand-made quills from the geese and ducks, and their paint brushes were made of horse and badger hair, and because they had no electricity they could only work when the natural light was right. Sometimes on winter days it was too dark and cold to work at all. They had no compasses to help them make these perfect graphics, only steady hands."

It exploded out of the page at us, and I noticed that one of the artists was dyslexic: the L in the right hand corner was backwards. I smiled and saluted him across the ages.

"Look Scarlet, I've got my own book of the Earth." I pulled out another well-worn book.

"Oh look, it's a book." *It's very beautifully made; the cover is woven in shot silks of ocean colours . . .* We opened it up, and looked at the old treasures: a poem, "The Strange Horses," by Edwin Muir. Pressed fern and hazel leaves from the forest. The class photo. "Look, that's me, at school, and there's Pearl and Dean. All this comes from Sussex, look at these . . ." A pink jay's feather, thin birch-bark, some dried seaweed (not entirely crumbled to pieces yet), a drawing of a Peace Dove, a Celtic knot of gold and green thread. All bits of my local landscape—sheep's wool, horse-hair, moss—still intact, still beautiful.

"Who made it for you, Mummy?"

"My class-mates. They were pretty good artists too."

It was so cold while I was waiting around for the kids to come out of school that I was forced to take refuge over the road in the Brompton Oratory. "Our Lady of Comfort Shopping and Commerce" just didn't feel like a holy place, but I lit a candle for St Michael—"Oh Michael the victorious, I make my circuit under thy shield"—and then another one for his dragon. Then I went over the road for a cappuccino in Patisserie Valerie. I was struggling with an overwhelming desire for Cream of Magic Mushroom Soup when my heart skipped a beat: I saw Alex, sitting up at the bar, a moment before remembering that he was dead. This was happening all the time, whenever I saw someone who looked even vaguely like him.

The little ones were in the back of the car. "I've thought of a great way to get rich," said Harry. "You run as fast as you can and bang your head against a brick wall so hard that all your teeth fall out, and then you get a load of money from the tooth fairy!" Scarlet and Katie laughed derisively. I put on the Sharon

Shannon tape. Maybe that was the answer: change my name, wear a miniskirt and become a fiddle legend. "Connie Connemara, a legend in her own mind!"

My son, gangly and gaunt, had become a blond person. Noticing that most of the younger inmates had become blond too, I managed to button my lip tight and not say a word for about a second. "Hi Minu, you look like that guy in Blade Runner."

"Thanks Mum, you look like Brad Pitt."

"I suspect that subconsciously you're just trying to emulate me . . . You didn't see the dolphin programme by any chance the other night?"

"Yes, I most certainly did, brilliant, I think Miles or some old boyfriend of yours once took me to see them in Brighton, years ago when I was little. I can't remember if you were there or not."

"No I wasn't, but it's wonderful that they've been released after all these years in captivity." (They took the dolphins back to the Caribbean expecting it to take ages for them to rehabilitate, but they swam off as if they'd never been away.)

"I wouldn't mind going to the Caribbean to rehabilitate, either. It's all very well this security one gets in the daily routine here, but I would like to be doing things for myself. Christ almighty, Mum, I would give a lot to be out now."

"But you will be, very soon. It's only another few weeks, I think we've got one more visit to go."

"Is that true, Sunny?" interrupted Leo. "Just one more visit? Shame, I kind of like it in the countryside."

"This isn't the countryside, you prat, it's nowhere at all."

"Sorreee Sorrel, lighten up will you?"

Trying to change the subject, Minu said, "Mum, I don't suppose you read that article the other day about teenage mothers. I can't understand why they are so negative about them. They need all the help they can get, it's a cheap trick to attack people who are already down. I wanted to write back about you and me, because we've gotten along fine and I have a lot of exams. But then a letter from this address wouldn't look too good!"

"And your Mum is not a teenager..."

"Thanks Sorrel. But you're right. You rarely meet anybody who has actually been directly helped by the government in any way. Au contraire, they seem to make it as hard as possible for people who are already in trouble: teenage parents, disabled people, or children with learning difficulties and the special needs kids, or housing."

"That's because there is no financial return from investing in them," put in Leo.

"Yeah, that's about it really. The treasury seems wide open for people who already have money, like big businesses," added Sorrel.

"I know. My mates here in the prison are convinced that there's some deal going on, with this 'every child should have a computer' mallarky, when it seems obvious that kids should have some decent teachers who are properly paid. But they won't put the money into human beings."

"That's just it," I said. "Most of the problems being a young mum are ones of poverty, not age. I wish that I hadn't had to work so hard when you were little. Still, that's life. And there are plenty of bad parents in all age brackets, so maybe being a good parent is a character thing..."

"I don't even remember you working. I mean, I was always with you, and I had really good time. Except when we left Sussex because it all fell apart, and we moved up to Scotland. I hated it there."

"I know you did. That's why I didn't push to stay longer. But I just had to go where the work was... Anyway, here are the reviews of my children's tape, four of them now. One of them from the best Irish harp player in the world, which is quite an honour. And look this one says how "unique and appropriate" your cover design is. This means loads more children will know about it... They better like it."

"Hey Mum, that's so cool. Can I keep these reviews, please?"

One of the things that had changed about Minu, since he'd been in jail, was that he never criticised me anymore. Quitebloodyright too, you should never criticise your parents.

Goethe said that every plant has an archetype it strives towards being, and I like this idea. And according to Steiner, every tree is connected to a planet and a metal, which I like too. For example, oak trees—Mars and iron; birch trees—Venus and copper; and conifers—Saturn and lead, which makes sense to me, because when you stand in a conifer plantation you can tell that their planet is a long way off; the trees are so tall and they don't make proper leaves, and the stillness is immense.

He also says that beech trees are linked with Saturn as well, but sitting up there in the big tree I didn't experience that at all. I wonder if he ever actually climbed into a huge old beech tree to just hang out there, or carve his name in its yielding bark. Because he might have found it more Venus than anything else.

If you scramble out from here onto the orangey clay path and follow it downhill across the wooden bridge that spans the ironrust stream, and if you carry on through the hushed Forest, fork right and walk about another thirty yards and then scramble left past some bushes and trees, you come to the Lily Pond. Apart from it being a really nice place, it's also the last place I can remember being at peace with myself before I spoiled everything . . . What I needed was a long appointment with Doc Martin, like maybe fifty or sixty quids' worth. It would take me that long to talk it through. If I could get myself to at all, that was.

"You see Dr Martin, I was living with a man. Well, two men, actually."

"Yes, you told me. Go on," he says. (For Christ's sake, don't blow it. Get a grip and take advantage of this person who is waiting for you now.)

"After my marriage with Minu's father I decided not to

have any more relationships, and if you find it hard to relate to people, erm, if you've got two of them it means you don't have to relate to either of them properly. Meanwhile you can adjust your heart and get over your troubles."

"Oh, therapy," he says.

"Yes, and it was fine, except I got pregnant . . . And had an abortion. It's against everything I'm into. I'm a creative person and I like children. It would have been all right if I'd kept it."

"Hm. You say that with hindsight, but people make mistakes, you know. You're being awfully hard on yourself." (Dr Martin is trying to tell me it's OK, but it isn't.)

"I never let myself be talked into anything I didn't want to do before, but somehow I just let it happen. I let myself down. I didn't want to but I got into a panic about childbirth—scared of it from the time before, and unable to face my fear. That shouldn't have stopped me . . . And what's more, you know, my Mum she didn't have one, and here I am."

9

... Deep in the heart of the Forest lies a quiet, still pond. At one end stands a dark yew; oak, chestnut and beech trees enclose it all round. The whole place lies in a hollow, and its peacefulness works on us. Luke in his waders stands in the middle, surrounded by a cloud of water-lilies and attendant dragonflies. He stands perfectly still, like a blue heron, before gently bending down to pick the five lilies he has come for, a present for his friend. This is a lasting image ... Because the next morning when I woke up, I threw up.

"Miles, I'm not feeling well at all. Actually, I feel ghastly."

"Better see the doctor, then."

"Look, I think I'm pregnant." Miles tried to hide his horror, mainly at the idea of the commitment; this threesome had its advantages for all of us. "It's all right," I said. "You wouldn't have to take responsibility, I can manage on my own."

"I knew you would say something like that, but I don't think an abortion is any different from contraception if it's done early enough." It hadn't even occurred to me to have an abortion; I didn't know what to say I was so surprised, but he didn't want this kid, that was clear.

"I'll go and see the doctor then, and have a test and talk to him, all right?"

It was my old family doctor—that was good, we could talk. "When did you have your last period, Sunny?"

"That's just it, only a couple of weeks ago."

"Well, it's too soon to know then."

"No it isn't, I know that I'm pregnant."

"All right then, how do you feel about it?"

"I'm not sure . . . I think I'm going to need an abortion. No support, you see."

"How old is your little chap now?"

"He's three."

"Yes, and you are the same age as my son, twenty-one now. Go away and think about it, we'll do a test, and when you know what you want to do come back."

And all this time, in their pool under the promenade, Marlon, Missy and Babe the dolphins had been swimming around, jumping through hoops to catch fish suspended from the mouths of various trainers and singing "Happy Birthday" to liars, and all just for our entertainment. (I didn't know they would have to stay there forever.)

That's where Miles and Minu were now, and I wished I was too.

The abortion clinic looked out over the sea and Brighton; it was one of those new smart buildings surrounded by bushy conifers and shrubs, anonymous, like a bank. There were rows of women waiting here. Lots of them were only young, about fifteen, or younger; some were very distressed and crying, some trying to be tough, and others completely fine. Some changed their minds before the anaesthetist got to them; others were waiting impatiently. And although there were lots of us there I felt completely alone, and I think the others did too. The whole place was so soulless and sterile, like an empty vessel. "Hello,

I'm the anaesthetist," he said, slipping the syringe into my arm. "Goodbye," I replied, because this stuff was already working.

I came swimming up from the anaesthetic struggling and sobbing, in total despair, because I knew I had done the wrong thing. I had fallen from grace. Bereft, full of grief, I quieted myself down and listened to others, some of whom were sobbing too. I wanted to help them, but felt so woozy myself . . .

It took me ages to get over the anaesthetic. I carried on living with Miles and Crispen, but had to wrestle with this sadness. I kept up my teaching, and cared for Minu, and when the sadness became overwhelming I took heroin. I didn't tell a soul, not even my best friends like Liza, because I was ashamed. Up until that point I had mostly felt that I was not wanted on the Earth, and that my real home was a spiritual one, but from then on I felt that they wouldn't want me in heaven either. I was no longer good enough, because I had sent that soul back. If I'd known how it would feel I would never have done it.

10

1977. The December rain fell in sheets on the Regent Street Christmas lights. Evening shoppers scurried past the cheery shop displays, and Santa beckoned little children to visit his grotto; the Salvation Army band huddled in a shop porch with tubas, trumpets, drums and trombones sticking out at all angles. My four-year-old travelling companion was deeply thrilled to be in a taxi, overwhelmed and dazzled by the whole experience. "Off to somewhere nice for Christmas, then?" the cab driver asked. "Scotland, I've got a job there teaching." He dropped us off at Euston Station; the pavement was awash and the rain kept falling. "Will there really be bunk beds in the train? Can we get on now? Can I sleep on the top? Will they really wake us with a cup of tea? Come on Mum, I can hear a whistle!" "OK Minu, hold your horses . . ."

We found our compartment, stored our scanty luggage, and Minu went up and down the ladder about ten times and made sure that the taps were all in working order before settling down to sleep. Then, as the train gathered speed, a quavering voice from above said, "Mum, my dog Sammy. He's gone back to Mellow Cottage," and the little chap started to cry at

the loss of his imaginary friend. "Come and sleep with me then."
"Er . . . Mum, would you mind coming up here?"

From the outside, it looked like the Marquis de Sade's second home, but inside it glowed, a dragon's cave. Heinrich and Adelheit had made it warm; the colour-washed walls of orange, yellow and red were hung with paintings and woven rugs, anything wooden had been sanded down, bleached and stained into light honey-coloured hues, potted plants grew on every available shelf. Fires blazed in the fireplaces, Norwegian stoves flickered in dark recesses, and Advent wreaths gleamed wherever a bit of room presented itself.

It was a very small community of twenty-one maladjusted and deprived children, mostly from Glasgow and Dundee. They called their school "Occult Tower," an apt name for that dour Victorian house. Minu and I lived in the converted stables along with eight kids, Adelheit, and Greg, an enthusiastic American. A neat market garden lay buried in snow, the ponies Jupiter and Mars pawing the frozen ground, and behind them the view opened out towards the hills. The children showed us round, and I had difficulty understanding some of what they were saying, their accents were so strong. "Hi, what's your name?" I asked a boy of about eleven, who had a long ponytail of black hair down his back and very bright blue eyes. "I'm Heidi," he said, looking me straight in the eyes to see if I was going to fall for it. "Hi Heidi. Pretty name for a pretty girl," I replied, deciding that I was going to call him Heidi forever.

Miles was on the phone, oblivious to the grief and shame of the abortion. But I didn't blame him or harbour any kind of resentment; no sense in that, and ultimately it was my decision. "How are you, love, did you get there safely?" he asked.

"I'm fine, just fine, it's great up here."

"Good, I'm so glad to hear that." He was trying to sweep our break-up under the carpet so that everything could be nice and friendly; Miles didn't like to look at the dark side of life. "So you're all right, are you?" (I had already shut him way out of my life, and felt an enormous distance between us, even though only two days ago we had been taking our time and making love in a relaxed sort of way.)

"I'm fine and thanks for calling, take care, speak to you soon." I hung up. So long, farewell, aufiedersehen, goodbye.

It was a different kettle of fish working with the maladjusted and deprived kids to working with the handicapped. I was delighted at the immediate feedback in the classroom, often unasked-for, sometimes pushing it; this lot were completely on the ball, buzzing with energy, sharp and funny. Some were gifted with music. We could actually play traditional tunes together, and I learned new tunes from them; dextrous on tin-whistles and recorders, they picked up guitar chords easily. A few of these kids could really paint beautifully too, and it was good to be working with them. Others needed help with their writing. "Relax your hand, it doesn't matter what it looks like, try and get it to flow a bit more, yeah that's better, relax. Look, that's fine. You know what, where I went to school it was pretty similar to here, but I had to make my first pen from a goose quill."

While I taught in the mornings, Minu went to nursery school, and in the afternoons he tootled around with the younger children helping in the kitchen or playing out side. But he wasn't that happy there, and watching a train go by in the distance he would ask me, "Mummy, is that the train to Sussex?"

The children in my house were a pretty independent lot, capable in the kitchen and around the house: setting the tables, making their own beds, and helping themselves to snacks. A boy called Jo booted the humming fridge, quoting eloquently, "Ask not for whom the fridge hums, it hums for thee." They were banned from most of the local facilities such as the phone-box (because of phone-tapping), and they were constantly helping themselves to free Durex, chocolate and cigarettes from slot machines which they had a gift at fiddling. Only one at a time was ever allowed in the local shops, and even then they still managed to nick something or other. Ranging from five to eleven years old, many of them had had to fend for themselves from a young age, and some had been roughed about. We were trying to get them back into mainstream education for the last year of primary school, and usually did. I was glad that this Steiner school had its feet firmly planted in the world.

Heinrich was showing more then a passing interest in me, which was a nuisance.

Not all the children were from deprived backgrounds. Some came from quite wealthy middle-class families with every material thing a child could wish for, but none the less they presented all the same problems as the others. Many with truly horrendous family histories had brothers and sisters who were coping very well at home . . . The only truth I know is that each child is different.

It didn't do to be authoritarian with those independent souls either. They reacted to it like I did at school: "Fuck off bastard, what do you know?" You needed to be funny, light on and ready for the occasional set up.

"Sunny, do you know what sexual intercourse is?"

"Yeah, it's a form of communication. Like talking." He ran off laughing, "Sunny thinks that sexual intercourse is talking!" (I'm going to get him back for that.)

"Excuse me Heidi, but shouldn't you be using the girls' loo?"

"That's it, I've had enough of all you fucking shitheads, I'm running away and I'm never bloody coming back!" screamed Lynn.

"Well hang on a sec, you'll need something to eat. I'll make you some sandwiches."

Then Adelheit added, "I'll go and pack some things for you, it's a long way to Dundee."

Finally Lynn stood lonely and sobbing in the middle of the drive with two suitcases, a knapsack and a sleeping bag. "I hate yous," she said, shuffling back into the house. "And I hate him, too," she added, glaring at the only picture of Rudolf Steiner the place had. I liked Lynn; she was a great girl, and artistic too. By the next day, Dr Steiner had grown a luxuriant moustache.

> Dear Sunny,
>
> What happened to you? I didn't even know you had gone to Scotland. Your Mum just told me you got a job there and left right away. The thing is, I've got my emigration papers to go to Australia and a job nursing out there. I've had enough of Woodbrook, and it's time to make my own life now. I'm going in the summer hols, perhaps we'll get a chance to say goodbye then? Sunny you'd better bloodywell get in touch, OK?
>
> Love,
> Liza.

Jo, Daniel and Lynn were hanging out in my room, and I got to hear bits and pieces about their battered lives. In between the larking around and general chit-chat, I listened with interest to what was really going on inside them, and sensed this deep longing to put it all right. Why was it that the victims felt that it was their responsibility in some way to make things good, while the perpetrators were often unaware of the damage they had caused. "I've got very nice foster-parents now, so it's much better for me," said Dan.

"That's true Dan, they are really nice, and you know what?

It's eleven-thirty, everybody else has been asleep for hours, and I've got to get some sleep too."

"Go on, light a cigarette and give us a drag before we go."

"You're a drag. Nice try, sleep well, goodnight".

"Aw . . . Hey Sunny, do you really think that sexual intercourse is talking?"

There's this thing called physical literacy that these kids often had. It's a total control of your physical body: an ability to walk across the horizontal pole above the swings, or to climb up a lamppost and hang from one arm off the cross bar, to skip the light fantastic across the fallen tree, to run barefoot along the yawning precipice, to swing and somersault off the trapeze. We watched each other, in recognition of a silent challenge.

My kids there were awash and drowning in a sea of emotional needs, smarting from violence and deeply hurt in their souls. I felt very akin to them. But watching them and teaching them, listening to them and living with them, I become aware that I was no longer a child. I did have some control over my life, and I realised that it was no use saying, "My father didn't do this for me, my mother doesn't understand, my teachers let me down," etc., etc. If I wanted to move forward I realised I had to say, "This is what I've got, these are my strengths, and are now the tools with which I can help others." I decided never to be in a violent situation again, and that I would not let things just happen to me in life. I would always stand behind my actions and any major decisions that I needed to make, I would be responsible for myself, and put it all behind me. And I did, almost; well, very nearly.

> Dear Sunny,
> I hope you are well and that Minu is enjoying Scotland. I have some very happy memories, riding over

the moors, on my pony, the lovely purple heather and the river Dee.

I have decided to move to London, now that you have all left home. I can continue with my practice there, perhaps take on fewer patients. I am looking for a place close to the Albert Hall, it has always been a bit of a trek, going up to town for the opera and concerts. This house is far too big for one person, and does have some lovely memories of you all growing up and many happy times, but it also has some very unhappy ones too.

I am looking forward to a whole new stage of development in my life, and seeing all sorts of property at the moment.

Love to you,
Mother.

Dreaming about Tycho Brahe, I recognised him immediately. He came into my room and looked around, and I was delighted to have such a distinguished visitor. Curiously, he seemed to be on a an electrical appliance fact-finding mission, and pointing to my tape recorder he asked, "What's that?" So I put on a tape for him, Bach's flute sonatas. Tycho listened for a while, and then asked me how it worked. I shrugged. Then I had to boil the kettle for him, and make a cup of tea. "How does that work, Sunny?" I ended up hoovering my room and switching the lights off and on for him. He was fascinated by it all, but always asked me the same question. Finally he said, "It's no good Sunny. You have got to know how things work in this world." Which I understood to mean that it was time for me to leave the Steiner community, and learn more about the real world.

When I first worked with the very handicapped kids, they were always put into institutions, but that's not necessarily so any more. More and more parents don't want them put away somewhere but like to keep their children at home, often adapting their houses to their child's needs, and wherever possible they go the local school. These families work hard to get them participating in as much of a normal life as they can. And low and behold, many Down's Syndrome kids can read and write now. Where I used to work we taught everybody everything, but mostly children in need of special care did not get an education at all. Some of us have always thought that it's socially good for "normal" kids to be educated alongside people who need more help than them. And vice versa. For example, I—a "normal" kid—was finally taught to write by a child with Downs Syndrome. Nowadays it's becoming different, and about bloody time too.

My job in Scotland lasted for a year. Before leaving, I gave Heinrich a night of pure joy and ecstasy... From which he's still recovering, I hear.

Then Minu and I went to live with Romany, back in Sussex. I got my first job in the "real world", doing music for a BBC Radio children's programme. Minu enjoyed having Misty and Phoebe and their older sister Ariel to boss him around again, and the luxury of the leafy forest. A succession of William Morris students (always a good source of interesting and exotic boyfriends) used to visit. Even back then we used to sit around Romany's Aga stove, underneath the perpetual array of drying knickers, trying to get our heads around making up our own millennium ritual, trying to decide how best to celebrate it and express ourselves at the same time. "I have to move house soon, what do you think of Wales?" "Nothing. I never think of Wales at all if I can help it." "But it's expensive and overcrowded in the south of England." "Why don't we just burn down your house, Romany. We need fire if we're going to do a ritual, along with earth, water and air, of course." "Is your house insured?" "I don't know..." "We've got to include the directions too." "Directions to where, might I ask?" "No, you lumpfish—North, South, East, West. And up and down."

The house was a perfect place for children, warm and very social. We had a fine old time, despite having no money—painting a lot, chatting a lot, and laughing together, as we sometimes still do. And that's when I first met Finn . . .

11

It was a pity that Dr Martin had grown a beard, because he had a really nice face, and now you couldn't see it, or tell what was going on with him so easily. "Look, about the abortion. It really bothers me, and it was my fault that I got pregnant. I didn't do what I was supposed to do, and I knew perfectly well not to take that kind of risk. I am responsible for the whole thing."

"What if it had been your partner's fault?"

"That didn't occur to me. But the abortion changed my whole relationship to everything."

"Have you talked to anybody else about it?"

"Not really. Where I was bought up, it amounted to murder, and perhaps they were right. It's been a real problem for me, 'specially as my Mum did not have one. I've got these really great women friends, and some of them have had one too, but they don't seem to feel so badly about it. Sometimes I tell myself that it's part of human experience to have known some bad in your life, but I worry about that soul and carry it about within me, and maybe that would explain the craving for hard drugs . . . I would like to put this burden down now. Not because I don't want the responsibility of what I've done, but because I can't move on with it, and it stops me dead with this hopeless feeling."

"Well, it sometimes affects people that way. Is this what you came to tell me?"

"Yes."

"Look, I really think that psychotherapy could help you. (He's pushing me away again, and pulling the carpet out from under my feet.) How would you feel about that?"

"I don't want to do that."

"Well, think about it," he said.

"I'm not going to."

Doc Martin's ratings dropped so low they went off the bottom of the page. Bollocks to him anyway, and homeopathy could fuck off too. I told him all about myself and what did I get? Nothing.

I was wandering through our house in horror and despair. The sitting-room was wrecked, furniture lying upturned and ripped apart, paintings hanging skew-wiff and a freezing wind pouring through the broken windows. In the kitchen, food lay scattered all over the place, and the cupboards that I had so recently built hung half-way off their hinges. I ran upstairs to the first floor. Scarlet's room, once so beautiful, was devastated—in particular the things that I had made for her: her bed, the Noah's Ark, the curtains and her dolls. The small spare room had been turned upside down. The bathroom taps were running and the sinks hung from their pipes, and Finn's study, oh my God, his beautiful books—including, perhaps especially, the ones he wrote—had been mutilated. My heart sank as I realised that because I had broken my promise of long ago to my father ("Don't tell ze others, darlink"), he had done this to me. I plodded up to my studio and bedroom, which had received the same treatment; but propped-up in a corner, under a pile of old newspapers, sat my father. He pointed his finger at me and said, "There is only one person to blame for all this destruction. Look what you have done." I woke up thinking, but that isn't what I've been doing, is it? I'm trying to sort it all out. I reached out automatically for Finn, and then remembered he'd buggered off. I got up and made myself a cup of tea.

I fell asleep again in the early hours of the morning, but when I awoke, out of the blue, the name and address of someone I had the feeling would be able to help was in my mind. I phoned her up. "Just come over now if you're not doing anything."

This woman had clearly been through a thing or two; perhaps fighting a terminal illness? We liked each other immediately, and she was gentle and confident. I told her about everything and how Dr Martin and I had worked through almost all of it with a fine-tooth-comb. That when Minu had been led away by the two policewomen in court, I'd wondered where they were taking him to, and how we'd got to this point in our lives. Almost as if Minu could not come out of jail until every little thing had been sorted through and found it's rightful place. About how I wanted to come to terms with what I'd done when I'd had the abortion, to find a way through somehow.

We talked and talked, and then she said, "Well, it seems to me that you have cared and worried about this soul, just like you would have if he or she had been born, and through your creative work and work with children. You really couldn't have done more. You know, he would be twenty years old now, and you would have to start letting go of him anyway. Perhaps you could try and think about it in those terms. Which doesn't mean losing your commitment to him . . ."

Then she gave me a meditation to do. This was something I could really work with. I thought about what she'd said. It was going to be a lot like when Minu left home—we separated off, but I'm still committed to him. It made sense and she was right.

I walked home in peace through the still and quiet of night.

12

The phone rang. "Mum?"

"What's the matter, what's going on Minu?" I could tell that he was not OK.

"I want to come home Mum, I want to come home where I belong, oh please help me." (He was crying, and suddenly so was I. What could I do for him?) "Now don't cry Minu, just tell me what's going on."

"They found an extra phone card in my room, and some extra unexplained prison clothing, I don't know myself what it was doing there. And Mum, they've added an another week onto my sentence."

"Oh what, for a phone card? Hey, it's OK, we can manage a week. You'll be home in only 17 days even so." (The time had clearly come to get that Home Secretary, and superglue him stark naked onto that spare plinth in Trafalgar Square.) "Now cheer up Minu, it's ok, and Scarlet wants to talk to you."

Then Scarlet took the phone, with the kitten under her arm. "Hello Minu, how are the horses? I'm looking forward to you coming home, do you want to speak to Twinkle? I've got his ear right on the phone . . . Speak up, we can't hear you."

"Hello Twinkle, is that you?" he bellowed. I could see his fellow inmates pointing at their heads and rolling their eyes.

"Scarlet, lets go to the Tate and look at some pictures." She put her elbows on the table, cupped her chin in her hands and sighed like she was about eighty years old. "Well all right Mum, but only if we can look at some great big colourful pictures that make me feel really happy."

We were soon standing in front of one of Pierre Bonnard's paintings of his wife in the bath again (did she live there?), but there was more to this woman then met the eye. Her body lies half submerged in water, one leg stretched out taut, the other passive, folded beneath it. One of her arms moves the water, the other relaxed and still. How many colours has he used to paint her? There are shadows and outlines of grey, blue, brown and ochre that run along her body; he has used orange and pinks to give her a soft but active tension, and black, umber, yellow, pink, red and blue in her hair and on her face. In other words, pretty nearly all of the colours are here. She is painted in fine, precise lines and rough brush strokes, considered details and obscure hidden features, making her immediately accessible but also full of hidden secrets.

"Well, I never knew that all these colours and all of these things were in the ingredients for making a woman," said Scarlet.

"You mean like a cake?"

She giggled. "Yes. Take one women and add yellow and blue . . . some water . . . a spoonful of shade . . ."

At home, I forced myself with a will of iron to paint again. "Get into your painting. Go on, try—you've got to do something creative again," I told myself. "Every single creative thing you do helps to fight the forces of destruction, remember?" So I did. And in the very first one, the leaping impala jumped right out of the bright warm colours.

From then on I painted every day; often at night too. The

pictures came easily, I could hardly keep up with the flow of images and ideas as they tumbled out: birds of the air, fish from the depths, dolphins, a flying squirrel, abstract landscapes of the soul, the galloping horse, a Kraken from the deep . . . The colours shone, and I let each creature speak for itself. They were the strongest paintings I'd ever done I learned as well that through painting and music I had another voice.

When I was a kid, I can remember being outraged at that passage from the Bible that goes: "Whosoever hath, to him shall be given; and whosoever hath not, from him shall be taken even that which he seemeth to have." But it's true, so don't ever give up. If you lie down and let yourself go nothing will happen for you, the well will dry up and your power lines will be cut. But provided you make an effort, it will be met, the phone will ring, work will appear, and inspiration will come.

One night, lying alone in bed, my mind turned back to another experience of hope and pleasure . . .

Finn and Scarlet lay sleeping in the Dingle Hotel. It was seven o'clock in the morning, and I was walking down to the harbour for a date with an old boy-friend. The early September skies were blue, not one cloud. My heart, full of eager anticipation, was bumping along at quite a rate. A fisherman waited by the pier for me. "Mornin'. Wet suit?" "No, I never wear one." "OK, all set. Let's go then." As we left the harbour, the sun rose like a radiant lover over the sleeping green hills. We lit up, and I took over the wheel guiding the boat across the bay, heading for the open Atlantic swell, as he tidied up. Out at sea, we slowed down and chucked out the anchor. Finn McCool, are you out there somewhere? We watched and waited. And suddenly there he was, his blue fin speeding through the spangled water, his smile at the side of the boat, eighty-three teeth grinning from ear to ear. I was over the side in a flash. Into the magic, into the light.

The dolphin stayed with me for two hours while I went in and out of the water. It was damn cold, but after the first five minutes you warmed up. I got thoroughly dolphinized, and I'd forgotten how great it felt, being probed by his sonar, rolling in the salt water, under and over, playing with you—an honour—he fed the soul, and left you with peace and well-being in your heart . . . A brother from the sea.

The phone rang. I hesitated to pick it up what news of fresh disasters would it bring? "Sunny McCabe, this is the oral hygienist. (Help! The oral sadist.) Where have you been for the last year?"

Sitting there, at her mercy and feeling about five years old, she exhorted me to dedicate my life to cleaning my teeth. "What's happened to your teeth? Don't you clean them any more? Are you flossing daily?"

"Yes, I floss them once a day, and yes, I clean them after every meal. Sometimes I even get up in the middle of the night to give them an extra go."

"Oh. Let's see how you floss them, then." I gave a very credible flossing demonstration. "Well, I can't understand why your teeth are such a mess," she sighed. What was wrong with my teeth was that I was lying right through them.

I read in my *BBC Wildlife Magazine* that "after giving birth, the female seals leave the beach for the open sea, where they fish and swim freely for the rest of the year . . ." Mmm, sounds lovely. And this time, I actually managed to finish the article.

> Dear Mum,
>
> I'll be out so soon now. Why has Finn moved over the road? When I get back, I'll be there with you and Scarlet, don't worry. Finn's so weird at the moment, it may be a good thing. I don't know how you feel about it, but I get the impression he walks in and out of the

house as he pleases and does what he likes, with you paying the price for his 'freedom'.

Freedom is something I've thought about a lot. It's not circumstantial, it's an inner attitude. The only thing we have some control over is how we react inside ourselves to the things that happen to us. That doesn't change if we are in jail or out in the world. Obviously it's far more pleasant not being in jail! But ultimately it's up to you whether you want to remain a free individual true to yourself, or get taken over by the system.

I've thought about that judge too. Really it's him who's imprisoned, by his prejudices. Not me.

All my love
Minu.

Dear Minu,

Thank you so much for your letter, you're so right. I hope you will always be a free individual, and true to yourself. You are a bright and generous spirit, and I love you for that. Mum.

"Sunny, do you feel like coming out? We're going to the Pelican Cafe."

"I'd love to, what time?"

"7:30."

"It's a bit early for me, but Finn can come over and put Scarlet to bed tonight. OK, see you there."

The girls were all there, and having a rip-roaring argument about teenage sex. Most of them were against it, which was pretty rich. "You can't look at it through grownup eyes, for a start," I pointed out. "It's a completely different thing, as you might remember, when you're a teenager to when you're an adult. I think it's perfectly fine among teenagers, so long as they've got contraception and all that jazz."

"I suppose you're right, really. But mine are at it all the

time, in the house, and they smoke dope and lie about the place stoned out of their minds with their boyfriends when they've got school the next day. Maybe if I sold up and moved to Herefordshire they'd be out of temptations way."

"Romany, you've been saying your going to sell up for twenty five years, and Herefordshire is just the same as everywhere else. We're not talking heroin addicts here, a bit of sex and drugs is good for you."

"I suppose you're right . . . Now Sunny, why are you letting Finn walk all over you like this?"

"Have you been in touch with Minu recently? Look, I'll try and explain. My parents have not spoken to each other for twenty-five years, and even now when I go to visit my Dad my Mum really doesn't like it. Minu does not have his father either, which hasn't exactly helped him. I am determined not to follow my parents' example, for Scarlet's sake. She loves her father, as is right, and has a good relationship with him, so we are trying to maintain a good parenting relationship on her behalf." (Also he helps me with my spelling.)

"Well, we shall just have to see then, won't we? Death to all men, is what I say!"

"Well thanks for the solidarity, but Romany you and Crispen have been divorced for years and still work pretty well around the needs of your girls, don't you?"

Finn never did come back. He just climbed the stairs and turned the key, but he did not, unfortunately, fall asleep for a hundred years. First he really put me through it, and then complained about being miserable. He came over for supper, went off on trips, got in a tangle over his affairs and then, heartbroken, asked to come back. But I said no. I tried not to imagine him in bed with somebody else, sharing the love that we had had. But he had broken something that was whole and complete. He just said that he couldn't help his feelings.

"That's complete pants Finn. Why I know certain women who feel like murdering people when they have PMS. If they couldn't help their feelings, there would be a trail of dead bodies from here to eternity." And yes, I loved him very much, but the only time in our life that I had needed real emotional support, he was not there for it, for whatever reason. I think if he had been, our relationship could have moved on to a whole new thing. As far as I could see, he didn't have a place in his life for me except as slave, and I would rather be alone than compromised.

By the way, I guess if you want to find out if Finn and I ever did get around to doing it up the big tree, dripping with love and lust, you'll just have to climb up it and see if his name is up there, won't you?

When Finn left though, he took away more than just himself. Not that our relationship was ideal, it's just that when we were together I could always see what love could be. Now that's gone.

The little folk sat in the back. Harry had election fever, and exhorted people through the open window to vote Conservative. "Harry, if you say that one more time, you can bloody well walk home." "Right, let's get him," Scarlet said to Katie, and they started to pull off his trousers. When I turned around to look, poor old Harry was hanging on to his trousers with both hands in a life-and-death struggle with the girls, who were winning. It was better not to interfere in these situations, I felt. After a while, I heard Harry's chirpy voice saying, "Scarlet, will you give me mouth-to-mouth resuscitation?" "No!"

Rudolf Steiner said, "A properly composed book should awaken spiritual life in the reader, not merely impart a certain quantity of information. Reading it should not be mere reading, but should be an experience of inner shocks, tensions, and solutions." Well, that's OK then. They are going to be so pleased with me!

"Sunny, this is your mother here." (Mum's messages always sound like she's reporting from the trenches.) "Bad news, I'm afraid. The police have confiscated my car for a week for reckless driving." Oh, I wish! Seriously though, this is what she said about me and Finn breaking up: "Poor Finn, I'm so terribly fond of him. Anyway, dear, the really amazing thing is that you managed to maintain a relationship for so long."

Thanks, Mum.

It felt like I hadn't been very well at all. And I still had to choose my days out carefully. Sometimes I found myself suddenly sensitive and overwhelmed by the busy crowded streets, or feeling that I shouldn't be out in this wind, or that I needed to take it easy today . . . It's as though there is a piece of me missing somehow. I don't think I'm ever going to get it back, either.

I opened the front door and my father-in-law stood there, in his best suit, with about twenty white lilies and white gladiolas in his arms. He looked really well, and much younger. Then he gave me the flowers and said to me, "I'm OK, Sunny. It's all right now, I'm OK." And in the night sky, behind him, there twinkled an array of golden stars, and a crescent moon. I woke up and thought, they put that background in so that I couldn't argue about exactly where that dream had come from. I had been worrying about him, after what I'd read about death, and people who don't have a spiritual life.

Later that morning I went off to the Russian Orthodox Church. I lit a candle for the dead and for St Michael. "Be thou at my back, thou ranger of the heavens, thou warrior of the king of all." Because we both had fought a dragon, and I think he had been at my back.

I thought a lot about what the psychotherapist said, about separating off from the soul I sent back. It's going to be OK now, I'm trying to learn to look at it that way. This does not mean one can be forgiven oneself or any body else either for that matter; we are after all responsible for our actions. But I can let it go and give it over, because ultimately, forgiveness is not in our hands at all, but in the hands of the gods. Only they can do that.

When you become eighteen and ready to leave the court of your school, you sit around a table with the circle of your friends, to read the final part of *Parzival* together . . .

Eventually Parzival's quest took him to Gawain's Castle of Wonders, where he stayed for a while until one morning he set off again in search of the Holy Grail. Riding into a forest, he met a very powerful heathen knight. They engaged in battle, and were equally matched until the unknown knight broke Parzival's sword. This knight turned out to be Parzival's half-black, half-white brother Fierefiz, who had conquered twenty-five armies over which he now had complete control: a man of action and great will-power. Upon recognising each other after battle, Parzival took Fierefiz back to Gawain. Then the sorrowful thoughtful man, the joyous man of feeling, and the powerful man of will embraced each other. Thinking, feeling and will conjoined to make a complete man and then the way to the Grail lay open wide to them.

But here is something I learned for myself from reading *Parzival*: it isn't only developing thinking, feeling and will that opens the way to the Holy Grail. Parzival could not attain the Holy Grail without including his heathen brother Fierefiz. In other words, whatever colour or religion we are, there are no steps forward unless we are willing to bring everybody along with us. Self-development is non-selective; there are no chosen few.

Sunday morning. Finn was over to see Scarlet, and I set about making something nice for Dr Martin, to thank him for helping me so much. I got out my tools, turned up the Van Morrison, and sang along in perfect harmony, "When that rough god goes riding, when that rough god goes riding, riding on by . . ." and started to engrave some fish around a Japanese glass bowl when the door-bell rang. Scarlet flew off to open it, and look who's here: Minu! "Hi everybody, got off a day early, step lively Mum."

"Let me in, you slimeball," said the beaming Sorell, squeezing past him and hugging me. We were both grinning like Cheshire cats. Finn hugged Minu and had enough sense to put the kettle on. Ignoring Sorrel, her main competition, Scarlet wrapped herself around Minu's shoulders like a scarf, saying, "Have you finished your stupid job in the country?"

"Yes darling, I have."

"Really, are you back then, bongo-brains?"

"Yes, I'm back."

I smiled inside, warm and alight.

. . . Faithful Henry had been so unhappy when his master was bewitched, that he caused three bands of iron to be placed around his heart, so that it would not break . . . When the carriage was driving along the road the King heard a crack, he thought the carriage was breaking, but Faithful Henry said "It is only one of the iron bands, springing from around my heart . . ."

Now that my boy-man was out of prison, I could see that he was going to need a lot of warmth and love. He was vulnerable, fragile, and struggling with it. Neither of us abandoned ourselves to festivities; we needed to take it easy with our emotions; learned that lesson with the home leave. He stayed for a while but soon found a place to live a few streets away, and popped in almost every day. I tried to give him what he needed, carry him for a while. I supposed that for him, his experience would be one of those you get over but at the same time carry within you for the rest of your life.

"Hi Mum, can I use the washing machine, the jigsaw, the electric drill, got any spare curtains left over, what about the roller, got any Polyfilla, can I borrow the fish kettle, my probation officer is on the same road as me, do you think I should aply for housing benefit? How do you make Salmon Teriyaki?"

"Slow down, Minu. I hope you never take speed, because you may find (like I did) that it's really slow compared to your normal state of being. And careful when you open the fridge door, you never know what might be in there."

"Mum, I'm going to the travel fair at Olympia to get some tickets to travel around South America and visit Uncle Jake..." But he came out with tickets for a three-month trip around India. "Look, it includes two internal flights, and a trek somewhere or other on elephants. It's such a good deal!"

"That's great Minu, good for you... Erm, does this mean you're going to get a lot of vaccinations?"

"No!"

I sat in my studio thinking about Nicky and all the work we'd done here. He would be in the company of the best musicians now, side by side with the likes of John Lennon, Jimi Hendrix, Nick Kossoff, Tim Buckley, Mama Cass, Sandy Denny, Brian Jones, Janis Joplin, Bob Marley... It could be a mistake I thought, to expect heavenly harps in the Sweet By-&-By. So I wrote this song:

> "I'm dancing with your shadow, your echo,
> I'm reaching for your hand,
> The gentle snow that falls now, so warm now,
> Lies muted on the wasteland
>
> And you stole away, so softly
> Across the border line.
> And your wings are wet with rain now
> Climb the ladder you have to climb.
>
> I'm holding you in my heart, my head
> I'm waiting, marking time,
> The tide has turned, it's falling and falling
> All along the shore line.

And you stole away so softly
Across the border line.
And your wings are wet with rain now
Climb the ladder you have to climb.

I'm dancing with your shadow, your echo
I'm reaching through the sky,
The gentle snow, so warm now
I wish we'd said goodbye.

And will the lovers rise again
On the day of the dead?
Do you get to see your departed
Or light a tiny bright flame instead?"

Then I sent it out, hoping he could hear it.

"Mum, that's a great song. I wish I'd been at his funeral, somehow I don't think putting flowers on his grave is quite adequate, but can we do some sort of ritual for him?"

"Yes, let's think about it."

'Two pints of milk, one line of cocaine and half an ounce of your best quality hash today, please . . .' Minu had made a little wooden boat, and we filled it with flowers, laying a small bottle of wine, a twist of cocaine and a lump of hash among them. I wound a guitar string around the song I'd written, and coiled up his leather bondage dog collar. Minu stuck lighted candles in the holes he'd drilled out for them. And then we launched it on the Thames from Dove Wharf, where Nicky had lived for so long. It floated away beautifully, then caught in the midstream current, and disappeared out of sight under Hammersmith Bridge.

On our way back we stopped by at St Paul's the Divine Comedian to see how the Circus was getting along with the rehearsal for Aladdin. I opened the church door just as Scarlet flew by full tilt on a high unicycle, with Aladdin and a gang of stilted Arabian brethren in hot pursuit. Triumphantly brandishing her stolen trophy, Aladdin's jewelled and twinkling lamp, she circled the entire church at top speed, shouting, "I AM RICH BEYOND MY WILDEST DREAMS.... I AM RICH BEYOND MY WILDEST DREAMS... I AM RICH BEYOND MY WILDEST DREAMS!"

That's Scarlet, and she's right I thought. And a glimmer of an idea began to light up the way ahead. We had enough talent between us to have a fine theatre troop of our own, with Saskia head of make-up, Marlene in charge of the dance department, Romany purveyor of exquisite scenery and costume design, Ariel in charge of the symphony orchestra, with her sister's Phoebe on fiddle and Misty on Cello. Shane had become obsessed with juggling and his Mum Charley could be our manager and cook. Minu could spin the discs. The possibilities were infinite! Bet they'll all be up for it—high time to get this show on the road.

See? This is how it's meant to be, you bastards. Are you proud of yourselves, punishing and trying to wreck us all? What has this taught us, may I ask? What did we have to learn anyway? What we learned about was British justice, and your so-called family values, and broken hearts. But we also learned about surviving, and freedom... And most of all, love. So up yours.

... It's six o'clock, the waters break, I push and you are born. Quite simply and easily, you leap into the world like a flying fish. A few days later I am bringing you home. I hold you close, as I have been doing more or less continuously since you were born. We are both relaxed and fine...

SORTED.